GUY GARCIA

OBSIDIAN SKY

A NOVEL

SIMON & SCHUSTER
New York London Toronto Sydney Tokyo Singapore

SIMON & SCHUSTER
Rockefeller Center
1230 Avenue of the Americas
New York, New York 10020

Designed by Carla Weise/Levavi & Levavi
Manufactured in the United States of America

1   3   5   7   9   10   8   6   4   2

Library of Congress Cataloging in Publication Data

Garcia, Guy
Obsidian sky: a novel/Guy Garcia.
p. cm.
1. Aztecs—Antiquities—Collection and preservation—Fiction.
2. Mexican Americans—Journeys—Mexico—Fiction.
3. Anthropologists—Mexico—Fiction. I. Title.
PS3557.A67028   1994   94-361
813'.54—dc20   CIP
ISBN: 0-671-86479-3

Para Carlos Fuentes,
que me llevó a la ventana

OBSIDIAN
SKY

Donato Negrete heard his wife scream and opened his eyes to see the face of God descending. A more devout Catholic might have been killed in the time it took to make the sign of the cross, but Donato, who prided himself as being a rational man, only raised his hand to deflect the falling statue, which lost one hand and most of its head as it crashed against the floor.

A second scream, this one from his mother-in-law, pierced his ears. "It's the end of the world," Doña Luz cried, pointing in horror to the decapitated Christ.

"No, it's not," Donato told her, watching the clay pot that Luisa used to make menudo pitch like a drunk and the framed pictures of Benito Juárez and John F. Kennedy slip off their nails. "It's an earthquake."

As the earth danced beneath him, Donato staggered to where Luisa and her mother were cowering against the wall and led them out of their two-room house and into the relative safety of the street.

Then, as suddenly as it began, the earthquake ended. In the eerie quiet Donato could hear children crying and the mindless yapping of the widow Muñoz's black mutt. Except for the haze of dust that hovered above the treetops, the town seemed oddly unchanged, as if the land had been lifted and then carefully dropped back into place. A few feet away, Doña Luz was on her knees in the dirt, praying, her eyes wrinkled with rapture. Donato pursed his lips in disapproval, sensing the start of another family argument. He was saved by López, his neighbor and occasional drinking partner, who ambled over from where he was standing with a knot of other men.

"Qué chingada," he said, shaking a confectioner's dusting of adobe off of his shirt. "Anybody hurt?"

"No, how about you?"

"Nah," López said, a lopsided grin pasted on his face. "The chicken laid a few extra eggs but that's all. Did you hear that noise it made? Like a wounded animal."

"Yes," Donato answered, but his mind was on other matters. "Listen, I've got some business to take care of, so . . ."

"Of course," López said with a mocking bow. "See you later, jefe."

Donato hurried into the house and changed into his uniform. Standing before the chipped mirror in the bedroom, he pinned on the badge that identified him as a deputy of the Mexican National Tourist Office, Division of Anthropological Treasures. Seeing himself in the guise of a government official never failed to give him a lift. At such moments he didn't even notice the potbelly and jowls that caused some of the townspeople to ridicule him behind his back. Though the job amounted to little more than a glorified security guard, Donato's position nevertheless provided him a modicum of self-respect, a sense of purposefulness that he found singularly lacking in the lives of López and the pious Doña Luz. Let others waste their time on liquor, lotería and the Virgin Mary, not him; he had better things to do. Donato was fully aware of how lucky he was to be living in the midst of some of the world's greatest wonders, as splendid and awesome as the crumbling pyramids of Egypt or the bone-white temples of the Greeks. More than once he had given impromptu lectures to the tourists who spilled over from the nearby and more famous ruins at Uxmal. Some were merely curious about the gruta de Loltún, the mysterious cave with its underground spring and fifth-century Maya shrine. They arrived in rented jeeps and station wagons, young and old, laden with maps and travel books or simply lost. Donato often kept them spellbound with his tellings of the Maya myths, always ending his stories about ancient dynasties with the declamation, "and you have lived to stand on their graves."

The aroma of chorizo and coffee called to him from the kitchen. But his longing for Luisa's savory huevos rancheros could not overcome his sense of duty; he knew he must go to the cave and report any damage to the proper authorities as soon as possible. On his way out Donato gave his wife a peck on the cheek and shot a final frowning glance at Doña Luz, who was bent over her bed with a rosary clutched in her fingers.

Outside, the cool morning air was a balm on his nerves and he sighed with relief, glad to be free of the old woman's superstitious mutterings. He started down the dirt path that led to the cave and with every step Donato's mood brightened. Despite the morning's rude awakening, it was turning into a promising day. The tremor was, after all, a minor disturbance, though the experts would soon know for sure. He and his family were unhurt, his house was still standing, and any damage to the cave was sure to be minimal. In fact, he was no longer certain that there had been any earthquake at all; such things only happened in Mexico City and the northern states. In any case, a prompt and thorough report would no doubt please his superiors, increasing the chances that he might someday be promoted to the head of security at the beachside temples of Tulum or some other scenic ruin. Buoyed by his thoughts, Donato looked up as he hustled his bulk down the path, enjoying how the sunlight splintered through the green forest canopy, like the beam of an old-fashioned movie projector.

The path widened into a small clearing bordered by a chain link fence and metal gate. Donato unlocked the gate and surveyed the entrance to the grutas. He approached the yawning mouth of the cave and flicked on the master light switch. Nothing. The power must still be out. Fumbling in a wooden box hidden outside the lip of the cavity, he found his flashlight and thumbed it on, aiming the beam into the shaft. The light cut a thin swath through the gloom, illuminating the narrow passage to the shrine. As he was about to take another step, the earth shuddered. Donato froze, sure that the jaws of the abyss

11

were about to snap shut around him. He could feel goosebumps rising on his arms as his will to continue shriveled in the moist air, which now felt like the fetid breath of death itself. The events of the whole morning seemed suddenly ominous: the freak quake, the old woman's fear—were they premonitions of his own demise? His immediate impulse was to run back outside before another aftershock sealed his doom. But he willed himself to remain, consciously fighting the animal urge to flee into the sunlight. To turn back now would be a victory for Doña Luz and her ilk and a defeat for the forces of enlightenment and progress—everything that he stood for. The very notion of defying the old crone gave him strength. Mustering his determination, Donato pushed deeper into the murky recess. The official tour usually took two hours, but Donato knew enough shortcuts to cut the time down by more than half. A step at a time, he drew closer to the inner sanctum, all the while searching for cracks in the clammy limestone. The squeal of a bat echoed in the dimness. His stomach grumbled. Donato kept moving; he knew he had passed the point of no return. He heard the temple before he saw it, the steady plunk of water dripping slowly into an underground pool. The flashlight found an urn that bore the face of Tláloc, the giver of rain and life, god of plenty, lord who is the wine of the earth. Though he had seen it a hundred times before, the grim visage, with its long hair and blunt features, never looked more forbidding.

Elation surged through Donato's heart. Except for a few loose boulders strewn on the floor, the shrine appeared unscathed. In spite of himself, he silently thanked the gods and took a last sweep of the vault. That's when he saw it. At the far end of the room, behind a column of stalactites, a fissure had opened up in the wall. The hole was about three feet tall and one foot wide, extending from the floor to the level of a man's knee. Donato moved closer and shone the light into the crack. He found himself looking into another, larger enclosure. Something glinted. Stooping for a better angle, he could make out the shapes of several objects, some of them close enough to touch. He waited. Seven drops echoed in the chamber while he came to a decision. Then, summoning every last vestige of his courage, he leaned forward and reached into the darkness.

1

The sun was high in the Mexican sky as Brian Mendoza crossed the zócalo and arrived at the heart of the Aztec universe. Before him lay the excavated ruins of Templo Mayor, the sacred sanctum of Tenochtitlán, the Navel of the Moon, earthly intersection of the Nine Underworlds and the Thirteen Heavens. The crumbling corpse of Templo Mayor had lain buried beneath the expanding grid of modern Mexico City for centuries. Then, on February 21, 1978, employees of the municipal electric utility had stumbled on it while digging a tunnel for an underground power line. Now a web of metal ramps zigzagged over the site, which covered the better part of a city block. From his vantage point on the central square Brian could see the serpent heads that guarded the twin temples of Huitzilopochtli and Tláloc, and behind them the modern cement and glass slab of the museum.

Brian looked at his watch. He was half an hour early for his appointment with Xavier Zapata. He could have spent the extra time looking for an apartment, but Brian didn't want to risk being late. There was too much riding on this meeting.

Brian straightened his tie before continuing across the busy plaza to the public entrance. The intent stares of the taco vendors made him uneasy until he realized that they were only hoping he would buy something. Reflexively reaching into his pocket, he felt the leaden heft of the Mexican coins he had received at the airport exchange booth. An elderly woman with a red ribbon in her hair raised a bottle of Fanta orange and smiled solicitously.

"No gracias," Brian said, hoping he didn't sound too much like a gringo tourist. His Spanish was actually more than serviceable, but a totally convincing accent still eluded him. Yet the language barrier was really the least of it. In his interactions with the Mexicans at the airport he had noticed a cool reserve, a subtle distance that ineluctably marked him an outsider, a half-breed pocho, a Chicano.

He felt it again in the appraising glance of the girl who sold him an admission ticket in the small entrance hall. Seconds before she had been chatting amiably in Spanish with one of the guards, but as Brian approached her face became a mask of politeness.

"Gracias, señorita."

"Enjoy your visit, sir."

Brian passed through the turnstile and traced the steel steps to the southern corner of the excavation, where a portion of the circular Coyolxauhqui stone had first blunted the tools of astonished workers who were digging a ditch for the electric utility. Zapata, then a subdirector of the National Museum of Anthropology, was quick to realize the importance of the discovery. His deft and well-documented restoration of the ruins made him a national hero and catapulted him into the firmament of his field.

Now, more than two decades later, another stroke of serendipity had thrust Zapata and Templo Mayor back into the spotlight. In an effort to keep the adjacent cathedral from sinking further into the spongy lakebed over which Mexico City was built, municipal engineers had decided to dig under the northeast corner of the church and install a raft of cement pontoons, as they had already done once before. But the laborers had dug down less than thirty feet when their shovels struck solid stone. When a chunk was brought up to the surface, Zapata had confirmed it as a fragment of the shrine of Quetzalcóatl, the Plumed Serpent, an ancient and powerful god of many guises who was associated with the birth of mankind. The work on the cathedral was halted until city officials could formulate a plan to preserve the integrity of both the newly discovered Aztec temple and the church, each of which represented powerful—and opposing—poles of the Mexican psyche.

Brian turned to look at the neighboring house of the Catholic god and he could see where a whole corner of the building had been carefully shrouded in scaffolding and a canvas, as if to shield the viewer from an act of architectural sacrilege. Continuing along the corrugated ramp, he came upon a gaggle of tourists gathered in front of the twin staircases that marked the oldest part of the site. The group was raptly listening to a man with a pencil-thin mustache etched on his lip. The guide was light-skinned and slender with thick eyebrows that closed the triangle of his pointed chin.

"Templo Mayor was the spiritual and geographical locus of the entire Aztec empire," the guide was saying, "and these two pyramids formed the sacred ceremonial center of Templo Mayor. One temple is dedicated to Huitzilopochtli, the warrior sun god, and the other to Tláloc, the god of rain and fertility." The guide pointed to a weatherworn carving of a hare and two dots. "That glyph over there denotes the year 2 Rabbit, which corresponds to about 1390 A.D. on the Christian calendar. As the Aztec empire grew, newer and larger pyramids were built directly over the original ones. After the Conquest, the Spaniards tore down the outer pyramid that once stood here and used the stones to build a cathedral but, as you can see, the original temples escaped destruction and have survived nearly intact."

The guide leaned on the rail and gestured to a sloping shelf of stone at the tops of the pyramids. "The platforms at the summits were holy spaces used for religious rituals and human sacrifice. The victims would be beheaded and pushed down the stairs. But first their hearts would be torn out and offered to the gods."

The teenagers in the group tittered and gasped.

"How gross!"

An adult in a lime tank top raised his hand. "I read someplace that some of the Spaniards were sacrificed."

"It's true," the guide confirmed. "When Hernan Cortés and his men entered the gates of Tenochtitlán on November 8, 1519, they were so impressed with the city that they wondered if they were dreaming. Motecuhzoma, the Aztec emperor, welcomed the Spaniards even though his wise men had foreseen the destruction of the city at the hands of enemy invaders. But Motecuhzoma refused to heed the omens. Some believe that Motecuhzoma mistook Cortés for the god Quetzalcóatl, who, according to Aztec myth, had disappeared into the sea vowing to return one day in the form of a light-skinned man and claim the king's throne. In any case, Motecuhzoma became a puppet for Cortés, who had him enslaved. The Aztecs were so enraged that they stoned their emperor to death and attacked Cortés and his men. Some Spaniards were captured and sacrificed, along with many Aztecs, on the great pyramid that once stood here."

"Wait a minute," a woman in a Mets baseball cap objected, "I can understand why they killed the Spanish, but why would they murder their own people?"

"It wasn't murder," the guide explained. "At least not in the way we define it. The Aztecs believed that without sacrifice the sun would no longer rise and the world would end. At least that's what they thought."

"But it did end, didn't it?" Brian had spoken the words almost before he realized it.

"Excuse me?" the guide said, looking for the source of the question.

"I said that the Aztec world did actually end, in the form of Cortés and the Conquest."

Heads turned in Brian's direction.

"Well, yes," the guide allowed, "in a certain sense that's true. But that really has more to do with the myth of Quetzalcóatl, the Plumed Serpent. If you'd like to pursue your idea further, there are some very good sources on the subject available at the bookstore."

Satisfied with his rebuff, the guide started to turn away, but Brian wasn't finished. "You mean Ce Acatl Topiltzin-Quetzalcóatl, the ruler of Tula who was overthrown by his brother Tezcatlipoca, the Smoking Mirror, and vowed to someday return and reclaim his rightful throne. Motecuhzoma, after all, believed that he was descended from the Toltec kings."

"That's very interesting," one of the tourists chimed in.

The guide was staring with open hostility now, but Brian couldn't resist pressing his point. "What I'm getting at is simply that Motecuhzoma's capitulation to Cortés could have been at least partly motivated by the Aztec tradition of self-sacrifice established by his Toltec ancestors."

Their eyes locked for a moment.

"There is absolutely no scholarly evidence to confirm that theory," the guide said acidly.

"Yes, but isn't that only because—"

The guide held up his hand. "Sir, I suggest that since you are so keenly interested in this subject that you sign up for one of the classes available through the museum." He turned away from Brian and addressed the group. "Sorry for the interruption, ladies and gentlemen. Now if you will please follow me . . ."

Brian checked the time and silently cursed. He was five minutes late for his appointment. Forcing himself not to run, he hurried through the glass doors into the cool, dimly lit interior of the museum. He was halfway across the lobby when he recognized a stout, swarthy man standing off to the side with a young woman in a smart navy skirt. As Xavier Zapata spoke, the woman scribbled in a notebook, nodding her head. Even from twenty feet away he knew that she was extraordinary. At first, because of her height, Brian thought she might be American, but as he drew closer he registered her caramel complexion and almond eyes. She must have sensed him staring because she looked up and caught him. As Zapata turned to see who had interrupted their conversation, her gaze implicated him like a rumor, rooting him to the glossy floor.

"Professor Zapata?"

He peered at Brian through thick gold-rimmed spectacles.

"I'm Brian Mendoza." Zapata's expression remained blank. "Your new research assistant. From Berkeley. I have your letter . . ."

"Oh, yes, yes, of course." Zapata was nodding vigorously, pumping Brian's hand like a long-lost uncle. "I'm glad you're here. You're just in time to witness me being interrogated by the media. *The Globe*, to be exact. It's our largest English newspaper. And this is their star reporter, Marina Soto."

"Hello," she said in fragrantly accented English.

Brian nodded, tongue-tied.

"Mr. Mendoza will be joining my staff for a few months," Zapata told her. "He has a very interesting theory about Motecuhzoma and the Conquest."

"Oh really?" she said with genuine interest. "I'd like to hear it sometime."

"I'd be honored."

At the other end of the lobby, a photographer was waiting to take Zapata's picture against an installation of human skulls. "If you don't mind, Professor," he pleaded.

Zapata excused himself and took his place before the camera. The photographer held a light meter up to his face, then to the skulls. "It was my idea," Zapata intoned as the strobe froze him in an electronic burst of light. "Does wonders for an old man's vanity don't you think?"

"You're far too modest, Professor," Marina Soto replied.

The camera flashed once more.

Marina Soto was writing again, but Brian could tell she was watching him. Lowering his voice so that only she would hear, he asked, "Are you always so kind to your interview subjects?"

She looked up from her notebook. "If I find them interesting."

"So I take it you find Professor Zapata interesting."

"Don't you?"

The question caught him off guard. "Well, sure, but I hardly know him."

"I don't think you have to know someone well to find them interesting, do you?"

"No," he agreed, as the rest of the room dissolved for a moment. "Certainly not."

She rewarded him with a fleeting smile, and he watched her add a card to her mental file.

Zapata was blinking as he rejoined them. "I always suspected that fame would be a debilitating experience," he said gruffly.

"Yes, Professor," Marina Soto said, "but like fame itself, the effect is only temporary. About fifteen minutes, I think."

Zapata grunted with amusement. He turned to Brian. "Brains and beauty, too. And to think I almost declined to be interviewed."

Brian looked at the girl for her reaction, but her attention was focused on Zapata. "I just have a couple more questions, Professor."

"Would it be better if I come back later?" Brian asked.

Zapata shook his head. "That won't be necessary. Arturo Torres, my deputy director, is expecting you for an orientation tour. He'll be your supervisor while you're with us here. I suggest you hurry and catch him before he leaves for lunch. His office is on the third floor."

Taking his cue, Brian excused himself and started for the elevator. Marina Soto. Her name was still echoing in his mind as he entered the administrative offices and asked to see Arturo Torres. The receptionist told Brian that Mr. Torres was due to be in shortly. Then she showed him a vacant desk and a telephone that he could use in the cramped quarters that housed the museum staff.

Except for a few tagged idols perched on tables against the windows, the area looked like any other postmodern workplace. At the dozen or so desks scattered about the room an equal number of young, well-scrubbed researchers pored over open texts, bound printouts and folders or sat mesmerized by scrolling columns and charts on glowing computer screens. At first no one paid any attention to him, but as Brian tried out the swivel chair and pulled open the drawers, a few staffers came over and introduced themselves. Only two made a lasting impression: Laura Castillo, a skittish epigraphist with ebony pigtails who specialized in translating Aztec and Maya codices, and Guillermo Orellana, an affable Guatemalan who headed the restoration department. Even if he hadn't been interested in their work, there was a natural warmth about them that he instantly liked.

"So you're joining the slaves of Templo Mayor," Guillermo said cheerfully.

"It looks that way. I'll know more after I get my marching orders from Mr. Torres."

"Then let me direct you to the commandant's quarters." Guillermo gestured down a long hallway that opened into a labyrinth of steel bookcases. "It's on the other side of the library," he said. "You might want to leave a trail of bread crumbs."

Brian thanked him and entered the stacks, which true to Guillermo's warning, was a chaotic maze of bookcases, files and towering pillars of cardboard boxes. Torres's office was a windowless rectangle at the end of the last aisle. Empty. The door was open so Brian stepped in, immediately noticing the stark, colorless decor and fastidious alignment of the folders and papers that covered the gun-metal desk. The only bit of color came from the ruddy hue of a miniature Chacmool that sat next to the stapler. Brian was reaching out to touch it when a voice accosted him from behind.

"What are you doing here?"

He turned to see the tour guide from the ruins, glaring as if Brian had offended him all over again.

"Hi," Brian said. "I'm waiting for Arturo Torres."

"I am Arturo Torres," the guide growled. "Who are you? And what are you doing in my office?"

"I'm Brian Mendoza," he said, taken aback by the outburst. "Professor Zapata has taken me on as a research associate. He told me to report to you for an orientation."

Torres looked like someone trying to wake up from a bad dream.

"I guess it looks like you'll be giving me a tour after all," Brian joked, but Torres's expression didn't change. "Look, I'm sorry about what happened earlier," Brian said, offering to shake. "I hope there aren't any hard feelings."

Torres looked at Brian's outstretched hand as if it were a foreign object.

"If this isn't a good time, I can . . ."

"No," Torres said, moving to his desk with great reluctance. "Let's get this over with." He reached into the top drawer and produced a plastic ID card. "This will get you into the museum and Templo Mayor."

"What about the new dig?"

"That is off limits."

"But I thought . . ."

Torres took on the manner of an adult forced to reason with a difficult child. "Only those with special clearance are allowed into the excavation zone."

"So how do I get special clearance?"

"Forms must be filled out and approved by Professor Zapata. It can take weeks, even months. Even then you must be accompanied by a senior staff member at all times."

The battle lines were clearly drawn. As far as Torres was concerned, Brian was an unwelcome nuisance, a burden that would be tolerated, but only if he abided by the rules. And the rules, Brian now knew, were not designed to be bent by interlopers from the United States.

"I'm sorry," Torres said without the slightest sign that he was, "but things are different here than where you come from."

"I've noticed."

Torres stood and pressed his long, delicate hands down the front of his shirt. "Come with me," he said, "and I'll finish the tour we started this morning."

With a brisk efficiency that stopped just short of rudeness, Torres led Brian through the main museum exhibits and then outside into the dead narrow streets of Templo Mayor. A jet made a pale scar in the sky over the disinterred temples and Brian was struck by the jarring juxtaposition of ancient and new, seen and unseen. Torres unlocked a small access gate and Brian followed him onto the ground level of the exhumed necropolis. As they made their way through the sacred precinct of Tenochtitlán, Brian could feel the present peeling away from his skin, until even the dust on his shoes seemed charged with an ineffable aura of consequence. Moving along the shaded alleys of hand-hewn rock he found himself holding his breath, as if immersed in an alien atmosphere too rich for his lungs, as if were he only quiet enough, still enough, the stones themselves might deign to share their secrets. Human noises, modern and harsh, broke the illusion. Above and around them a fresh herd of tourists was swarming over the ruins, pointing cameras in every direction, scurrying along the observation ramps like denizens of some Mesoamerican rat maze.

Torres paused at the foot of a stairway guarded by stone frogs. "The Frog Altar," he announced with the same pedantic voice he had used on the tourists. "We estimate that this sector was built during stage IV-B, around the middle of the fifteenth century, under the reign of Axayácatl. It was dismantled by the Spaniards after the Conquest of course."

"Of course."

They continued along a narrow channel, under the metal cat-walks, to a flight of stone stairs at the base of the twin pyramids of Huitzilopochtli and Tláloc. "This part is much older," Torres said as they climbed. "Circa 1375 to 1427. All the artifacts found here conform to the basic scheme of Aztec cosmology." He held his arms out like a scarecrow and turned ninety degrees to face each of the four cardinal directions. "East: the place of dawn. West: the region of experience. South: the home of the gods. North: the barren place of evil."

It seemed to Brian that the last had been a barely veiled accusation, a mythological slur against Mexico's northern neighbors.

"Excuse me," Brian said. "But isn't north also the direction of Aztlán, the mythical homeland of the Aztecs?"

"Yes," Torres answered, "but we Mexicans have always suffered from a tendency to idealize our past."

Had Brian detected a touch of irony in his voice? Maybe he wasn't such a stiff after all. Torres pointed to a blunt object embedded in the platform. "The sacrificial stone, which marks the fifth direction."

"And the center of the universe."

"Correct."

A gust of wind ruffled their clothes and sent dust devils spinning over the court of the Eagle Warriors.

"The victims were bent backward like this." Torres arched his back. "And held down by four priests. The fifth used an obsidian knife to slice open the victim's chest."

"Dad, look!" A boy was pointing from a ramp about twenty feet away. "That dude's gonna get sacrificed!"

Torres straightened up and self-consciously smoothed his hair. "The heart was torn out of the chest cavity," he continued, "and stuffed into the mouth of the statue of Huitzilopochtli, or placed in the belly of the Chacmool over there." He nodded toward a reclining stone figure with a bowl-shaped abdomen. "We are fairly certain that the victims and priests were heavily drugged during the ceremony, probably on a combination of natural narcotics and hallucinogens. Interestingly, only males were dispatched in this manner—"

"Women were decapitated, dismembered and cast down the stairs," Brian interjected, "in a ritual reenactment of the death of Little Hummingbird's sister, Coyolxauhqui."

"That's right," Torres confirmed.

Brian leaned over to touch the chiseled chunk of black tezontle. It was difficult to fathom the river of blood that had flowed from this innocent scrap of volcanic rock. During the Conquest, after the notorious Night of Sorrow, the Spaniards had cringed in horror listening to the screams of their captured comrades as their chests were split open and their hearts lifted out. But even Cortés and his men could not have been fully aware of the Aztec appetite for human sacrifice. Though ritual killings had been performed in ancient Teotihuacán and Tula, it was the Aztecs who elevated the rite to an artful obsession, devising a multitude of different ways to stab, flay, dismember, burn and boil their victims. Cannibalism was rife amongst the upper classes, and human flesh was enjoyed not only by kings and priests but also by Aztec nobles who traded favorite recipes for its preparation. The very thought conjured images as hideous as the most gruesome horror film. Yet Brian felt anything but disgust; he knew there was meaning as well as method behind the Aztec madness. His conviction that the Aztecs were inherently no more bloodthirsty than any other culture had driven him to study their ways and, ultimately, had led him to this very spot. He looked toward the canvas awning draped against the cathedral. "And that must be the new Quetzalcóatl site."

"Yes," Torres said. "The carbon samples of the interior walls support Professor Zapata's initial conclusion. Of course the digging has been halted, for the moment anyway. According to the dates on the artifacts, the chamber was used for several years beginning around 1518."

"Only three years before the fall of Tenochtitlán," Brian noted. "I would have expected it to be much older."

"So did we."

"How do you account for the discrepancy?"

"We can't." Torres's pedantic tone was gone, replaced by a scientist's ardor for the unexplained. "We know that the various levels of

Templo Mayor were built right on top of each other like a wedding cake, the oldest layers on the bottom. Right now our guess is that someone was using this chamber for his own private worship."

"A secret altar dedicated to Quetzalcóatl?"

Torres nodded.

"But why?"

"When we know the answer to that," Torres said snidely, "you can read all about it in *Science* magazine."

Brian barely registered the rebuff. He was too busy digesting the implications of what Torres had just told him.

"Was there any sign of sacrifice inside the chamber?"

"Not that we could find. Why do you ask?"

"No reason." There was no point in sharing his thoughts with Torres; the less he knew about Brian's intentions the better.

As they waited for the elevator, Brian turned to his boss and summoned all the sincerity he could muster.

"Torres?"

"Yes?"

"I just want to thank you for the tour and for giving me the chance to work with you. I may not always show it, but I do realize how lucky I am to be here."

Brian extended his hand and this time Torres shook it. "Just remember that you are a guest here," he warned. "If you keep your eyes open you might even learn something."

"I feel that I already have."

There were three messages waiting for Brian on his desk. The first was an embossed gold card inviting him to a cocktail party at Zapata's home in the fashionable Coyoacán district on Friday night. The second was a telephone memo telling him that Marina Soto had called to make a lunch appointment for the following Monday at one of the high-rise hotels on the edge of Chapultepec Park. The last message was from Brian's Berkeley roommate and best friend, Greg Stone. "If you're reading this I guess you got the job," it said. There was a check in the box marked WILL CALL AGAIN.

Shouting forced its way in through the windows overlooking the zócalo and Brian stood up to see what was going on. A commotion had broken out near the cathedral, where a group of pro-government

24

workers was waving banners emblazoned with the likeness of President Nava. As the demonstrators marched toward the National Palace, a second group rushed forward to confront them. The opposing mobs faced off near the center of the plaza, separated by about thirty feet of charged space. At first the antagonists seemed satisfied with a theatrical display, shaking fists and hurling insults across the narrow no-man's-land. There was a tense lull as each side waited for the other to make a move. Then a collective gasp of outrage as the antigovernment group set fire to a pro-Nava placard. Brian watched in disbelief as the police moved in, their billy clubs blurring as they chased the dispersing crowd across the plaza.

Looking behind him, Brian was amazed to see his co-workers still seated at their desks, apparently oblivious to the chaos outside.

"If anyone is interested," Brian announced to the room, "there's a riot going on in the zócalo."

Guillermo rose nonchalantly from his desk and came over for a look. "It's the third time this month," he said dryly. "Like a bullfight put on for us by the politicians and the media. Instead of capes and swords it's tear gas and guns. The best thing is just to sit back and try to enjoy the show."

"Do you agree with him?" Brian asked Laura, who had joined them at the window with a stack of books in her arms.

"No, I'm not that cynical," she said, setting the volumes aside. "But some people still remember the last revolution and it makes them afraid of change."

"Are you afraid of change?"

She bit her lip. "The wrong kind of change can be dangerous sometimes."

"But people can at least try to avoid repeating the same mistakes," Brian said. "That's what we're talking about, don't you think?"

"Yes," she agreed grudgingly. "At least I hope that's what's happening."

Brian glanced at the books in Laura's arms. The dust jacket of one volume showed a detail from a pre-Columbian codex. There was no mistaking the colored pictograms and rounded symbols scrolling across the bark-paper pages like an otherworldly cartoon strip. "I understand you're an expert in translating Aztec and Maya codices."

Laura dipped her head and her eyes retreated behind long black lashes. "Well, I don't know if I would call myself an expert exactly . . ."

"Of course she wouldn't." Guillermo affectionately squeezed her shoulders. "She's much too modest."

Laura squirmed in his embrace, refusing to meet Brian's eyes. "Guillermo, por favor."

"I'll let you go, but only if you tell him about your work."

"All right," she said, her cheeks like polished apples. Then to Brian, she added, "I love him but he exaggerates everything."

"I'm not exaggerating," Guillermo scolded. "Forget about the hot-heads in the streets. What you're doing is really revolutionary. The art of translation will never be the same. I'm not kidding. Show our friend while I go get us some coffee."

As Guillermo loped off, Brian said, "It really does sound fascinating."

"You're very kind, but I wouldn't want to bore you."

"Not a chance. I'm really very interested."

She regarded him warily, calculating his sincerity. "All right," she relented, her diffidence succumbing to professional pride. "Come over to my desk and I'll show you."

In the corner of the room Laura had staked out an oversized table, which lay buried under several layers of texts and color enlargements of Aztec codices, as well as an assortment of maps, history books, dictionaries and nature guides with photos of Mexican flora and fauna. In the middle of it all, like some futuristic relic, was a computer and laser printer.

Brian peered at the figures displayed on the iridescent screen. "Isn't that part of the Dresden Codex?" he asked, referring to the renowned book of Maya pictograms.

"Yes. It's a computerized copy. The original was discovered in the library of the King of Saxony in the seventeenth century. I have most of the known codices and several native language dictionaries stored on the hard disk. It saves a lot of time, but electronic cross-indexing has its limitations, since a single glyph can have more than one meaning."

"How is that?"

"I'll show you." Laura punched a few keys and a glyph depicting a bat's head came on the screen. "This glyph can represent a syllable or a whole word, depending on the context. It can be read either as 'zotz,' the word for bat, or as the phonetic syllable 'tz-i.' "

"So how do you know which it is?"

"Well, as I said, it depends on context. Carvings on temples and monuments, for instance, tend to be about real people and are told with the cadences and grammatical structures of real speech. The codices tend to be more symbolic, except in cases where they are meant to record epic events."

Brian nodded to show that he followed.

"The Aztecs, like the Maya, recorded their history in stone artifacts and glyphs, which have symbolic and ritual meaning, and codices, which can contain numbers or pictograms, or some combination of both. Aztec historians also recorded their thoughts in Nahuatl, the Aztec language, and, after the Conquest, some were transposed phonetically into the European alphabet. Up until now, the analysis of these sources has tended to be literal and discreet."

"Wait a minute, you've lost me now."

"I mean that when a symbol was decoded as a bat, it was assumed that it meant bat and nothing else."

"What else could it mean?"

Laura pressed her dainty hands together. "Oh, so many things," she chirped, punching more keys on the computer. "Depending on the geographical area, the time of year and so forth we can determine that the sign of the bat could have represented a portent of doom, a sign of good luck or even a person. The next step is to establish the relevant context."

The computer screen showed two columns of text. The left one contained a column of pictograms, the right one historical and linguistic notes.

"You mean like if there was a war going on at the time? Or a famine?"

"Yes, but that's just the beginning," she said with the alacrity of a schoolgirl. "The translated glyphs give us the outline of what happened." Laura scrolled the two columns down on the screen. "Then these secondary sources can be used to finish the picture. What flowers were in bloom? What was the weather like? Who was the king and what were his beliefs? What gods were dominant and what powers did they have? What social values did they represent? The codex provides the main thread. Then I take the glyphs, the Nahuatl commentaries, the Spanish glosses and anything else I can find and weave them together."

"You mean you can actually reconstruct a historical narrative? A story with characters and a plot?"

She beamed at him. "That's right, like a history book, or a novel."

Brian regarded the pig-tailed prodigy before him. He'd heard talk about such an approach to translation, but it had always been theoretical, too cutting-edge for anyone to risk their reputation on. Yet he'd also known it was only a matter of time before someone tried. And now this bashful maiden, who probably still lived with her mother, was actually doing it, breaking new ground with an ingenious concept whose time had finally arrived.

"I don't think Guillermo was exaggerating at all," Brian said, his eyes still on the computer screen. "I think what you're doing is very exciting. My thesis is on Aztec ritual sacrifice, and so naturally I'm very interested in the Quetzalcóatl excavation."

Laura quickly touched a button on the keyboard and the screen blinked off. "I'm sorry, but until the translation of the Xotl codex is finished, only the professor and Señor Torres are allowed to see it. Not even me. I mean, I only get a few pages at one time."

"I see."

"Perhaps if you ask him he'll agree to show it to you."

Brian willed himself to stay calm.

"You mean he keeps a copy in his office?"

Her silence told him yes.

"So Torres will eventually have the only full translation. And Professor Zapata, of course."

Laura's eyes widened in alarm. "Please don't tell them that I told you. I was expressly forbidden . . ."

"Laura, please excuse me," Brian apologized. "I'm still getting used to how things work around here. The last thing I want to do is compromise your work or get either of us in trouble. So, if it's all right with you, I'd appreciate it if we kept this conversation between the two of us."

It was as if a cloud had lifted from Laura's face.

"Thank you, Mr. Mendoza."

"My friends call me Brian."

"I'll remember, Brian," she said as Guillermo was back with their coffee.

"Well," he said, handing a cup to Brian, "was I right?"

"I'm very impressed," he said, and Laura blushed again.

"De nada, amigo," Guillermo said. "But don't think you can get away without telling us something about your own work. From what I hear, you have some groundbreaking thoughts yourself."

Laura nudged her boyfriend in the ribs. "Don't be presumptuous, Guillermo. Maybe he's not ready to talk about it."

"No, I don't mind at all," Brian said. "It's just that some people think my ideas are a bit unorthodox."

Guillermo began nodding enthusiastically. "Those are the only kind of ideas worth having. We scientists are all iconoclasts by nature. Except in our case, instead of destroying the icons we bring them back and try to translate them. If it weren't for all the paranoid secrecy around here, Laura would have finished by now."

"Guillermo, *por favor*," she whispered.

"What are you worried about, woman? We're all colleagues here," he said and segued into a digression on the religious persecution of Copernicus during the early sixteenth century.

"Guillermo," Laura interrupted. "Maybe Brian would like to get back to work. I know I would. So if you gentlemen will please excuse me."

As they left, she shot Guillermo a final warning glance but he ignored her. "I'm sorry," Guillermo said after they were out of earshot, "that woman worries too much. You would think we were working on the hydrogen bomb or something. Torres is the worst. Everyone knows he keeps the key to his desk under the Chacmool. That man thinks he's living in a spy novel. It's so childish. I think it makes him feel more important—a silly exercise of ego. I mean, who cares?"

"Not me," Brian said, hoping he sounded convincing.

But Guillermo's thoughts had already moved on. "You were going to tell me about your theory?"

"Well," Brian began, trying to redirect his thoughts, "the basic notion is pretty simple, actually. I wrote a paper about it that was published in *Archaeology Digest* last year."

"Yes, of course," Guillermo broke in. "I read it: 'Real Blood, False

Conclusions: The Role of Self-sacrifice in the Spanish Conquest of Tenochtitlán.' A wonderful premise. Please correct me if I'm wrong, but as I recall your hypothesis was that the Conquest was actually a reenactment of the self-sacrifice of Ce Acatl Topiltzin-Quetzalcóatl, the king of Tula."

"I don't know what amazes me more," Brian said, "that you read it or that you remembered it."

"You shouldn't be amazed," he said. "It was a very provocative piece, very bold. I think the correlation between Motecuhzoma and Quetzalcóatl's tradition of self-sacrifice was well postulated, but lacking in proof." He stopped himself. "I'm sorry, I'm being rude, aren't I?"

"No, you're right," Brian said. "I do need more proof. It's only half a theory, right now. I came here to find the other half."

"I have no doubt that you will," Guillermo said with assurance. "Now, I really should let you get back to work. May we continue this discussion another time?"

"I'd like that," Brian said. "By the way, I was wondering, is it possible to use the building at night? I mean, in case I need to work late?"

"Oh yes. If you have your pass the guard will usually let you in."

"Usually?"

"If he's not snoring," Guillermo explained. "But after midnight the doors are locked until morning."

"Thanks," Brian told him. "And thanks again for the coffee."

He emptied his cup and went back to his desk, but the electric buzz in his veins was not from caffeine; the idea was already germinating in Brian's mind. He was sure that the Xotl Codex Laura was working on had come from the Quetzalcóatl dig and that it was a gold mine of raw data. Yet he was equally positive that Torres would never let him see it.

Brian decided to spend the remainder of the day in the library. As he browsed through the rows of books, he could see Torres at the end of the stacks, hunched over his desk, shuffling papers with a self-important air, no doubt devising new ways to belittle his subordinates. Brian couldn't find a single reference to an Aztec scribe named Xotl, even under 'sh,' which was the phonetic pronunciation of the Aztec letter 'x.' On the other hand, there were dozens of volumes devoted to Quetzalcóatl, the many-faced deity that Xotl had worshipped— and Motecuhzoma had justly feared. Did Xotl believe that Cortés was Quetzalcóatl, too? And, if so, why would he have felt the need to worship him in secret, perhaps even after Cortés had entered the gates of Tenochtitlán? As Brian walked back to his desk, the riddle went round and round in his head without a beginning or end, like a spinning Aztec calendar or a plumed serpent devouring its own tail.

2

The pink stucco wall rose flush against the cobbled street and vaulted toward the sky like a pastel fortress. Brian approached the latched wooden doors of Zapata's property and pressed the intercom button. Presently a woman wearing a white apron appeared and wordlessly led him through a shady portico filled with potted banana plants and blooming fuchsia. Only after he had passed through a second wrought iron gate did Brian get a view of the house, a multi-leveled structure of concrete and glass surrounding an emerald square of lush lawn. The imposing geometry—simultaneously modern and archaic, grandiose and severe—reminded Brian of the reconstructed Maya temples at the National Museum of Anthropology.

Zapata, nattily attired in a beige silk jacket, was waiting for him in the tiled foyer. "Welcome, Mendoza," he said, giving Brian's hand two efficient pumps. "I'm so glad you could make it."

"My pleasure, Professor. Incredible place you've got here."

"Thank you. It was designed by the great architect Luis Barragán. He had a talent for expressing the extreme simplicity that derives from both the Indian and Colonial cultures."

"Does that include the ten-foot walls?" Brian said lightly.

"Especially the walls," Zapata said as he steered Brian toward the living room. "The Indians used walls to create sacred spaces, the Spaniards to separate the conquerors from the conquered, the rich Mexicans to divide the poor from the rich. But Barragán saw the wall not as a division but as a bridge, a means of communication."

Unlike its flat facade, the interior of the house was warm and inviting. The airy rooms were furnished with rough-hewn antiques and low leather couches. There were Olmec reproductions on the coffee table, abstract paintings on the clay-colored walls. The guests sported the sober hues of the affluent: dark suits and dresses interrupted by a fleeting glint of gems or precious metal.

"And how do *you* see the walls, Professor?"

Zapata surveyed the room as if from a great height. "I see them as a way to protect the rest of the world from these social cannibals. Take away their clothes and their money and they would eat each other alive."

Seeing the surprise on Brian's face, he added, "Don't misunderstand me. Without their financial support, we would still be chipping at the stones of Templo Mayor with our fingernails."

"So this is a fund-raiser for the museum?"

Zapata crossed his arms. "I prefer to think of it as a small cocktail party I am throwing for my well-endowed friends," he said. "If some of them are moved to contribute to the museum, who am I to stop them?"

"Your indulgence is admirable," Brian said. "And thanks for inviting me. I have to admit I feel a little out of place."

"Nonsense," Zapata retorted. "Talent is one thing that even money cannot buy. Besides, there are some people here that I think you should meet. Now please have some champagne and join the party while I go raise some money."

A servant materialized with a bottle and filled Brian's glass to the brim. He took a sip and stole a look at the label. French and undoubtedly expensive. Whatever else he might be, Zapata was no ivory tower ascetic.

The event fit the pattern of what Brian had always heard about Zapata: brilliant, ambitious, unpredictable—a learned man of science and administrative acrobat. He was also a glutton for controversy who never ducked a fight. Guillermo had told Brian about how the discovery of the new Quetzalcóatl temple had touched off a three-way power struggle among the city bureaucracy, the Roman Catholic church and the Ministry of Cultural Affairs—all of which claimed jurisdiction over the site. Zapata, who was no friend of the clergy, had caused a small scandal by accusing the mayor of helping the bishop reenact the Colonial suppression of the country's native heritage. Now Zapata was toasting his adversaries in his own living room, using the lure of celebrity to raise money for the Templo Mayor research foundation. Zapata's growing notoriety had sparked rumors that he harbored political ambitions, but the professor seemed to relish the role of the gadfly too much ever to become an insider. Academic and architecture buff, political provocateur and social magus, clearly Zapata, like the mercurial Quetzalcóatl, had more than one guise.

The party was reaching critical mass, that faintly electric buzz that confirmed the guests were into their second drinks and planning to stay for a third. Brian scanned the throng and spotted Torres, whom he had expected to see, and Marina Soto, whom he had not.

Brian meandered through the room, admiring the art and smiling pleasantly, steadily working his way toward Marina. He was halfway there when a woman suddenly turned and reached across his chest to tap Zapata's shoulder, pinning Brian between them.

"Professor," she teased, "it seems like centuries since your last party. I was afraid we had lost you to the pyramids."

The woman was on the downward slope of voluptuous and slightly stewed. Zapata turned and, as if wounded, exclaimed, "Sonya, you do me an injustice. The pyramids are no match for the mysteries of a beautiful woman."

"Really?" Sonya frowned at Brian. "For years I've begged him to take me along on one of those famous expeditions . . ."

"Excavations," Zapata corrected.

". . . yes, that's what I meant," she said petulantly. "But he never takes me."

Zapata raised his eyebrows. "I didn't think you were the kind of woman who enjoys getting dirty, Sonya."

"Why, Doctor!" she said, pretending to be shocked. "Who was it that said, 'The greater the wealth, the thicker the dirt'?"

"Galbraith, I think," Brian interjected as Zapata waved to someone across the room.

"Hello," the woman thrust her hand out at Brian. "I'm Sonya Velásquez."

"Brian Mendoza."

"I'm sorry," Zapata said, "I'm forgetting my manners. Brian has just joined us at Templo Mayor. He's visiting from the U.S. Would you both excuse me for a moment."

Sonya sighed and took a sip of her drink, her features magnified by the heavy crystal. "So," she intoned with a cracked veneer of interest, "another archaeologist."

"Anthropologist."

"What's the difference?"

"Anthropology is the study of man," Brian told her. "Archaeology is the study of human remains, particularly as they relate to past cultures. They used to be two entirely different fields. But nowadays, to be honest, the lines are pretty blurred."

"Oh, my God." Sonya rolled her eyes. "He's being serious."

Brian recognized the type: professors' wives, usually. Once beautiful and vivacious, years of living in their husbands' shadows turned them into bourbon-swilling cynics who flirted with junior faculty. Their fermenting bitterness made them ruthless and unstable, equally adept at come-ons and cutting remarks. For them, drinking was often the best revenge; Lady Macbeth with a splash of vermouth.

"My dear handsome man," she said, apparently willing to give him a second chance, "are you enjoying Mexico City?"

"Very much, except for the pollution. It reminds me of Los Angeles."

Sonya stirred her ice until the cubes were spinning in a drowsy vortex. "It's not so bad, really. The smog, I mean. You'll get used to it. People can get used to anything."

Across the room, Marina caught Brian's eye from where Torres had her cornered against a bookcase. She raised her glass in a silent toast. Torres followed her glance and gave Brian a chilly nod.

"Besides," Sonya was saying, "the minister of the interior claims that the new regulations on auto emissions are already having an effect."

"I don't know about the new regulations," Brian answered, "but someone should tell the minister to look out his office window once in a while."

Sonya threw back her head in a silent laugh. "Do you think so?" she purred. "In that case, why don't you tell him yourself?" She nodded toward a group that included Zapata and several others. "He's right over there."

"You're kidding."

"Not always, darling," Sonya said as she hooked Brian's arm and pulled him over to join the clique. Everyone was listening to a man in an elegant black suit whose easy, measured tone gave his words innate authority. He was fiftyish, tall and lean with flinty gray eyes and a patrician nose. Brian noticed that he was the only male in the room not wearing a tie.

". . . you may laugh," the man was saying, "but the signs are unmistakable. First the earthquake in '85. Then the flooding in Michoacán and Tabasco. Famine in Africa. Social disintegration in Eastern Europe. Economically, Mexico has made progress, but our political infrastructure—no offense to present company—is a disgrace. This could be interpreted as confusion among the kings and their people. Scientists—the soothsayers of modern times—have long predicted catastrophe in the form of overpopulation, global warming and depletion of the ozone layer. And there's our continuing pollution problem—the writings are quite explicit about dead birds dropping from the sky."

"It's true that we have many problems, Alejandro," one of the men agreed, "but what makes you so sure that they signify the end of our civilization?"

"Portents of the end of the Fifth Sun," Brian broke in. "The Aztec prophets predicted that the water would become poison, the animals would die and the sky would turn black, blotting out the sun."

The gray eyes flashed at Brian. "Exactly. According to the codices and other sources, yes, there is a clear correlation between the omens of the early-sixteenth-century Aztecs and our own culture today."

"That is all very fascinating, Alejandro," Zapata said, "but these omens you mention are a fait accompli. To be really convincing you must make a prediction, or at least tell us about something that is not already common knowledge."

"Very well. The Aztec prophets predicted a ball of fire would cross the heavens and light up the night sky."

"The Alpha Centauri asteroid," Brian said. "It's supposed to come close enough to Earth to be visible in a few weeks."

The group grew larger as others gathered around to listen.

"Ah, there you have it," Alejandro exclaimed, "a flaming fireball from the heavens that will send us all the way of the dinosaurs. Did you know that the meteorite that ended the Jurassic period collided with Earth just off the coast of the Yucatán peninsula? They know because they've discovered a huge hole in the ocean floor near Cancún. The odds of it happening again become greater each year."

"It's true," Sonya confirmed. "I saw a program about it on television. I just hope it doesn't fall on top of Mexico City. Dios!"

"Alejandro, you are a true oracle," a balding man said. He paused a beat before adding, "Or maybe you just read the science section of *The New York Times*." The group exploded with relieved laughter.

Alejandro patiently waited for the laughter to end. "It's not just me, you know," he answered. "According to the Maya wise men, the apocalypse will take place on December 23, 2012, which marks the folding of the twenty-year katun and the completion of the great cycle that began on August 13, 3114 B.C. On that day, the Maya believed, the sky will be divided, the land will rise and the world will be destroyed by the Ninth Lord of the Night. Is that specific enough for you?" His words were met by a nervous quiet. "Besides," he continued, "it is only the end of the world as we know it, Mr. Minister. The demise of the old always clears the way for the birth of something new."

"Are you referring to the national elections?" another man asked.

"I said something *new*," Alejandro replied. "Our present political system is still mired in the past."

"Well," the minister huffed, "that will be decided not by you or I but by the will of the people."

"Or the will of God."

"But *whose* God?" Zapata interjected. "You've no doubt heard the story of the Spanish friar Bernardino de Sahagún, who was trying to explain the concept of heaven and hell to an Indian convert. 'Heaven,' explained Sahagún, 'is where God is, and hell is where the devil is.' 'Where,' asked the Indian, 'are the Spaniards?' Sahagún reflected for a moment before answering, 'The Spaniards are in heaven, my son.' 'In that case,' the Indian replied, 'I think I'd like to go to hell.' "

Everyone laughed, and Zapata excused himself with an abbreviated bow. Brian marveled at the professor's social ease, the way that his anecdote had artfully defused the tension without taking sides. Maybe he was a political animal after all.

As the group broke apart, Alejandro was still looking at Brian. "Your comment about the meteorite was very astute," he said. "It would have had to drop on their heads before they'd have made the connection. They really are no different from the dinosaurs."

Brian smiled. "Well, not everyone likes to ponder their own demise."

"So you agree that we're all going to die."

"Eventually."

Alejandro laughed. "Touché, Mr. . . . ."

"Mendoza. Brian Mendoza."

The man took Brian's hand in a firm grip. "Alejandro Villalobos, at your service. Tell me, is your interest in anthropology intuitive or professional?"

"I've just joined the staff of Templo Mayor as a research assistant to finish my Ph.D."

"And do you have a particular area of interest?"

"Aztec ritual sacrifice."

Villalobos's interest seemed to rise a notch. "I'm a businessman, an investor let's say, and something of a student of anthropology," he said. "These parlor games can be amusing, but my affinity is genuine and I'd like very much to hear more about your work. If I may, I'd like to invite you to my home for dinner sometime."

"Sure. That would be nice."

"Good. My assistant will call you at the museum to set a date."

Free at last, Brian strolled over to the bar where Marina Soto was waiting for a drink. The corner of a notebook protruded from her handbag. He got as close to her as decorum would allow and whispered, "Does your editor approve of drinking on the job?"

"It's only a spritzer," she replied reprovingly as the bartender handed her a drink. "But tell me, are you always so moralistic?"

"I'm sorry," he said. "I don't mean to be presumptuous. I guess I was just surprised to see you here. Very pleasantly surprised."

"So am I," she said. And Brian felt it again, the intoxicating tension and, beneath that, a faint sexual glow.

Marina indicated the crowd with her eyes. "So how does it feel to be rubbing shoulders with the Mexican elite?"

Brian stood beside her and faced the room. "Oh, is that what they are? Seem like your ordinary group of apocalypse-loving capitalists to me."

"Oh really?"

"You don't agree?"

He watched her as she coolly appraised the well-coiffed crowd. Reflexively, several males turned, and Brian realized she was easily the most beautiful woman in the room.

"Some of them, yes," she said finally. "But there is nothing ordinary about Alejandro Villalobos. He is one of the richest men in Mexico. Old money and the new right. Very intelligent. A bit mysterious—there are rumors that he is a shaman. I've been trying to interview him for months."

"Really? I'm sure Professor Zapata could arrange it for you."

"Not very likely."

"Why not?"

"Well, for one thing, they hate each other."

"But I thought—"

"Don't be deceived. Look at them. They are like two sharks circling each other in a small tank."

Brian looked over his shoulder to where Zapata was presiding over a cluster of listeners, earthy and animated, his stubby fingers stabbing the air to emphasize his words. As if to illustrate Marina's point, Villalobos was at the opposite end of the room, pale and serene, a paragon of aristocratic poise as he conversed with a man in a green linen jacket. To Brian they seemed less like competing predators than two entirely separate species, each descended from a different branch of social evolution.

"But who will take the first bite?" Brian speculated.

"Who knows? Probably the first one who smells blood. It's well known that both have powerful allies and political ambitions. That's another reason I'd like to interview Villalobos."

"What about you," Brian teased. "What are your ambitions?"

"For myself or for others?" she said flatly.

"Is there a difference?"

The playfulness in her voice evaporated. "Yes, a big difference. I should be offended, but you are a foreigner. You see, Mexico is not like the United States. The games of power are not played in the media, or even in the national assembly. The important decisions are made by a small group of men who live behind walls in houses like this one."

"And have names like Villalobos," Brian said. Marina nodded as she sipped her drink. "Have you tried asking him? For an interview, I mean."

Her expression told him it was a stupid question. "People like Villalobos do not speak to the press," she said curtly. Her disenchantment was palpable. Brian groped for a way to redeem himself. "Then maybe I'll put in a good word for you. He's invited me to dinner."

She offered him a nod of congratulation, but her eyes were mocking. "You would do that for me?"

He shrugged. "I happen to believe in the idea of a free press." He waited a moment before adding, "Of course, it could be dangerous. We'd be forced to meet incognito. You know, crowded bars with loud music and smoky, dimly lit cafés."

"How dim?" she asked, submitting to the private argot that was forming between them. It was no small victory, Brian knew. Words mattered. Language was the breath of civilization, as a professor of his liked to say. The same principle applied to the harsh consonants of long-dead empires and to the lexicon of love that bloomed between two strangers. This secret code bound them to each other, marked them as members of the same binary tribe.

"So dim that you need to rely on other senses," he said.

She shifted her weight and regarded him warily. "Very subtle, Mr. Mendoza. I thought Americans were supposed to be so direct about sex."

The words were on the tip of his tongue.

"Miss Soto?" It was Torres. "I see you've met our visiting, ah, associate," he said, ignoring Brian. "I'm ready to continue whenever you are. I'll be over there."

"Yes, of course," Marina said. "I'll join you in a moment." Torres backed away, but the spell was broken. "I'm sorry," she said. "But I must get back to work."

"I can't say I envy you," he said.

"Buenas noches, Mr. Mendoza."

Brian looked into her smiling, defiant eyes. "I'm looking forward to our own interview," Brian said, "provided, of course, that you're still interested."

"It's my job to be interested."

"Then let me get you another drink."

"Sorry," she said, as she began to walk away, "it's against my morals."

He kept his eyes on her until she had reached the other end of the room. Then he consulted his watch and drained his drink. A few minutes later, Brian slipped away from the party without saying goodbye and took a taxi directly to Templo Mayor.

I enter the world gasping as Venus rises on the day of 7 Snake and marks my destiny. Still wet with the fluids of creation, I am carried outside and held up to the heavens so that Quetzalcóatl's star can bathe me in its divine light. The day and moment of my birth have already determined that my name will be Xotl and that I will grow up to be a priest, a man of learning and celestial worship, a caretaker of the gods who will be expected to claim his place in the highest strata of our society. As if troubled

*by the weight of such lofty expectations, I begin to cry, my brows tied to-
gether in a knot of infantile anguish. Rocking me in her arms, my mother
asks, "Why are you so sad, my little one? What is it that troubles you so?"
But my only answer is a pitiful wail followed by another wave of incon-
solable sobbing.*

*My father, Tlacpan, is a great warrior who has brought honor to our
family in the war against Chalco. During the long and costly campaign,
Tlacpan captured six warriors, who were sacrificed to Huitzilopochtli,
the Little Hummingbird, defender of the Fifth Sun. The prisoners were
marched up the steps of the old temple and placed upon the sacred stone
one at a time. Four priests, their long hair and black robes encrusted with
blood, held down the prisoner's arms and legs while a fifth tied a rope
around his neck. After the sacred chant, the king raised an obsidian knife
high above his head and stabbed it down into the heaving body. The heart
was still throbbing as the king yanked it out and held it aloft, sprinkling
the hot blood in the direction of the sun, ensuring its movement across the
heavens. Then the heart was jammed into the open mouth of the Little
Hummingbird, nourishing him while the next prisoner was readied to offer his chalchiuhatl, or precious water.*

*To die such a death is not considered a misfortune; instead, it is
looked upon as a privilege. For without death there is no life, and those
who are kissed by the sacred knife are allowed to ascend to the Thirteenth
Sky, where the world was born and the gods reside. My father speaks of
the victims with envy, adding that if he were not so valuable on the battlefield he would gladly follow in their footsteps and place his own chest
on the tezontle altar.*

*This I learn during a childhood of privilege and plenty, made pos-
sible by continuing victories over our neighbors in the Flowery Wars,
which bring booty and blood to our table. As the son of a decorated warrior, I am entitled to attend a calmecac, a school for the offspring of the
noble classes and a basic requirement for anyone wishing to enter the
priesthood. The day I am to leave, my father takes me aside and speaks
to me, a mixture of pride and concern on his face. "Listen, my son," he
says, "you are not going to be honored or respected or esteemed. You are
going to be looked down upon, humiliated and despised. Every day you
will cut agave thorns for penance, and you will draw blood from your
body with these spines and you will bathe at night in cold water and be*

forced to go without food. My son, you must harden your heart to the pain, and deaden your skin to the cold, and you must defeat your hunger like a warrior defeats his enemy. For then will the elders say, 'Look, it is clear that he is the son of Tlacpan.' "

My father's words summon a great sadness within me because I suddenly know that I will never see him again. And even though I am still very young, I force myself not to cry. Mistaking my emotion for homesickness, my father smiles and says, "Don't worry, my child, I know you will not fail me, and one day you will become a great priest of the god Quetzalcóatl." Then my mother embraces me tearfully and I climb into the litter, looking back one last time to wave good-bye to my parents and to my childhood.

During the ride to the calmecac, I gaze out at Tenochtitlán, a city embraced by the Lake of the Moon, cradled by the Valley of Mexico, surrounded by slumbering volcanoes. My eyes trace the great causeways, canals and roads, all woven together like the stitches of the finest tapestry. The people themselves are like colorful beads embroidering the streets and lining the bustling waterways. I envy the carefree laughter of children my own age playing games in the dirt while their parents shop along the stalls that sell silver and pottery, woven baskets, candies, fruit and chickens. Here and there, over the flat roofs of the white houses, a small pyramid rises up, defining the spiritual and physical center of the neighborhood. And up ahead, taller than all the others, stands the Great Temple itself, its magnificent walls marking the crossroads of the kings and the intersection of heaven and earth.

My father has not spoken falsely; life at the calmecac is harsh and devoid of pleasure. Dressed in loincloths and simple white tunics, my fellow students and I are sworn to a code of monastic discipline. At midnight we are roused from sleep and told to pierce our earlobes and tongues with cactus thorns as a sign of penitence. Before the dawn we are awakened again to bathe in the cold waters of Lake Texcoco. It is at the calmecac that I learn about the history of our people, who long ago emigrated from Tula, the home of our ancestors, the Toltecs. Our tribe, the Mexica, descended from the paradise Aztlán in search of a new home. When the pilgrims saw an eagle eating a serpent, they knew the gods had sent them a sign, and on that spot they founded Tenochtitlán, which means the place where cactus grows in rock.

At the calmecac we are also lectured in astronomy, politics and writing. But the majority of our time is devoted to worshipping the Aztec and Toltec gods. Our patron is Quetzalcóatl, the Plumed Serpent, protector of priests and vengeful guardian of civilization, and who also manifests himself as Venus, the Morning Star, and Ehécatl, the god of wind. We also pay tribute to the other gods, including the warrior Huitzilopochtli and Tláloc, the bringer of rain, Tezcatlipoca, brother of Quetzalcóatl, lord of darkness and confusion, and a host of deities representing fire, fertility, women, music, dance, pulque, flowers and gold. We learn that the realm of man, the One World, lies between the Nine Underworlds and the Thirteen Skies, beginning with the First Sky, which was the home of the moon, and continuing up to the place of the supreme beginning.

I work hard and try to honor my parents but it is not until years later that my true calling is revealed to me. On that day I am in Quetzalcóatl's shrine, praying for his eternal guidance and wisdom. To show my humility, I take a thorn from my satchel and push it into my earlobe. As the blood trickles down my neck I see my father bleeding on the battlefield. He is a brave man who does not fear death but he is trembling, an expression of abject dread on his face as his hand opens and a gold charm in the shape of a hummingbird falls through his fingers. When I leave the shrine an elder is waiting outside with his head bowed. Before he can speak, I say, "I know: my father is dead." The elder is so surprised that he does not speak, but only kneels before me in a sign of respect.

News of my vision spreads quickly through the calmecac and it is said that the gods have blessed me with the gift of divination. But instead of becoming one of the king's soothsayers, I ask to be named a keeper of the shrine of Quetzalcóatl. A few weeks later my request is granted. The authority of my new post gives me free access to the religious precincts of Templo Mayor, which are being enlarged to reflect the growing power of the empire and our gods. I devote myself entirely to the teachings of Quetzalcóatl, who is worshipped as the link between earth and heaven and who is honored by the presence of several large serpent heads and a small circular shrine near the much larger temples of Huitzilopochtli and Tláloc. It is my task to help the other priests maintain the shrine and to ensure that he receives a proper amount of tribute from the people. But despite my holy responsibilities and exalted rank I suffer from a troubled conscience. For I know that Quetzalcóatl once preached against sacrifice *and yet the number of victims seems to increase by the day. How can the elders continue to kill and not expect Quetzalcóatl to be angry? And how can a priest expect to enforce the god's will with the blood of Huitzilopochtli's victims on his hands?*

Despite the gravity of my misgivings, I have little time to dwell on such thoughts. The new temple to Huitzilopochtli is finished and the Supreme Emperor Motecuhzoma has called for a great celebration to mark its inauguration. Nobles and kings from the most distant reaches of the empire are summoned to witness the spectacle, which is unprecedented in its dimensions. The streets and the plazas overflow with people, like the rivers after a storm. The number of victims to be sacrificed is almost as great. They are in four long lines that reach from the temple to the outskirts of the city. Out of view from the populace, the leaders of our neighboring nations sit behind flowered screens, feasting on meats, fruits, candies and other delicacies while they wait to witness the slaughter. For centuries this tradition has ensured the respect of our enemies and the loyalty of our allies, Tlacopan and Texcoco. At dawn, the kings of the Triple Alliance take their places atop the temple and a great silence descends on the multitudes. As the rays of the sun ignite the peaks of the volcanoes, the air shakes with the sound of beating drums and the first victims are led to the altar. Two by two their chests are ripped open and their hearts torn out. Then their bodies are kicked down the steps, where they collect in a steaming heap. After the butchers and cooks are done with the corpses, the skulls are mounted on wood racks for all to see and enjoy. The killing continues all day and into the evening. After nightfall, torches are lit and placed along the steps of the temple creating a fiery avenue of death. By midnight the kings are exhausted by their labor and the high priests are ordered to take their place and continue the killing.

The second day dawns red with the blood of hundreds and I realize it is only a matter of time before I will be called upon to help with the grisly duty. As I expect, a messenger from the high priest of Huitzilopochtli appears and orders me to don my ceremonial robes and wait at the base of the pyramid. To be asked to assist in the sacrifice is a great honor and my peers come forward to congratulate me, but I do not feel fortunate. As the appointed time draws near I push through the crowds until I am standing at the base of the temple. One after another the bodies roll past me and I silently pray to Quetzalcóatl for guidance and strength. A goblet of blood and sacred herbs is offered to me and I drink, knowing that it will take me closer to the gods. After a while I hear my name and mount the steps as if in a dream. My feet feel nothing but the blood-soaked steps, my ears hear nothing but the shuddering drums, my eyes see nothing but the plunging knife in the glistening hands of the high priests. I reach the summit of the temple and look down. A crimson waterfall flows down the steps and into a shallow pool, where it spreads out to touch the feet of the watching hordes. The knife is placed in my hands and I feel the cape of quetzal feathers being lowered around my shoulders. I avert my eyes as the captive is held down before me and stripped. The obsidian blade feels heavy and slick in my hands. My nostrils fill with the scent of fresh blood and my senses reel. To fail now would mean my own death but my limbs have lost their strength. It is then that Quetzalcóatl saves me. He shows me the spirits of the dead, smiling, running in fields of green maize. They look at me and laugh, their white teeth flashing. I understand my god's message: these are not men but ghosts who have already lost their lives. To kill a dead man is not a sin. It is my duty to end their agony and set them free in the next world. Most important is the fact that Quetzalcóatl does not wish my death; he has other plans for me. My mind becomes clear—I know he will guide my hand. I raise the knife and utter the sacred words: "The sun has risen and gives us warmth. Deign to fulfill your function, complete your mission, O Lord." In a single stroke I plunge the blade toward a naked chest before me. Only in that fleeting second before the jagged tip pierces flesh do I actually look at the man I am murdering. He is trembling and his features are disfigured by horror. The man is a stranger yet I recognize his expression: it is the same one I saw on my father's face.

The next day I am visited by several Huitzilopochtli priests who tell me that they want to pay tribute to Quetzalcóatl. Wary of this sudden conversion by my religious rivals, I am at first reluctant to admit them. I ask, "Why would servants of the all-powerful Huitzilopochtli wish to pay homage to an ancient Toltec god?" The youngest among them identifies himself as Tonatiuh. "Huitzilopochtli is doomed and so is Motecuhzoma," he answers boldly. "We are sickened by the constant war and sacrifice that is weakening our empire and wish to pledge allegiance to the true and future god." Tonatiuh further explains that he recently journeyed to Texcoco, where the cult of Quetzalcóatl reigns supreme under the wise King Nezahualpilli. This I know to be true, but what he says next is a revelation. The Tecocoan king, Tonatiuh tells me, is predicting the return of Quetzalcóatl and the fall of Motecuhzoma, who will be punished by the gods for misleading his people. I tell Tonatiuh and the others that I will help them as much as I can, but that our meetings must remain secret lest the emperor accuse us all of treason. They agree and take their leave, promising to visit me again within the fortnight.

I return to my chambers in a state of extreme agitation. Could this be the purpose that Quetzalcóatl has spared me for? That night I dream that a white cross appears atop the Pyramid of the Sun just before the city is engulfed in flames. I see the bridges burning and enormous beasts carrying gods who shoot lightning bolts from their fingers. I see women and children butchered to bits and people with terrible sores on their hands and faces. Then I begin to rise above the carnage and move with a gentle wind that blows me south toward the paradise of Tlalocan, the place of Tláloc. As I drift southward, the air becomes warm and scented with the nectar of a million flowers. It is a land of blossoming forests and lush mountain valleys. This is the source of all rivers, springs and water, both hot and cold, and I can see streams and waterfalls pouring into shimmering lakes filled with silver-skinned fish. There can be no hunger here because the fields are heavy with fruit, maize, beans, onions and flowering plants. The hills ring with the songs of painted birds and the croaking frogs, which ensure that Tláloc remains awake and sends a steady flow of life-giving rainfall down to earth.

Something bids me to look up and I see Tláloc himself, resting on a cushion of clouds, resplendent in a gown of green, white and red feathers. He wears a jade choker with red flowers decorating the edge and gold bands on his arms and legs. Tláloc points downward and a gust of air sends me toward the ground and into a cave where I know Quetzalcóatl is waiting. I hear a sound like the rushing wind and shield my eyes from the brightness of his robes. The rays of light emanating from his hands reach out like fingers until they touch my face and I know that he is pleased with me but that there is much more for me to do. Without speaking he holds up the symbol of totality and I instantly understand. I feel his concern for the hardship that lies ahead of me and I know that no words exist to express my emotions.

When I awake the candle has gone out and my chamber is dark. I go *outside and look out over the city. With tears in my eyes I listen to the gentle commotion of families gathering for their supper, watch the lights of Texcoco twinkling across the blue-green lake. The world is the same yet I have changed, like a blind person who has regained his sight or an infant who has taken its very first breath.*

Someone was coming down the corridor. As the lock turned in the door to the outer office, Brian quickly replaced the codex translation and the key, killed the lamp in Torres's office and crept into the library stacks. He felt foolish crouched down on the floor on his hands and knees, skulking around like a common thief, but to be caught flagrantly breaking the rules would be even worse. Footsteps echoed briskly on the linoleum floor, and Brian recognized Torres's silhouette moving past the stacks and into his office. The light clicked on and there was the sound of the desk drawer being opened followed by a shuffling of papers. He heard Torres cough, then the whisper of pages being turned. After a minute the light went out again. The footsteps retreated. A jangle of keys, the muffled slam of the door. Silence.

Brian remained hiding for another minute just to make sure before standing up and stretching his legs. He wondered what could be important enough to drag Torres away from the party. Did he suspect what Brian was up to? If so, the risk was well worth it. Laura's lyrical interpretation of the Quetzalcóatl codex had already provided invaluable insights. Xotl, he now knew, was not a scribe but a priest. He had foreseen the arrival of Cortés in a vision. But the message of his vision was still unclear. The answer would probably be in the forthcoming sections. Already there was no doubt in his mind that Xotl's story was a major anthropological discovery, and that the priest's writings could have a major impact on existing perceptions of Aztec cosmology.

"Incredible," he whispered, just to hear himself speak, to make it more real. Brian's instincts hadn't failed him. He'd been right to sneak into the museum and break into Torres's locked desk. Despite his eagerness to know more, he would have to wait since the rest of the codex was still being translated. Besides, it was too dangerous to stay any longer. What if Torres came back again? Or Zapata? It would be better to come back later on to continue his secret studies.

Brian knew he should feel guilty, but instead he felt oddly exhilarated, lightheaded from the wine of his intellectual larceny. Still in the dark, he tiptoed to the exit and let himself out, half expecting Torres to be waiting for him in the corridor. But except for the faint sizzle of the fluorescent lighting, the hall was deserted. A minute later, Brian was in the downstairs lobby, striding toward the exit. The night watchman hardly looked at him as he groggily unlocked the doors and muttered buenas noches.

3

Torres was watching him. Brian could feel him tracking his movements whenever he took a book from the library or stopped to chat with Laura at her desk. At first Brian was afraid that his skulduggery had been discovered. But when Torres failed to confront him, he decided that the suspicion he saw in his rival's eyes was probably just a by-product of their instinctive enmity. Since Zapata's party, Brian and Torres had in fact barely spoken, which was fine with Brian, who knew that Laura had just completed another section of the codex because she had come in extra early and had spent the rest of the morning tidying up her desk. Brian immediately began planning another nocturnal foray, all the while pretending to be too absorbed in his work to notice that Torres instructed the secretary to hold his calls and locked himself in his office.

Brian's duties included making an inventory of objects that had been retrieved from excavations in the field. Somewhere in the basement of the building a team of technicians was painstakingly sorting, cleaning and assembling the objects, which were then catalogued in the museum collection for future exhibition. The artifacts were listed on computer printouts that identified their dimensions, location and chronological origins. Brian's job was to sift through the voluminous inventory of stone tools, broken idols and pottery fragments and direct them to the appropriate section of the museum. When the columns of artifacts began to blur on the page, his mind wandered ahead to his lunch that afternoon with Marina Soto. At Zapata's party he'd felt a subtle charge, an attraction that went beyond flirtation. It was almost as if under the superficial differences, despite their clashing nationalities, they were alike, both driven by ambition and the need to understand the hidden forces that shaped their fate.

In only a few days his habits had taken on an agreeable, if unremarkable pattern. Days were spent at the museum, punctuated by a conversation with Zapata or lunch with a colleague. Nights were for working on his thesis and long walks down the endless avenues of Mexico City. As the time inched by, the unfamiliarity of Mexico became less threatening and he began to recognize his own foreignness as a kind of freedom. Each new sight, smell and taste became a form of sensual liberation, a tiny triumph over the ordinary. His old life at Berkeley began to take on a distant quaintness. He pictured his fellow students sprawled out on the lawn, soaking up the California sun, and found it increasingly difficult to relate. It was almost as if there were now two Brian Mendozas. One continued to think like a typical American student; the other was a man without a face or a country, traveling on a temporary visa, listening for the spiritual echoes of a long-dead Aztec priest.

The call came just as Brian was in the midst of collating a list of ceremonial sea shells recovered from a section of the pyramid of Tláloc. Speaking in perfect English, Villalobos's secretary telephoned to invite Brian to spend the day at his country house in Tepoztlán, a small Indian village about an hour south of Mexico City. A car, she explained, would come to pick him up at 10 A.M. on Sunday. Before Brian could say anything else, the line was disconnected. He shrugged and went back to work. At the moment he was more interested in tracing the origin of a batch of ceremonial shells. The shells were believed to have come from Xoconochco, a distant province on the Pacific located near present-day Mazatlán. The various rooms and even the mortar between the stones of the temples were brimming with such objects, a physical and symbolic embodiment of the Aztec effort to assimilate and consolidate all the various cultures and peoples under its rule into a common hierarchy. It was a grand, even laudable impulse, but one that contained the seeds of its own destruction. Xotl, with his doubts and secret beliefs, was himself a small fissure in the Aztec cosmology. There had probably been hundreds, perhaps thousands of others like him, quietly chipping away at the metaphysical foundations of the One World, until the cement binding the Aztec empire together had finally cracked under the weight of its own presumptions. But there was something else, too, an emotion that seemed to come out of nowhere. He admired Xotl. For seeing the coming apocalypse and trying to understand it. For having the courage to act on his convictions. For daring to question. Brian knew he was treading on dangerous ground. The annals of anthropology were rife with examples of researchers who had compromised the truth by looking at the evidence through the distorting lens of their own values. It had long ago been accepted that a certain degree of cultural bias was inevitable, but it was still the anthropologist's duty to try to remain alert to such prejudice and eliminate it from his analysis. Was his insight into Xotl valid, Brian asked himself, or was he merely projecting his own perceptions onto the words of the Aztec priest, like a narcissist transfixed by his own reflection?

Then Brian's musings were interrupted by a voice from the much more recent past.

"Hello?"

"Hola." Greg Stone's high school Spanish was absurdly amplified by the long-distance booster. "Esté es tu viejo amigo, Pancho Villa."

"Buenos días, Señor Villa," Brian deadpanned. "Forgive me for being frank, but I was under the distinct impression that you were dead."

"Jez, I know." A raspy chuckle. "But hi jeest moved to Montana and opeened a Taco Bell stand. As you anthropologeests know, amigo, we dead hombres have a habeet of, ah, turning up."

"So do photographers. But I think you're confusing me with Louis Leakey, señor."

"How dare you get technical on me, Mendoza. Especially when I'm threatening to visit you?"

"Don't tell me you're coming here to try to overthrow the Mexican government, Señor Villa."

"From what I hear, the Mexican rebels don't need my help."

The flip banter was a signature of their friendship, cultivated by countless late-night rap sessions in their shared two-bedroom Berkeley brownshingle. Like a secret handshake, it defined the boundaries of fraternal complicity. The verbal preliminaries over, Stone filled Brian in on the details of his latest assignment. He had been hired by *Life* to photograph a religious sect in Montana that was digging bunkers in the mountains in preparation for the Final Judgment. Some three thousand followers of the Church of Divine Intervention had already sold their possessions and brought their families to live in the designated "holy zone." Meanwhile, the local townspeople were threatening to attack the church compound with tractors and shotguns, and journalists were flocking to the area in anticipation of "good color." Stone expected to be there for a couple of weeks before heading down to join Brian in Mexico. "While I'm there, I'm planning to do a few freelance jobs and gorge myself on mole poblano," Stone announced. "They say there are twenty-seven spices in the sauce alone."

"I didn't know that."

"You mean to tell me that you've never tasted mole?" Brian's best friend asked. "What kind of Mexican are you?"

The plastic dagger glinted in Brian's glass as he stirred his drink and waited for Marina Soto to spot him at the bar. It was still in his fingers when he rose to greet her.

"I know I'm late," she said, gesturing to the toy sword, "but isn't that a bit drastic?"

The comment had a double edge that he had come to expect from her. Nothing she said was offered at face value; even her apology had a teasing subtext.

"Not if you had stood me up."

She was wearing a simple black dress that might have been discreet on a less shapely body. A burgundy and gold scarf draped around her neck completed the ensemble. As she sat down he caught the faint incense of her perfume.

"Well, you can consider yourself saved," she said. "What are you drinking?"

"Aztec Elixir," Brian said. "Two parts ginger ale, one part cranberry juice."

She made a sour face. "You've got to be kidding. Only the tourists drink those things."

"Hey, don't blame me," Brian protested. "It's your country."

"Not this part," she said almost grimly. Then to the bartender, "Agua mineral, por favor."

"So why did you suggest we meet here?"

"I thought you'd be more comfortable."

Brian scanned the room, which was filling up with a mix of local businessmen, tourists and well-dressed women out for a ladies' lunch. "Do you really have such a low opinion of me?"

Marina tried to hide her smile behind her glass, but it was no use. "I'm sorry," she said at last. "It's really not funny."

"Yes it is," Brian said with feigned gravity. "I'm deeply offended."

She stood and reached for her purse. "Let's go then."

"Listen, I didn't mean—"

"I know a better place. It's not far."

Brian paid the bar bill and followed her through the lobby and out into the street, past the yellow rumba line of taxis waiting at the curb, across a busy avenue and into a one-story hacienda-style restaurant with tile floors, potted plants and wrought-iron bars across the windows.

After they were seated, Marina asked, "Does this suit you better?"

"Much," Brian said, marveling at her capacity to surprise him. "You know, I've never met a woman like you."

She drew back. "Should I take that as a compliment?"

"Absolutely."

Brian looked around. Bird cages dangled from the rafters and a trickle of water danced in a tile reflecting pool. He ordered broiled red snapper and a glass of white wine; Marina had a Caesar salad and more mineral water.

They talked about Colonial architecture and the vicissitudes of high-altitude weather. Then Marina took out her notebook and placed it on the table beside her plate.

"So what can you tell me about your boss?" Marina inquired in a no-nonsense tone that made his heart sink.

"You mean Professor Zapata?"

"Who else could I mean?"

"I thought you were here to interview *me*."

"Yes, that's true," she said tactfully. "But you knew I was working on a piece on Professor Zapata. I thought that much was understood."

"Well, I only started two weeks ago."

"I know."

"So why are you interviewing me?"

She leaned across the table and looked him in the eye. "My profile on Zapata is nearly finished. My editors want to run it now, but I have the impression that there's something he hasn't told me, an announcement of some kind. I don't know. I thought you might be able to help me."

Brian marveled at the power of female intuition. The Xotl codex had been burning a hole in his brain ever since he'd read it. He wanted to tell her, but couldn't risk it.

"I'd love to help, but at this point you probably know more than I do," he said. "I'm sure that when the professor is ready to issue a public statement, he'll be in touch with you. He seems to be quite aware of the power of the media."

Marina flinched at the phrase. "Yes, he's a very smart man, but his intelligence is being wasted. He could be one of the great leaders of this country but all he cares about is digging up old bones."

"You think that's wrong?"

"I think we must help the living before we help the dead."

"So you agree with the church?"

Her almond eyes widened. "The church? The priests are the worst ones of all. That is the real tragedy, all this religion and superstition, it diverts energy from making things better. We already have too many churches. What we need are schools, factories and truly democratic institutions. Mexico is not poor; it is very rich. But we squander our wealth with bad planning and corruption. Why do roads and bridges go unbuilt while we pour our resources into beach resorts for rich foreigners? Why must the masses forage in the garbage for food while their bosses lunch on veal in the Lomas of Chapultepec?"

Her anger was incandescent, a white hot filament of outrage. Brian was too taken aback to respond.

"I'm sorry," she said. "I've shocked you, haven't I?"

"No, not really," Brian said. "It's just that you seem to take it so personally."

"Tell me this, Mendoza. You've seen what our leaders are like, how much they care. If I, if we, do not take it personally, then who will? If no one takes responsibility, then how will things ever change?"

"I don't know," Brian confessed.

Their lunch arrived, but Marina only picked at her plate. "I'm sorry," she said. "I didn't mean to subject you to a diatribe. Enough about politics. And now I should do my job and begin our interview."

"Fine," he said, "but you can make it up to me by telling me a little bit about yourself first."

She seemed to weigh his motives for a moment, then something in her softened. "My father was a diplomat. I was born in Mexico but we were constantly traveling. My youth was spent in Paris, Washington, Bogotá. It was only after my father retired that we came to live in Mexico permanently."

"You make it sound so tragic."

"Don't misunderstand. I love my father very much and I would never live anywhere else. But Mexico will always be in some sense a foreign country to me. It's better really, because, unlike other Mexicanos, I'm always learning and I don't take things for granted."

"Is that why you became a journalist?"

"Yes, perhaps. I don't know. I've always been attracted to other people's lives, other ways of looking."

"I like the way you look very much," Brian said, and from the slight reddening of her cheeks he could tell that he'd finally gotten through to her.

"I think that's enough about me," she announced. "Now it's my turn to ask questions." She extracted a pen from her purse and held it to her notebook. "Let's start with some biographical details."

Brian cleared his throat. "All right. My name is Brian Mendoza. I was born in Los Angeles, California. I am an only child and my astrological sign is Gemini."

She scribbled on, ignoring his fatuity. "Tell me about your parents."

"My father, Miguel Mendoza, died when I was eight. My mother is Irish, Mary Sheahan."

"Irish. Is that where your green eyes come from?"

"I guess."

"What was your father like?"

"He was a good man."

She waited for him to continue. "He was a good man? Is that all you can remember about him?"

"I wish I could remember more. I worry sometimes that my memories aren't real, that I'm inventing things to compensate."

"What are your memories?" she asked gently. "Describe him to me."

Despite his initial reservations, Brian found himself opening up, trusting her, searching his mind for details. Did all interviews conjure this strange combination of sacramental confession and clinical psychoanalysis? He had read once about the tacit contract that existed between interviewers and their subject. The person being interviewed gave information—his or her life story, personal information and thoughts—in exchange for the chance to further a cause or grease the wheels of fame. But what, Brian wondered, could a journalist offer to someone who had no interest in exposure?

"He was strong—physically and emotionally, but also very gentle," Brian said. "He didn't talk much. Words made him uncomfortable. He would take me to football games and museums . . . ."

"It's hard for you to talk about him, isn't it?"

"Yes."

"And your mother?"

"She's okay."

Marina stopped writing. "Only okay?"

"We don't get along so well anymore. It's part of the reason I moved to Berkeley. To get away. My dad's death changed her. A construction accident."

"I'm sorry."

Brian shrugged. "It was a long time ago. I was only eight."

"Do you blame your mother?"

"No. Why should I? It's just that we've never been able to see eye to eye. After my dad died she lost her trust in people. Everything became a threat, made her nervous. She turned into a hypochondriac. That's probably why she wanted me to be a doctor."

"You didn't?"

"No, but it took me a long time to realize it. I took premed as an undergraduate major. I even got into medical school. I'd only been there two months when I discovered that I had no interest in medicine. I got physically ill, which is pretty ironic when you consider I was supposed to be learning how to heal other people. I started waking up in the morning with this terrible knot in my stomach. Then one day I just stayed home and the knot went away."

"So you went back to school?"

"Not at first. I drifted for a year, took dumb jobs, traveled a bit. I became a professional dilettante—my mother's words. Then one day I saw a television special on the Aztecs. I went out the next day and bought every book I could find. I applied to graduate school for the next fall. And to my utter surprise, I got in."

Marina rested her chin on her palm. "It sounds very romantic."

"It wasn't. It was tough going back, like someone who'd failed life and had to take it over again."

"Have you ever been married or had children?"

"That's two different questions."

"Well, one usually goes with the other."

"Not always."

"No, not always," Marina allowed. "What about now? Is there a woman in your life?"

The way she phrased the question annoyed him. "There are women, but no woman, if that's what you mean."

"Yeah, that's what I mean," she said, imitating him.

"Okay," he said, "I deserved that." He looked at Marina and the image of Linda receded. "Right now, my work is the most important thing in my life."

"Yes, but why Aztec sacrifice?"

Brian chewed his fish, wondering how to answer.

"One of my classes was on pre-Columbian cultures," he said finally. "I ended up writing my term paper on the subject. I got an A. My professor suggested that I submit it to a journal, and it got published."

Marina nodded approvingly. "You must have said something that the teacher liked."

"I couldn't believe that such an advanced civilization could at the same time be so barbaric. I still don't believe it. It's a question of cultural relativity. There are some anthropologists who think that the Aztecs—morally at least—weren't any more bloodthirsty than the average investment banker."

He paused to let her react to his joke, but the irony was apparently lost on her.

Brian continued, "I wouldn't go quite that far, but recent history argues that the Mesoamerican societies hardly cornered the market on mass murder. Right now, as we speak, lives are being sacrificed all over the world. The only difference is that instead of Huitzilopochtli, they are being sacrificed to the modern gods of money and technology. I don't think we've even begun to understand what was really happening up on those pyramids."

"And you do?"

"I think I can."

"You seem very confident. Does your Latino background help?"

"You mean being a descendant of cannibals?"

"That's not what I meant," Marina chided.

"What did you mean?"

"You're Chicano, right? Part Mexican."

He shrugged. "I guess."

"You guess? I would think that is something that you'd know."

He took another drink of wine before answering. "Look, you've got to understand that growing up in Los Angeles I was never particularly aware of my, ah, Mexican heritage. It was just there. I never questioned it. In grammar school, we studied Father Serra and the Camino Real and how California once belonged to Spain. My Anglo friends went to Taco Bell and ordered burritos just like everybody else. So I never had any reason to see myself as a foreigner. That's not who I am."

"So who are you?"

"Just a scientist trying to do his job. Why are you shaking your head?"

"Because I don't believe you."

"Why?"

"Oh, I don't doubt your sincerity, but I think, on some level, you are kidding yourself. I think you are afraid."

"Afraid of what?"

She was holding her glass with both hands, peering at him over the rim. He felt like a rabbit caught in the crosshairs. "Afraid that you're wrong, afraid of what you might find if you let your instincts lead you."

Brian put his fork down and pushed his plate away. "Is that what Torres told you?"

"I'm sorry," she said. "I didn't mean to upset you. Torres is a vain bureaucrat who sees you as a potential threat. You know: the Yankee Usurper. Intellectual Imperialism. He lives with his head in the ground—literally and figuratively. You're not like him—and Zapata knows it."

"What do you mean, he knows it?" Brian asked.

"He told me that you might be on to something, something important. You seem to have made an impression on him."

For the first time, Brian became aware of music. A group of musicians was strolling from table to table, singing requests for the diners. "What else did he tell you?"

"He said you were working on a new theory about Aztec sacrifice that could be very controversial."

"Controversy is Zapata's middle name."

"That doesn't make him wrong about the significance of your work."

"What makes you so sure he's right?"

Marina smiled indulgently. "Let's just say it's a seasoned reporter's instinct."

Brian felt himself arriving at a crossroads. "Can I trust you to keep a secret?"

"Of course."

He waited until the waiter had cleared away their dishes. "This is strictly off the record, right?"

"Absolutely."

"Hold your story."

She searched his face. "Can you at least tell me why?"

"No, I can't."

"Maybe I already know."

Brian sidestepped her bluff. "It can be misleading to read too much significance into things," he said evenly.

Her eyebrows arched. "Are you referring to something in particular?"

"Well, your name for example. Marina. It happens to be the Spanish name for La Malinche, the Indian who became Cortés's translator and lover, a woman who was despised as the betrayer of her own people."

Marina frowned. "There was a time when I thought my name was a curse. Naturally, I developed the urge to know more about La Malinche. I learned that she was beautiful and very smart. Being able to speak both Maya and Nahuatl, she eventually learned Spanish too and became Cortés's translator and most trusted advisor. Mi lengua, Cortés called her. My tongue. I also discovered that she eventually gave him a child, perhaps the first mestizo baby. In that sense one could argue that she was the mother of the modern Mexican nation. Does that sound like someone who should be despised?"

"My point exactly," he said. "You can't always trust your first impression. Besides, I happen to think Marina is a very beautiful name."

A burst of applause signaled the end of another song. The musicians, who wore dark matador's suits and white ruffled shirts, approached their table.

"A song for the señorita, señor?"

"Why not?" Brian said, ignoring Marina's halfhearted protest.

"Would you like to make a request, señor?"

"How about a love song?"

"All Mexican songs are love songs."

"In that case, maybe we should let the lady decide."

The singer turned to Marina.

" 'La Guacamaya.' "

"Con gusto, señorita."

The players launched into a boisterous melody that galloped over strumming guitars. The music evoked lonely, rugged vistas, where men escaped the heavy burden of life through the fleeting pleasures of the flesh. A man at the bar was moved to join in, clapping an off-beat accompaniment.

Brian leaned over the table toward Marina. "I thought Mexican love songs were all tragic ballads?"

"Don't let the tempo fool you," she answered. "The words are quite sad. The Guacamaya is a parrot with beautiful tail feathers."

She began to translate for him:

> *Poor Guacamaya, oh what a pity*
> *Oh what a pity, poor Guacamaya*
> *The cactus fruits are all gone now*
> *What will you eat?*
>
> *Fly, fly, fly, Oh how I flew*
> *When I was taken prisoner, señorita*
> *All because of you.*

"You seem to know it well," Brian said after the musicians had moved on.

"My mother used to play it for me when I was a little girl."

"And I'll bet you were already luring young men into your cage."

"I don't believe in cages," she said curtly, and signaled for the check. Outwardly, her attitude toward him had reverted to a journalistic level, but under her perfunctory manner he sensed an emotional shift, an openness that hadn't been there before.

She insisted on paying, despite his protestations. He relented only after she agreed to let him return the favor sometime. They strolled out through the patio together and Brian resisted the urge to touch her. "Thank you for a wonderful lunch," he said, gesturing to their surroundings. "And for giving me a taste of the real Mexico."

"This is not the real Mexico," she averred. "This is better than the tourist hotels but it's not the Mexico I love. Sometime I will show you how chilangos have a good time."

"Chilangos?"

"That's a slang term for the people who live in Mexico City."

They were soon standing at a busy intersection, an island of two in a sea of blaring noise and motion. "It was so relaxing in there I almost forgot where I was," he said.

"Yes, I know what you mean."

As they walked back to the hotel, Brian craned his head up at the white sky. "No sign of the meteorite. I thought it was supposed to be visible in daylight."

"I dreamed that I saw it last night," Marina said. "It crossed the sky and disappeared over the volcanoes."

Brian became thoughtful. "Villalobos told me it was an omen of the apocalypse. Did it look like the end of the world?"

"No," she said, her voice dreamy. "It was beautiful. Like an angel with a train of diamonds."

"I like your description much better."

"So do I," she said, handing her parking ticket to the attendant. "Can I give you a lift?"

"No thanks. I feel like walking. Maybe the angel will show herself to me."

They shook hands and he held hers until she pulled it away. "I hope we can get together again sometime, on a personal level," he said.

She gave him a probing look. "Are you serious about learning more about Mexico?"

"Absolutely."

"Lesson number one: never proposition a lady in public."

He still had some time to kill before heading back to the museum, so Brian decided to catch a cab to the Zona Rosa. From there he could walk along Avenida Reforma to Calle San Jerónimo, where he'd taken a two-room flat on the third floor above a clothing store. The second floor was occupied by his landlady, La Madre Conchita, a loquacious woman with billowy hips and a penchant for parrots. She had answered the door in her nightgown with a full-grown macaw on her shoulder, the bird eyeing Brian like a greedy accountant as he negotiated the rent down to the equivalent of four hundred dollars a month. La Madre had turned the building's courtyard into an aviary and as she unlocked the door to the vacant flat he heard the dry rustle of feathers through the open window. "Very nice neighborhood," La Madre kept repeating as he inspected the closet-sized kitchen and tubless bathroom. When a loud screech resounded through the apartment she immediately dropped the price. As Brian reached for his wallet, La Madre complimented him on his bargaining skills and good judgment, adding parenthetically that her birds provided the extra benefit of scaring away mice. Her words were lost on Brian, who was too busy fumbling with the unfamiliar currency to listen. In any case, what had clinched the deal was neither birds nor mice but the fact that the apartment was only a few blocks away from Templo Mayor.

"Argentino?" the driver asked as Brian paid his fare.

"Californian."

The driver nodded with vigor. "I like California very much."

"Me too."

Brian ambled past the slick towers and high-heeled shops of the Zona Rosa to the monument of Cuauhtémoc, the last Aztec emperor. A nephew of Motecuhzoma, Cuauhtémoc had inherited the throne of a dying civilization. Besieged by smallpox and surrounded by enemies, the young king had led the final defense of Tenochtitlán from the attacking Spaniards and their allies and survived to see his people defeated and forced into bondage. But even with his armies annihilated and his nation in ruins, Cuauhtémoc had managed to win a significant victory over the invaders. After the sacking of Tenochtitlán, Cortés had gathered Cuauhtémoc and the other surviving Aztec chiefs and publicly interrogated them about the whereabouts of the vast fortune in gold and jewels that the Spaniards had been forced to leave behind when they retreated from the city on the so-called Night of Sorrow. The Aztecs claimed that they had dumped the gold into the lake and could not retrieve it. Convinced that they were lying, Cortés kept searching for the loot, but the treasure of Tenochtitlán was never found. The story of the lost fortune had lived on through the centuries, however, and there were those who believed that it still existed, buried in some secret hiding place, waiting to be discovered.

From his pedestal above the twentieth-century chaos of cars and pedestrians, Cuauhtémoc stared out over the world's largest metropolis, a mute gaze fixed on the outer reaches of his lost empire. Brian focused on the sea of brown faces flowing around him. It was there, too—the simultaneous condition of triumph and defeat. The Spaniards had conquered the Indians, but the blood of the vanquished had taken refuge in the veins of the invaders, spawning a hybrid race of mestizos, the Mexicans, many of whom had migrated north to mix again. Some, like Brian's father, had been born U.S. citizens and married Anglo women, their ethnic identity subsumed into the American mainstream, their children media-savvy products of a mass culture that made them at home in any foreign city and strangers in their own ancestral land.

Brian kept walking. He wandered along wide avenues and narrow streets, past expensive jewelry stores and tin shacks selling cigarettes and chewing gum, past businessmen in Italian suits and barefoot families huddled on the steps of steel and glass banks. Skyscrapers stood next to vacant lots where buildings had been before the great earthquake of 1985 shook them into mass graves. Brian remembered the news accounts of the disaster, which left thousands entombed in the pulverized rubble. The people had rallied and, in spite of the government's ineptitude, an amazing number of victims had been rescued. Even so, it was said that many of the survivors still suffered from nightmares of being buried alive.

Heading east on Arcos de Belen, Brian came across an open-air market, its multi-colored awnings waving like flags in the breeze. He browsed the cluttered stalls of curios, jewelry and hand-painted pots, a gaggle of children and vendors in his wake. A basket weaver proved particularly persistent, following him into a covered cul-de-sac of stands that specialized in fireworks and plastic toys.

"For your wife, amigo," the man said, holding up a blue and green tote bag that Brian had made the mistake of admiring for more than a second.

"I'm not married."

"For your girlfriend."

"I don't have a girlfriend."

"Then this will help you get one. A young guapo like you should have a girl. Any woman would gladly make love to a man who gave her this."

The man held the bag aloft.

"It's very beautiful," Brian agreed, "but I don't need a handbag."

"The quality is good, the price very cheap."

"I don't want it."

"How much do you want to pay, amigo?"

A boy was tugging on Brian's finger, his palm upraised as if offering to share his need.

"Nothing, amigo."

"Here." He pushed the bag into Brian's hands. "Feel the material."

"I don't want to feel."

"Please."

Brian looked around for a sign of sympathy. But the expressions of the other vendors told him that only a fool would refuse to buy such a gorgeous and reasonably priced gift. Defeated, Brian paid the man and made his escape. He had gotten a great deal on a handbag he had no use for, but to refuse was to pay a higher tariff in the hard currency of guilt. On his way home, he stopped and bought some basic provisions and a copy of *The Globe*.

La Madre was sitting on the stoop when he got back, a chartreuse and aqua parakeet snuggled in the crook of her arm. "How much," she inquired, raising her eyebrows at his acquisition.

"Thirty pesos."

She let a puff of air pass through her lips. "Too much. He wants bags, I can show him where to buy them cheap. Todo muy barato."

"I don't even want this one."

"Why not?" she asked with comic severity. "It's very pretty, just like Esmeralda."

"Take it. It's yours."

"Qué me dices?" La Madre asked warily. "You are sure?"

"I'm sure."

She accepted the bag with her free hand. "Thank you, thank you, Mendoza. Qué dios lo bendiga. Isn't he a nice man?"

Brian was in his room before he realized that she had been talking to the bird. He could hear Esmeralda's cousins chirping and cooing in the courtyard, the sound punctuated every now and then by an assertive squawk. He closed the window and tried to concentrate on the newspaper.

The lead article was about the ongoing effort of President Francisco Nava to ferret out corruption in his government. A cabinet minister had been forced to resign for taking kickbacks on a federal housing project. The action had prompted grumbling in the ruling conservative Patriotic Revolutionary Union, better known as the URP which had just lost a gubernatorial race to the opposition for the first time in sixty years. Though popular with international banks and the foreign press, Nava was under fire from both the Mexican right, which saw him as a dangerously idealistic reformer, and the left, which considered him a puppet of the status quo. The economy, thanks to a massive influx of foreign investment, was booming. But in spite of that fact—or possibly because of it—a populist movement had taken hold in the northern provinces. The upsurge of material expectations, rather than pacifying the public, was inflaming the country. Demonstrations and street battles like the one Brian had witnessed in the zócalo were increasing and pessimists talked of another civil war. Brian scanned the other headlines: . . . A blight on the vineyards of Australia . . . A massive beaching of whales on the coast of Alaska . . .

His eyes moved to the bottom of the page, to a story illustrated by a picture of a man wrapped in white bandages:

JUNKMAN'S "WHITE MAGIC" CASTS
A SPELL OF DEATH
by Marina Soto

Marina's article told the tale of a poor scavenger from the huge slum of Nezahualcóyotl named Pancho Chávez. Chávez, who owned his own junkyard, was searching through a dumping site with his sons one day when he discovered a heavy machine that he was sure he could sell for scrap metal. Using crowbars and sledgehammers to tear the machine apart, Chávez was delighted by what he found inside— a glowing capsule that he decided was "a white magic stone" sent from the gods. Chávez took the magic stone home and gave chips of it to grateful relatives and friends who hoped that a little of the junkman's luck might rub off on them, too.

A few days later, Chávez came down with flulike headaches, stomach pains and vomiting. His seven-year-old daughter, Lydia, was the next to succumb to the mysterious ailment. In addition to her father's symptoms, blisters broke out on Lydia's hands and mouth. When her condition worsened, her worried parents rushed her to the hospital, where she was diagnosed as suffering from advanced radiation sickness caused by exposure to cesium 137, a material used in medical diagnostic equipment.

Dr. Gilbert Ortiz, a physician who examined the Chávez family, described their radioactive contamination as "comparable to victims of the Hiroshima bomb." Public officials investigating the case feared that as many as several dozen people had been exposed to the cesium 137, which could also cause hair loss, loosened teeth and internal bleeding. Meanwhile, the entire Chávez family was in the hospital fighting for their lives. The prognosis was poor.

Brian tore the article out of the paper and folded it into a square. It was impossible for him to imagine being so destitute that a piece of glittering refuse would seem like treasure, so unlucky that a brief moment of happiness would bring slow, agonizing death. For all its human tragedy, the tale was most disturbing for its atavistic quality, a nagging sense that Chávez and his family were not so much hapless victims of cruel chance as merely the latest innocents to be sacrificed to the gods of science.

It is soon after my dream that the omens begin. The first sign is a fiery comet that lights up the sky, like a flaming ear of corn or the blaze of daybreak. The light seems to bleed fire, drop by drop, like a wound that will not heal. It is wide at the peak and narrow at the bottom, like a dagger piercing the very heart of the heavens. The people run in the streets wondering aloud what the comet could mean, but how can I tell them that the gods have sent an unmistakable message of catastrophe?

A few days later, Tonatiuh returns as promised. The Flower War against the Huexotzincos is faring badly, he reports, and Motecuhzoma is in a foul mood. More significant, however, is the recent visit to Mote-

cuhzoma by the Tecocoan King Nezahualpilli, who warns him of terrible calamities to come.

In the weeks that follow, more dark signs appear. The temple of Huitzilopochtli suddenly bursts into flames, though no one has been inside to light the fire. The next day Motecuhzoma himself stands upon the smoldering cinders and orders that the temple be rebuilt as soon as possible. But those who are standing nearby say that his voice is shaking as he vows to avenge the Little Hummingbird. Motecuhzoma orders doubling of the number of victims being offered to the sun, but the omens persist. That spring the harvest is poor and a cow gives birth to a calf with three heads. Then the wind whips the lake until it boils with rage, as if trying to shatter the world reflected in its once calm surface. It rears up and lashes at the walls of the houses and sucks boats into the water, where many fishermen perish.

Then comes a different kind of calamity. Convinced that he needs a larger sacrificial stone to pay proper tribute to the Sun God, Motecuhzoma orders a search for a boulder large enough for the task. One is found at the edge of the lake in Chalco and is chiseled on the spot to the appropriate shape and size. But while it is being brought to Tenochtitlán on huge rafts, the ropes holding it snap and it plunges into the water. The king orders the stone retrieved, but try as they might, the divers cannot locate it. Besieged by new nightmares of death and catastrophe, Motecuhzoma tells his personal priests, including Tonatiuh, to confess their own dreams. But when they deny having similar nightmares the king calls them liars and flies into a rage. He has the priests and their families put in chains, where they are to be left to starve. Fearing for Tonatiuh's life, I and several others from my temple use our influence to arrange for his escape. Despite the religious supremacy of the Little Hummingbird, there is growing sympathy for anyone who preaches tolerance, and the servants of Quetzalcóatl have always been held in the highest esteem by the people. We instruct the jailers to tell the king that the prisoners, being sorcerers, have made themselves vanish from their cells, an explanation that he duly accepts. As venerated priests of Quetzalcóatl, my confederates and I have access to parts of the shrine that are unknown to Motecuhzoma's agents. Once in the safety of our compound, I lead Tonatiuh to a private chamber deep in the bowels of the temple. Between offerings and my other duties I bring him food and continue to tutor him in reading and writing and the ways of the Plumed Serpent. Aflame with the passion of youth, he is impatient to act and on more than one occasion I have been forced to speak to him sternly. But his mind is quick and his spirit pure and the bond between us is not unlike that between a father and his son. With great satisfaction I watch his knowledge and respect for his teacher grow. In time it will be his turn to take up the quill and record the events that have altered the future and ended the past.

4

The snow-capped volcanoes rose like islands above the smog as the silver Mercedes-Benz sped south on the mountain highway to Cuernavaca.

"Popocatépetl and Iztaccíhuatl," the driver informed Brian, pointing at the peaks over the milky miasma that filled the Valley of Mexico. Brian nodded and inhaled deeply, grateful for the chance to breathe clean air.

Traffic was light and the Mercedes made speedy progress. They'd only been on the road for half an hour and already Mexico City's urban landscape was gradually giving way to open fields and patches of evergreen forest. As the car continued its ascent, the trees were joined by rugged cliffs that towered over deep ravines spotted with tufts of prickly pear cactus and sage. Brian felt the pressure building in his ears and tried to guess their altitude. As they began their descent from the summit of the pass Brian could see where the mountains flattened out ahead into a broad plateau that fanned out toward the horizon. The air became warmer and drier. Bird-of-paradise plants, splendid in the morning sun, sprouted from the embankment.

The road began to loop across a shallow valley and Brian gained an unobstructed view of oscillating foothills and the parched rectangle of a peasant ranchito with its whitewashed shed and solitary goat. They were in high desert now, the horizon disrupted by clusters of huge, misshapen boulders. The driver took a sharp left off the highway and onto a bumpy dirt road, past a small grocery store, a gas station and a few modest houses. A church tower came into view, then the rest of Tepoztlán, which lay cradled in a verdant niche between the mountains and the arid plain that stretched to Cuernavaca and beyond.

The Mercedes's tires vibrated against cobblestones as it arrived at the town square, which was bordered by low buildings and stalls selling avocados, pottery and handmade leather goods. The driver turned right and headed for the outskirts of town, past an old convent and a walled graveyard with its plastic flowers and cellophane wreaths, down an unpaved alley riddled with deep potholes. A cloud of dust engulfed the car and Brian was about to say something when the driver halted in front of a pair of bamboo gates and honked his horn. A man in a battered cowboy hat appeared and swung the doors back, motioning for them to enter and park.

Brian climbed out of the car and stretched his legs. Nothing during the one-hour journey or in the town had prepared him for what he saw. Before him was a stately hacienda ringed by a wide patio and flowered gardens. Off to one side of the property, the aqua glint of a swimming pool filtered through a grove of papyrus stalks. In the opposite direction were what appeared to be tennis courts and more gardens. The entire complex was enclosed by a wall at least twelve feet high, topped with a tangle of barbed wire and flowering vines. And looming above everything like a Hollywood backdrop, in such sharp relief that one could almost touch them, a range of chiseled rock faces, silent and Sphinx-like, vaulted toward the cloudless sky.

Brian was still trying to take it all in as Villalobos crossed the manicured lawn and grasped his hand. "Welcome to my secret paradise," he said.

"Thank you," Brian said, unable to tear his eyes away from the mountains.

"Don't bother with your bag, Diego will take it," Villalobos was saying. "Your trip from the city was pleasant, I trust?"

Villalobos was wearing a white guayabera, slacks and espadrilles. He was exactly as Brian remembered him, right down to his patient, vaguely amused smile. Villalobos touched Brian's shoulder and guided him toward the house. The entry and living room were formal in a rustic way, with exposed ceiling beams and sturdy antiques arranged against crimson walls. A suit of Spanish armor stood at attention in one corner. Voices drifted in from the patio.

"You must be thirsty." Villalobos gestured toward the open French doors. "Please join me for a drink and I'll introduce you to everyone. Then you can dust yourself off before lunch."

Brian's fellow guests numbered three: Octavio Esparza, Eduardo Raffa and his wife, Elena. Brian shook hands with each and ordered a rum and tonic from a servant dressed in white. "Octavio is a neighbor and the architect of this house," Villalobos explained. "Eduardo and Elena are artists, a painter and sculptor, respectively. But all that you really need to know is that they share my love for Tepoztlán and its many charms."

"Those mountains . . ." Brian began, unable to finish the sentence.

"Yes," Villalobos said knowingly. "They are very powerful. They give off a kind of energy, no?" There was a murmur of agreement from the group. "Ah, your drink has arrived."

Glasses were raised and everyone drank. Brian noticed that they all had the same distant expression and he sensed that he had interrupted something. He was starting to feel like a party crasher when Eduardo broke the silence.

"Alejandro tells us that you are working with Zapata at Templo Mayor." It was more a statement than a question, but Brian answered anyway.

"Yes. I'm here from California while I research my thesis."

The woman was about to say something when Villalobos broke in. "We'd all like to hear about Mr. Mendoza's work, but I think that for the moment we should let him unwind, as the Americans say. I'm sure that you are tired and would like a few minutes to relax and freshen up. Diego will show you to your room."

Brian's quarters were up a flight of steps and across a small tiled terrace that looked out over the grounds. The room was spare and masculine with white walls and blond furniture. A soccer ball and a tennis racquet were stashed in the closet, along with what looked like the gloves and padding from an ice hockey uniform. The sports paraphernalia told Brian that this had once been the room of a young man, probably Villalobos's son. If he had a son then he must also have a wife, but there had been no sign of a Mrs. Villalobos. Divorced or deceased? It suddenly occurred to Brian how little he knew about his host. The man was practically a stranger, yet here he was in his house, in his son's room, about to have lunch with his friends. And there was something decidedly odd about the way Villalobos had practically ordered him to his room before he'd barely had a sip of his drink. Was it concern for Brian, or something else? He hoped that his coming hadn't been a mistake.

To Brian's relief, lunch had none of the awkwardness that had marked his arrival. The meal was served on the patio at a long table laden with steaming platters of grilled chicken, black beans, quesadillas, tamales and bottomless carafes of wine. Villalobos's friends turned out to be amiable companions with a knack for amusing anecdotes. Octavio's story about a visiting Arab oil sheik whose mistresses took up a whole floor of the El Presidente Hotel segued into Elena's tale about disguising herself as a man during a trip to Saudi Arabia.

"Why not, the men are already wearing dresses," she said. "Actually, I think caftans on men are very attractive."

"You'll never get me in one," Eduardo said stubbornly.

"You see," Villalobos said to Brian. "Change does not come easily in this country."

"So I've noticed," Brian said. "There are demonstrations in the zócalo almost every day. Depending on whom I talk to, Mexico is either on the verge of democracy or civil insurrection."

"We will enter a new era, or we will tear ourselves apart," Octavio observed glumly.

"Or maybe both, if the gods are willing," Villalobos said.

Brian could feel the others calculating his reaction to Villalobos's remark, but he pretended not to notice. A few minutes later, the guests rose from the table and drifted off to siestas, until only Brian and Villalobos remained.

"Did you enjoy your lunch?" Villalobos asked after the dishes had been cleared away.

"Very much, thanks," Brian said. "I still can't believe we're only an hour from Mexico City."

"Yes," Villalobos said with satisfaction, "it's a remarkably tranquil oasis—the perfect antidote to the madness over the mountains."

"I'm a little surprised to hear you say that," Brian observed. "The way I've heard you talk about apocalyptic omens and civil insurrection it almost seems as if you welcome the madness."

"It's very simple," Villalobos answered. "I am a hedonist but also a pragmatist. The new era cannot take place without the destruction of the old. The end of the second millennium will open the door to the third, the demise of the Fifth Sun will give birth to the Sixth, just as the rise of democracy will ensure the end of the existing order and the start of our national future. To think otherwise is pure sentimentality."

"But the old guard will not go out without a fight, will it?" Brian asked.

"No," Villalobos said calmly. "A certain amount of struggle is inevitable."

"So you support the democracy movement?"

"That is for the politicians to decide. I have other things to occupy my time."

Before Brian could respond, Villalobos rose from his seat. Brian assumed that the audience was over, but to his surprise, Villalobos offered to give him a tour of the property. "My father used to bring me here as a boy," Villalobos said as he led Brian across the neatly clipped grass. "He told me that those mountains were alive, that they possessed magic. And he was right." They paused to look at the cliffs and Brian saw that the shifting sun had transformed them, highlighting certain contours, erasing others. Even the colors had changed. The soft browns and greens of morning had become harsher, the gaps between the stone peaks obscured by inky shadows. "See the way they lean against each other? The locals call them 'las montañas borrachas.' "

"The drunken mountains."

"Yes. It is also the birthplace of Tepozcatl, the god of pulque, the Aztec liquor. Some say it is the world's oldest alcoholic beverage. The Indians built a pyramid on the mountain in Tepozcatl's honor. I'll take you there if you'd like. But first, let me show you around the house. I think you'll find it interesting."

They entered a corridor that opened onto a rectangular courtyard filled with plants and a small gurgling fountain. "On the most obvious level," Villalobos began, "the house conforms to the traditional Spanish colonial structure, that is, arches, white walls, tile roof, and a cross-shape arrangement of wings connected by a central patio. But the design also corresponds—quite intentionally, I assure you—to the Aztec cosmology and conception of the universe." Villalobos paused. "Do you follow me?"

"I'm afraid not."

"You are no doubt familiar with Ometéotl?"

"Sure," Brian said. "The original creator of the universe."

"Precisely. Then you also know that Ometéotl and his female half bore the four principal gods who ruled the Aztec universe."

Brian recited the names of the four brothers: "Xipe Totec, the Flayed One, the god of fertility. Quetzalcóatl, the Plumed Serpent, the god of wisdom. Huitzilopochtli, the Little Hummingbird, the god of war. Tezcatlipoca, Smoking Mirror, the god of sorcery."

"Right," Villalobos confirmed. "And we also know that the manifestation of each of those four principal gods depends on his position in relation to the four cardinal points of the universe and their corresponding color, e.g. blue for south, red for east, black for north and white for west. We also know that the earth itself was at the center of this cosmic axis."

"I'm still not sure . . ."

"This," Villalobos pointed to the circular fountain, "is earth."

Suddenly what Villalobos had been saying made perfect sense. "So each wing of the house corresponds to a cardinal direction," Brian said, using the main corridor to orient himself. "The entrance of the house was decorated in red and faces east, the place of the rising sun."

Brian did an about-face. "My room, in the west wing, was white, the realm of Quetzalcóatl."

"Very good, Mr. Mendoza," Villalobos said. "And what you are thinking is also correct: the wing that includes the kitchen and servants' quarters is painted blue, the color of the south."

"That leaves north," Brian said.

"So it does." Villalobos motioned for Brian to follow him. Their footsteps echoed on the tile as he led the way up a stairway and pushed open a set of double doors. "The master bedroom is downstairs but, as you might guess, I spend most of my time in here."

It was one of the most impressive rooms Brian had ever seen. Gaping bay windows allowed a panoramic view of the mountains, which seemed about to burst through the glass. One side of the room was covered with bookshelves, the other half was taken up by a large antique desk and glass cases filled with a variety of pre-Columbian objects. The couch, chairs and lampshades were all jet black.

Brian walked over to the glass cases and perused the contents. From what he could tell, at least two of the pieces—a small jade sculpture of Xilonen, the goddess of maize, and a stone representation of Tezcatlipoca—were of museum quality.

"Fantastic," Brian said.

"This is my inner sanctum," Villalobos announced. "It is a space for serious thought and honest conversation."

"I can see why." Brian moved to the bookshelf. In addition to a considerable number of anthropological volumes, there were hundreds of books on history, literature and philosophy. "A person could spend their whole day in here," Brian said, flipping through a first edition of Foucault's *Archaeology of Knowledge.*

"Someday I hope to," Villalobos said, "but for the time being, my work demands that I spend the better part of my week in Mexico City."

"Not to be disrespectful, but I don't even know what your work is."

"I'm not sure I know myself," Villalobos said lightly, motioning for Brian to sit. "Will you join me in some tequila?" Villalobos went to the bar and returned with a cut-glass decanter and two shot glasses. "They say I'm a banker, an entrepreneur. But really my work is to keep the world in motion, to grease the wheels of industry, to keep money flowing into the right hands, to make sure that the financial center holds."

"That's a tall order."

"It's not nearly as formidable as it sounds," he said as he poured two neat shots. "It has made me rich, of course, but it provides no food for the soul. Power and money are necessities but, to paraphrase Karl Marx, they have no inherent value. Money is useless to man on a desert island. In the same way, power is pointless without the will to wield it. I would much rather be an anthropologist like yourself, speaking to the souls of the ancients, Mr. Mendoza."

"Brian."

"So tell me, Brian," Villalobos repeated amiably as he raised his glass, "have you read the new codex? Salud."

Brian let the tequila burn a path down his throat before answering. "Which codex?"

Villalobos clicked his tongue. "Oh, come now, Brian. I think we can be frank with each other. Naturally, I'm not asking you to divulge any details. But I know Zapata has uncovered something in the tomb of Quetzalcóatl. Just as I know that Quetzalcóatl is a key part of your thesis."

"I haven't seen it," Brian blurted. "Unfortunately, I'm not authorized yet."

"That's difficult to believe."

"I know," Brian said with genuine bitterness. "When I came to Templo Mayor, Zapata told me I would be at the mercy of the museum department heads. Torres, the dig supervisor, controls access to the site. I think he considers me some kind of threat."

Villalobos was staring at the chameleon shapes towering through the windows. "Maybe you are," he said before reaching to refill their glasses. "Did you know that his doctoral dissertation was a defense of the very theory you are trying to overthrow?"

"You're kidding."

"Arturo is a good scholar, meticulous, even brilliant, but he lacks"—Villalobos's fingers massaged the air—"imagination. Do you agree?"

"Humanity is more like it."

The thin skin around Villalobos's eyes crinkled with amusement.

"I like your spirit, Brian. I like a man who speaks his mind, who is capable of intuitive leaps, a man who would try to prove that Motecuhzoma was suicidal. Yes, I've heard about your theory. I think it's very provocative. But more important, I think it might be true."

Brian turned to look through the windows. "Why, because you identify with him?"

Villalobos was unfazed. "Partly," he said. "But also because it answers many questions, don't you agree?"

"That's what I'm hoping to prove."

"Yes, and that is why I've invited you here. To offer my services, to help you in any way that I can, as a partner of sorts."

"I'm flattered," Brian said, suddenly lightheaded. He was tempted to accept Villalobos's overture, which had the same magnetic tow as the mountains that loomed outside. But Brian knew that his best bet would be to remain noncommittal and wait until he had a stronger hand. He carefully placed the empty glass on the table. "I'm sorry, but I'm really not at liberty to share my findings, at least not yet. Meanwhile, I hope we can just be friends."

Far from offended, Villalobos nodded and sprang to his feet. "Of course," he said, "that goes without saying. We'll continue our discussion another time. Now come with me and I'll show you the rest of the property."

The grounds around the house covered at least a dozen acres and included the main building, a small guest house, the pool, riding stables and the tennis courts. A small army of gardeners was busy trimming the bushes and tending the flower beds as Brian followed Villalobos outside.

"Do you play?" Villalobos asked, indicating the tennis courts.

When Brian said that he did, Villalobos seemed delighted. "Then you must indulge me for a set. My other friends, I'm afraid, are into more sedentary forms of recreation. You'll find a racquet and some clothes in your room. They should be about the right size."

"I noticed," Brian said. "I didn't know you had a son."

If the subject was a sore one, Villalobos didn't show it.

"He's living in the U.S. with his mother. You remind me of him—impatient youth, questioning everything. I'll meet you back here in ten minutes."

Villalobos was right; the shorts and shirt were a perfect fit. By the time he got back to the courts, his host was changed and waiting for him. They agreed to play three sets. Brian won them all, but not without difficulty. Villalobos was fit for his age, and possessed a mean forehand.

"Tennis seems to be your game," Villalobos said. "You're quite good, but perhaps you'd like to try something a little more challenging."

Villalobos pointed through the wire fence and Brian realized that what he had mistaken for a second tennis court was actually a paved rectangle with steep angled sides.

"What did you have in mind?"

"How about a game of Tlacthli?"

"The Aztec ball game?" Brian could hardly believe his ears.

Villalobos slapped his back. "I knew I could count on you." He called to one of the gardeners and told him to fetch something from the house.

"But how . . ."

"It's based on the ball court at Chichén Itzá, only much smaller, of course."

"Of course," Brian repeated, too amazed to do much more than gawk. Villalobos had obviously done his homework. The playing area had been formed in a classic double-T configuration. Two carved stone loops protruded from either side of the court, the base of which was engraved with Aztec hieroglyphs. Brian was sure that it had cost a fortune.

"I trust you know the rules?" Villalobos asked sportively.

"Well, it's not my area of specialty, but if I remember correctly, the object of the game was simple enough: the team that first managed to throw a ball through one of those rings won. But the players were not allowed to use their hands or feet to touch the ball. Instead, they had to use their hips and their knees. To the Aztecs, the court represented the world, and the ball a heavenly body, usually the sun or the moon. It was a game strictly for the elite class, which routinely bet vast sums, even losing their own lives. On very special occasions the winning team was sacrificed to the gods in a kind of spiritual Superbowl."

"Excellent," Villalobos said, his eyes bright with excitement. "Very illuminating—and wittily rendered. But the Aztecs could also be sore losers. Ixtlilxóchitl tells how the emperor Axayácatl wagered against the lord of Xochimilco and bet the marketplace of Tenochtitlán against a garden belonging to the lord. The emperor lost and the following day Aztec soldiers appeared at the palace of the fortunate winner to pay him tribute. While they saluted him and showered him with presents, one of the soldiers threw a garland of flowers with a thong hidden in it around the lord's neck and strangled him on the spot."

Brian concluded that Villalobos was no anthropological dabbler: his interest in the historical and cosmological intricacies of the game was as substantial as his wealth.

The gardener returned with a burlap bag containing a ball and the leather padding and wooden paddles he had seen in his closet. "These are rugby pads," Villalobos said as he handed Brian a set. "They suffice nicely as a substitute for the protection that the Aztecs used. I've also bent the rules to allow kicking with the feet and the use of these paddles. It's a concession to the fact that the true version of the game has not been played for hundreds of years. Any objection to those terms?"

"None that I can think of," Brian said, attaching the pads to his knees and elbows. He picked up the heavy ball, which was similar in size to the ones used to play ordinary soccer but about ten times as dense. He gave it a test bounce and it sprang back higher than his head. It reminded him of a giant Superball. He began to understand why Tlacthli was considered by the Aztecs to be a dangerous sport.

"What shall we bet for?" Villalobos inquired as they gave the ball to the gardener and lowered themselves into the court. "Sacrifice is a little steep, don't you agree?"

"Wholeheartedly," Brian quipped, and saw that his joke had not been wasted on his host.

"In that case," Villalobos said, "let's say that if I win, you will have to honor my invitation to come and stay for the weekend sometime."

"That's not a very tough penalty. But what happens if I win?"

"I will give you my car and driver for a week." Though he was some forty feet away, Villalobos's voice was crisp and clear.

"The wager is a bit unorthodox," Brian called out as he stretched his legs, "but then so is the game. How do we start?"

"Chon will throw the ball on the divider line, and from that point on the ball is fair game. You'll be trying for the ring on your right, and I'll be aiming for the one on your left. Ready?"

"Ready."

The gardener hoisted the ball into the air and it made a hollow thud as it hit the dirt and bounced toward Brian. He started to reach out with his hands, then caught himself at the last second and opened his arms, letting the ball rebound off his breastbone and across the center line. It hurt like hell but Brian didn't complain. Villalobos was already in control of the ball, which he stopped with his thigh while coiling the other leg. The kick was solid but his aim was off and the ball ricocheted off the wall about a foot from the target. When it came toward Brian again he let it bounce against the wall and then whacked it with his shoulder, almost as if he were playing off the backboard in a racquetball court. The ball arched through the air and hit the ring, narrowly missing the hole.

"Good," Villalobos shouted and Brian felt he had acquitted himself from his bumbling start. After a few more volleys a rhythm developed as Brian got the hang of slapping the ball with the side of his knee to give it a horizontal spin.

Even with Villalobos's modified rules, the game was exhausting. They had only been playing a few minutes and Brian was drenched in sweat. Even so, he realized that the game was as much a mental as a physical contest. The trick was to anticipate the angle that the ball would come off the wall and use its natural inertia to guide its trajectory before it bounced. Villalobos had another near miss and Brian returned it wide. Caught off balance, Villalobos kicked blindly and sent the ball speeding back across the line of scrimmage. Brian lunged for it, missed and tumbled sideways against the stone wall. Villalobos was instantly at his side, helping him to his feet. "I'm okay," Brian said. "I'm just a little winded."

"Naturally," Villalobos said, "the altitude. It takes a while to adjust. Is anything sprained?"

"No," Brian said as he dusted himself off. "My shoulder might be a little sore in the morning, but otherwise I'm fine."

"It was my fault, I shouldn't have kicked the ball directly at you."

"It's not your fault. You won fair and square."

"It was a draw," Villalobos insisted. "But I hope you will still accept my invitation to spend the weekend here. Anytime. The offer is open."

Slightly dazed, Brian repaired to his room to shower. He began to feel better as the cool water streamed over his body. He leaned against the tiles, marveling at what had just happened. The rich were supposed to be eccentric but Villalobos was in a league of his own. What was more, Brian found himself quite enthralled. Wealth, intelligence, humor—Villalobos seemed to have it all, including a penchant for physical exertion that was contagious. Game or not, Villalobos had been totally immersed in the moment and, in spite of his initial skepticism, Brian had responded. The match may have begun as some sort of anthropological lark, but by the end they had been playing seriously. Nevertheless, Brian suspected that Villalobos could have played even harder.

When Brian came out of the bath, his clothes were laid out on the bed, freshly washed and pressed. Outside, Diego was already loading his things in the car. "It's a shame you can't stay for dinner," Villalobos said as he walked Brian to the Mercedes.

"Next time."

"So I haven't scared you away then?"

"Quite the contrary."

Brian slid into the back seat and Villalobos closed the door for him. "I'm glad you came," he said through the glass. "See you next time." As Diego eased out the drive, Brian turned to wave good-bye but Villalobos had already disappeared into the house.

The offices of *The Globe* were on the ninth floor of the Latin American Tower, a modern steel and glass skyscraper that Brian's cab driver informed him was the tallest building in the world, taller than even New York's Empire State Building or the Sears Tower in Chicago. "Ask me why," he insisted.

"Why?"

"Because the lobby is already seven thousand feet above sea level!"

He found Marina at her desk, simultaneously speaking on the

phone and scribbling on a notepad. When she saw him she registered surprise with her eyes and put her hand over the mouthpiece. "Please." She gestured to sit. "I'm almost done."

Brian moved a stack of magazines from the nearest chair and took a seat. From the speed at which people were moving he guessed that the paper was close to deadline. A woman hurried past with a black-and-white photo in her hand, her bracelets making urgent music. A man cursed quietly, a lady laughed. Phones rang without being answered. Off to the left, behind a makeshift wall of cardboard boxes, Brian could hear the staccato clatter of automated wire machines churning out copy.

From the tone of Marina's voice, the interview was not going well. Her lips were bent into a grimace, her attention focused on the conversation. He took the opportunity to watch her practicing her craft. She was dressed more casually than before in a loose black blouse, short skirt and boots. The effect was both utilitarian and sexy. With the phone still wedged against her neck, she leaned forward over the desk. Her hair fell across her face and she reflexively pushed the heavy strands behind her ear, which was perfectly shaped and embellished by a tiny diamond stud.

A few seconds later, she slammed down the receiver.

"An uncooperative source?" Brian asked.

"Dealing with the government in this country is like a bad production of Kafka," she exclaimed.

"*The Castle*?"

"No. 'The Metamorphosis.' The man is a cockroach who refuses to make a simple statement." She waited a beat before adding, "I didn't expect to see you again so soon."

"I was thinking about our lunch the other day—"

"Don't worry," she interrupted, "I was only using it as background."

"I don't care about that. This is a social call. I thought we might grab some coffee. But if you're too busy—"

"I'm always busy," she said, reaching for her purse. "But I've got to get out of here for a while or I'll go crazy. There's a place we can go across the street."

It was a disco-style diner, decorated with Fanta soda posters and neon tubes bent into the outline of Marina's building. Behind the

Formica counter, a radio played a Spanish version of "Hotel California." They sat at a corner table, facing each other, their knees almost touching. The waitress handed them menus and Brian noticed that the second page featured the same dishes translated from Spanish into bad English.

"I don't know which sounds worse, 'Cheese Tortilla' or 'Hamburgesa,' Brian said.

Marina shook her head. "I know; it's stupid. Anyway, I'm just having coffee." Brian ordered two cups and made an airplane out of his paper napkin. For the first time since they had met, he felt awkward in her presence. Their earlier meetings had benefited from having a built-in structure: she was the journalist, he was the anthropologist. There had been a psychological safety in their professional identities, roles to be played and played with. By coming to her office uninvited, he had broken the rules. Now he was on her turf, working without a net.

"So," he said, breaking the silence, "what's your story about?"

"Oh, nothing important." She massaged her temples and Brian imagined the silky texture of her skin. "It's a feature on Baja California, but Fonatur won't give me any statistics that aren't three years old. It's quite frustrating."

"Fonatur," he repeated. "It sounds like a name for the phone company."

"Yes," she said, relaxing a little bit. "I suppose it does. It stands for the National Fund for Tourism Development."

Their coffee arrived and he watched her meticulously stir in milk and sugar. Rather than let the conversation lag, he said, "You'd think it would be in the government's interest to give you what you need."

"It is," she said. "But things are never simple in Mexico."

"So I've noticed."

"And how are things at the museum?"

"It's reasonably interesting," he said, "but . . ."

"But what?"

"Let's just say I'm having my own encounters with the bureaucracy."

She nodded sympathetically. "I can imagine. By the way, did you ever meet with Villalobos?"

"I did, as a matter of fact. His house in Tepoztlán is incredible—it even has an Aztec ball court."

She sipped her coffee pensively. "So the rumors are true."

"We played a game. It was actually kind of fun. His interest in anthropology is anything but superficial."

"I'd love to hear about it."

Her interest was piqued, and Brian scoured his mind for details. Pulling out her notebook, she asked, "Do you mind?"

"Just don't use my name."

"I promise I won't. Who else was there?"

"A few others. An artist and his wife. An architect."

"Octavio Esparza?"

"Yes, Esparza. How did you know?"

"Not just anyone is invited to weekend with Alejandro Villalobos," she replied. "I told you, Mexico is ruled by a very small group of people. It might not be fair, but it's the reality."

"Yet reality can be misleading."

She tilted her head quizzically and Brian explained, "I'm talking about your story about the radioactive man."

"Pancho Chávez?"

"Right. It was an incredible story."

"You actually *liked* it?"

"It spoke to the anthropologist in me."

Intrigued, Marina leaned closer. "And what did it say to you exactly?"

"It said that for some people, magic—white and black—still exists. It said that religion and science are much closer than we generally realize. And it said that you are a very talented writer."

The change in her was subtle, but its effect on him was like pure oxygen. He could see her reorganizing the file cabinet in her mind, adding notes, reappraising him. She tilted her chin and the glare from outside ignited a spark in her eye. He could tell that his interpretation of the story had pleased her. And he was equally sure that it had drawn him one step closer to her. As if reading his thoughts, she said, "But you didn't come here to tell me about my article."

"No, I didn't. The other day you said you would show me how the natives have a good time. I'd like to take you up on your offer."

She put the notebook back into her purse. "I'd love to go out with you sometime."

"How about tomorrow?"

Her brow furrowed for an instant. "No. Here's your second lesson: the best night for us to go out is Saturday."

"Why?"

"Because that's the night I'm free."

It was raining when Brian went out looking for a place for dinner. The warm, sticky drizzle left an oily sheen on the pavement and seeped through the soles of his shoes. La Madre had recommended a place around the corner called La Paloma. The restaurant was a long, narrow space dominated by a flaming charcoal grill and a TV mounted on a stack of painted vegetable crates. Brian took a seat near the back and ordered a Tecate with lime and carne asada, the specialty of the house. While waiting for his food, Brian realized that every head in the place was turned toward the television, watching an undubbed video of *Raiders of the Lost Ark*. He was about to cut into his steak as the spirits emerging from the Ark transformed into ghoulish monsters and attacked the Nazis, their screams of horror meshing with the hiss of sizzling meat.

It was still early when Brian left La Paloma, so he decided to take a post-prandial detour toward Plaza Suárez and the colonial church of San Miguel. The rain had stopped but the streets were still slick, their shiny surface reflecting the lights of the city like a funhouse mirror. Try as he might, Brian could not find his own image in the penetrating stares of dark-skinned strangers. Yet he knew a part of him had been born here, had died and lived here. Like the La Brea tar pits of his native L.A., Mexico was an opaque surface that invited reflection even as it cloaked a deeper reality.

At the end of the block, Brian came to a shop that sold Indian ceremonial masks. The gallery of distorted faces grinned back at him through the glass. He could instantly tell that these were not commercial tourist trinkets; they were genuine artifacts, caked with mud and worn down by years of ritual use. Several of the masks had bird feathers attached to them, others were embellished with beads and small mirrors.

"Pase, señor."

"I'm just looking."

"The light is better inside."

A boy with thick Indian features and a luminous smile beckoned for him to enter. After hesitating a moment, Brian obliged and the boy shut the door behind him. The room smelled of mildew and wood and damp earth. Masks of every size and configuration hung from the walls and the ceiling, from intricate metal faces with engraved rays of hammered tin, to flat, almost featureless slabs of wood with narrow slits for eyes. Some seemed to be speaking, others had wooden snakes undulating from where their mouths should be. Spellbound, Brian moved along the perimeter of the store, the boy hovering at his elbow.

"Where did you get these?" Brian asked.

"From all over Mexico, señor," the boy replied. "They are the real McCoy."

Brian laughed and the boy did too. Encouraged, he began a sort of narration, explaining the geographical origin of each mask and the ceremony in which it was used. Brian was drawn to a wooden blue and red duality mask. Each half was painted a different color and twin serpents coiled around the eyeholes, their tongues converging on the lipless mouth hole.

"Where is this one from?"

"Yucatán, señor."

"I'll take it."

As Brian paid, the boy looked at his choice and made a grunt of approval.

"Did I choose a good one?"

The boy shook his head, his wide nose and deep-set eyes making another kind of mask.

"It chose you."

When he got home, Brian took the mask out of its brown paper wrapping and hung it on a nail over the bed, where the ghostly outline of a crucifix remained on the peeling white paint. Then he reread the tale of the radioactive man and climbed between sheets that smelled of detergent. The birds, for once, were quiet and he could hear a woman's voice, low and lustful over a Pedro Infante ballad, and behind that, the muted clatter of dishes being washed and children being bathed and bundled off to bed. An ambulance siren wailed on some anonymous avenue, answered by the plaintive howl of a nearby dog. Just before he drifted off, Brian became aware of another sound, a rhythmic vibration that passed through his pillow and entered his dreams. It might have been a passing train, or distant thunder, or the restless breath of twenty million souls, their fears and hopes heaving together like the lungs of a sleeping giant.

I am lighting a bowl of copal when Tonatiuh, his eyes wild with excite- ment, comes running into my chambers. Huge creatures with long white wings have been sighted along the coast of Cuetlaxtlan. Spies are sent to watch the invaders and they return with stories of a house on the water, from which emerged men with white faces and robes of many colors. The alien beings are also seen riding on the backs of fearful beasts and hold- ing long rods that spray fire. Motecuhzoma is well aware of the prophe- cies, but he wants to make sure that the foreigners are indeed Quetzalcóatl and his agents, so he sends emissaries laden with gifts of gold and a feast of roasted birds and fruit and chocolate. If the strangers accept the gold, it will prove that Quetzalcóatl has returned to reclaim his treasure. And if they eat, it will show that they remember the food of their native land. The invaders do both before sailing away in their ships and Motecuh- zoma is hopeful that they have heeded his request to take gifts and food and never again return.

But not long afterward the winged vessels reappear and the white strangers once again emerge from their floating houses. New emissaries are sent to meet the strangers, but this time they do not seem pleased by the gifts sent by Motecuhzoma. They take the envoys prisoner and demon- strate awesome powers. Then they release the messengers and instruct them to tell their king that they suffer from a disease that can be cured only by gold. When the emissaries return to Tenochtitlán, Motecuhzoma has them report to him immediately. "The supernatural beings possess a weapon of fire that roars like thunder," the envoys tell him. "And a thing like a ball of stone comes out of its entrails, spitting sparks and smoke and smelling of sulfur. And if the stone strikes a mountain, the mountain splits open. And if it strikes a tree, the tree shatters into splinters as if it exploded from within. Their costumes are made of metal. And giant deer carry them on their backs wherever they wish to go, holding them as high as the roof of a house. Their faces are as white as lime. They have yellow hair and beards, though some are black. And their dogs are enormous, with flat ears and tongues that hang out. They are savage, like demons, always bounding about."

Hearing this, Motecuhzoma knows it would be useless to attack the invaders. Instead, he orders that more treasure and food be sent to their camp by the sea. He also makes certain that this time a contingent of priests accompanies the delegation. Several keepers of the temple of Quetzalcóatl are invited to join the expedition and I accept, knowing that it will provide a chance to get a firsthand look at the strangers. The journey is long and arduous, over snow-capped mountains, windy plateaus and steaming jungles. At last we reach the sea, and everything the emissaries have said proves true. The invaders welcome us and the treasures we have brought and once again sit down to enjoy our emperor's bounty. As befitting exalted guests, the foreigners are offered human meat, which has been well seasoned and sprinkled with fresh blood. But the foreigners seem greatly offended by the special food and throw their plates to the ground in disgust. At this, the other priests look to one another and exclaim, "Only Quetzalcóatl, who disdained human sacrifice, would dare to refuse human meat from our king." There is a murmuring of agreement, but I remain silent. For I know that the bearded stranger is not Quetzalcóatl. I have seen Quetzalcóatl in all his shining glory, and this stranger, however powerful and cunning, does not share my god's visage. Nevertheless, it is clear that the invader possesses great magic and is surely a sorcerer. All of which leads me to conclude that the yellow-haired one is actually Tezcatlipoca, our Lord Quetzalcóatl's evil sibling. For who could impersonate the Feathered Serpent better than his own estranged brother, the god of black magic and deception? And who else but Smoking Mirror would have the guile to steal an empire that did not belong to him, as he had already done once before in Tula?

These thoughts I keep to myself as we journey back to Tenochtitlán under brooding skies. No sooner do we arrive in the city when word comes that Motecuhzoma wishes to see us at the palace. Still dirty and exhausted from our travels, we enter the gates of the imperial compound. The great hall of the palace is full and many chieftains and generals are also in attendance. Motecuhzoma himself sits on a gilded throne, dressed in fine robes of woven gold. A great plumed crown rests upon his head and jeweled sandals cover his feet. Though we are forbidden to gaze directly at the king, I steal a glance at his person and remember that he is small of stature with a sensitive face and delicate hands. My heart sinks; it seems impossible that this diminutive monarch could be a match for the cunning Tezcatlipoca.

Presently, Motecuhzoma's brother, Cuitláhuac, welcomes us and bids us to speak. The eldest among us recounts our experiences, including the bearded one's comments and his refusal to eat human flesh. Then the discussion turns to the question of whether or not the stranger is indeed Quetzalcóatl. My fellow priests share their observation that the invader's actions are consistent with the prophecies. An elder from Xochimilco then speaks, saying that the portraits of the intruders painted by Aztec artists do indeed bear a resemblance to our legendary Toltec ancestor.

But several of the nobles and warriors remain unconvinced. Cuitláhuac speaks for them when he forcefully states his belief that the strangers are not gods but men who come from a faraway land and whose only aim is to conquer Tenochtitlán and steal its riches. The conversation proceeds thus, with arguments being offered on both sides until I can no longer hold my tongue. Dropping to my knees I beg the Lord Motecuhzoma to listen. "Great Emperor and unquestioned ruler of the One World," I cry. "I beseech thee to listen to your servant, who has seen the stranger and knows him to be not the god Quetzalcóatl but his evil enemy, Tezcatlipoca, the Smoking Mirror. Strike him down with your warriors now, my liege, while there is still time or life as we know it will soon come to a disastrous end!"

My outburst causes a great commotion in the chamber and two guards are instantly at my side lifting me to my feet. Amid the confusion there are cries of "Heresy!" but my words have been spoken with sincerity and I hear Cuitláhuac command that no harm be done to me. Caring not for my own safety, I would say more, but hands are placed *against my mouth. As I am dragged out of the palace I see that Mote-cuhzoma has risen to his feet and that his features are torn by a terrible state of anguish.*

Several days later I hear that our emperor has decided to keep the invaders quarantined at their seaside camp, but the strategy fails when the bearded stranger is invited into the villages of the Totonacs, a vassal tribe of the Triple Alliance. In the ensuing months, rumors of rebellion and unrest echo across the Valley of Mexico. It is said that the bearded ones speak of another god, one who hangs on a cross, and bow to images of a woman who wears a cowl of blazing light. More ominous are reports that the strangers are recruiting allies from the surrounding states that oppose our empire. A ray of hope is provided by the news that our mortal enemies, the Tlaxcalans, have attacked the invaders, but that light is quickly extinguished when the two armies declare a truce and the bearded ones, accompanied now by thousands of enemy warriors, resume their march toward Tenochtitlán.

In a final effort to stop the invaders, Motecuhzoma sets a trap by luring the bearded ones and their Tlaxcalan allies into an ambush at the city of Cholula. But the plot is discovered by the white barbarians and the plan backfires, ending with the slaughter of thousands of loyal Cholulan troops. Word of the approaching invaders has by now spread throughout the city. There is weeping and lamenting in the markets and public places. People walk about downcast and greet each other with tears. They try to console one another and their children, but at night they toss in their beds, tortured by horrible nightmares.

One bright morning, the fitful fever of dread is shattered by the scream of blaring conch trumpets. The invaders have arrived at the gates of Tenochtitlán! Borne on a litter, our emperor leads the welcoming procession, which includes nobles, warriors and priests, and behind them, thousands of curious bystanders. The bearded ones, who ride atop their large deer, are accompanied by their Tlaxcalan allies and the woman named La Malinche, who speaks the tongue of the invaders as well as our own. The two groups meet at the great causeway and the stranger called Cortés attempts to embrace Motecuhzoma but is stopped by our guards, for no one is allowed to touch the emperor. Speeches are made, and Motecuhzoma leads the strangers inside the gates of Tenochtitlán, where they are invited to reside in the palace built for Motecuhzoma's father, King

Axayácatl. After the strangers have feasted, Motecuhzoma goes to the palace and tells them:

"We have always held that those who descended from Quetzal-cóatl would come and conquer this land and take us as their vassals. So because of the place from which you claim to come, namely from where the sun rises, and the things you tell us of the great Lord who sent you here, we believe and are certain that he is our natural Lord, especially as you say that he has known of us for some time. So be assured that we shall obey you and hold you as our Lord in place of that great sovereign of whom you speak . . ."

A strange paralysis grips the city. Ignoring the advice of his generals, Motecuhzoma continues to honor his exalted guests as equals, giving them treasure, slaves, women and free passage throughout the palace. The bearded ones seem genuinely awed by our mighty metropolis, and for a few days I dare to speculate that Smoking Mirror has abandoned his plan. Then Cortés and his men ask to see the pyramid of Huitzilopochtli, and Motecuhzoma agrees, leading them to Templo Mayor and up the 114 steps to the sacred altar. The two stone slabs atop the temple were still dripping with blood from sacrifices meant to appease the Little Hummingbird for the intrusion of foreigners into the sacred compound. It is there that Cortés angrily denounces Huitzilopochtli, calling our god a devil, and demands that the statue of the Little Hummingbird be replaced with one of a goddess the invaders call the Virgin Mary. Motecuhzoma refuses and our generals brace for war, but Cortés suddenly relents and the threat of battle recedes. The following day, the imperial guards are struck speechless by an amazing sight. What do they see but our king leaving the palace to reside with the foreigners in their quarters. Once again the suspicions of our generals are aroused, but Motecuhzoma insists that he is there of his own free will and that Huitzilopochtli himself bade him to live with the strangers so as to better instruct them on our customs. To assuage the people's fears, Motecuhzoma even appears on the balcony of the strangers' palace to proclaim that the people have no cause for alarm.

The sad illusion that all is well does not last long, however. Our king's brother, Cuitláhuac, and his nephew, Cacama, begin to plan an attack against the interlopers. But before they can act, Motecuhzoma learns of the plot and informs Cortés, who lures the rebels into his compound and has them arrested and put in chains. What happens next erases any doubts about the invaders' true intentions. Accompanied by a squad of his men, Cortés returns to the sacred pyramid of Huitzilopochtli and attacks the statue of the Little Hummingbird with swords and iron mallets. Hearing the commotion, I rush to the scene and arrive as our king begs Cortés to halt the desecration. By now the square is filled with hundreds of onlookers who can barely believe their eyes. The sight of the great Motecuhzoma reduced to a pitiful beggar is more incredible than if water were to reverse its course and run uphill. There are murmurings of outrage from the crowd. Perhaps sensing the danger, Cortés agrees to allow the effigy of Huitzilopochtli to be safely removed before the invaders replace it with a white cross and an altar to their Virgin.

I see the strange cross atop the pyramid and my blood turns cold. My Lord Quetzalcóatl's premonitions have all come to pass. As my dream comes true my old life becomes the illusion. Already the chaos has begun. People are shouting, running, their shadows scattering like phantoms. They flee to their houses and shutter their windows. Calmly, I return to the temple and begin making the necessary preparations for what I know will be a long and dangerous journey. In a few days I will leave my beloved Tenochtitlán, never to return.

One crucial task remains, and to that end I search the temples and the marketplace each day, looking for the serpent sign that marks the one I seek. She was shown to me by our Lord, but in the dream her face remained hidden behind a curtain of black hair. Only her bare arm was visible, revealing the coiled shape of her destiny. I search among the noblewomen lounging on the balconies of their houses and the merchant maids tending overflowing stalls of corn and beans and crimson stacks of chipotle chiles. I look for her among the stout washerwomen at the edge of the lake, the wives of the fishmongers mending their briny nets, the farmers' daughters lugging plucked hens to market. Then, when I least expect it, I am taken to her during a visit to Motecuhzoma at the palace of Cortés. We have been allowed to bring food and drink to our enslaved leader, who is too ill or heartbroken to eat or even speak. I hear sobbing and trace the wretched sound to a nearby cell where several naked women are huddled together. These are the strangers' concubines, presented to them as gifts from Motecuhzoma. "Why are you here?" I ask. A girl with a face like the waxing moon turns to me and answers. "At first our keepers were not cruel," she says. "But after our Lord Motecuhzoma was taken prisoner some of us tried to run away and the strangers caught them and killed them. Those who survived are kept here until they call for us. Please help us. We will die too if we stay here much longer."

As she speaks I glance at her arm and see the sign, like a snake prepared to strike from her flesh. I instantly know that I will arrange for her escape, that I will nurse her back to health and hide her like Tonatiuh until the proper moment comes. I also know that her name is Loma.

All at last is ready. Our party numbers seven: Tonatiuh and myself, Loma, and four slaves to carry our baggage. I descend to my private chapel and pray to Quetzalcóatl, asking him to guide me on the proper course and defend me from Tezcatlipoca and his sorcerers. We depart on foot at dusk, with the evening star shining above us. As we make our way south toward the outskirts of the city I feel pity, not for my homeland, which in my mind is already a crumbling ruin, but for the innocent people huddled in their houses, eating their dinners, unaware of the looming danger. I feel something else, too: a slim thread of hope intertwined with anticipation. For I know now that our mission will lead us far from the One World, across lands infested with enemies and demons, beyond the realm of mortal men, to the buried foundations of heaven itself.

5

The conflagration started on the tip of his tongue and quickly spread to his throat and sinuses, filling his mouth with glowing embers, until his eyes were watering and his whole head was on fire.

"Water," Brian gasped.

"No," Marina said, handing him the second of two small tumblers. "Drink this and mix it in your mouth before swallowing."

Brian quaffed the tequila and the flames of chile pepper were joined by the sharp stab of alcohol. For a moment, Brian just sat there as the two sensations collided into something wonderful. He swallowed, his throat still glowing with a spicy tomato tang.

"Now can I have some water?"

"Naturalmente."

Brian took a deep drink of mineral water. "Incredible," he said. "What do you call that again?"

"Tequila y sangrita," she told him. "Tequila with a little blood. It's sort of a Mexican Bloody Mary—basically tomato, lime and chile, with a little bit of orange juice for sweetness. You can get it in bottles, but it's much better fresh."

"I've never tasted anything like it. But you might have given me some warning."

"You're right," she said without regret. "My uncle always started his weekend with a tequila y sangrita, so I thought you should, too. Did you like it?"

Brian nodded. "I think I'll have another one."

Marina opened her eyes wide. "Ay dios," she exclaimed, "I think I've created a monster."

"Hey, you were the one who wanted to turn me into a real Mexican, right?"

"I agreed to try."

"So how am I doing?"

Marina glanced around. "I don't think a single person here suspects that you were born north of Tijuana."

"Good," Brian said.

The room was large and well lit, with high ceilings and arched windows. The tables were arranged in a semicircle around a raised wooden platform. It was nearly midnight yet the place was just beginning to fill up. The other patrons were well dressed, mostly couples in their thirties and forties. And as Marina had promised, there was not a tourist in sight.

"What's the platform for?" he asked.

"You'll see."

"Have you ever brought anyone here for an interview?"

"Certainly not."

"How about for a sangrita?"

Offended, she asked, "What makes you think that I would?"

"Nothing." He was still getting used to her tendency to take him literally. "What I meant is that I like this place. It reminds me of that Hemingway story, 'A Clean, Well-Lighted Place.' You know, 'Our father who art in nada, nada be his name . . .' "

"Mexicans read Hemingway, too, you know," she said dourly.

"I didn't mean to sound—"

"I know," she said. "It's just that when most Americans think of Mexico—if they think of Mexico—they only see nice beaches and illegal immigrants, not necessarily in that order. It must be terrible to be treated like a stranger in your own country, a second-class citizen."

Brian shrugged. "I guess that's true for some Latinos, but it's not my own experience."

"What is your experience?"

"Am I getting interviewed again?"

"I'm sorry. I don't mean to make you self-conscious."

"Of course you do."

She smiled and looked away.

"Marina, we're both talking in English but sometimes I'm not sure we're speaking the same language." She still wouldn't look at him, but he knew she was listening. "Yes, my name is Mendoza and my father's parents came from Mexico. But that doesn't make me a Mexican. I was born and raised in the United States of America. Some people would say that makes me a Chicano, or a Mexican-American. What does that mean? I don't know. But if you want to know anything about me then you have to realize that there's a gap between who I am and where I came from."

"Don't you mean between where you are and who you were?"

Brian's irritation dissolved in the dark pools of her eyes. "All I care about right now, is being right here with you."

"I'll drink to that," Marina said and raised her tequila for another sip.

"Salud," Brian said, following suit. "And I do know that means 'to your health.' " This time the tequila went down so easily that he almost forgot the chaser.

Marina narrowed her cat eyes and motioned for him to drink again.

"Are you trying to get me drunk?" he asked.

"What if I am?"

"Nothing, except that I might not be responsible for my actions."

"Is that a promise or a threat?"

They were like a couple of wary champs, jabbing, ducking, circling each other without landing a punch. He was seized by an impulse to get inside her defenses, to touch whatever it was she was protecting.

"You know, you're a lot like this drink we're having—fire and ice, cool and hot at the same time."

"Really?" she asked, reaching into her purse for a cigarette. "Is that good or bad?"

"I'm still deciding." He struck a match and held it to her cigarette. "I didn't know you smoked."

"There are a lot of things you don't know about me," she said, inhaling deeply. "Actually, I'm trying to stop. But old habits die hard."

She exhaled, the blue tendrils curling away from her lips. Their eyes met again and he almost understood. She was offering something, but he sensed that it was up to him to find out what it was.

"When I was a kid," Brian said, "we used to play a game called Truth Serum."

"Were you CIA or KGB?" she asked.

He laughed because the question was absurd and they both knew it, because the god of tequila was singing in his veins, because he was in a nightclub in Mexico City with a beautiful woman and he had no idea what would happen next.

"The rules were simple," he said. "Each player took a sip of Kool-Aid and then had to answer one question as truthfully as they could. Then the other player would do the same and so on until the Kool-Aid ran out."

"Or until there were no more secrets," Marina interjected.

"Whatever."

"I would play with you," she said, "but we have no Kool-Aid."

"We have something better," Brian said, raising his glass. Over her shoulder, a group of musicians was setting up on the wooden stage.

"Since I just had one of these little firecrackers, I think ladies should go first this time," he said. Marina nodded and, holding her glass in both hands, drained it in one swallow. The man at the next table saw her and shouted, "Andale, muchacha!"

She brushed her hair away from her face and said, "Okay, ask your question."

"Why did you bring me here tonight?"

"That's easy. I wanted to show you how chilangos have fun."

Brian waited a few seconds before saying, "Now tell me the real reason."

When she realized he meant it, she said, "Because you're not threatened by my intelligence or my independence, because you don't try to control me."

"Is that what most Mexican men do?"

"I'm sorry," she chided officiously, "only one question per drink, please. Now it's your turn."

Brian gulped his drink and folded his arms. "Okay, shoot."

"Why did you come to Mexico?"

"To work on my doctoral thesis with one of the world's most renowned anthropologists, to test myself in a foreign country, to brush up on my Spanish . . . to meet you."

"That's a very good answer," she said. "Now give me the real reason."

The mellifluous sound of a harp laced the air. The plucking was joined by a guitar and a bass, the instruments weaving a buoyant, joyous melody. Marina ignored the music and kept her gaze locked on to him.

"During my first year in graduate school, I met somebody," Brian confessed. "We were together for two years. There was talk about getting married. Then something went wrong. We said some dumb things. Then it was over. Or at least I thought so. When you're trying to avoid running into someone, Berkeley can seem like a very small place. It became obvious that one of us had to go. So here I am."

He impulsively took her hand. "It's also true that I find you extremely attractive."

She smiled and the effect was like lace peeking out from under a suit of armor. Brian's spirits soared with the music. He wanted to give her something in return.

"Did your editors hold the story?"

"Yes," she said.

"Your instincts were right. He's found something under the cathedral, something important." Marina lowered her glass, waiting for him to continue. "It's an anthropological bombshell. A new codex. It's going to be big news when it becomes public. That's all I can tell you."

Marina put her hand over his. "Don't worry," she said warmly. "I appreciate what you've done."

There was an expectant hush as a pair of dancers mounted the platform. The man wore a peasant's white shirt and red kerchief, the girl an embroidered blouse and a flowing skirt. Then the band launched into a boisterous fandango of harp and strumming guitars. As the macho held his hands behind his back and stamped his boots in time with the music, the señorita kicked her heels and twirled her skirt, revealing layers of brightly hued petticoats. The couple moved together until they nearly touched, then parted to dance alone at the opposite ends of the stage. Whenever the dancers came close, the crowd erupted with hoots of approval. The song ended and the dancers retreated. After a brief pause, the band started another song and the dancing began anew.

"It's incredible," Brian said. "I've never heard Mexican music with a harp."

"This style comes from Veracruz," Marina explained. "It's known as jarocho and the dancing is called zapateado. Most of the people you see here are from Veracruz. This is the music of their home."

As if on cue, a man from the audience jumped onto the stage and joined the dancers in a stamping frenzy. Another couple followed, prompting more cheers.

"That looks like fun," Brian observed.

"Would you like to try it?"

Brian raised his hands. "No way. I'm a lousy dancer."

"Not after tonight."

"You're crazy," he said as she grabbed his arm and dragged him out of his chair and toward the stage. He made a valiant effort to turn back, but she insisted, and he finally gave in, too drunk to really care. He put his arms behind his back and stamped his feet, trying to follow the movements of the other men. Marina drew close to him, and he felt the pull of sexual attraction. But when he tried to kiss her she coyly spun away.

"Is teasing Mexican, too?" he shouted.

"Very," she answered and threw back her head, showing him the soft skin under her neck. The rest of the room became a blur as he watched her dance, watched the supple lines of her body flow with the music and beckon to him. Then he closed his eyes and abandoned himself to the bounding rhythm.

The jarocho was still ringing in his ears as they stumbled onto the sidewalk.

"You were wonderful," Marina said.

"So were you." She leaned against him and he could feel the heat of her body through his clothes. "I should get you home. It's late."

"It feels early."

She twined her arm in his and they walked along the shuttered streets like lovers out for an evening promenade. Every now and then, Marina would lift her head from his shoulder to point out a landmark or give him the history of a particular building or avenue. When they came across an all-night food stand, she insisted that he sample a taco made with barbecued goat meat. They walked a few more blocks and stopped at the door to a modern apartment building.

"Would you like to come up for a nightcap?" she asked.

"Where I come from an invitation to a lady's apartment at this hour could have certain consequences."

"I appreciate the warning," she said. "But you're in my country now."

"Still the teacher instructing the student?"

"Class isn't over yet."

In the elevator he pressed against her and she squirmed away. "Not here," she told him, and he wondered if he would ever be able to read her signals clearly.

The apartment was decorated in high-tech Mex—a leather couch and glass coffee table, Tezio lamps, ebony pottery from Oaxaca, hand-woven Indian rugs. An office was set up in a small alcove off the living room. A personal computer, its orange screen glowing, was hemmed in by stacks of notebooks, newspaper clippings, and back issues of *The Globe*. Thumbtacked to the wall were photographs of Marina standing with people he didn't recognize.

"Don't look in there, it's a mess," Marina called out from the living room as the strains of "La Guacamaya" emanated from the stereo. She had dimmed the lights and lit candles.

"My favorite song," he said and took her in his arms. They danced a few steps, casting elongated shadows on the walls and the ceiling.

He leaned forward to kiss her and this time she didn't stop him. They moved to the bedroom and he undressed her slowly, gingerly, as if a sudden motion might cause her to change her mind. Then he removed his own clothes and drew her down to the sheets.

The light filtering in through the window gave her body an iridescent sheen, like the Day-Glo-on-velvet nudes that were hawked to gringo tourists in Tijuana. As he guided her fingers, her touch was surprisingly tentative, like a student of Braille. It hadn't occurred to him that he could be her teacher, too, that physical release could be its own lesson.

She gasped and bit her lip hard enough to break the skin. He drew back, resting on his elbows.

"Do you want me to stop?"

She answered by pulling him forward and Brian tasted blood as he buried himself inside her.

He awoke to the sound of pealing church bells, each tintinnabulation reverberating louder until it seemed that the clapper was his own brain, bashing dolorously against the inside of his skull.

Brian groaned.

He could hear movement in the kitchen. Running water. The clatter of cups and plates. Then the reviving aroma of fresh coffee. Without opening his eyes, he lay motionless in the damp cotton sheets, his head impacted in a pillow, while he recalled the sensations of the night before. He fast-forwarded the videotape in his mind to their lovemaking and felt himself stirring again.

"Good morning," Marina called out from the kitchen. "You have ten minutes for a shower before breakfast is ready."

Playing dead, Brian waited. He had almost drifted off to sleep again when he felt her weight on the mattress. She smelled like soap and fresh flowers. Her hair brushed his neck and shoulder. Then he felt her hand tickling his chest, trailing down his stomach until her fingers found what they were looking for.

"My God," she asked, pretending to be surprised, "you still want more?"

"I always want more."

"No," she chided, "your eggs will burn."

"They're already burning," he said. Her laugh was full and slightly throaty, as if sex had loosened something in her larynx. Brian grabbed her wrists and tried to pin her beneath him but she wriggled out of his grip and fastened her robe. She stalked to the kitchen turning at the last second to glance back at him from the doorway.

After breakfast, they emerged into the limpid light of morning, strolling hand in hand among the families leaving church in their Sunday best. Brian watched the mothers and fathers surrounded by gaggles of squealing children, saw the frowning matrons dressed in black, erect with God-fearing piety. Marina looked girlishly fine in her white cotton dress and Brian felt a prideful pleasure in their secret communion.

They walked aimlessly and without hurry, browsing through the bustling Sunday market, past stalls that sold radios and shoes and garish plastic robots and movie magazines and candles with the Virgin Mary painted on them. There were women in flowered aprons toiling over mounds of steaming tamales and tacos and huge brimming pots of frijoles and red rice and plastic containers with glistening slices of mango and papaya sprinkled with chile and fresh lime juice. Just as Brian's hangover began to reassert itself they arrived at the leafy extremities of Chapultepec Park, the verdant lungs of Mexico City, where they bought sodas and sat on a knoll above the glassy lake. Partly hidden by the gracious boughs of an elm tree, they kissed and fondled each other with the impunity of young lovers. It was then that Marina turned to him and said, "Tell me about her," and he knew that the time for evasion was over and that he would confess the whole story of Linda, the woman who had carried his child, a child that he had never allowed to be born.

"Does she hate you?"

Brian followed the flight of a bird as it swooped low over the water and felt himself skimming along the surface of something deep and cold.

"Yes." He shrugged. "I don't know. I guess I can't blame her if she does."

Then Marina had reached for his hand and kissed it and the touch of her lips was an act of absolution, a type of forgiveness that only a woman who just made love to you could bestow. He wanted to embrace her again and thank her for her compassion, but instead he said, "I was scared. It seemed like the only reasonable solution at the time."

"It's hard for me to imagine ever thinking of that as a reasonable solution."

Propped up on one arm, Brian twirled a blade of grass between his fingers. "I can't explain," he said, "but things are different in America. People are different. I'm different." In fact the old Brian Mendoza was becoming harder and harder for him to identify with, as if his past and future life was not really his own but one belonging to a stranger or a distant relative with whom he no longer kept in close touch.

"Still thinking about the past?"

"No." Brian pulled his gaze away from the lake. "I'm thinking about the present, actually. Mexico. Last night was like a wonderful dream, but it was real. I never thought I could feel so at home in a foreign country."

"Sometimes a person needs to get away from familiar things to find out who they really are," Marina said. "Tell me, do you like the beach?"

"I love the beach."

She tousled his hair. "Have you ever been to Cabo San Lucas?"

"No, why?"

"It's very beautiful. Desert and ocean. Fonatur has finally decided to send me there for my travel article. I've got an extra ticket. I want you to come with me."

"Are you serious?"

"Extremely."

"For how long?"

She put her lips to his ear and he could feel her sweet breath flooding his senses.

"For as long as it takes."

A shaft of light slanted across the twin towers of the church of San Miguelito as Brian greeted the day on Calle San Jerónimo. La Madre was sitting on the stoop, drinking café con leche and smoking a skinny cigar the color of wet leather.

"Buenos días, Doña Conchita."

"Buenos días," she replied. Then, as he ambled down the street he heard her say to the parrot nestled in the folds of her blouse, "Mira, Esmeralda, allí va el amante." Look, there goes the loverboy.

Laura was standing by his desk when he got to the office, her hands fluttering like nervous birds. "Oh, Brian, I'm so glad to see you. Señor Torres said he wants to see you right away."

"Was he waving a machete?"

"Oh my, no," she exclaimed, covering her mouth with her hand. Brian enjoyed making her laugh, particularly when it was at the expense of their boss. His snide comments about Torres never failed to make her eyes dilate with alarm, as if lightning would strike anyone who uttered such slander. Then she would hurry back to her desk, as if even listening to his remarks made her an accomplice in his insubordination. It was not hard to picture her in church, her pigtails hidden by a lace veil, praying to the Virgin. The image was difficult to reconcile with the Aztec ghost whose words she was bringing back to life. He had tried to get her to talk more about it, but each time he raised the subject she had grown flustered and withdrawn.

He had better luck with Guillermo, who displayed a fondness for American slang, and did his part for the cause by drawing caricatures of Torres in grotesque positions. One day he heard Laura's guilty giggle and looked over his shoulder to see Guillermo holding up a picture of Torres defiling a maiden atop Templo Mayor. Their behavior was barely a notch above schoolchildren writing obscenities on the blackboard behind the teacher's back, but it helped to pass the time and, more important, it provided Brian with a way to win the trust of his colleagues.

He looked at Laura, so girlish in a starched white blouse and pleated skirt, and wondered how she'd react if he told her that he'd been surreptitiously reading the results of her work. Thanks to her he now knew that Motecuhzoma had been warned about Cortés not being Quetzalcóatl. But Xotl's diary had still not answered the critical issue of whether the Aztec emperor had consciously orchestrated his own demise, or merely fallen victim to a monarch's delusions of infallibility. The question gnawed at Brian like a grain of sand trapped in an oyster. What if he confided in her? Would she keep his secret or turn him in?

"Laura, I was wondering . . ."

"Yes?"

He hesitated on the brink of confession. "Never mind," he said. "I don't want to interrupt your work."

"Don't be silly." She smiled sweetly. "Is it about your thesis?"

"Yes, that's right. I'm having a little trouble tracking down the exact date of Topiltzin-Quetzalcóatl's birth. Depending on which account I read, he was born in the central plateau of Mexico at Tollan, or a hundred kilometers to the south at Amatlán, in the year 843, 895, 935, 947 or 1156, and died at Uxmal in 1208, or was cremated in Tlapallan, or disappeared into the sea off the coast of Yucatán and turned into Venus, the Morning Star."

Laura nodded vigorously, her brow furrowed with professional concern. "Yes, it's very confusing, isn't it? I think part of the problem is that there are so many different manifestations of Quetzalcóatl, but you might also consider the possibility that they are all right."

"How could they all be right?"

"Well, I once read a paper that suggested that Ce Acatl had been impersonated many times through the centuries by pre-Hispanic zealots."

"You mean impostors?"

"Not impostors, exactly, more like apostles who claimed his name and spread his teachings."

"And they all went by the name of Quetzalcóatl."

"Or one of his other manifestations—the Plumed Serpent, Venus the Morning Star, Xólotl, the Evening Star or Precious Twin."

"Xólotl?"

"Yes, Venus, the evening star. There are two principal myths that pertain. The first deals with the time before the creation of the Fifth Sun, when the sun and the moon were static in the sky. Quetzalcóatl transformed himself into a warrior and fired a dart at the sun, which set it into motion, thus changing him into Venus, the Morning Star, or the Lord of the Dawn. But at sunset he descended into the Underworld and became Xólotl, the star that falls on its head, the Dog Star. Xólotl struggled against the forces of darkness until the morning, when he would reemerge once again as the Lord of the Dawn.

"Another version tells how Quetzalcóatl went into the Underworld to ask Mictlantecuhtli, the Lord of the Dead, for the bones of mankind. He complied but tricked Quetzalcóatl into falling into a deep hole, where the bones of mankind were scattered in the dark. Xólotl, who could see in the dark, helped Quetzalcóatl gather the bones into a pile and take them to the Place of Origin. There, Quetzalcóatl and the other gods poured their blood over the bones and the new race of men was born. There are several other variations but they make the same basic point."

"So Xólotl is associated with the creation of the Fifth Sun?"

"Yes. And also the color white, which signified the transition from death to life, the moment of renacimiento—rebirth or resurrection."

"Mil gracias, Laura. That's all very helpful."

"De nada. Now you'd better get going before somebody blows his top."

Before reporting to Torres's office, Brian sat at his desk and wrote down everything Laura had just told him. The word almost jumped off the page as he silently mouthed it: *Shol-o-tel*. The name of the Aztec priest and Quetzalcóatl's alter ego seemed too similar to be a coincidence. It was possible, of course, that "Xotl" was a faulty transposition of "Xólotl," but he knew Laura would never make such a dumb mistake. Could the Aztec priest have assumed the name and then intentionally altered it to confuse his enemies? As Laura herself had pointed out, it wouldn't be the first time an Aztec had named himself after a god.

The pieces of the puzzle were still tumbling through Brian's mind as he knocked on the glass door of Torres's office and braced himself for the worst.

"You asked to see me?"

"Yes," said Torres, who was looking at Brian as if his very existence posed a conundrum that defied any reasonable explanation. "You have been granted authorization to visit the cathedral dig."

Brian forced himself not to look jubilant.

"I don't suppose I have to tell you," Torres continued, "that it wasn't my idea. The cathedral dig is an extremely delicate situation already without visiting, ah, associates, wandering around."

"I'm sure it is."

Torres used his index finger to trace the clipped whiskers on his lip.

"I am leaving with Professor Zapata this afternoon to attend the Guadalajara conference, so I've asked Guillermo to accompany you. You understand that you are to remain with him at all times while in the dig area."

"Of course." Brian could hardly believe his luck. By telling him when he would be away, Torres had unwittingly handed him another chunk of the Xotl gloss.

A few minutes later, Brian and Guillermo were in the elevator heading down to the museum lobby.

"So what is it like sleeping with Zapata's daughter?" Guillermo asked casually.

Brian blinked at the Guatemalan. "I didn't know he had a daughter."

"Well, you must have done something to get him on your side. In the two years I've been here I've never seen anyone get around Torres like this. The order had to come directly from Zapata, or even higher."

Brian smiled and shrugged as the elevator reached the lobby. "Maybe they've noticed my respect for authority figures."

Guillermo smirked at his joke and pushed open the doors to the outer courtyard. He squinted and crinkled his nose at the brown blanket of air. "I don't know what I'm doing here, letting the poisons kill me," he said peevishly. "If I'm going to die anyway, I'd rather die in my own country."

"You miss Guatemala that much?"

"I'd be there tomorrow if I thought it was safe to go back."

Brian turned to see if Guillermo was kidding, but his features were drained of levity. "I didn't know Guatemala was a dangerous place for archaeologists."

Guillermo shook his head with grim amusement and leaned against the balustrade that overlooked Templo Mayor. When he spoke his voice was low and corrosive. "Guatemala is a dangerous place for anyone who speaks his own mind—or gets in the army's way."

"You don't have to talk about it unless you want to," Brian said, but Guillermo's attention remained fixed on the slanting ruins.

"We were working at a small site about thirty miles from Dos Pilas," he continued, "me and two colleagues from the university. After a few days of digging we managed to uncover a pre-Classic subterranean Maya tomb, not too different in size from where we're going now, but much older of course. We found some stone carvings, a few of them museum quality. We were elated, naturally, and we went into the local village to celebrate, a bit too loudly perhaps, because the next morning we found several of the locals at the site doing their own dig."

"Poachers?"

Guillermo nodded. "The local Indians, especially the younger ones, know that artifacts bring dollars from tourists and foreign collectors. From their perspective, we are no better than poachers ourselves. The distinction between turning them over to a museum and selling them for profit is lost on them. They have families to feed. One can't really blame them.

"Anyway, when they saw us coming they ran and we gave chase. We eventually caught up to one of them, just as a two-man army patrol arrived on the scene. At first we were actually glad to see the soldiers. We explained the situation and the second soldier went off in search of the other poachers. We figured that the soldier who stayed would give the poacher a good scare, or at the most arrest him. But then he told us that the man was a rebel and that he should be made into an example. He raised his rifle and took off the safety. I am no hero, believe me, but when I saw that guy about to be shot in cold blood . . ."

Guillermo flinched at the memory. "Suddenly I knew that the stories I'd heard about innocent people being slaughtered were true. I couldn't let him do it."

"So what did you do?"

"So I yanked the gun away from the soldier and threw it into the bushes." Guillermo emitted a dark chuckle. "Then I ran, because I knew that I would be his next target. I know he found his gun because a minute later I could hear the bullets ripping through the leaves around me. Luckily, I knew the area well enough by that time to be able to circle back to the village and get a ride out before the soldiers came back. When I got to Guatemala City they had already been to my house and told my parents that I had joined the rebels. I was a pariah in my own neighborhood. People were afraid to be seen with me—it was too dangerous. Some friends of mine knew the owner of a boat that was sailing for Mexico. Money was exchanged and I left an hour later. The Mexicans granted me political asylum and it wasn't too long before I was introduced to Zapata through mutual friends. I told him my story and he offered me a job."

Guillermo was slumped against the rail, as if the telling had sapped his strength. Brian tried to imagine what it would be like to be a fugitive from his own country, marooned in Mexico without the option of going home. Compared to what Guillermo was facing, his own problems seemed trivial.

"I had no idea," Brian said. "Have you seen your family since then?"

"My sister came to visit me a few months ago. It only made me more homesick. We write letters . . ."

"Maybe things will change."

Guillermo gave Brian a dubious look, but his natural buoyancy had returned. "In Latin America nothing ever changes," he said as they resumed walking. "That is one thing that the Aztecs had absolutely right. They saw the pattern that formed their world, the pattern that would continue despite wars, famine, earthquakes, even the end of civilization as they knew it. Today it's nuclear Armageddon, pollution, global warming. We are doomed to repeat our past. The pattern continues. Nothing is altered, only the names of the gods are different."

They had arrived at the northeast corner of the cathedral. In addition to the ropes and canvas awning Brian had seen before, a chain link fence had been erected to keep the curious away. Off to the side, an electric pump belched a stream of dark fluid into the gutter. Guillermo fished in his pockets for a laminated identification card and showed it to the guard, who waved them inside. Then Guillermo handed Brian a flashlight and motioned for him to follow. The excavation area was an archaeologist's paradise: the stone floor was covered with objects—pots, masks, shells, small statues and knives, most of them still encrusted with greasy black mud.

Guillermo turned to Brian. "What do you know about the discovery of the site?"

"Only that it was found by workers who were trying to keep this corner of the cathedral from sinking."

"Right. The subsoil here is very unstable. It took days just to get the water level down far enough for us to go inside. What's the matter?"

"That mask," Brian said. "It looks a lot like one I bought a few weeks ago."

"I hope you washed it off before you took it home."

Guillermo motioned to a low arched passageway. From the type of stone around them, Brian guessed that they were inside the foundations of the church. The floor of the next room had been dug out, revealing a pit about ten feet deep with a metal ladder resting against its side.

"The workers got this far," Guillermo pointed about two feet into the pit, "before they realized that they were no longer shoveling just mud. The first objects that turned up were some shell ornaments and the remains of a ceramic bowl. But what really tipped them off was the change in the stone. You can see where it becomes porous and much older."

"I'm surprised they didn't think it was just part of the original church that burned down."

"Well, in fact they did," Guillermo explained. "Until they found that." He pointed to a piece of carved tezontle resting against the wall. Brian stooped and shone his light on it for a closer look. The stone was broken in half and badly chipped, but it was unquestionably part of a serpent's head.

"As you know," Guillermo continued, "it had been suspected for years that the original church had been built directly over the temple of Quetzalcóatl. As soon as the carving was found, Zapata ordered a halt in the digging. Normally, a formal excavation would have been authorized and a restoration plan devised."

"But the church stepped in."

"Put its foot down is more like it," Guillermo said. "Hours after the temple was discovered the Cardinal began pressuring the museum to abandon its plans on the basis that the site is Holy Ground."

"Can the church do that?"

Guillermo nodded. "Even though the Constitution forbids the church from owning property, Mexico is a Catholic country and the Vatican still wields considerable influence in secular affairs. The government has responded by sealing the site until it can find a permanent solution."

"So that's why the artifacts are still here," Brian mused. "But why would the church risk a confrontation with the museum? Why not let the museum take what it wanted and then continue with the structural repairs?"

Guillermo wagged his finger at Brian.

"That, as Shakespeare would say, is the rub. The original church on this site was built in 1525, but despite the rumors that jewels had been mixed into the mortar, it was eventually deemed too modest for the capital of New Spain and was torn down. The present structure was begun in 1573 and not fully completed until the early nineteenth century. The first effort to keep it from sinking was initiated in 1975, when hundreds of supports were sunk 130 feet into the ground. At the time the workers reported hitting many air pockets with their drills. The director tried to have the work halted back then, too, but after much prodding the church finally admitted that the cathedral had been built directly over the foundations of the original, and that a maze of catacombs was known to still exist under the building. Not even the church knows how many there are or what exactly they contain. Some people believe that the catacombs were used as torture chambers during the Mexican Inquisition. In any case, you can understand why the Bishop might be a little sensitive about the prospect of scientists crawling around down there, possibly discovering things that the church would rather leave unmolested. And so it was, until the church went ahead and dug its own grave, as it were."

"And now the Pandora's box is open and both sides are caught in a deadlock over who has the right to explore the contents."

"Exactly," Guillermo answered. "But who is Pandora and what is in the box? It was Zeus who created Pandora and sent her into the world as an act of revenge against men. Do you believe that the curiosity of women will be the doom of us all?"

"It's always better to know the truth."

"Undoubtedly," Guillermo agreed. From the rim of the pit, he turned and bowed. "Visitors first."

Brian felt a tingle of anticipation as he peered into the dank orifice. Stuffing his flashlight in his back pocket, he lowered himself a rung at a time, careful not to touch the sides of the shaft. The floor was coated by a pulpy mass that gave under his shoes. A few seconds later, Guillermo was at his side. They passed through a series of interconnected cells and Brian had to crouch to keep from scraping his head on the ceiling. Some of the passages had been blocked with makeshift plywood barriers.

"Couldn't they just have put up a few KEEP OUT signs?" Brian mused.

"Contrary to its teachings," Guillermo said sarcastically, "the church does not always leave it to God to protect its interests." He aimed his beam at an opening in the wall about three feet square. "It's in there." As Brian crawled through, something oozed through his fingers. He wiped his hand on his pants and kept going.

The chamber on the other side was surprisingly large, about ten feet wide and almost tall enough for him to stand. A lone electric lamp lit the damp interior. There were glyphs on the walls and a raised platform that looked like it could have been used as an altar. At its base, a few flat stones lay next to an open cavity.

"It looks like it was used as a hiding place," Brian observed.

"It's possible," Guillermo said obliquely. "A number of objects were found in this chamber."

"But you can't tell me what they were."

Guillermo raised his hand in apology. "My orders were to escort you to the dig, nothing more."

"I understand."

"So now I'll tell you anyway," Guillermo said. "Some pottery. Incense burners. A few ritual objects. You already saw most of them up above. And then of course there's the codex."

He waited for Brian's reaction.

"I already know."

Guillermo seemed delighted. "That's good. I knew you were too smart not to figure it out. They are fools to try to keep it a secret. It's only a matter of time before word leaks out and then the caca will hit the fan."

"Has Laura shown any of it to you?"

Guillermo shook his head. "Are you kidding? The woman has too much integrity to bend the rules, even for her boyfriend. It's one of the things I love about her."

"So everything of interest has already been taken out."

"I wouldn't say that exactly," Guillermo said. "They had to leave the walls."

Brian pointed his beam at the side of the chamber and almost dropped his flashlight. The glyphs were badly faded and still covered by a thin film of grime, but they were readable. Brian recognized several symbols associated with Quetzalcóatl, including a serpent pierced by an arrow, the symbol of self-sacrifice or drought, and a figure offering bones to a deity. Off to the side, a circle had been drawn between two flared triangles, the Aztec sign for movement. There was something next to it and Brian had to wipe away more mud to get a better look.

"It's probably best if you don't touch anything," Guillermo said, his voice weirdly amplified by the thick walls.

"Right," Brian said. "It's just that I've never seen anything like this before."

"I have," Guillermo said. "At Atetelco, near Teotihuacán. It's quite an impressive site, and it's only an hour away by car. I'd be happy to take you there. I'm sure Laura would like to come along, too."

"How about next week, after I get back from Cabo San Lucas?"

"Cabo San Lucas," Guillermo repeated. "Somehow I doubt you'll be going there to fish."

"I'm going there with a friend."

Guillermo made a sly face. "A female friend, by any chance?"

"As a matter of fact, yes."

"It sounds like our visiting colleague has fallen in love. Is she beautiful?"

"Let's just say I think I've found my own Malinche."

"Qué bueno," Guillermo nodded his endorsement. "I'm very glad."

Brian refocused on the glyph. It was hard to be absolutely sure, but it looked like a figure with a triangular bonnet and the symbol for the Thirteenth Sky.

On their way out, Brian paused to examine the objects that had been found in the chamber. He picked up a small smooth stone with a hole drilled through it.

"What do you make of this?"

Guillermo studied the stone closely, rubbing his fingers over the surface. "Looks like a pendant of some kind. There's an image etched on one side. It's too damaged for me to be certain, but my guess is that it's another representation of Quetzalcóatl."

"Mine, too," Brian said. He took the pendant and let it dangle from his fingers. The image flipped into an inverted position, as if diving toward the Underworld.

6

His dreams were broken by the boom of muffled thunder. The noise came again, a rolling concussion that vibrated through the tile floor and rattled the sliding glass doors leading to the patio. Brian listened to the thudding breakers of Cabo San Lucas, visualizing his position on a map at the blunt tip of Baja California. After picking up a jeep at the airport in San José, he and Marina had spent the next hour racing between the desert and the sparkling sea, Marina's hair flickering in the wind like a black flame. He couldn't remember the last time he'd felt so carefree and relaxed; then she had reminded him that he was, nominally at least, back in California, the *other* California. Pinning the map down on her lap, she had directed him past Cabo proper, a ramshackle assemblage of condo developments, sushi restaurants and beer billboards, and on to the rocky point where the Pacific raised its voice against the Sea of Cortés.

Pulling up to their hotel, Brian dropped the bags in the lobby and went out to gape at the spectacle of glassy blue-green waves rearing up against honey-colored cliffs. Their room was on the edge of the complex, where careful landscaping yielded to the brazen desert. The porter had barely accepted Brian's tip and closed the door before he and Marina were at each other like the young couples who gave Cabo its reputation as a honeymooners' hideaway.

Brian swallowed and rubbed the sleep from his eyes. They had neglected to open the windows and the room was stuffy with sex and hotel disinfectant. Beside him, Marina was still napping, her profile tinted by ruddy afternoon light. Careful not to wake her, he pulled on a pair of shorts and slipped out. A stiff shore breeze was blowing and Brian could feel grains of sand lash his ankles. As he walked the strand the breakers reared up and curled like question marks before answering themselves in a frenzy of white foam. There was not a single swimmer in sight, and he remembered the manager's friendly warning to stay out of the water or risk being swept out to sea by the cape's greedy currents. The tide must have been coming in because every now and then a wave would fan across dry sand like an animal off its leash before retreating back into the wash. Brian turned and started back toward the hotel. He could see the low white buildings against the looming escarpment, and off to the right, the natural rock arch that marked the southernmost point of the cape. There was something exhilarating about the conjunction of ocean and sand, the bracing contradiction of elements. Or maybe it was just his state of mind; a beatific high brought about by the fusion of opposites.

Up ahead, Brian spotted a man standing knee-deep in the foam, evidently determined to catch the sunset on his video camcorder. As Brian watched, a wave coiled and struck, pulling the man off his feet and into the roiling surf. When Brian started running toward the thrashing figure the man shook his head, yelling, "No, not me! The camera!" Brian looked down just as a yellow rectangle tumbled out of the wash like high-tech flotsam.

Brian waited as the camera's owner thrashed toward him through the surf. He was about forty-five, still handsome in a grizzled way, with the body of an aging Apollo and the callow grin of an eternal adolescent. Just the kind of grown-up who took his toys seriously.

"Here you go," Brian said. "But I'm afraid the thing's pretty soaked."

"No problem." The man wiped his face with the crook of his arm and reached out to accept the soggy Sony. "Thing's totally waterproof. Those Japs are frigging geniuses."

By now a few people had come out to see what the commotion was about. A youngish brunette pushed to the front of the crowd. "Are you okay, honey?"

"Yeah, I'm fine," the man answered, pointing the Sony at Brian. "Thanks to this good Samaritan who saved my life"—he winked—"and my camera."

Brian tried to back away but he could already hear the tape whirring in its hermetically sealed casing.

"What's your name, amigo?"

"Brian."

"A good American name," he said. "Say hi to the folks back in Scottsdale, Brian."

"Hi."

"Hey, what do you think I've got here, an Instamatic or something? This is moving pictures, pal. C'mon, wave!"

But all he saw through the viewfinder was Brian's back receding out of focus.

Marina, her hair swept up in a towel turban, was already getting dressed for the evening. Fonatur had set up a whole itinerary for them, including a sunset cruise and dinner at one of the better Cabo restaurants. They left the jeep at the hotel and took a five-minute taxi ride to a cement jetty bristling with masts and deep-sea rigging. Cabo was also renowned for its big-game fishing and the kiosks along the harbor were papered with snapshots of vacationing gringos proudly posing with eighty-pound marlins.

"Pobre pescados," Marina said as they walked past the photos and boarded a flat-bottomed craft with the words LOVE BOAT stenciled along the gunwale. The crew—a jaunty quartet of Mexican youths in tank tops and surfer jams—welcomed them aboard and passed around plastic cups of spiked punch as reggae thumped from stereo speakers. They nodded hello to their fellow passengers—mostly American couples with money belts around their waists and matching dabs of zinc oxide on their noses.

"Is this your idea of an authentic Mexican vacation?" Brian asked. Marina told him to hush and scribbled something in her notebook.

The engine cleared its throat and the "Love Boat" pushed away from the docks, gliding past the luxury yachts anchored in the bay, toward the painted rocks at the point. In their own crude way, the music and drink were having the desired effect. Brian inhaled the salty breeze and reached down into the water, letting it shove against his open palm as it rushed past. Marina was staring off into the distance, lost in thought. Brian sidled closer and put his arm around her shoulders. "Come on, lighten up, you snobby chilanga," he teased. He saw her make the effort to push aside whatever was on her mind. Hugging him back, she said, "You're right, I'm not going to let work spoil our vacation."

The bow shuddered against the swells as they headed toward open water. Brian steadied himself and measured their progress against a pale crescent beach nestled in a natural cove. "Lover's Beach," the first mate announced and a few passengers responded with raised cups and applause. The natural arch depicted in so many postcards was dead ahead and people began moving toward the starboard side to get a better view. Dark shapes lolled on the boulders. "Seals!" came the shout. This brought even the most blasé passengers to their feet. There was a chorus of oohs and ahs. Cameras clicked. Then the boat cleared the point and the sun came into full view. Brian stared at the bloated orange orb, which seemed close enough to singe the sails of any ship foolish enough to sail toward it. The crew turned off the music and cut the engine, allowing the boat to drift with the tide. Craft and current moved as one, the vertical motion of the waves measured by the black waterline that stained the base of the arch. The seals began to bark, their canine voices clearly audible over the sloshing sea. "There it goes!" someone cried as the lower rim of the sun dripped into the ocean. Like the minute hand of a clock, the pomegranate disc sank below the horizon at a speed that was imperceptible at one moment and obvious the next, until only a small arc remained, then a piercing, luminous dot vainly resisting the earth's declivity, then nothing.

"Look at the moon," Marina murmured. And to Brian's surprise, it had already risen, like a child forced to wait until the exit of a brighter sibling to be noticed. The sun's pale sister took charge of the sky and asserted itself over the sea, which the twilight had tinted iridescent shades of iodine, purple and green.

Brian looked into Marina's eyes, which were ablaze with the same nameless color.

"Thanks for bringing me here."

"De nada."

That night, after dinner at a fish house on the bay, the moon was still with them as they walked together along the vacant beach.

"When I was a boy," he told her, "I actually believed that it was made of cheese. I think I got the idea from a cartoon. I asked my father about it and he laughed and said, there's no cheese on the moon because the man ate it all, which is how he got so fat. And even now, whenever I look at it I always see him."

"What man?" Marina answered. "I see el conejo, the rabbit."

"The rabbit?"

"Mira," she said, taking his hand in hers as she outlined the body, head and ears. "There. Can you see it now?"

Brian forced his eyes to give up what they expected. It was there, just as she claimed: a profile of a hare perched on its haunches, its ears jutting out from an oval head. "Yes, I think so," he said. "But can you see the man?"

She nodded as he described the cratered eyes and mouth. "But I still think it's a rabbit," she said.

"I guess it's both." Brian picked up a piece of driftwood and flung it into the sea. The surf had calmed down and the palms, deprived of an onshore breeze, looked haggard and limp. Mariachi music wafted from the hotel bar, but the beach was dark and deserted.

"I wonder if this is what the rest of California was like, before the freeways and the tract houses," Brian said.

"Do you miss it?" she asked.

"No, I don't."

She tugged playfully on his arm. "Not even those wild California girls?"

"I'm with a wild California girl—a Baja California girl."

She laughed and leaned against him. "Very good, Mendoza."

Brian saw something dark near his feet and almost stumbled as he tried to step around it. Behind him, Marina stifled a giggle. He turned and lunged for her but she was too quick and he ended up on all fours in the sand. Brian threw his head back and the motion made the stars swim in the sky.

"Estás borracho," she chided.

"And whose fault is that?"

They had ordered two rounds of margaritas, then a bottle of wine with dinner. The waiter had opened the chardonnay with a theatrical flourish, proffering the cork for Brian to sniff and dribbling some wine into his glass. When Brian told the waiter that the lady should taste the wine since she had selected it, the man had pretended not to understand. Calmly but firmly Brian repeated himself, this time in Spanish. Red-faced and frowning, the waiter had grudgingly obliged, as if enology was beyond the realm of female discrimination.

"So tell me," Marina asked, "why did you insist that I taste the wine tonight?"

He peered into the shadows, trying to pinpoint her location. "Did I embarrass you?"

"Not in the least. But you did embarrass the waiter."

"He embarrassed himself."

"You haven't answered my question."

"Because it was appropriate," Brian said.

Marina's voice rose above the surf. "And you do think that your own ideas of propriety entitle you to offend other people?"

"He deserved it, he was being a chauvinist."

"You're awfully sure of yourself, aren't you?"

She was so close now he could touch her.

"I know how to deal with waiters, if that's what you mean."

"That's part of what I mean. The other part is that you and the waiter are quite alike in a certain way."

"Alike?"

"Yes. You both assumed that you knew what was best and you both exercised your will without once asking me what I wanted."

"But I thought . . ."

"I know what you thought. And you were basically right, but if you had really cared about my feelings you would have asked me. You never did."

"Are you asking me to apologize?"

"Don't be silly." Her words, inflated by irony, floated to him over the sand. "I've hurt your pride haven't I?"

"No."

"That's the other part," she said.

"What other part?"

"Your stubbornness. That and your supreme self-confidence, the conviction that you are always right—it's very American."

Having his words turned against him like that suddenly soured his mood. Hadn't he behaved like a gentleman? What more did she want? "Look, I'm tired," Brian said, trying to conceal his annoyance. "So if it's all right with you, I'm turning in."

He took two steps before Marina blocked his path.

"No," she said, "not until you listen."

Brian dug his heels into the sand and crossed his arms. "Okay. Shoot."

"You think I'm being critical of you, but I'm not. I'm just trying to get you to understand. You can dress and eat and drink like a Mexican, but you will never be a Mexican until you think like a Mexican. I don't expect you to ever do that; I wouldn't want you to. I like you the way you are. I'm just asking you to open your mind up a little. Look at things from the other side sometimes. Try to see the rabbit, Brian."

He looked up at the moon with its random arrangement of mountains, craters and blotchy seas.

"Listen to me," she said. "Do you know what it means for an unmarried Mexican woman to travel alone with a man? Good girls do not run off to Cabo for the weekend."

"Marina . . ."

"Do you know what my mother or my priest or the people in my neighborhood would say if they knew I was here with you? They would say that I no longer care about my family, or my religion or my upbringing. They would say that I have no scruples or morals. They would say that I was beyond salvation."

She was standing so close to him now that he could feel her

breath, but it was too dark for him to read her expression.

"Do you understand?"

"I understand."

"Good," she said.

Then she unzipped his pants, sank to her knees and took him into her mouth.

Brian was thirsty when they got back to the hotel, so he pocketed the room key and took the palm-shrouded path to the palapa-covered bar, where he ordered a Superior, served Mexican-style with a wedge of lime. Brian squeezed some lime into his beer and took a long swig. The dinner crowd had dispersed and, perhaps owing to the momentary dearth of American customers, the satellite TV was tuned to a Mexican news station. It was hard to hear the newscaster's voice above the whining piña colada blender, but he gathered that the antigovernment forces were gaining momentum in various sectors of the country. There had been another large rally in Mexico City led by the campesinos who were squatting in a tent city near the zócalo, and protesters had clashed with police in Querétaro, Guadalajara and Apatzingán. Most ominous were reports that Maya dissidents in Yucatán and Chiapas had mobilized a revival of the Cult of the Talking Cross, an armed anti-Colonialist movement that had kept the Spanish and the Mexican government at bay for forty years during the first half of the nineteenth century. The rebels were calling for secession from the Mexican republic and an abrogation of the peace treaty that had been negotiated with President Porfirio Díaz in 1876. Already there had been scattered incidents of tourists being ambushed and robbed at gunpoint by the guerrillas, who painted white crosses on their chests and called themselves Cruzobs.

"Just the fellow I was looking for."

Brian felt a hand on his shoulder and turned to see the man with the Sony camcorder beaming back at him. He was wearing flip-flops, acid green spandex shorts and a Corona beer T-shirt. "Richard Rattner," he announced, extending his fleshy paw.

Brian shook it.

"Brian, right?" Rattner's index finger was extended like a gun barrel.

"Right."

"I just wanted to thank you for what you did today," Rattner said, plopping down on the adjacent stool.

"You're welcome, but I didn't do a thing."

"I know you didn't save my life—that's our little joke. But you did help me get my camera out of the deep six. The least you can do is let me buy you a drink, okay? Dos Coronas, por favor! Rapidamente! That means on the double."

"I know."

Brian kept his eyes on the TV screen, wishing that Rattner would rewind himself to his own room.

"Watching the news, eh?"

"Yeah."

"Anything happening back home?"

"Hard to say."

Their drinks arrived and Rattner lifted his beer at Brian. "I'll drink to that." He chugged half the bottle and held it up with the studied aplomb of a liquor ad. "Mexicans make excellent beer," he said. "And their beaches here are the best. The whole coastline is just gorgeous—Hawaii without the humidity. And not only that. They've got minerals, oil, you name it. It's only a matter of time before they get their beans in a row, if you know what I mean."

Brian didn't answer.

"Not that it isn't happening already," Rattner added. "I've been coming down here for twenty years and, boy, I can tell you this place has really changed. Back in the seventies, you *had* to rent a jeep to get around—no cars—the roads were so bad. No TV, either. Now they have streetlights, condos, new roads. In town, you can even get sake and a Baja California roll to go. Show me a country with take-out, I've always said, and I'll show you an advanced civilization."

"I guess it depends on how you look at it."

"Exactly," Rattner agreed, misconstruing Brian's words. "Where we live, in Arizona, there's a pretty big Hispanic population. Brian, where in the States are you from?"

"California."

"So there you are. You know what I'm talking about. My main line of business is manufacturing, light industrial stuff, and most of my employees are immigrants. I'll say this, because I know, they are hard workers, honest people, the nicest folks I ever met. For years I've been helping them get papers so they can stay and get work and feed their families. Now the tide has turned. All the money is going south. Hell, I'm thinking about moving my own factory down here. Funny how quick things flip around."

The newscast ended and a Mexican commercial came on. Brian noticed that all the actors in the ad were light-skinned with European features.

"I guess."

"Let me illustrate by asking you a question. Why do all the Mexicans in the U.S. send their money to Mexico?"

"To help their relatives?"

Rattner imitated an electric buzzer.

"Not! Wrong answer. Try again, pal."

"To pay the national debt?"

"Maybe," Rattner agreed dubiously, and it dawned on Brian that this man would do almost anything to keep the conversation going. "But you know what caused that debt in the first place?"

"Colonialism." Brian knew he was being rude, but he didn't care.

Rattner recoiled. "Well, historically speaking," he allowed. "But I'm talking about right now. Something that's going on at this moment."

"Revolution?"

"No, come on," Rattner jerked his head to and fro. "You know what I'm getting at—interest rates, profits, capital gains! A country with six percent growth for the past four years must be doing something right. That's why the Mexicans send their money here, because it's just plain smart. And, I'll tell you this: it's not just a good move for savvy investors."

He nodded his head at the man washing glasses behind the bar. "That guy over there probably has a big family and a sick mother to support. Without this hotel he would be unemployed, his wife and kids out begging on the street. That goes for the maids, the clerks. Multiply that by hundreds of thousands. Did you know that tourism is the second largest source of income for the whole country? That's right. Second only to oil. We're talking five, maybe ten billion bucks by 2005. I'm talking grande dollars here."

"You sound like you have a personal stake in it."

"You bet I do." Rattner beamed at Brian. "You know that cove around the point, the one they call Lover's Beach?"

"What about it?"

"It's just been zoned for a new development. I'm a limited partner with a consortium of Polish banks. A hundred and fifty rooms. Super-deluxe. I figured it was time to give something back to this country."

"And make a tidy profit."

"Hey, there's nothing wrong with making money," Rattner took another slug of his beer, "as long as it benefits the people and helps the economy. Investment equals jobs equals profit equals investment. Capitalism 101. That's what made America great. And that's why this new president they've got—"

"Nava."

"That's why Nava is good for Mexico. Out with the old, in with the new. He's been cracking down on corruption, keeping the economy open to foreigners. You watch, he'll make Mexico into the next Japan. Just give him a few years."

Brian pushed away his drink and looked at Rattner's weathered face. "He might not have a few years," he said. "The opposition is trying to throw him out. They say there could be another civil war pretty soon. Could be bad for business."

Rattner waved his hand as if shooing away an insect. "That's just politics—a bunch of old guys wagging their peckers at each other. Everybody knows that this country is thirsty for dollars. The Mexicans would never do anything to kill the goose that lays the tourist egg. If there's one thing these people understand, it's the value of old-fashioned hospitality."

"Maybe so," Brian answered, "but Maya guerrillas have started attacking tourists in Yucatán."

"Where did you hear that?"

"It was just on the news."

For the first time since he'd sat down, Rattner was mute. They stared together at the TV, which had been switched to a soccer match. The crowd roared as the ball arced through the air and bounced off a player's head before continuing its trajectory to the goal.

Brian thanked Rattner for the beer and stood up.

"It won't change anything," he muttered.

"I'm sorry?"

"They can't stop progress." Rattner was staring into his beer as if it were a crystal ball. "Not even with guns. Condo developments are being planned from here to the Guatemalan border. You can already see the foundations going up. In five years this place is going to look just like Honolulu."

The brown skin of the desert stretched against the sea as Brian drove Marina to her interview with the deputy sales manager for Quinta Sol. Pulling up to the unpaved entrance, they passed a group of Mexican laborers digging along the shoulder with picks and shovels. The workers had glanced up for only an instant, but it was enough for Brian to register the hot mixture of curiosity and contempt. Brian maneuvered around dump trucks and tractors toward a cluster of tile roofs along the water. "It's the first stage of the government's long-term plan to build Baja into a major resort," Marina explained.

Inside the air-conditioned office a cardio-correct young man in a black polo shirt and white tennis shorts bounded in to greet them. "Miss Soto," he said, extending a tanned, muscular forearm. "Hi. I'm Adam Cruz." They all shook hands and Cruz invited Brian along for the tour. Cruz was a Mexican-American, third generation, born and bred in the coastal community of Manhattan Beach, where he had grown up "grooving on the waves." A surfing trip with some pals brought him to Cabo and he had resolved to remain and make it his full-time home.

"Quinta Sol is a self-contained, ecologically sound, fully integrated leisure community," Cruz began in accentless L.A. argot. "The goal is to provide maximum comfort and security in a health-oriented atmosphere. Each unit has its own climate-control system, built-in utilities, sauna, whirlpool and fiber-optic fax . . ."

As Cruz led them along the manicured footpaths, Brian felt a stab of cultural dislocation. The man's roots were Mexican yet everything about him, from his fashionably cropped hair to his designer tennis shoes, conformed to the cultural cutting edge. Like artificially flavored tortilla chips, Cruz combined and transcended both cultures. He was the vanguard of a new race flourishing on a low-cal diet of tuna-steak flautas, cayenne pepper health supplements and Japanese oysters with cilantro vinegar: Neo-Pacific Man.

Brian realized that Quinta Sol was just a single manifestation in a much larger evolution of the whole peninsula. The jeeps, the sushi bars, the heated Jacuzzis and tennis courts were all part of the Master Plan. The new order had even brought its own religion, the "Lifestyle" that Cruz was describing with such missionary zeal. Richard had been right: eventually there would be no difference between Cabo and Honolulu. It was merely a matter of time.

Brian decided to head back to the hotel while Marina finished her interview. Cruz had gallantly offered to drive her back to the hotel in time for lunch. On his way out, Brian slowed down where he had seen the laborers, but the gaping ditch was abandoned. They would be back—maybe. So much of Mexico seemed to be in a state of perpetual midconstruction. An unfinished country for an unfinished people, he thought.

Heat waves rose from the rocks and Brian felt a rivulet of sweat inch down his chest as he cut across the grove of spiky yucca to the chlorinated oasis behind the main lobby. The pool was empty except for a few early drinkers at the swim-up bar. He dove in and did a few laps, then hauled his dripping body onto the cement deck and lay there in the expanding puddle of warmth. As Brian listened to the pulsing surf his mind conjured absurd images of a Mexican-style amusement park, featuring such attractions as the Speedy Gonzáles crash cars and the Aztec temple flume ride.

When he opened his eyes again, Marina's face was gazing down at him. "I saw this handsome guy out by the pool and I thought I'd introduce myself."

"Adam Cruz," he said, extending his hand and flashing a Pepsodent smile. "Damned nice to meet you."

Marina laughed and shook her head. "Don't tell me you're jealous."

"Are you kidding?"

"Are you hungry?"

"I'm starving."

"Then why don't you get dressed for lunch while I get us a table."

After pulling on dry shorts and a cotton shirt, Brian ducked into the gift shop and bought a copy of *The Globe*. He was surprised to see Zapata's picture on the front page. The accompanying profile was pegged to the controversy over the Quetzalcóatl excavation. Halfway down the second column, Brian read something that made his stomach clench. The article hinted that Zapata had found a manuscript which he had not yet made known to the public, and even quoted an unnamed source at Templo Mayor saying that the Templo Mayor director had uncovered "an anthropological bombshell." The article concluded with the speculation that Zapata might be hoarding his "bombshell" as ammunition to use against church officials who dared to stand in his way. The byline was waiting at the bottom of the story in bold type: Marina Soto.

Brian reread the words, as if repetition could somehow change their meaning. Anyone who knew he and Marina were seeing each other would assume that he had been the source of the anonymous quote.

Marina was already seated at their table, reviewing her notes. "Working on your next exposé?" Brian asked. "I hope Cruz knows a good lawyer, because he's going to need one after being interviewed by you."

"What are you talking about?"

Brian tossed the paper on the table.

"This is what I'm talking about."

She reached out and gingerly picked it up. He waited while she read it, her lips silently mouthing the words. He knew when she had gotten to the bombshell part because she looked up at him and said, "Brian, I'm so sorry."

"Sorry isn't enough, sorry is too late."

"You don't understand," she pleaded. "I didn't write that."

"Oh come on, Marina. Don't insult me by lying again."

"Brian, listen to me, I'm not lying to you."

Heads were starting to turn. Brian sat down and lowered his voice. "You didn't write that?" he sneered. "Didn't you tell me yourself that you were working on a story about Zapata?"

"Yes, but—"

"But what?"

"The editors wrote that in while I was gone . . ."

Brian ignored the throb in her voice.

"If the editors wrote it, they had to have gotten it from you. That was my quote."

"Yes, it was your quote, but they weren't supposed to use it, not like that. I told them just so that they would hold the story until I could get more information."

"And that's when you decided to invite me on this little vacation, just to make sure I didn't see it. Or maybe you figured a little sex, a little sun and who knows what he might tell me. Is that how you get your scoops, Marina? By sleeping with your sources? Maybe you are La Malinche after all."

She covered her eyes with her hand. Brian couldn't stand to look at her anymore so he walked out of the hotel, got into the jeep and started driving. He drove automatically, going nowhere, anywhere. He needed to move, to clear his mind. Turning onto the main highway he pressed on the accelerator until the wind was hard against his chest. He sped through several small towns, not even slowing down as mangy gangs of dogs gave chase, until all he could see was cacti and brush and brown hills wilting under the scorching sun. He pulled over to the shoulder and stopped, overheated and lost. The anger was all driven out of him, and the vacuum he felt inside matched the desolation of his surroundings.

He sat stock still for a while, sweating through his shirt and listening to the arrhythmic plink of the cooling engine. Then he noticed the clump of yellow buds sprouting through the pavement and the soothing hum of insects buzzing through the weeds. The warm breeze, which moments before had only smelled of dust, carried the minty scent of sage and the essence of a thousand different flowers. Brian considered the possibility that he'd overreacted, that she was telling the truth. He imagined her alone in their room, waiting for him to come back and accept her apology.

A flock of small birds fluttered overhead and he watched them fly north until they had been swallowed by the sky. Brian climbed out of the jeep and walked over to a bush dotted with brilliant red blossoms. He saw one that he liked and broke it off at the bottom of the stem. Then he did the same to another and another, until he had enough for a bouquet.

It was almost dusk by the time he pulled into the hotel parking lot. The management was hosting "Fiesta Night" for the new batch of arrivals and Brian had to dodge hovering trays of margaritas on the way to their room. The lights were still on—a good sign. But as soon as he pushed the door open he knew she was gone. He put the flowers down and picked up the note Marina had left for him on the dresser.

> Brian,
> I'm sorry things didn't work out. I've gone back to Mexico City. The room and the jeep are paid until Monday. After that you're on your own.
> Marina

Brian sat on the bed and considered his situation. It was certainly too late to catch her at the airport and he was equally sure that there wouldn't be another plane to the capital until morning. He was stuck for the night, in Cabo, which at the moment was the last place on earth he wanted to be. He wasn't in the mood for company but he didn't want to be alone either so he got back into the jeep and drove into town. After considering his options, he settled on a noisy cantina called the Giggling Marlin, which was lively enough to forestall boredom yet large enough to offer anonymity. Brian took a seat at the warped wood bar and ordered a double tequila. A mariachi band playing South of the Border standards was strolling among the tables of sunburned fishermen. There was a poignancy in the lamenting melodies, a blue tint to the blaring horns that made the music an ideal soundtrack for serious drinking. No wonder so many Mexicans are drunks, he thought sourly, downing his tequila with a diligence that quickly earned the bartender's respect. The bartender's name was Paco and he performed his job with a gravity that meshed perfectly with Brian's objective.

There was a ruckus at one of the tables and Brian looked over in time to see a man being dragged from his chair. At one end of the room several waiters readied a noose hanging from a large pulley attached to the rafters. It seemed for a second that Brian was about to witness a public lynching. But instead of putting the rope around the victim's neck it was looped around his feet. The waiters heaved on the rope and the man was soon dangling upside down. A hearty cheer reverberated through the room as the man twitched helplessly, hoisted into the air like the human catch of the day.

No sooner had the man been lowered to the floor when a shout came forth from a different table. This time the victim was a young woman, who put up a good struggle before she was overpowered by several men in her party. Up she went, and even Brian was impressed with her efforts to keep her dress from falling back over her head. Eventually, she went limp with embarrassment, like a fish with all the fight wrestled out of it, as the flash from several cameras illuminated her panties.

Across the bar, Paco was shaking his head, and for a few seconds Brian was actually ashamed to be American. A half-serious thought crossed his mind: was he finally starting to think like a native? Too bad Marina wasn't here to share the moment.

"Beats the hell out of Mexican TV, eh?" said the stranger standing next to him.

"Sure," he said. "If you like seeing people make utter fools of themselves."

"I think maybe you're taking it a tad too seriously, pal."

"And I think you're a tad too full of shit."

The man's posture went rigid. "Go to hell," he said.

"After you," Brian retorted. The stranger moved down the bar to join his friends and Brian sensed the dull heat of several hostile glances. No longer feeling welcome, he paid his tab and charted a course toward the exit.

He was debating whether to try another bar or call it a night when his ears picked up the amplified twang of live music. The sound drew him across the street to where the locals were gathering for a neighborhood dance in the small municipal bullring. Outside the entrance, men huddled in groups drinking beer under strings of naked light bulbs. There were a few muttered comments as he stood in line to pay the admission but otherwise no one bothered him. A platform had been set up for the band, which made up in verve what they lacked in talent. The music was oddly familiar to Brian, a kind of hayseed polka played with electric bass and guitar. Several of the men wore cowboy hats and he felt like he had stumbled on some sort of mestizo hoedown. As the musicians played, the dancers twirled on the dirt floor of the ring, sending a small cloud of dust rising toward the stars.

To get a better view, Brian jumped up on the risers and limned the bullring. He heard some girlish noises off to his right and turned to see a quartet of women huddled together, trying to disguise their interest. The prettiest one, in her ruffled red dress, reminded him of Marina and Brian felt a pang of longing. As he approached the girls he could see their heads bobbing together in a kind of murmuring panic. The one in red stood and started to flee, but Brian caught her hand and held it.

"No, wait," he said. "What's your name? Cómo te llamas?"

"Alicia," the girl whispered, and looked away as if ashamed of having spoken. Her long black hair was combed into braids with black ribbons tied at the ends. She was skittish and breathtakingly fragile in his grip, and Brian almost turned her loose. But then the band struck up "El Rancho Grande" and he was seized by a desire to dance.

"A bailar?" he asked. "Por favor. Uno nomás."

Brian pressed gently on her hand and she went with him willingly. Alicia's friends, who had been watching raptly, started clucking like worried hens as they passed but she ignored them.

The dance floor smelled of dung and straw and Brian, remembering its other use, could almost detect the faint stench of blood and dried viscera. Alicia stood back and held her skirt like a matador's cape. Brian stepped forward and put his hand on the small of her back, doing his best to imitate the other men as they swiveled and stamped their feet on the ground. It was difficult at first, but after a few bars he got the hang of it and he saw Alicia smile as he dipped his shoulder and skipped to the polka beat.

When the song was over, Alicia smiled and made a coy curtsy and he held her hand and told her that he wanted to buy her a limonada. She smiled and nodded and he had just turned to see where he might find one when somebody put his hand on Brian's chest and pushed hard, making him bump against several other couples. Brian whipped around to his adversary, who was about his own age and wore dusty cowboy boots and jeans and was handsome in the same dark, sinewy way as the ditch diggers he had seen by the road earlier that day. Brian laughed, knowing as he did that it was stupid. Unfortunately, there was no time for him to explain that he was laughing at no one's expense but his own, that the tickle in his ribs came not from mirth but from the sudden knowledge that there was something both fitting and inevitable about this showdown with his Latin Other, that every second of the day had been leading up to this fight, just as this hotheaded macho had been waiting his whole life for the chance to punch the daylights out of some tourist stupid enough to come onto his turf and make a pass at his girl. Fortified by the tequila still singing in his veins, Brian stepped forward and took the first punch. The blow was aimed at his opponent's jaw but missed and connected with his collarbone instead. The cowboy staggered back in surprise before responding with a roundhouse right that left Brian's ear throbbing. Other hands grabbed him from behind and he felt the concussion of several unblocked jabs to his stomach and face. Then he folded to the ground and tasted the bitter grit of defeat as they kicked him a couple of times for good measure. Just before slipping into unconsciousness, Brian saw Alicia hurrying out the exit with her girlfriends. He watched her leave and felt neither loss nor pain, only the dull pointless throb of regret.

7

All churches, even Mexican cathedrals, reminded Brian of his mother, a woman who incorporated the hushed reverence of prayer into every aspect of her life. Her devoutness formed a permanent aura that both protected and enclosed her, like the cloying smell of incense and candle wax that clung to her clothes after Mass. Mary Sheahan was a literal Catholic, the kind who believed that if she obeyed the Commandments and followed the sacraments she would be rewarded after her death by a passage to paradise. Her faith was redeemable but, for Brian, nontransferable. Mary had prayed that her son would become an altar boy or maybe even a priest, and always made sure that they arrived at church early enough to find a good seat in the front pew. But after his father's death, Brian had resisted the church and questioned its teachings, preferring the indifferent canons of science to the cruel compassion of the Holy Ghost.

"Is God good?" Brian had once asked his mother.

"God is very good."

"And does God make everything happen?"

"Yes, God makes everything happen."

"Then why did he kill my dad?"

In his own childish way, he knew that his question would hurt her, and the disappointment in her eyes was something he had eventually come to regard as penance for his own lack of faith.

Brian pushed open the iron-hinged doors of the Metropolitan Cathedral and stepped into the realm of a God he no longer recognized. The cavernous nave was bordered on both sides by chapels to the Virgin Mary and the revered saints, each one enclosed by an iron gate and furnished with cushions for kneeling supplicants. The air was heavy with incense and the ardent echo of unanswered prayers.

Brian moved past the lacquered pews and batteries of flickering votive candles toward the gilded extravagance of the Baroque altar. Twisted gold columns rose to the ceiling where angels flocked around saints in swirling plaster robes. In the midst of it all hung the impaled Christ, his face twisted in divine agony.

Aware of his echoing footsteps, Brian self-consciously took a seat. As he gazed at the bleeding martyr he couldn't help thinking about his father and the catacombs buried just a few feet below. It vexed him to think that all the splendor before him was nothing more than an illusion for the masses, a fancy facade to make them forget their pain and the heinous crimes that had been committed in the name of Christ. "Damned hypocrites," Brian said aloud, and his blasphemy prompted several worshippers to include him in their prayers.

Brian was eight on that blistering July day when his mother called him in from the yard and ordered him to wash his face and put on a clean shirt. He knew something was wrong because of the way she had clutched his shoulder, as if using him for support, as they walked to the car. Once the two-toned Buick had cleared the driveway, she turned to face him, wisps of blond hair whipping against her cheeks, and said, "There was an accident on the job and your father is in the hospital, understand?" Brian nodded, even though he didn't.

The light turned red and she reached out to pat his leg reassuringly. He saw the tears in her eyes and he felt fear like a hand on his throat, making it hard to swallow. Brian stared at the road as his mother drove to the hospital. "Honey," she was saying, "please talk to me." Brian wanted to answer, wanted to be comforted, but his tongue was swollen and refused to budge. Instead he kept his eyes on the broken white line, which was now distorted into a quivering blur on the pavement. He kept staring at the line as if his father's life depended on it, as if his continuing to look was the only thing that kept it from disappearing.

Brian stood and headed for the exit, but an elderly man wearing a striped bow tie blocked his way. The old man raised a bony finger at the chapel dedicated to a black figure of Christ nailed to the cross. "We call him Nuestro Señor del Veneno, Our Lord of the Poison," he explained. Brian nodded politely and tried to pass, but the old man wouldn't budge. "The legend says that someone once tried to murder a bishop by putting poison on his body," he continued. "But when the holy man knelt to kiss the feet of the Christ, the statue shriveled from the poison and turned black, and the bishop was saved. Un milagro. A miracle." He regarded Brian with eyes like polished black marbles, and the deep lines in his face sketched a pattern of secret amusement. "Would you like to make a donation?"

Brian reached into his pocket and offered him five pesos. But the man pushed Brian's hand away. "Give it to the Christ, it's his story after all."

Brian dropped the coin into the metal collection box, pausing to look into the face of the black Jesus, its plaster features molded into a frown of ineffable sadness. My mother would love this place, Brian thought to himself. The old man nodded and stepped aside with a slight bow. "Don't worry," he said with a smile. "He knows that you don't believe.

Guillermo's yellow Volkswagen bug darted between two trucks, belched a cloud of white smoke, and sped north on the toll road to Atetelco. From the back seat, Brian eyed the speedometer and tried to remind himself that eighty kilometers an hour was not as fast as it sounded.

"Is there too much air?" Laura asked from the passenger side, her pigtails flying in the breeze from the open window.

"No, I'm fine," Brian said, raising his voice above the roar of Saturday afternoon traffic. "These cars remind me of when I was a teenager."

"They are not very large or luxurious," Laura said with a flash of white teeth. "But they are perfect for getting around in the city."

Over his shoulder, Guillermo said, "The biggest Volkswagen factory in the world is in Mexico, just outside of Puebla."

"That's true," Laura confirmed, and Brian noticed her admiring glance at Guillermo. It was difficult to believe they were not lovers, but Guillermo had assured Brian that their romance was strictly platonic, since Laura was personally opposed to sex out of wedlock. Privately, Guillermo had complained bitterly to Brian about Laura's "damned backward country-girl morals." Yet the tug of affection in his voice betrayed him, and at times his torment seemed to Brian more like that of a uxorious husband than a frustrated lover.

When Brian had confided to him about his troubles with Marina, mentioning everything except the reason for their breakup, Guillermo had nodded sagely. Then, slapping his hands together, he'd announced that a day trip to Atetelco would be just the thing to take Brian's mind off matters of the heart. "That is the great thing about being a professional man," Guillermo had said. "When the rest of your life turns to shit, you always still have your work."

As Brian had expected, Marina's article caused a big stir at the museum, and there were whispered rumors that a security crackdown was on the way. Yet, if Guillermo and Laura suspected Brian of being the source of the leak, they'd been much too considerate to mention it. The only clue came from Laura, who seemed relieved to hear that Brian and Marina were no longer seeing each other. "Good riddance," she'd said with uncharacteristic vehemence. "I knew that woman was trouble from the first second I saw her. You're better off without her."

Brian leaned back in his seat and watched the city relinquish its grip on the landscape as the trees and shrubs shook free of concrete and the air took on the sweet smell of mint and wild grass. The muscular brown hills stretched out under the capacious blue sky and every now and then they passed an adobe hacienda, its sprawling acres dotted with grazing cows and horses. As he drove, Guillermo filled Brian in on the basic facts. Dating back to 1500 B.C., the Palace of Atetelco was located less than a mile away from the famous pyramids of Teotihuacán. Like the adjacent structures of Tepantitla and Tetitla, Guillermo explained, Atetelco was probably used to house the elite classes and priests who presided at Teotihuacán, a civilization that predated the Aztecs by a thousand years.

"And what about travelers, pilgrims who were visiting from another city," Brian asked. "Would they have stayed there as well?"

"It's certainly possible," Guillermo answered as the Temple of the Sun came into view. "There's Teotihuacán."

The inverted V of the pyramid rose above the foothills, at once challenging and mimicking the dormant volcanoes in the distance. "Wow," Brian said. "It's even more impressive than I imagined."

Incredulous, Guillermo and Laura both turned to look at their passenger. "You mean you've never been there?"

Brian shook his head.

"You should have told us, hombre. We would have left a lot earlier. Now there won't be enough time . . ."

"Qué lástima . . ." Laura lamented.

"It might be too late to see anything," he said with a shrug. "But we could always have dinner and stay for the sound and light show."

Laura dipped her head and giggled. "Dios mío," she exclaimed. "It's so ridiculous, all these sound effects and colored lights, just to impress the tourists, as if the pyramids weren't beautiful enough already. Besides, I think the show has been closed since the rebels bombed the lights and speakers."

"Maybe they did us all a favor," Guillermo said. "But if the restaurant is still open we could have dinner, and Brian could at least get a closer look at the pyramids."

Brian indicated that this was fine with him, "As long as you show me the drawings first."

"That," Guillermo said as he pulled into a dirt parking area, "is what I am about to do."

Brian got out and stretched his legs. From where he stood he could make out the remains of a stone patio and, beyond that, a group of low buildings bordered by a grove of flowering trees. Except for a solitary sign near the road there were no markers and Brian felt like a trespasser, half expecting some irate resident to shoo them away. But no person or animal came forward to break the oppressive quiet. Even the wind was dead. They moved through the ruins like spirits haunting a necropolis.

"Atetelco means 'on the stone wall by the water,'" Guillermo informed him as they navigated the labyrinth of doorways and paved courtyards. "The San Juan River is just beyond those trees. As for the wall, only the foundations remain, but the main structures have survived. By Mesoamerican standards, these houses were elaborate mansions, signifying a highly developed social hierarchy. The other remarkable aspect of this place, of course, is these murals."

Ducking under an arched threshold, they entered a square enclosure decorated with two facing sets of painted frescoes. Vivid in the reflected light, the figures and patterns seemed to dance across the plaster walls. "Who do you suppose lived here?"

Guillermo leaned on one knee and dug his heel into the dirt. "Hard to say. It could have been a guesthouse for visiting nobles, or maybe a love nest for the Lord's concubine." Laura gave her boyfriend a quick jab in the ribs, and he doubled over in a pantomime of pain. When she rushed forward to apologize, he ensnared her in his arms and tried to give her a kiss.

"Eres salvaje!" she protested mildly.

Brian left them to inspect the murals, which averaged ten by fifteen feet in size and were cordoned off by a low slatted fence. Jaguars, their mouths open in an eternal roar, cavorted on two of the sloping borders. Below, a glyph of a human heart dripped red tears of blood. Diamonds containing priestly figures, each one different from the others, marched along the top of the wall. One carried a bird's head, another the symbol for Tláloc. The third wore a pendant of Xólotl, the diving god.

"That's what I wanted to show you," Guillermo said. "It's very similar to the one under the cathedral, don't you think?"

"Yes," Brian agreed, stepping over the fence for a closer look. He ran his fingers over the Xólotl glyph.

"Hey, you shouldn't touch that," Laura scolded.

"It's been repainted."

"What are you talking about?" she asked, her curiosity piqued. "Guillermo, watch out for guards while I see what he's talking about." She pulled a small magnifying glass from her purse and held it up to the glyph.

"Yes, it's been restored," she agreed, "no more than twenty years ago."

"So, there's no way of knowing if the original was painted in 500 B.C. or 1521 A.D."

"I've seen this symbol before," Laura said matter-of-factly.

"In the Xotl codex?"

Laura opened her mouth, but didn't speak. A few seconds later, in a low voice, she said, "I never told you that."

"You didn't deny it either."

Laura acted as if he'd uttered an obscenity. She was silent on the walk back to the car, and Brian knew she was trying to decide if his comment had been a lucky guess. She seemed torn between curiosity and the fear that his answer might somehow incriminate her further. Brian felt bad about causing her distress, but marveled anew at the transparency of her feelings. Her emotions were as pristine as a glass of spring water.

Understanding that Laura was upset but not why, Guillermo tried to draw her out with jokes and gentle prodding until she became cross and wouldn't let him hug her anymore. Brian suggested that they call it a day but Guillermo wouldn't hear of it, insisting that they stay for "Motecuhzoma's multi-media revenge."

As Laura had predicted, the light and sound show was closed for repairs, but they decided to have dinner anyway and took a table near a glass picture window overlooking the pyramids. In the orange and indigo twilight, the stout triangles vibrated with geometric power, and Brian could understand why men through the centuries had been drawn here to trade and worship and share the arcane art of divination. At the summit of the stone apex, overlooking the puny tribulations of earthbound men, what mortal would not feel a few steps closer to heaven?

Ignoring Laura's silence, Brian concentrated on the view while Guillermo did most of the talking, mostly descriptions of Teotihuacán as an ancient center of the obsidian trade and a mecca for the cult of

Quetzalcóatl. "That causeway between the Pyramids of the Sun and the Moon is called the Avenue of the Dead," he said. "The Pyramid of the Sun is almost as large as the pyramid at Cheops in Egypt. The Aztecs believed that under the base of the pyramid are caves that reach down all the way to the Underworld. The caves do actually exist, it turns out, and they remain largely unexplored. I would love to go down there someday, wouldn't you?"

When Laura excused herself to go to the ladies' room, Guillermo cut short his commentary, studying the beer in his hand as if trying to ascertain its exact origin. "Is somebody going to tell me what's going on," he asked. "Or do I have to consult a psychic?"

"I think I scared her a little bit," Brian said.

Grinning, Guillermo drained his beer and sighed. "You mentioned the Xotl codex."

"Just barely."

"You see, Laura is fundamentally too honest to understand that sometimes rules need to be broken. You can't blame her for getting a little nervous. She knows that Torres is a pig, but she also loves her job. She's too good for the museum. I would try myself to talk her into quitting if I wouldn't miss her so much."

"Don't you think she would miss you, too?"

Guillermo hunched his shoulders. "Quién sabe."

"Have you asked her?"

"If she'd miss me?"

"If she'd marry you."

Guillermo shook his head sadly. "She deserves better than to marry a foreigner with no future."

"I think that's unfair—to both of you. Just follow your heart."

"Maybe." Guillermo sighed. "But as the latest casualty in the war of the sexes, you are hardly in a position to be dispensing romantic advice."

"Touché," Brian said, his ribs still smarting a bit as he saluted Guillermo with his glass. "We all make mistakes, but that's no reason to stop trying."

"What mistakes?" Laura asked, back from the ladies' room.

Guillermo rose and held her chair. "We were just talking about the folly of men throughout the ages," he said. "They build monuments to their gods in the hopes of being protected. But the gods always fail them, and only the monuments remain. History is littered with the dreams of whole civilizations turned to dust." He gestured to the pyramids glowing in the Mexican night. "The people who built them are gone; all that's left is the mute carcass."

"But sometimes their voices can still be heard, don't you think?" Laura said, her eyes flickering at Brian. "So maybe they were not so foolish after all."

"I think we are fools if we don't listen," Brian said.

Laura's expression thawed a bit, but she still seemed miffed. As they rose to leave, Brian touched her arm. "Laura, I'm sorry if I've put you in an awkward position," he told her, "but it was the only way for me to find out what I needed to know. I'm positive now that Xotl stopped at Teotihuacán and stayed at Atetelco."

Laura slowly lifted her gaze until, to Brian's astonishment, she was looking him straight in the eye. "So am I," she said.

Early on the third morning of our journey, after a breakfast of atole and beans and fried cactus, I climb to the crest of a nameless hill and fall to my knees in prayer. Before us lies the sacred city of Teotihuacán, a sight of such welcome glory that my companions cry out in amazement. Through the tears in my eyes the twin tributes to the moon and the sun are like the tips of shimmering arrows piercing the heavens, flying upward from the doors of the Underworld to the gates of the Thirteenth Sky. It has been many years since my last visit to this place, and already I feel its power entering my soul like a potent tonic. At first, Tonatiuh and Loma had resisted this northern detour, but now the veil of doubt has been lifted, and their faces have opened like young flowers in the clean morning light, their eyes closed in divine rapture.

"Come," I say, leading the way down the trail. "We have much to see and do before resuming our journey south. The eternal city of Teotihuacán is a feast for the senses as well as the spirit."

Descending to the Street of the Dead, our trail converges with a dozen others, each one adding the stamp of a few more tired feet, until the ample avenue is filled with pilgrims of every description. Once the center of the ancient world, this holy ruin still inspires worship, and its importance is such that Motecuhzoma himself once came to pay tribute. For it was here that the first world of men was born and died, planting the seeds for all that came after, including the Fifth Sun and the rise of the Aztec nation.

These thoughts fill my head as we arrive at a pyramid decorated with exquisite carvings of the Plumed Serpent. "This is the house of Quetzal-cóatl," I say. Trembling, Tonatiuh touches a ferocious fanged muzzle and looks to me for explanation.

"Our Lord has many faces," I tell him. "No one is more compassionate or loving, but he can also be merciless and fierce. The serpent, who crawls on his belly, is connected to the earth and the Nine Underworlds. The quetzal bird, with his graceful wings, soars through the gardens of the Thirteenth Sky. Together they represent the union of heaven and earth, man and God."

Tonatiuh nods and I see that he has taken the lesson well. What better way to illustrate the duality of our savior than to let him actually touch it? "We will return to this place later," I say, resuming our walk toward the Pyramid of the Moon. "But first we must find a place to make our camp."

Rejoining the throng on the Avenue of the Dead, we browse crowded stalls offering pottery and silver, cotton tunics and woven blankets. Here are farmers selling chickens and pigs, and mounds of fresh beans, and bushels of chiles, pointed green ones and short red ones and some a luscious shade of deep purple. From boiling clay kettles and glowing ovens come the aromas of piping tortillas and carne asada, black mole and green salsa de tomatillo.

Little Hummingbird has climbed high into the sky to cast arrows of heat at our heads and the jostling crowds have kicked up a cloud of brown dust that stings my nostrils. I wipe the sweat from my brow and feel a tugging at my sleeve. "Father," Tonatiuh says to me, "Loma has fainted!"

I turn and see the poor child draped on Tonatiuh's shoulder. "Help me get her into the shade," I shout, spying a shop that sells fresh lime water. I give Tonatiuh a few cacao beans to make the purchase and lay Loma's limp body on a mat of woven straw.

"What is wrong with that girl?" a man's gruff voice demands.

"She is ill," I answer curtly. "And, besides, her predicament does not concern you."

"On the contrary," he replies, "since I own this shop, you are on my property, and I am therefore entitled to an answer."

I turn to face my verbal antagonist, who is reclining in a chair of sapling branches. Neither young nor old, the girth of his belly suggests a man with a weakness for food and the means to indulge it. A wispy beard clings to his cheeks like cobwebs but he is dressed in fine robes. Jeweled rings of silver and gold sparkle on his surprisingly delicate fingers.

"You appear to be a wise man," he says to me, his eyes narrowing with concern. "And a wise man does not turn away help for his sick daughter."

"She is not my daughter," I answer as Tonatiuh returns with a cup of cool limonada.

"And I suppose this handsome young man is not your son?"

Bristling at the man's mocking tone, Tonatiuh turns and proclaims: "We are pilgrims from Tenochtitlán, and Xotl is a great priest from the temple of Quetzalcóatl leading us on a sacred mission."

"Hush, my son," I say.

The man places his hands on his knees and leans back until the sapling chair creaks in protest. "Well, well, it seems that I have misjudged you," he says with new respect. "I have heard of the great priest Xotl, who saw his father's face at the moment of death. Allow me to introduce myself. My name is Becan, and you are welcome to stay in my house at Atetelco for as long as you wish. We have a small temple there, and I can summon a physician to treat the girl while you worship."

"I have heard of you, too, Becan," I tell him. "You are a merchant who grew rich on the obsidian trade."

"Quite so," Becan says. "I hope you do not disapprove of my profession."

"On the contrary, it is one of the reasons I have come here."

"Excellent." Becan slaps his dainty hands together. "Then you will be guests in my house and tomorrow I will personally escort you to the artisans quarter."

Before I can demur, Becan has ordered his servants to carry our things to Atetelco. A litter is ordered for Loma while Becan, Tonatiuh and myself follow on foot. Along the way I learn that Becan is a devout fol-

lower of Quetzalcóatl and a descendant of the families who ruled Teotihuacán in its glorious past. As we pass the temple of our Lord, I silently
say a prayer of thanks to him who guides our every move.

Our rooms in Becan's mansion are comfortable and clean. Best of
all, they open onto a small courtyard with a private shrine. After a plentiful dinner and a night of rest, Loma is feeling better, and I am confident that she will soon be strong enough to resume our journey. In the
meantime, Tonatiuh has begun an addition to the drawings on what Becan calls his "gallery of distinguished visitors." It is a symbolic marker
of our journey and I am pleased to see that his adroitness with a brush
continues to develop. I am also glad to do something in return for our
amiable host, who gives us everything and asks for nothing.

True to his word, Becan escorts us to the quarter where obsidian is
sold, on the edge of the main marketplace. Traders from the nearby mines
at Navajas are arriving from the countryside, their bags weighted with
polished cylinders of gray, black and rare green obsidian. The sight of so
much precious glass makes Tonatiuh visibly nervous.

"Don't worry; looking is free!" Becan bellows, slapping him on the
back. Then to me he says, "Great teacher, you are no doubt interested in
something of ceremonial quality?" I nod, fingering the cacao beans in my
purse; the bag is nearly a third empty and our journey has scarcely begun. We arrive at a final row of shops dedicated to the sale of finished
sculpture, jewelry and finely honed blades. Becan bids hello to a merchant, who in turn greets him with great deference. The man rushes to display his wares, which are wrapped in sheaths of thick cotton. He unwraps
the knives one at a time, and each is more beautiful than the last. Finally,
he reaches into a long deerskin pouch and pulls out a double-edged mas-
terpiece. I lift the dagger by its silver and green stone handle, and it hews
naturally to my hand.

"Do you like it?" Becan asks.

"No, it's not what I'm looking for," I lie, trying to avoid Tonatiuh's
stare of utter astonishment. "Perhaps another time."

Crestfallen, the vendor replaces his wares, but Becan's good humor
is only momentarily dimmed. "Perhaps you would like to shop for some
supplies for your journey?"

"Yes, that would be useful," I say. I don't know how long our currency will last or even if the beans will have any value where we are go-

ing, but the knowledge that I have not squandered it all on a handsome knife is comforting as we head to the market.

On the final night of our stay, Becan holds a great feast for us at his house. There are musicians and dancers and tables piled high with smoked meats and exotic fruits and chile stews. For once I allow myself to indulge in a glass of pulque, but only so as not to insult our host. At the end of the evening I perform a blessing ritual for Becan, who has proven himself magnanimous and pure of heart despite his gross habits. As a parting gift, Becan insists that we accept the services of his slaves, two warrior guards and a guide who will take us as far as the barren wilderness of the south. I gratefully accept and realize that our Lord has once again taught me the value of humility: never again will I let piety blind me to the essential goodness in my fellow man. After the ceremony, Becan kisses my hand and I embrace him knowing that the cult of our Lord is safe as long as he and his heirs walk the sacred streets of Teotihuacán.

At dawn the next morning, our things are already packed and ready. Standing at the door of his house, Becan waves good-bye until his hearty bulk has shrunk to the size of a pea and disappears behind a grove of pepper trees. On our way through Teotihuacán, we pay a final visit to the temple of Quetzalcóatl and pray for our safe passage through the uncharted regions. I gird myself for the travails ahead, knowing that the trip will seem doubly hard after our recent life of luxury. How soft we have become in just a few days! Every pebble seems to seek out the space between my sandals and my tender feet and the blaring sun singes the tops of my ears. Then I realize that my discomfort is a necessary penance for all the fine food and pulque, and I once again remember how to draw inner strength from my corporeal pain.

We are already a day's walk away from Atetelco, and the porters are setting up camp for the night, when I reach into my bag for my pipe and feel the exquisite touch of the deerskin pouch.

It was nearly midnight when Brian left the museum and ventured into the starless night. The crowds that jammed the zócalo by day were gone and the bustling shops along Calle 20 de Noviembre shuttered. Across the plaza, he could see soldiers at their positions outside the National Palace, huddled in small groups, smoking cigarettes.

Directly before him, the cathedral was a massive blot against the phosphorescent sky. Seeking a shortcut to where he could catch a cab, Brian turned right onto a side street that bordered the tent city of the campesinos. His intention was to cross quickly through the squatters' camp, but it was much larger than it looked from outside and before he knew it he was surrounded by a labyrinth of cardboard barriers and burlap screens that blocked the sidewalks and blotted out the streetlamps. He pressed on blindly, figuring that he would eventually emerge on the far side of the zócalo. Then, as he stooped below the endless web of neck-high guy ropes, Brian noticed human shapes, silent and eyeless, drifting toward him in the dark. The voice seemed to come out of nowhere, a hoarse whisper that wrenched the soul.

"Señor, ayuda, por favor."

It was joined by another, then a third. Brian was surrounded by the talking shadows, phantoms of deeper black floating in the gloom, circling him like tombstones, blocking his way. He lurched to the side and collided with one, the impact taking his breath away. Brian gasped, inhaling the thin air of panic.

"Señor . . . señor . . . ayuda . . ."

As he lunged toward the lights of the Hotel Majestic, he caught a whiff of rank odor and started to run, leaving the dark shapes behind as he hailed an empty taxi. He was back at Calle San Jerónimo, fumbling for the keys to the door, by the time he recognized the smell of his own fear.

8

Brian stared at the patch of plaster directly over his chair. It had initially appeared to be featureless and smooth, like a blank fresco. But after a while he noticed the hairline crack that ran diagonally across his field of vision, the small bubble of congealed paint, and the sloping line that defined the intersection of the ceiling and the wall, which was the same luminous shade. White, the color that contained all colors, the color of purity and self-sacrifice, the ritual color of Quetzalcóatl. It was also the color that Villalobos had chosen for his son's room, a room that Brian was beginning to think of as his own.

Brian had arrived in Tepoztlán early that morning, only to be told that Villalobos was tied up in an unexpected business meeting and would join him as soon as possible. Brian was shown to his now familiar quarters in the west wing, where he'd used the time to catch up on his reading, waiting for the knock on the door that would summon him to an audience with his mercurial host.

Brian closed the book in his lap and looked out the open window. The red bougainvilleas of Villalobos's garden reminded him of Marina and Brian felt the recurring pang of emptiness. Since their trip to Cabo the week before, he'd tried several times to reach her at *The Globe*, but she was always away from her desk and never returned his calls. Their affair, at least in Marina's mind, seemed to be over. Maybe Guillermo and Laura had been right about him being better off without her, maybe he should just turn the page and get on with his life. But try as he might to push Marina out of his mind, it was impossible for him to accept the possibility that he'd never see her again.

The revving of a car engine and the slamming bamboo gate told him that Villalobos's meeting was over. Brian went downstairs and found him alone on the patio, reading from a stack of newspapers. Dressed in pale green slacks and a white shirt, he seemed genuinely happy to see Brian again.

"I'm so happy you could come," Villalobos said, rising from his chair. "Did you have a pleasant drive from the city?"

"Very pleasant, thanks."

"I hope you will forgive me for not welcoming you this morning. There was a troublesome matter that urgently needed my attention. I hope the wait wasn't too tedious."

"Not at all. It was actually very relaxing. Just what I needed."

"I'm very glad," Villalobos said. "Will you join me for a late breakfast?"

Soon the table was covered with platters of eggs and sweet toast and fruit and steaming pots of coffee and tea. Brian was ravenous and as he ate he recounted the story of his recent trips to Cabo and the pyramids. Villalobos listened with fascination to the account of his trip with Marina, interrupting only to ask a factual question or make a noise of agreement.

"So this femme fatale," he asked when Brian had finished, "have you spoken to her since?"

"No."

"But you know where she is."

"I think so."

"Then you must find her and tell her that you love her."

Brian was astonished. "Love her? I'm not sure I even know her."

"A man does not start a fight in a bullring over someone he does not know," Villalobos observed. "What is this Cleopatra's real name?"

"Marina Soto."

"La Malinche," Villalobos said, as if the name revealed everything he needed to know about her. "The Indian consort and silver-tongued translator. A very complex and fascinating woman. Imagine, a Maya noblewoman who was abandoned by her parents and given as a gift to Cortés."

"She was Maya?"

"Putun Maya, from the Gulf Coast region of Xicalanco. She became Cortés's guide and mistress and bore him a son. Her intelligence and resourcefulness helped him win many battles. If not for her, the Spanish invasion might not have succeeded."

Brian felt the subject leeching at his mood. "If it's all the same to you, Don Alejandro, I'd really rather not discuss it."

"Of course," Villalobos said, folding his napkin and rising from the table. "I understand completely."

It was a clear, sparkling morning and Villalobos invited Brian for a stroll around the property. This time they walked past the stables toward a muddy creek that meandered through the woods. A series of cement barriers jutted out from the banks, forming a string of shallow pools.

"It is called the Río Seco," Villalobos said, "and in the dry season it lives up to its name. I designed these dams to hold the water, but to be truly effective the dams should extend upriver for another thirty miles. My neighbors, the people who own the river beyond my property, do not believe in planned irrigation. I've even offered to pay the cost of the work, to no avail. So every year this creek turns into a dry ditch."

"I would think that a man of your resources would be able to persuade his neighbors to do anything."

"Never underestimate the power of tradition," Villalobos said as he stared into the murky water. "It controls our lives from before our birth until long after our bones have turned to dust."

"You really believe that?"

"Yes. And I think you do too."

The surface of the pond was like a polished black mirror and Brian found himself staring at his own reflection. The face in the water was the exact opposite of his own, like a photographic negative. The undulating image drew him in until he lost his balance and had to steady himself. The dizziness was so fleeting that Brian wasn't even sure he had experienced it. When he looked again, the face had disappeared into the rippling current.

"I really should be getting back to the city," Brian said. "I've been in Mexico a month and I've hardly done any work on my thesis."

His host waved away the thought. "There is no hurry. Diego can drive you to the museum on Monday morning. No major discoveries will happen without you. Besides, I am leading an expedition into the hills tomorrow. It's very beautiful, but it takes all day. I think you will enjoy it."

Marina was waiting for him. Brian could see her atop the temple of Tláloc, surrounded by robed figures. He wanted to speak to her, to explain that he no longer loathed her, to ask for her forgiveness, but she was too far away to hear him. Stepping onto the metal observation ramps, he saw that Templo Mayor had changed. It was no longer a ruin. The magnificent structures were totally restored and painted in brilliant shades of red, green and yellow. Feathered banners waved from the highest pinnacles and serpent heads protruded from the sloping walls with gleaming white teeth and crimson tongues. As Brian drew closer, he could hear words being spoken in a language he didn't understand. The incantations wafted to him on the breeze. It was an Indian tongue, guttural and hewn by hard consonants. He strained his ears to listen but the words were still too garbled. As he hurried forward the ramp under his feet started to wiggle until it was writhing like a snake. He jumped off and began to run down the maze of narrow streets around the temple. It was difficult to see where he was going and he kept getting lost. Again and again the dead ends forced him to retrace his steps, running in circles. Just when he was about to give up, a bird flew across his path. It fluttered and sang as it led Brian to the base of the pyramid, where it turned into stone. Using his hands for balance, Brian began to climb the steep steps. A scream pierced the silence. Looking up, he saw Marina, her body draped in gold and feathers, waving to him. Zapata, Villalobos and another man stared down, their expressions distorted by the oblique angle of his ascent. The words came again, a prayer that explained why the gods had called him to Templo Mayor, and why Marina must die. Brian kept climbing and the stones under his fingers turned wet and sticky with blood. The higher he rose the more blood poured down, until his body was bathed in a warm torrent. He felt his fingers losing their grip and then he was sliding down the face of the pyramid, groping for some way to stop himself. Just before he hit the bottom, the base of the pyramid opened into a huge crater. The earth swallowed him and he kept falling, helplessly, soundlessly, gathering speed as he tumbled head over heels into a deep, fathomless void.

Brian awoke to a discreet rapping on his door. "Come in," he called. But all he heard was the sharp tap of footsteps retreating on tile. As he showered and dressed, the high priest's litany was still reverberating in his mind. But the harder he tried to recall it the more elusive it became, until all that was left was the vague impression that something important had slipped through his consciousness.

It was still dark outside as Brian closed the door of his room behind him. His watch broke in Cabo and he hadn't had a chance to replace it. But he didn't need a chronometer to know it was ungodly early. Even the roosters were asleep.

He found Villalobos in the living room, warming himself before a crackling fire.

"Good morning," he said to Brian. "Ready for a hike?"

"Absolutely."

"In that case, please join us for some chocolate."

"Us?"

Villalobos motioned to the sofa. "Octavio is coming along. I hope you don't mind."

With a high-pitched chuckle, Octavio Esparza sprang to his feet and crossed the room to shake Brian's hand. Shorter and more Indian than Villalobos, he had an earthy, ingenuous manner and ironic black eyes.

"Good to see you again," Brian said, accepting a cup of the thick brown liquid. The chocolate was unmistakably Mexican—dense, sweet and laced with cinnamon.

"Good to see you too, Mr. Mendoza."

"Brian."

"Yes, Octavio," Villalobos said. "There are no formalities among travelers out for a sunrise walk."

"By the way," Brian inquired. "Just how early is it?"

"Around four o'clock."

"Four twelve," Octavio corrected. "The locals think we are lunatics," he added cheerfully.

"Yes, it may seem a little extreme," Villalobos agreed. "But as you will soon see, there is a point to our early-morning madness." He drained his cup and extended his arms. "Shall we?"

Outside, Diego had the Mercedes warmed up and waiting.

"I thought this was a walking trip."

"It is," Villalobos reassured him, "but Diego is going to give us a head start. You'll understand soon enough."

Diego eased the car out of the drive and jostled over the cobblestone streets of town. Despite the hour, shadows moved across the curtains and thin wisps of smoke rose from the chimneys of the adobe houses. In front of the old convent, a group of men were busy hanging lights and erecting a wooden stage. "It's the preparations for the Santa Candelaria," Villalobos explained. "On January 5, Catholic Mexicans commemorate the arrival of the Three Kings bringing gifts to the Christ child with a holiday called Día de Los Reyes. On that day a cake is served. A plastic baby is mixed into the batter and whoever gets the piece of cake with the child inside must throw a fiesta on February 2, which is called La Candelaria. That's tomorrow."

"You mean today," Octavio corrected.

"Yes, today," Villalobos allowed. "There is also a ceremony in which the women of the town carry baby dolls to the church and have them blessed."

"The people may be starving," Diego groused, "but they will always find money for a fiesta, even if they have to hawk their mule."

The road twisted into a one-lane track, then narrowed further until the pavement abruptly ended. It was there that the Mercedes came

155

to a halt, its headlight beams illuminating a dirt path that disappeared into the woods.

"We get out here," Villalobos announced.

Diego put the car in reverse and a minute later they were alone in the predawn dark, climbing the lower slopes of the hills above Tepoztlán. Villalobos took the lead with Brian following second and Octavio bringing up the rear. Though it was still quite dark and he carried no flashlight, Villalobos walked briskly, sidestepping roots and loose rocks as if by instinct. Off to the east, the sky announced the coming dawn with a luminous swath of blue. They were climbing too fast for conversation as they zigzagged up a series of steep switchbacks and Brian found himself working hard to keep up. After another hour or so the trees began to thin out and the ground beneath their feet became rock. "We're almost there," Villalobos said as they mounted a natural stairwell between two boulders, where the elements had scooped out a shallow bowl. Brian lifted himself the final few feet and joined Villalobos and Octavio, who had already turned to face the view.

The vista before him spread southward in a 180-degree arc that swept from the valley of Tepoztlán to the distant southern flatlands. Brian watched in awe as the first rays of day cleared the horizon and fanned out across the sky in golden beams that ignited the peaks around them. Down in the valley, where it was still night, he could actually see the pockets of lingering darkness, like nocturnal pools stranded by the advancing dawn. It was only the beginning of another day, no different from any other morning, yet Brian was flooded by a powerful sense that he had witnessed something monumental.

"I call this place the throne," Villalobos said quietly.

"I can understand why."

A cock crowed and the sounds of the stirring town drifted up to them. One by one the lights of the houses blinked off. Doors slammed. An engine coughed. An old man driving a horse and wagon clattered over the cobblestones on his way to market.

"Look," Octavio said, pointing to a small clearing directly below them. A man had emerged from his house holding a machete in one hand and a thrashing chicken in the other. They watched him slice the bird's neck with one neat stroke and carry the limp body back into the house. The slaughter had an unconscious perfection to it, as if the swinging blade was an act of nature that transcended human intention. Perched on a rim of the rocky ledge, Brian teetered on the brink of revelation before backing off to more familiar ground.

Villalobos indicated a conical peak off to the east. "That's where we're going," he said. "We'll walk along the trees on that ridge. It's one of my favorite trails."

They left the throne and set out along the green spine that linked the mountains. The terrain was much more varied and lush than Brian would have guessed. Grasses, evergreens and flowering plants sprouted everywhere. The scenery was constantly changing and every turn in the trail yielded some unexpected discovery. Nothing, in fact, was quite what it at first seemed. A spherical boulder, seen from a different angle, turned out to be less than a foot thick. Caves and barrancas appeared in what had appeared to be solid rock. And as the sun climbed in the sky, the mountains changed again, transformed by the devious play of light and shadow.

Villalobos and Octavio were knowledgeable and considerate guides, constantly pointing out waterfalls, interesting rock formations, and identifying the variations of flora along their path. Brian learned that Octavio was an amateur botanist, and he often stopped to inspect a plant or shrub, which he then clipped and stuffed into his rucksack. Villalobos, for his part, was well versed in the local lore and showed Brian a sheltered valley that rebel armies used as a hideout during the Revolution. As the day wore on, Brian found himself admiring their appreciation of the land and their willingness to understand it on its own terms. For them, hiking in these hills was not simply a pleasant form of physical exercise, but a treasured excursion into the essence of Mexico itself.

They reached the base of the second peak around eleven o'clock and Villalobos suggested that they take a rest before embarking on the final leg of their ascent. They squatted Indian-style under the shade of an ancient oak with a clear conspectus of the valley. From his rucksack Octavio produced a plastic container of pulque. The viscous liquor stuck in Brian's throat but he swallowed anyway before passing the bottle. Octavio also produced three oranges, which he proceeded to juggle expertly before tossing two of them over to Brian and Villalobos. It took Brian a few seconds to accept the fact that his orange was already peeled.

"How . . . ?"

"Don't ask," Villalobos said soberly, "it only encourages him."

Octavio seemed to find his friend's comment hysterically funny.

"These mountains are very special," Brian said, meaning not just the beauty of their surroundings, but the way they honed the senses until even the most mundane moment was magnified and transformed.

His guides nodded sagely. Normally the dearth of conversation would have made Brian uncomfortable. But here, in the dusty embrace of the enchanted hills, their silence seemed eloquent. The pulque came around again and this time Brian drank deeply.

Looking at Villalobos, Octavio remarked, "He's almost ready, don't you think?"

"Ready for what?" Brian asked.

Villalobos stood and dusted off his pants. "Follow us and you'll see."

The hills were shuddering with heat as they left the shade and began climbing the flanks of the pointed peak. Ignoring the fatigue in his legs, Brian sped up until he had taken the lead position; he wanted to be the first to reach the pinnacle. If Villalobos had chosen it as their destination, then there had to be a reason. Brian concentrated on making his legs defy gravity, his eyes locked on the last few feet of trail. Then something told him to look up and he found himself standing on the lower edge of an angular arch. The gap was a nearly perfect rectangle measuring at least twenty feet wide and thirty feet tall. Looking through it, he could see a small village perfectly outlined in a frame of chiseled rock. A hot desert wind blew through the hole and made a low whistle as Villalobos and Octavio clambered up beside him.

"It's called La Ventana," Villalobos explained. "The Window." He pointed back in the direction they had come. "During the equinox, the setting sun shines through this hole and directly toward the Pyramid of Tepozcatl—"

"The god of pulque," Brian interjected.

". . . yes. On the summer solstice, however, the sun comes down in this direction . . ." He held out his arms on a tilted axis from west to east. ". . . and the window illuminates the site of a small ruin a few miles beyond this town, which is called Amatlán."

"What kind of ruin?"

"According to the local legend," Villalobos said, "it is the birthplace of the god Quetzalcóatl."

Brian felt lightheaded. "Is that possible?"

"I was hoping," Villalobos said, "you might be able to tell *me*."

Brian gazed out through the stone keyhole, asking, "Have you seen these ruins?"

"There's nothing there. Just a few crumbling stones on the remains of a foundation."

"There is a monument to Quetzalcóatl in Amatlán," Octavio chimed in. "At the church of Santa María Magdalena."

"We'll show it to you," Villalobos said. "Diego is waiting there for us."

Amatlán was a hamlet of a dozen or so ramshackle houses and a nondescript general store clinging to the foothills beneath La Ventana. The perforated peak loomed over the rutted streets and the whitewashed bell towers of Santa Magdalena, a sixteenth-century chapel that seemed made of spun sugar. The central plaza had been swept clean and twine festooned with paper flowers extended from the church to the surrounding houses. As they entered the town limits, a pack of yapping mutts ran up to greet them, but the villagers stayed out of sight.

They turned the corner toward the front of the church and Brian spotted the Mercedes parked off to the side with Diego behind the wheel, snoring.

The church stood alone on a plot of land enclosed by a low stone wall. It seemed abandoned, so Brian pushed open the rusty gate and the trio let themselves in. The monument to Quetzalcóatl was cast in some sort of greenish alloy and mounted on a cement pedestal. Brian immediately recognized it as a representation of the Plumed Serpent, its body coiled as if ready to strike. A human face protruded from the serpent's yawning jaws. Judging from the material and the rectilinear style of the monolith, Brian figured it was no more than twenty or thirty years old.

"Does it tell you anything?" Villalobos asked Brian.

"Only that the person who made this has been to art school. The original monument, if there ever was one, was probably destroyed to build the church."

Villalobos nodded at the statue. "So this Quetzalcóatl is an impostor?"

"Well, maybe. But there's another possibility. Assuming the dates are correct, and that the original Quetzalcóatl traveled through Amatlán on his way south, this other Quetzalcóatl would have had to be somebody who knew the teachings of the original and wanted to continue his message after he had gone. That and the age difference suggests that the second Quetzalcóatl could have been a devoted acolyte, a kind of apostle or chosen one among his younger followers."

"Or his son," Villalobos said.

There were voices coming from inside the church and Brian followed them into the shaded vestibule. The interior of the chapel was windowless with rough wooden pews. An ornate ceramic statue of the baby Jesus presided over the altar, which was smothered with hundreds of bright plastic flowers and votive candles flickering in rows of tall glass jars.

Octavio was sitting at one of the pews, talking to an old Indian dressed in white trousers and a faded sarape. They were speaking the same guttural language as the people in Brian's dream.

"It's Nahuatl," Villalobos said matter-of-factly.

"His name is Marcos Petén," Octavio announced. "He has lived in Amatlán all his life. He says that there was something here before the metal statue was erected—a piece of stone that was brought from the Quetzalcóatl altar."

"Does he remember what it looked like?" Brian inquired.

Octavio spoke again to the old man, who nodded slowly. His lips barely moved as he uttered the words. Then he brought his gnarled hands together into the shape of an inverted steeple.

"The descending god," Brian said before Esparza could translate.

"Yes." Octavio was amazed. "Do you speak Nahuatl?"

"No," Brian said as he started to pace before the altar. "His hands told me."

He could feel Villalobos watching him as he moved about the room. "It's one of the manifestations of Quetzalcóatl," he explained.

"He's the one who helps to retrieve the bones of mankind from the Underworld. Ask him if he knows what happened to the stone."

Octavio translated the question, but this time the old man shook his head.

"Could it have been returned to the site?"

"No," Villalobos said. "I've searched many times. There's nothing there."

Octavio and Villalobos had turned to leave when Brian went to where the old man was sitting to thank him.

"Gracias," Brian said, and for the first time he noticed that the sunken eyes were clouded by cataracts. He grasped Brian's hand and pulled him near until he could feel the old man's fetid breath on his ear. The word came from his purple lips like a smothered gasp. He said it again before Brian pulled himself free and stumbled toward the door, away from the darkness and into the blinding afternoon light.

The plaza outside the church was no longer empty. People were hurrying about, carrying chairs and pots of food and boxes of soda and beer to a line of tables across the street. Children chased each other beneath their mothers' skirts while the older boys lit fireworks in a ditch by the side of the road.

"What's happening?" Brian asked. Villalobos told him that the town was getting ready for the fiesta that would begin when the parade arrived. Off in the distance, Brian could hear the distant sound of a brass band making its way up the hill from the neighboring village. The dogs came first, tails and tongues wagging, stopping every few yards to look back at their masters. Then the boys and young men lighting firecrackers and skyrockets, and groups of young girls waving branches of burning incense, followed by matronly women in flowered dresses. The rear was brought up by the band, a cacophonous combo of trumpets, tubas and drums that seemed to be playing several kinds of music at once. Brian detected bits of John Philip Sousa, mariachi and unintentional Stravinsky in the horns, while the percussion section vacillated between military cadence and a full-throttle samba. In the middle of all were several dozen women carrying infants in their shawls. Some were praying, others singing, as they walked and swayed to the music. Brian smiled at a young woman and she responded by offering him her baby. Aghast, Brian tried to refuse but the woman insisted, shoving the bundle into his arms. She laughed and turned away, leaving him in the middle of the road with an orphaned toy doll.

"I think she was trying to tell you something," Octavio said as they climbed back into the Mercedes. "Maybe it needs to be breast-fed."

"She even has your eyes," Villalobos teased. Brian looked into the plastic green pupils and the other men guffawed.

More dark sedans were waiting in the drive when they got back to the house. Without having to ask, Brian knew that Villalobos would be missing dinner.

"Thank you, Alejandro," Brian said. "For having me here, and for taking me up there."

Villalobos responded with a slight bow. "You're very welcome. It's always a pleasure to open the window for a new friend." He draped his arm on Brian's shoulder. "The house is yours. Why don't you take a swim, relax. Take your time at dinner, then come to the study and we'll have a brandy."

A few minutes later Brian was diving into the inky cool of the black-bottomed pool. He did a few laps, then flipped onto his back, floating on the surface as a pair of metallic green dragonflies hovered against the notched bluffs. It was hard to believe that only a few hours ago they had been up there, grazing the clouds at the rarefied altitude of eagles. The mountains seemed less ominous now that he had shared some of their secrets. It was the same way with Villalobos; Brian felt that he had crossed an invisible line and been shown a side of his host that few were allowed to see. Yet Brian also sensed that Villalobos's patronage had its limits. There was a psychic cohesion between Villalobos and Octavio that Brian knew he could never share. Their pranks and wordplay, accented by the unsaid, only emphasized Brian's status as an outsider.

He lifted himself out of the pool and toweled himself off. As he crossed the lawn, he could see several male silhouettes in the living room. Brian doubted Villalobos had ever taken any of his business associates hiking in the mountains. He tried to imagine them cavorting on the cliffs in their twelve-hundred-dollar suits, assistants and secretaries in tow, punching out their office numbers on cellular phones. Back in his room, Brian propped some pillows in his bed and tried to make some headway into a paper on Aztec burial rites before dinner. He hadn't finished the first page before slipping off into a deep, dreamless sleep.

The voices drifted up from the patio, nudging Brian awake. "There isn't much time," someone was saying. "He has already moved against Javier and Aurelio. Any one of us could be next."

"Let me talk to him again," he heard Villalobos say. "He's a reasonable man . . ."

The rest was garbled, then an agitated baritone Brian hadn't heard before. "We've been over this, the time for words is past. Something must be done." The voices moved away from the window.

Brian didn't have to work for the government to get the gist of what he had just heard. It was a side of Villalobos that Brian found ominous. Brian knew from Marina that Villalobos's influence was vast and his interests myriad. A man like that would have many enemies both in and out of the government, piranhas constantly nibbling away at the fringes of his authority. But the discussion outside Brian's window had not been about small fry. Anyone who posed a threat to Villalobos and his associates would by definition be a very big fish.

After a solitary meal of enchiladas and red rice, Brian mounted the stairs to Villalobos's study. The door was ajar so he pushed it open, only to find Villalobos in midconference with two other men.

"Excuse me," Brian said. "I'll come back later."

"No, it's all right," Villalobos insisted. "My associates are on their way out."

The men rose and left the room with a perfunctory nod at Brian. One of them looked familiar, though he couldn't say why. It seemed odd that Villalobos had made no effort to introduce him to his visitors, but Brian pretended not to notice.

Villalobos waved Brian to a seat and went to the bar to pour them both a brandy. He seemed a different man from the one who had been hiking in the woods that morning. His smile was still warm, but his eyes were bloodshot and his shoulders sagged from fatigue.

"If this is a bad time . . ." Brian began to say, but Villalobos waved him silent.

"I've been tortured all evening by these hyenas in three-piece suits," he said. "What I need now is a bit of stimulating conversation to calm my nerves."

"I hope that whatever the problem is, it gets resolved in your favor," Brian said.

"Thank you for your concern, but I'm afraid that my favor has nothing to do with it. The great fallacy about power is the notion that it serves the powerful. It's just the opposite really—the powerful are servants to power. With position comes responsibility. Royal jelly is fed to the queen for the good of the whole hive."

The drift of the conversation was starting to make Brian uneasy.

"This is not the United States," Villalobos continued. "The civil infrastructure, if it isn't corrupt, is usually inept. It is incumbent upon the elite to make sure that the buses have gasoline, to make sure that the factory will open and the workers will get paid, to make sure, if you will, that the sun rises."

"I thought that only the gods could do that."

Villalobos's smile was weary. "You think I'm succumbing to megalomania."

"I know you're too intelligent for that."

"Intelligence," Villalobos repeated, as if Brian had said something important. "Correct me if I'm wrong. After all, you are the scholar on this subject. But isn't it true that ever since the beginning of time the gods have always existed to do one thing, and that is to perpetuate the universe. When the sun did not move and time stood still, Ehécatl, the wind god, blew with all his might until it crossed the sky. When drought threatened to kill mankind with thirst, Tláloc, the god of rain, commanded the heavens to pour down on the crops. When the Fourth Sun ended, and the world ceased to exist, it was Quetzalcóatl who drew his own blood and risked his life in the Underworld to retrieve the bones of man and give birth to humanity." His metallic eyes drilled into Brian. "Isn't that what the Aztecs believed?"

"You know it is," Brian said, suddenly aware that his initiation into Villalobos's world was not over; their mountain walk had just been a primer for the main lesson.

"I'd like to show you something," Villalobos said, releasing his visual grip. "Something that very few people have seen." He went to one of the glass cases, unlocked the door and removed the small figure on the bottom shelf. Then he pressed his fingers against the mirrored backing of the case and slid it back to reveal a hidden chamber. When he returned he was holding a knife on the open palms of both hands, like a priest making an offering to a higher power. The handle was in the form of a crouching figure, inlaid with what looked like a mosaic pattern of turquoise and mother-of-pearl. The figure's arms extended forward to grip the serrated shaft of the dagger. Even in the artificial light, the obsidian blade sparkled like black ice.

Brian couldn't take his eyes off the thing.

"It was one of the presents that Motecuhzoma gave to Cortés," Villalobos explained. "It was sent back to the emperor, Charles V, and became part of his private collection. It remained in Europe for more than four hundred years until it was recovered. I won't bore you with the details of how it came into my possession. Would you like to hold it?"

Brian accepted the knife, which fit perfectly in his hand. Brian touched the blade and a thin line of blood sprouted on his finger.

"Be careful," Villalobos warned. "The blade is extremely sharp. Sharper than a scalpel. Did you know, for example, that some ophthalmologists are using obsidian blades for eye surgery? You see, they've learned that volcanic glass holds a fine edge better than the strongest steel. For all their love of gold and silver, the Aztecs knew this, and to them a prime piece of obsidian was more valuable than diamonds."

Villalobos's voice became a hoarse whisper. "You can imagine how easy it would be to slice a man's chest open with such a knife. You have imagined that, haven't you, Brian?"

Brian placed the knife on the table between them. Villalobos smiled. He was purposely baiting him, trying to get under his skin, and the provocation gave Brian the courage to ask the question that had been in his mind since their first meeting.

"What exactly is it that you want from me, Alejandro?"

Villalobos took a sip of his brandy, rolling the liquor around his mouth before swallowing. "You say that only the gods can make the sun rise, and that is true. But that is only the half of it. They also make the sun set. No man, no religion, not even science, can change that.

What you said the night we met at Professor Zapata's party indicated to me that you understood this, the cosmic strands of fate converging on one time and place. The sun is setting on the world as we know it, Brian. There are forces at work, forces that neither you nor I can stop, that will usher in a new era." He leaned forward and his eyes glinted like chrome. "Every civilization, like every human being, has a birth, a life and a death. We are all helpless before that fact. Nobody can change it. All man can do is try to understand. What you offer me, Brian, is knowledge."

"About the end of the Fifth Sun? You know as much about that as I do."

"Perhaps. But what if the Fifth Sun hasn't yet ended?"

Brian felt the mountains moving closer, pressing up against the windows.

"That's a very intriguing thought, I grant you," Brian said, trying to clear the dark shapes from his head. "But I still don't see why my opinion is so valuable to you."

"Ultimately, my motives do not concern you," he said. "All that matters is that we can help each other in our quest for the truth."

"Yes, but why go through the trouble of getting a graduate student to visit a dig when you could just as easily do it yourself?"

Villalobos seemed surprised by the question.

"Who says I haven't?"

The words hit Brian like a physical blow. Villalobos shook his head in disappointment.

"I should have thought it was obvious," he said, waving his hand at the library around them. "I don't need *information*." He virtually spat the word. "I have access to every book or article ever published. Several different museums have made offers for my collection of artifacts. What I seek is youthful insight. That is something that money— even my money—can't buy. Am I right?"

"Yes," Brian said, but he knew that Villalobos was wrong; humankind was not helpless in the face of fate. It created its own future, just as surely as the Aztecs had foreseen their own demise. There was no telling how much he had spent trying to acquire the truth, as if it was something that could be put in a glass case to admire. Brian wondered if that was the price of having everything for Villalobos, to live in constant fear that some important trophy had eluded him, that some crucial depth had gone unplumbed, when in fact what had failed him was the ability to trust his own imagination.

Villalobos was waiting. Brian knew he no longer trusted him enough to tell him about the Xotl-Xólotl connection or the old man in the church. But it would be foolish to alienate him before he could learn more about his intentions. Whatever happened, Brian knew that everything hinged on his next words.

"So," he said as casually as possible, "what exactly is it that you want to know?"

Villalobos was already gone when Brian packed up to leave the next morning. The cook offered to make him breakfast, but Brian asked only for coffee and some sweet rolls. He was anxious to get to the office and learn if there would be any belated fallout from Marina's article. Torres and the professor had been at a conference in Palenque the week before and were due back this morning. Then again, it was just as likely that no one had connected him to Marina. After all, his quote could have come from any number of sources, including Torres. As before, the car was warmed up and waiting in the driveway. This time, however, it was not Diego behind the wheel, but another man that Brian had never seen before. Unlike his gregarious predecessor, the man was a laconic professional who kept his eyes on the road and his opinions to himself. Before long they were out of the mountains and weaving through the congested streets of the capital. Brian found himself welcoming the tumultuous rush of the city, the freedom of being just one among millions. The car pulled abreast of the zócalo and Brian jumped out with his weekend bag in tow. Not bothering to wait for the elevator, he bounded up the museum stairs and walked in on the morning staff meeting.

His abrupt entrance triggered a few smiles and Torres's blank stare. There was a charge of tension in the room, like static electricity.

"Your timing is excellent, Mr. Mendoza," Torres said. "I was just briefing the staff about the new security policy. No staff members are to speak to the press on or off the record or grant interviews of any kind without first clearing it with either myself or Professor Zapata.

Is that clear to everyone?" There was a general muttering of acknowledgment. "Also, until further notice the office will be closed on weekends to anyone without special authorization. That's all. Thank you very much. Oh, and Mr. Mendoza, would you please come to my office for a minute?"

Brian followed Torres to his office like a condemned man. The deputy director took his place behind his desk without inviting Brian to sit.

"I understand that you were away most of last week."

"Yes, visiting friends in Cabo San Lucas."

"I hear it's very beautiful there."

"Yes, it is," Brian said, well aware that Torres was not fond of chitchat.

Torres's expression became solemn. Here it comes, Brian told himself. Torres reached into his top drawer and handed Brian an envelope that had already been opened.

"This telegram came for you while you were away. The secretary would have gotten it to you sooner, but she didn't know where to reach you. I'm sorry."

Brian unfolded the flimsy yellow paper. Normally he would have been furious at Torres for violating his privacy, but instead he just stood there staring at the page, as if he were having trouble deciphering the ten neatly typed words:

YOUR GRANDPA DANIEL HAS PASSED AWAY. PLEASE HURRY. LOVE, MOTHER.

9

The fly ball hit a streetlight and grazed a telephone wire before falling back to Alta Avenue, where a lanky outfielder knocked over two trash cans to make the catch. Brian swerved to avoid hitting the boy racing across the smooth blacktop and felt a twinge of nostalgia. Not so very long ago, he had raised his mitt on the same street, darting between traffic or scampering after a grounder in the gutter. Back then, cars were an acknowledged complication of urban sport, and every passing vehicle had signaled an automatic time-out. But even from half a block away, Brian sensed that the rules had changed. As Brian's car approached the blue chalk diamond, the pitcher shifted his weight and his slouch took on an attitude of belligerence. Staring straight at Brian, he coiled, aimed and whipped a blistering fastball at the windshield. "Oh," his mother exclaimed, jerking her hand up to protect herself. But there was no fastball, no explosion of broken glass. Just as Brian had guessed, the pitch had been a feint, a ruse designed to psyche him out. The once friendly rivalry of boys and cars had become a war of nerves. Determined not to be cowed, Brian kept his foot on the accelerator. When it was clear that Brian wasn't stopping, the players ceded the street grudgingly. Brian looked in the rear-view mirror, half expecting to glimpse a rude gesture, but all he saw was the players' lean bodies closing ranks behind him.

"The neighborhood has changed," his mother said to the passing houses.

"No kidding."

The corner convenience store Brian had frequented as a youth was now a unisex hair salon, its walls defaced with graffiti glyphs. Across the street, the empty lot where Johnny Calderon had kept dirty magazines hidden under the cushions of an abandoned couch, charging a penny a look, was filled with garbage and the charred skeleton of an immolated Camaro. Only his grandmother's house—a Spanish one-story with a red tile roof and pink stucco arches located in the middle of the block—remained untouched by time. Her garden was green and tidy, enclosed by a four-foot chain link fence that gave the yard a slightly besieged look, as if the wire barrier was the only thing holding back the encroaching tide of drugs and violence.

Brian parked the car and escorted his mother to the porch, which was crowded with succulents planted in clay pots. Though it was already February, Christmas lights still hung from the eaves, and the front window was smudged by a greasy frost of ersatz snow. It was hard for Brian to believe that he had started the day at the airport in Mexico City. The flight had been uneventful and fast. Too fast. There had been no time to adjust to his surroundings, and he still felt the cultural dislocation of a visitor to a foreign land.

Mary rang the bell and while they waited Brian could hear the murmur of subdued conversation inside. Then the door swung back and his grandmother was peering at them through thick glasses.

Mary held open the screen door and pointed at her companion. "Mira, Nana. Look who's here."

Sara beamed at her grandson.

"Grandma, I'm sorry," Brian said as he leaned forward to hug her.

Her bent fingers clasped his back with affection. "Thank you, m'hijo. Come in. Por favor."

Several dozen people were crammed inside the tiny living room. Some of the faces were familiar, but Brian had trouble attaching names to most of them. The smell of fresh tamales wafted in from the kitchen and he noticed several people bent over paper plates piled deep with nachos, chile verde and chicken chimichangas. At the other end of the room a makeshift bar had been set up and Brian went over to make himself a drink. He was sipping his vodka when a tall man with reddish sideburns walked up and held out his hand.

"You're Brian, right?"

"Yeah. I'm sorry, I don't—"

"Walter. I used to work with your dad."

"Sure, I remember." Brian returned the firm grip, and felt the calluses from years of manual labor. "You used to sneak me sips of beer when my mom wasn't looking."

Walter shook his head with chagrin. "Gee, I hope I wasn't a bad influence or anything."

Brian smiled. "I don't think so."

"No, you seem to have turned out all right. Mikey would be proud. Mikey—that's what we used to call your dad at work."

"I know."

"The last time I saw you you were just a little guy. I remember you sitting in the church like a toy soldier, taking care of your mama. Everybody noticed."

Walter took a swig of his beer, and Brian watched his Adam's apple jiggle like a piston. He nervously tapped the top of the can. "Your dad was a great guy."

"I know."

"I'm sorry about your grandfather. I didn't know him too well."

"Me neither."

"So," Walter said after a pause, "I hear you're in graduate school up north."

"Actually, I'm living in Mexico while I finish my dissertation."

Walter took a half step back and whistled. "Wow, you must be pretty smart to be doing something like that."

"Sometimes I'm not so sure."

"Well, it can't be easy. You gotta have the smarts for that stuff." Walter squeezed the beer with his thick fingers and stared at the crumpled can as if unsure how it got that way. "I won't be going to the cemetery," he said. "I just wanted to say hello. It was good to see you, Brian. Good luck."

He shook Brian's hand again and started to turn away.

"Walter?"

"Yeah?"

"What happened? The day my dad got hurt, I mean. You were there weren't you?"

Walter's wide shoulders seemed to sag inside his flannel shirt. "It was the worst day of my life," he said quietly.

"I never got the whole story. Mom won't talk about it."

"Well, you were just a little guy. . . ." He looked around in vain for a trash can.

"Here, I'll take it."

"No, that's okay. I'll just hold it. Anyway, we were working on that Savings and Loan on Beverly Boulevard, stacking and welding the infrastructure on the tenth floor. Your dad and me, we were buddies, you know, we liked to work together, and we were laying the support beams for the floor. It was almost lunchtime so I went back to the tool box for another box of bolts. My back was turned when I heard a shout and a crash." Walter paused again, his ear to the past. "The strange thing was, he didn't make a sound. No scream for help or nothing. I couldn't figure out where your dad went. I was kind of pissed off actually, because I thought he had gone to lunch without me or something. Then I looked down and saw the people running."

"It was just the two of you up there that day?"

Walter's eyes darted toward the coffin.

"I still blame myself a little. I used to have nightmares about it."

"What do you mean?" Brian asked as the lights in the room seemed to do a little jig.

"That day, I'd brought a couple of beers up with us . . ." Walter's drinking hand fretted at his side, then up around his collar before finally getting banished to his pocket. "Your dad never did booze on the job. I'll swear to you on the Bible, kid. But that day I made him have one with me. Just one. He didn't even finish it. But I kept think-

172

ing, afterward, maybe the beer threw him off balance. I don't know how, it's crazy, but maybe with the wind . . ." Walter's voice trailed off. "He loved you a lot, Brian. He always talked about you."

"I know."

Walter's eyes had gone pink around the rim.

"I loved him too. He was my best friend."

"I'm sorry," Brian said.

"Don't be sorry. I'm the one who should say he's sorry. I told all this to your mom already . . . Listen, I mean it, if there's anything at all I can do, financially or—"

"No, no," Brian stopped him. "Thanks for telling me. It helps."

Walter wiped his eyes with his sleeve. "I owed Mikey that much. He would have wanted you to know. His son. My buddy, he used to call you. How's your mother doing?"

The question was innocent enough, but Brian knew what he really meant.

"She's fine," Brian answered, and he was aware of the defensiveness in his voice. "Considering."

Out of the corner of his eye, Brian noticed Mary watching them from across the room.

"Good," Walter said quickly. "I'm glad to hear that. I keep meaning to drop by but . . ." He shrugged and motioned to the bar. "Ready for another?"

"No thanks."

"Okay. Another time. I always wanted to tell you, but you were too young and then there was no time. Anyway, I'm glad we talked."

"Me too." He watched Walter go to the bar, open another beer and drink it down like a man dying of thirst.

The living room was elbow to elbow with neighbors, uncles and aunts, once or twice removed. No sign of Mary. She must have gone into the kitchen to help with the food. He'd never realized before how small the house was; as a child it had always seemed like a mansion. He went over and sat in his grandfather's E-Z rest chair and smiled politely at the people who came over to offer their condolences. He listened attentively to their respectful descriptions of Don Daniel, the good father, the hard worker and loyal friend, the patriot and pillar of the community who gave generously to the local church and treated his employees well. He knew he was expected to offer his own glowing testimonials, pay homage to his granddad's ghost. The fact was that his grandfather was a mean-spirited bastard, whose moments of tenderness or compassion were the exception rather than the rule. Brian tried to recall the last time he had seen him alive. Don Daniel was sitting in the same E-Z chair watching his beloved boxing matches on the Zenith console. His face was flushed and his teeth were clenched around a soggy cigar as he shouted, "Nail the son of a bitch, you pendejo!" True, he had loved Brian in his own gruff way, but he was just as likely to reach out and cuff his grandson as hug him. Despite Don Daniel's attempts to atone for his temper, Brian had never trusted his grandfather, and now his death seemed redundant, as if in some significant way he had long ago ceased to exist.

Mary was motioning to Brian from across the room.

"What did that man want?" she asked in the tense voice that he hated.

"That was Walter, he was with dad the day of the accident."

"I know who he is."

She would never ask him directly; it was not her way. Her eyes searched his face.

"What is it, Mom?"

"That man is a drunk. You shouldn't be talking to him."

"Why not? Afraid he might tell me something I don't already know?"

The question made her flinch. Then her expression went blank and Brian could feel the wall come down.

"The limousines will be here to take us to the church in about ten minutes," she said curtly. "I want you to ride with your grandmother. Hold her arm, make sure she doesn't fall."

"I'm not going to the cemetery, Mom."

Mary glared at him. "You'll break Nana's heart."

"No I won't. I already told her and she said she understood."

"Then just do one thing for me."

"What's that?"

"It's Albert, Connie Peña's son."

"I didn't know he was here." Albert was Brian's second cousin. He was two years younger than Brian but they had been playmates as children. Quick-witted and handy with a basketball, he was one of the few relatives with whom Brian had ever felt any kinship. After graduating from USC, Al had gotten a job as a Hollywood screenwriter. Brian had seen one of his movies once, a generic detective drama where the bad guy met his end in a vat of toxic chemicals. There had been others since then, mostly steamy thrillers with unhappy endings.

"Connie thinks he's smoking pot in the backyard," Mary said reprovingly. "Please go talk to him. I don't want a scene. Your grandma has suffered enough."

"I'll try."

On his way to the back door a woman hooked his arm and hugged him against her breasts.

"Do you remember me?" she demanded, holding him like a bear trap.

"Sure."

"What's my name?"

"Ah." He struggled in vain to get free. "It's on the tip of my tongue."

"I knew it." The woman released him and put her hands on her hips. "You don't remember."

"Yes, I do," Brian stammered. "It's just that—"

"I can't believe you forgot!" she exclaimed. "I used to baby-sit for you."

"I'm sorry—"

"Annie Dalton! I used to clean house for your grandparents when you were a baby. I still do sometimes, but I just got my degree as a beauty consultant."

"Oh, right. Congratulations. It's been a long time."

"You're telling me," she said. "You're no baby anymore."

"Nice to see you again."

He was halfway out the door when he heard her add, "I'm in the phone book if you know anyone who needs a quick makeover."

Al was standing near the rose beds, partially hidden by the lower branches of an orange tree. As Brian approached, he could smell the sweet stench of high-grade hemp.

"You're busted, pal."

"Says who?" Al casually peeked out from behind the leaves. When he saw Brian, he let out a low chuckle. "Hey, it's Brian the expat. A rare sighting." Al was wearing black jeans and cowboy boots and a black linen jacket a size too large. His hair was cropped short and his eyes were hidden behind a pair of round tinted shades.

They stood back to regard each other. "Life seems to be treating you well," Al said. "What's it been? Ten years?"

"Something like that."

"I hear you're living in Mexico."

"Yeah. For a few months anyway."

"You always did show signs of intelligent life." Al took another hit from the joint and offered it to Brian. "Take a puff, it's springtime," he said.

"Actually, I came outside to ask you to put that out. The grown-ups are starting to freak."

Al cocked his head to the side. "I will, but only if you take a hit. C'mon, for old times' sake."

Brian took a toke and the harsh smoke seared his lungs. "Now will you put that thing out."

"A deal's a deal." Al dropped the roach into the soft earth and buried it with his heel. "Remember when we used to fight World War II back here?"

"It was more like the U.S. Marines vs. Godzilla."

A blue jay fluttered in the branches and took wing over the house. Brian looked around at the small garden of fruit trees, bushes and flowers, saw the selfless dedication that had kept it all growing. The signs of Sara's green thumb were everywhere. Even the pine stakes holding up the tomato plants were in neatly spaced rows. Without realizing it, Brian had missed this place. And for the first time in many years, he was glad to be home.

"You always were big on reptiles," Al was saying. "Said you wanted to work in a museum and play with dinosaur bones. I guess you got your wish."

"Not exactly. I'm in anthropology."

"Oh right, like Margaret Mead. You should write a book called *Coming of Age in Fullerton*."

"Maybe I will." Brian broke off a leaf and held it to his tongue, tasted the bittersweet tang of orange and chlorophyll. "How about you? How's the film trade?"

"It's fine, really swell. I've got a script for a gang movie in development." Al smirked. "Which is another way of saying that I no longer have any control. A big star is interested in the lead part. Sorry, but I can't tell you who."

"I'll bet your mom's really proud."

Al pursed his lips. "Mom doesn't approve. She doesn't understand why I have to live all the way out in Santa Monica. She thinks the movie business is all about drugs and sex."

"Isn't it?"

"No, it's about money too."

"I'll bet it is," Brian conceded. "Maybe I'm in the wrong business."

"I don't think so. You were smart to get out of this cow town."

"Sounds like you got out too."

"Yes and no. I'm still freeway close."

A car horn sounded from the front of the house.

"That's probably the limo," Brian said. "We'd better get going."

Al shoved his hands in his pockets. "I think I'll skip church, if you don't mind. It only aggravates my Satanist tendencies."

"I know what you mean," Brian said, "but it's really different down there. In Mexico, I mean. People still believe."

His cousin's face turned serious. "It wasn't easy to do what you did. To give it all up and go back to school. I envy you, what you're doing. I've always wanted to climb a pyramid."

"It's easier than you think," Brian said. "All you have to do is set your next script south of the border."

"Yeah," Al said dryly. "I could do a historical drama with Mel Gibson. Mad Maximilian."

They shook hands. "It was really good to see you, Al."

"Listen, how long are you going to be in town for?"

"I'm not sure. A couple of days. I was thinking of making a quick trip up to Berkeley before I fly back to Mexico."

"I'm asking because my parents are throwing a party at the house for some friends of theirs tomorrow. It would be great if you could stop by, show a little family solidarity."

"Maybe I will."

"No you won't."

"What makes you so sure?"

The smirk reappeared. "We're more alike than you think."

The house that Brian grew up in was part of a terraced development on a dirt bluff once ruled by drilling rigs and coyotes. Bulldozers pushed out the rigs and leveled the hills into orderly streets with neo-Hispanic names like Via Camille and Arroyo Drive. Brian remembered the day his mother bought the house, picking from a list of five plans in the sales office that had been set up in the garage of the flagship unit. They had chosen Model B, a Spanish-style two-story, two-bedroom with indirect lighting, central heating and a built-in pool. Only a year earlier, the place would have been impossibly beyond their means, but the insurance settlement from Miguel's accident together with Mary's income as a legal assistant had lifted them into a higher tax bracket. The house became symbolic of a fresh start, a way to put the past behind them. Back then even the treeless streets seemed to give off a freshly minted sheen. But the novelty had eventually worn off, and by the time Brian left home for college the neighborhood had become just another middle-class encroachment on the landscape, virtually indistinguishable from the thousands of cookie-cutter tracts that stretched from Ventura County to the Mexican border. Brian parked Mary's car outside the three-car garage and let himself in with his own key. He found her in her nightgown, watching the news in the upstairs den.

"The car's in the drive."

"That's fine," she said, her eyes still on the flickering screen. "I left you some roast beef in the fridge. You can eat it cold or heat it up in the microwave."

"I'm not hungry."

"So what was so important that you had to leave your grandfather's funeral?"

"Nothing. I just couldn't take all those people asking how I was all the time."

"It doesn't matter. I'm used to making excuses for you. But you could have at least stayed for Sara's sake."

"Grandma understands. She misses Dad too."

Mary clicked off the set. She was still a pleasure to look at, with creamy skin and high cheekbones. Her hair was down and in the soft light from the table lamp she looked at least twenty years younger than the brittle woman he had seen standing in Sara's living room.

"I knew it," she said accusingly. "It was talking to that man, wasn't it?"

"Don't try to blame Walter, Mother. It's nobody's fault that Dad's dead. But it still hurts sometimes."

"It might hurt less if you didn't turn your back on your family and God."

"Mother, would you please spare me the religious crap, just this once?"

"That crap is what's kept me alive all these years."

"Really? I'm not so sure."

She flinched and he felt the old pattern taking over, a self-perpetuating cycle of recrimination, anger and guilt. The wound of Miguel's death was still fresh, unhealed.

"I didn't mean to say that. It's just that I want to understand," he explained. "I *need* to understand. We never talk about it without ending up in a fight."

Mary went rigid. "What is there to fight about? Your father's death was an accident."

"I know that. But that doesn't make the subject taboo. It's the secrets and half truths of this family that have caused pain. I used to blame myself for Dad's accident. It's irrational, I know, but I did anyway. You've blamed yourself too. You've mourned him long enough. Now it's time to stop punishing yourself and get on with your own life."

The words had just tumbled out but now he realized that he had been right—she did blame herself, and maybe him too. He knew that he had earned his fair share of guilt, especially by moving out as soon as he graduated from high school. That was her hook in him: the abandoned widow, the deserted mother. The plain truth was that he'd made a conscious decision not to apply to a local college. He'd feared her neediness, her festering fear, the way she nibbled away at his self-esteem. He knew that if he'd stayed she would have devoured him little by little, one piece at a time.

"That's easier said than done," she said, staring at the dark television screen. "You try being alone sometime."

"I am alone," Brian said, but she had blocked out his words like a radio tuned to a different station.

Mary Sheahan had loved her husband with a ferocity that found instant approval by the patriarchal Mendozas. Long-limbed and strong-willed, she met Miguel during high school, when he came to work as a dishwasher at her father's pub. Their clandestine romance had remained a secret until after Miguel had graduated and landed a job as a welder for a downtown building contractor. Even then, Casey Sheahan, a ruddy second-generation Irish-American who owned a thriving bar and cafeteria on Figueroa Street, might have withheld his blessing if not for the intercession of Daniel Mendoza, himself the proprietor of a popular taco stand on Atlantic Boulevard. Daniel arrived at Sheahan's Pub one night with a bottle of tequila and the intention to have "some straight talk about your girl and my boy." The exact details of the conversation were never revealed by either man, but a few hours later Don Daniel was demanding that Miguel get his lazy ass out of bed. "If you ever make Mary unhappy," a slurring Dan had warned Miguel, "you'll have to answer to me."

The newlyweds moved into a one-story stucco apartment on the back lot of the house that Daniel and Sara owned on Alta Avenue, in the epicenter of the East Los Angeles barrio. A devoted son, Miguel dutifully spent every Sunday afternoon helping his father improve the property. The two men were often seen toiling together in the yard, a six-pack at their side, building a new planter for Sara's herb garden or repaving the cement driveway in front of the garage. Mary, for her part, did her best to ingratiate herself with Daniel and Sara, who asked only that she make their son happy. That wish was guaranteed by the birth of Brian, who was named after Mary's great-great-uncle, Brian Donnally. A restless romantic who had joined the U.S. Army during the American war against Mexico, Donnally was among a group of Irishmen who, deciding that the U.S. aggression toward its weaker neighbor was unjust, had switched sides and joined the Mexican Army. Donnally died of chest wounds a hundred miles south of the Texas border, but the Batallón de San Patricio, or St. Patrick's Battalion, bravely fought on until its last stand at the outskirts of the capital, where the Mexicans later erected a monument in its honor.

The California sun was already burning through the marine layer, promising a good beach day. Brian found the keys to the Buick on the kitchen table along with a note from Mary saying that she had gone to church for a parishioners' luncheon. He dressed and drove over to the International House of Pancakes, stopping in the parking lot to buy a newspaper before treating himself to an All-American breakfast of coffee, orange juice and silver-dollar pancakes slathered in raspberry syrup. While he waited for his food, Brian scanned the headlines. He was not surprised to read that the antigovernment riots in Mexico had intensified. Three more people had been killed in demonstrations and the opposition was advocating civil disobedience on a national scale. Meanwhile, threats from a Colorado senator about the possibility of the U.S. Army invading Mexico to restore order were causing diplomatic convulsions on both sides of the border.

The same page carried a brief update from Reuters about the radioactive accident in Nezahualcóyotl. It was now suspected that hundreds of people had been contaminated and Mexican officials were reportedly considering evacuating the whole slum. There was no byline on the story but Brian couldn't help wondering if Marina had written it. Was she still in the capital, or had she been sent off to cover the violence in the provinces?

Brian finished eating and paid the check. Then he drove south on Beach Boulevard, past cars crammed with kids on their way to the beach, past gargantuan shopping malls and discount stereo stores, until he reached the side street to Connie Peña's house. Mariachi music beckoned from the backyard and Brian followed it through the side gate and into an ersatz-adobe patio festooned with balloons and oversized sombreros. Cardboard cutouts of a colonial church and barnyard animals lined the perimeter of the yard. Against the house, under the red tile awning, servants dressed in white peasant garb and red kerchiefs tended bar and served standard Mexican fare. The band was set up on a raised platform behind the pool overlooking the sixth hole of the Fullerton Country Club golf course. Brian felt a tug on his pants and he looked down to see a little girl in a peasant dress offering up a tray of margaritas. "Lime or strawberry?" she asked.

Brian bent down and took a cup of green slush.

"Thank you."

"De nada," the girl said and moved on to the guests walking in behind him.

"Brian! I'm so glad you came, honey!" Connie Peña was wearing yellow cowboy boots and a red and black dress that clung to her torso before unraveling into a profusion of petticoats. The effect was more saloon madame than Mexican señorita, but the stern glances of the older women only seemed to fuel her exuberance. Connie's fearless pursuit of a good time had already cost her at least two marriages, but Brian knew her as a generous, nurturing soul whom he considered a kind of unofficial godmother.

"How the hell are you, dear?" Connie smothered him in a hug. "It's great to see you again. Al went out for more tequila but he'll be right back. Did your mother come with you?"

"I'm afraid not. She's still a little under the weather."

"I don't blame her, poor thing. Funerals are such a downer. To tell you the truth, I always thought Daniel was kind of a stick in the mud. Maybe now that he's gone your grandmother will let her hair down a little and start enjoying life."

"I'll drink to that," Brian said.

Connie pinched his cheek with real affection. "You know, I'm beginning to think there's hope for this family after all. You still seeing what's-her-name? You know, the blonde at Berkeley."

"Linda."

"That's the one. Nice girl."

"We broke up about a year ago."

"I'm sorry to hear that. Seemed like you guys were going hot and heavy."

"Maybe too hot and heavy," Brian said.

Connie pulled him close. "Don't you fret, hon. There are plenty more fish in the bowl, especially for a good-looking guy like you." She batted her eyelashes. "And believe me, this old barracuda knows what she's talking about."

"Thanks, Connie."

"So give me a smile. That's better. I want you to forget your troubles and have a good time today. Is your drink okay? Good. Now please excuse me, I've got to go welcome the guests of honor."

Brian watched as Connie sashayed over to greet an older couple dressed as Carmen Miranda and the Frito Bandito. "Somebody call the sheriff," Connie shouted and the man played along by drawing his guns and pretending to shoot.

"Doesn't anyone remember the Alamo?" Al was standing in the sliding glass door with a jug of margarita mixer and a bag of ice in each hand.

"Boys!" Connie was clapping her hands at them from the rented dance floor. "Listen up. I want all the men over here. It's time for the Mexican hat toss!"

"I think that's our cue to fade out," Al said. He motioned for Brian to follow him into the house. They passed through a shag-carpeted living room and out the front door. When Al pulled out his car keys, Brian said, "Hey, where are we going?"

"I want you to meet a friend of mine," Al answered. "Consider it social research."

Al lit a joint as he eased his jeep onto the San Diego Freeway, northbound to Santa Monica. With one hand on the wheel, he used the other to slide in a Los Lobos CD. The singer's bittersweet voice was like a balm on the jangling electric guitars:

> *Oh sacred night*
> *On quetzal plumes*
> *Of dying suns*
> *And purple moons*

"So how does it feel to be back in the Big Orange?" Al asked, passing Brian the joint.

"It feels strange."

"Yeah," Al agreed as he steered the jeep through the rushing river of metal and glass. "It sure as hell does."

They exited on Wilshire and drove north for another twenty minutes, crossed Melrose and finally stopped in front of a modest bungalow nestled in the corner of a cul-de-sac. The facade of the house, which was half hidden by a pair of dwarf palms, had been fashioned out of jagged pieces of Mexican tile. Through the window he could see the interior walls were painted in pastel shades of pink, turquoise and lime. Al knocked and a minute later a bearded man in a black T-shirt and camouflage army pants came to the door and ushered them into a living room full of junkyard art, Mexican crafts and religious kitsch. One entire wall was covered in polished hubcap covers, and blinking strings of jalapeño chile pepper Christmas lights dangled over the doorways.

"This is Rico," Al said. "His parents called him Jimmy Ramírez, but that's all in the past. Now he only has one name because he's an artist. Artists aren't supposed to have more than one name, are they Rico?"

Rico yawned theatrically, and Brian guessed they'd been through this routine before. "This is my cousin Brian," Al continued. "He's working on his degree in anthropology down in Mexico."

Rico gave Brian a critical stare. "You don't look like an anthropologist."

"And you don't look like an artist."

There was an elastic tension, then Rico nodded approvingly. "Your cousin," he said to Al, "is okay." As Rico rummaged through his record collection, he asked Brian, "So what do you think of my house?"

"As a dwelling?" Brian asked.

Rico looked at Al. "Where did you find this guy?"

"Picked him up at a funeral."

"A little plot research, Al?" Rico laughed at his own pun as the record began to play. Strings in a minor chord, joined by primitive drums, then a woman's voice, by turns birdlike and guttural, fluttering over the orchestra. It reminded Brian of the soundtrack from an old King Kong movie.

"Yma Sumac," Rico announced. "Claimed to be the descendent of Peru's Inca kings. In the thirties and forties she was bigger than Madonna—and just as controversial."

The drums picked up a savage tempo and Sumac growled like an animal. "Wild stuff," Brian said politely.

"You two have something in common," Al remarked. "Brian's Ph.D. thesis is on Aztec ritual suicide."

Rico raised his eyes toward the ceiling in an expression of gratitude, then slowly raised his arm until his finger was pointing between Brian's eyes. "You've got to see my studio," he commanded.

Rico led the way to what used to be the garage, and as they entered Brian gagged on the toxic perfume of turpentine and oil paint. Several large paintings were leaning against the walls and as soon as he saw them Brian understood why Al had brought him here. Each of the canvases depicted a moment of Aztec-style sacrifice with Rico himself in the role of high priest. But the most startling aspect of the pictures was how the killings were juxtaposed with ordinary scenes from contemporary American life. "This one," Rico pointed to a scene of a woman's heart being ripped out while she waited at a grocery store checkout stand, "is titled *Express Line. Ten Items or Less.*" Another showed him in the guise of a teacher jabbing a blade into the chest of a young girl spread over the desk of a high school classroom. A third was a businessman cutting off the head of his secretary in a brightly lit office complex.

"These are just extras," Rico explained. "The best ones are being shown this week at the Pyramid Club."

"It's a nightclub downtown," Al explained. "All the bartenders wear loincloths and feathers."

"I danced my ass off with a black leather goddess last night," Rico said. "The title of my show is 'The Sacred and the Mundane.'"

Al lit another joint and the three men passed it around as they perused the paintings. For Brian, the cannabis high only enhanced the sensation that he was having a bad dream.

"Well?" Rico demanded, unable to contain his curiosity.

"I've never seen anything like it," Brian said diplomatically.

"Yes, I know," Rico said proudly. "They're utterly original. But I'm talking about the victims. I mean, are the methods authentic?"

"What methods?"

Rico waved his arms in exasperation. "The methods of sacrifice—decapitation, stabbing, evisceration . . ."

"The Aztecs did that, yes," Brian said. "But it was done in a very different context."

Rico's face fell. "What do you mean?"

"For the Aztecs," Brian explained, "sacrifice was not an act of class or racial consciousness, it was a way of preserving the cosmic order. They killed not to glorify death, but to perpetuate life."

Rico shot a nervous look at Al, who was slouching on a paint-splattered stool, the remains of the joint dangling from his mouth. Brian's cousin exhaled a cloud of blue smoke before speaking. "I think you'd better call *Artforum* and offer to make a retraction."

"Not constructive," Rico said curtly.

Al laughed. "You just blew Rico's rap right out of the aesthetic water," he said without a trace of sympathy.

"It's just my opinion," Brian said, trying to soften the blow, "from an academic perspective. It doesn't necessarily have any bearing on your work. Science and art have different rules."

"Exactly," Rico said with a rebuking glance at Al. "The impact is visceral, not intellectual. Who cares why the Aztecs sacrificed people to the gods? The point is that they did it."

The phone rang in the other room and Rico left to answer it. When he was gone, Al asked, "Why'd you let him off the hook?"

"I didn't have the heart."

"Very funny," Al said.

"Besides, I thought he was your friend," Brian added. But before Al could answer Rico had returned. "That was the Pyramid Club," he announced. "Some Japanese journalists are there and they want me to pose for pictures."

"We were just leaving," Brian said.

As he walked them out, Rico invited them to come by the club and preview his show. "I'll make sure you're on the list so you won't have to pay or stand in line."

"I'd really like to," Brian said, "but I'm leaving for Berkeley first thing tomorrow."

"Too bad," Al said. "Maybe next time Rico will let you watch him prepare his palette. He mixes some of his own blood into the red paint."

Brian looked at Rico, who just grinned.

"You had me going there for a second," Brian said. But when he shook Rico's hand he couldn't help noticing the flesh-colored Band-Aids on his fingers.

10

An impromptu jam session was warming up on Sproul Plaza as Brian stepped through the south entrance of the Berkeley campus. Two conga drums spoke first, a throbbing dialogue that was quickly joined by bongos and nattering maracas. A handful of students, their book-filled backpacks slung over their shoulders, paused to listen, their tanned bodies swaying to the undulating rhythms.

He found Larry St. Cloud at a picnic table outside the Bear's Lair pub, hunched over two stacks of manuscripts. A tenured professor of religious studies and Brian's Ph.D. advisor, St. Cloud was famous for his definitive study of Native American vision quests. He was also renowned for holding his office hours al fresco over a cup of black coffee and a stack of French fries. It was a high-cholesterol habit overlooked by his students, who tended to regard him as a modern-day shaman who had somehow infiltrated the sterile halls of academia.

Brian took a seat across the table from his mentor and before he could utter a word, St. Cloud said, "You could have at least sent me a postcard."

"I thought I'd wait until I could talk to you in person."

St. Cloud lifted his eyes from the sheaf of papers. "Do you expect me to believe that?"

"No."

"Well, at least I've taught you something."

St. Cloud was the mixed-breed issue of an Indian mother and a French father, raised on a Minnesota reservation and educated at the Sorbonne. He had come to Berkeley five years earlier to escape the brutal Midwestern winters and the deeper chill of his first marriage. St. Cloud had high cheek bones, a square, dimpled jaw and laughing blue eyes that belied his gruff demeanor. The consensus was that he was somewhere near fifty, but there was no way of being certain, since his aura was ageless. Brian watched as St. Cloud emblazoned a B+ on the top page and placed the manuscript on the second pile.

"Exam time?"

"Midterms for my Native American film class. Tyros don't know *Little Big Man* from *Batman*."

"So things haven't changed since my own undergrad days."

"Not much," St. Cloud muttered. "Except that I no longer award *A*s to Freudian profiles of George Custer."

"You sure seemed to like it at the time."

"I've become wiser," St. Cloud retorted. "And harder to fool."

Across the plaza, two men had started up a game of Frisbee. The aerodynamic disc sailed like a UFO over the plaza to where a bare-chested man in a wheelchair nabbed it with one hand, and with a quick flick of his wrist sent it whizzing back toward his partner.

"I'm listening," St. Cloud said.

Brian brought him up to date on the temple excavation, his encounters with Zapata and Villalobos and his hunch that Xotl and Xólotl were possibly one and the same.

St. Cloud gave Brian one of his rock-steady stares. "So you intend to get your degree on the basis of a typographical error," he said, but Brian could tell that he was intrigued.

"If I can document the link between Xotl the priest and Xólotl the god," Brian said, "it'll open a whole new chapter in the literature of Aztec sacrifice. The fact that Xotl believed that Cortés was Tezcatlipoca is already ground-breaking stuff. Now there's a chance that Motecuhzoma might have thought the same thing. It backs up my original hunch in spades. If I can reconstruct the route of the priest's pilgrimage, I'll have enough material for two degrees."

St. Cloud inspected a sliver of fried potato before popping it into his mouth. "How," St. Cloud asked as he chewed, "do you propose to go about doing that?"

"Doing what?"

"Tracing Xotl's route."

"I know it won't be easy," Brian allowed, "but I've already got some strong leads. The Quetzalcóatl codex, from what I've read, shows pretty conclusively that Xotl's mission was to resurrect Quetzalcóatl's spirit in the belief that only the Plumed Serpent could save the Aztecs from their enemies."

"A kind of Aztec ghost dance," St. Cloud mused.

"Something like that. Anyway, since Ce Acatl Topiltzin-Quetzalcóatl supposedly migrated to the Yucatán peninsula, I think it's safe to assume that Xotl was headed there too."

"How do you know he wasn't headed to Teotihuacán?"

"Well, as a matter of fact, I'm pretty sure he went there first before heading south. I found glyphs dedicated to Xólotl in one of the outlying temples. I think the implication is pretty clear."

"Try me," St. Cloud said.

"Larry, I'm no epigraphist, but I have corroboration from a Mexican colleague that the glyphs at the cathedral and the glyphs at Atetelco were painted by the same hand. I found the symbols for Tlapallan—the Aztec name for Yucatán—on the same wall."

"You're saying that the same guy painted two pictures a thousand years apart?"

"Actually the Atetelco glyphs were recently repainted, but I'd bet good money that the fragments underneath are exactly the same age as the ones under the cathedral."

St. Cloud wiped his mouth with a paper napkin and leaned across the table. "Okay, let's see if I've got this right," he said. "Xotl—or

Xólotl—is a priest at Tenochtitlán circa 1521. Through religious revelation or deductive reasoning he comes to the conclusion that Cortés is not Quetzalcóatl. He flees from the Aztec capital on a mission to find and resurrect the original Quetzalcóatl. Along the way, he detours to Teotihuacán and draws the glyphs you found, then continues his journey south, presumably to Chichén Itzá."

"I'm not sure about Chichén Itzá yet. Maybe Uxmal."

St. Cloud looked up and stared into space. Brian waited, knowing that this was a crucial test. St. Cloud could be brutally honest if he thought a hypothesis was weak or scientifically unsound.

"Personally," St. Cloud said at last, "I think you've got some interesting stuff here. But your theory won't hold water without concrete proof. Take away the codex and you've got nothing. Zapata has clout, and not just in Mexico. If he wants to stop you, he has more than enough power to get you kicked out of the country. I don't have to explain the effect this could have on a budding career. So whatever you do, don't cross him. Play by his rules. The other caveat is theoretical. You'll have to do a lot more basic groundwork to be taken seriously. You might want to take some notes."

"Right." Brian produced a pen and a small notebook from his pocket.

"Your case has to be airtight or it'll be shot down before it ever flies," St. Cloud continued, "so you might as well get used to defending your ideas. Here are just a few questions that you should be prepared to answer: For starters, where in the Yucatán did Xotl go? Who went with him? What type of ceremony did he plan to perform? How and where did he die? Where was he buried? Does he appear in any of the other codices? How does this change Xólotl's ranking in the Aztec pantheon? In other words, who was this guy?"

Along with his questions, St. Cloud gave him the titles of some recommended reading. "If you can't find them in the bookstores, let me know and I'll lend you my copies."

The conga players had been joined by a flutist. The instrument's airy voice fluttered over the roiling rhythm. A small crowd had formed around the musicians. A woman in tie-dye writhed to the music. Someone passed around a hat.

When Brian had finished writing, St. Cloud inquired, "How's your financial situation?"

Brian shrugged. "I've got about half left."

"You're going to need more before this is over. The Americas Society is offering a grant for three thousand on Mesoamerican cultures. I'll recommend you. Drop by the office before you leave and I'll give you the application." St. Cloud picked up another fry. "Do you need a place to stay?"

"I'm camping out with my old roommate. But thanks anyway."

A redheaded woman in a white halter top approached their table. "Hi, Larry?" she said sheepishly. "I'm really sorry to be so late, but my dance class ran long. Would it be all right if we rescheduled for tomorrow? I'm already late for poli-sci. By the way, I really enjoyed your lecture on burial rites. I'm a molecular biology major and it's just so refreshing to sit in a class that doesn't have anything to do with valences."

St. Cloud turned to Brian. "What do you think? Should I give this charming young lady a second chance?"

Brian pretended to give the matter serious consideration.

"The day 3 Serpent is a good time for talking."

The woman's eyes shifted uncertainly between St. Cloud and Brian.

"Mendoza is climbing the great mountain," St. Cloud told her. "I trust his inner vision."

The woman seemed to grasp that her leg was being gently pulled.

"Thanks a lot," she said to Brian with a sour little smile.

"Glad to be of service," Brian said.

The girl turned to St. Cloud, "And professor, I guess I'll see you on, ah, 3 Serpent."

St. Cloud smiled politely.

After they had watched her walk away, St. Cloud scowled at his pupil. "Three serpent is a good day for talking?"

Brian shrugged. "It was all I could think of. Well, I guess I'd better be going."

"First tell me something," St. Cloud asked. "You mentioned that this Xotl had someone else traveling with him."

"Yeah, a younger priest named Tonatiuh. He's a disciple of some sort."

St. Cloud shook his head. "Never heard of him. It might be worth doing a bio search before you go back to Mexico."

It was an obvious idea and Brian was chagrined that he hadn't already thought of it.

"I'm leaving tomorrow," he said. "I'm afraid I might have already missed something important, something that could put me on Xotl's trail."

"That trail has been sitting there for five hundred years," St. Cloud remarked. "It'll wait another day."

There was a shout from across the plaza. Brian looked up and saw the Frisbee hovering toward him. He stood and tried to catch it, but the spinning blue disc remained suspended in the air, just beyond his reach.

Greg Stone was sprawled on the sofa watching President Nava address a news conference on TV. He was urging calm and asking the Mexican people to have faith in the party that had successfully ruled the country for the past six decades. The news soundbite ended by noting that interventionist sentiments were on the rise in the Congress.

"You have to admit," Stone said sardonically, "it's a much better place for a war than Vietnam, or even the Persian Gulf. Not only is the food better, but just think of the convenience of invading a country on our own border. We'd save millions on transportation alone."

"I think Mexico has enough problems without the U.S. Army getting involved."

"Well, it looks like they might not have a choice."

Brian found himself resenting Stone's flippant attitude. "Maybe not, but you do," he said. "Are you sure you still want to come?"

"Are you kidding? Wild burros couldn't hold me back. I'll be there in two weeks. Besides, my ticket's nonrefundable."

They had met during their junior year, as roommates at a north-side co-op that featured communal dinners and a rooftop pot garden. Brian had opened the door to a blinding flash from Stone's Nikon and the resulting mug shot was the first of hundreds more. The next term they had found their own place, a two-bedroom brownshingle off Telegraph Avenue where they regularly hosted tequila and psilocybin Monopoly tournaments. The Boston-born son of a Ford auto parts manufacturer, Stone told Brian that he had come west to "piss off my parents and get a tan." Stone was successful on both counts, and also managed to maintain a 3.7 grade point average while working as a staff photographer for the school paper. By their senior year, Stone was getting his work published in several Bay Area magazines. But his big break did not come until after graduation, when he'd posed as a skinhead and joined a neo-Nazi group headquartered in the Haight-Ashbury section of San Francisco. His photo essay of the group's scarification rites had been picked up by *Black Star* and Stone quick-developed into a darling of the international Ektachrome set.

Like most California boys, Brian had grown up thinking that only sissies went to prep school, but he soon learned that Stone had no qualms about risking his life for a good picture. In his fearless pursuit of a "fortuitous frame" he was willing to climb mountains, buildings and bridges, endure alpine snowstorms and confront herds of charging elephants. Despite Stone's capacity for self-absorption, Brian was flattered to be drawn into a circle that exuded social aplomb and financial insouciance, two traits that did not come naturally to a scholarship boy from the East L.A. barrio.

"By the way, thanks for letting me use your couch," Brian said.

"Don't mention it." Stone picked up a mah-jongg piece and pondered its placement. "Planning to call you-know-who?" he asked.

"Nope."

"Look, I know it's none of my business . . ."

"That's true," Brian said.

". . . but does she even know you're here?"

"No."

"How long has it been?"

"About a year, I guess."

"Isn't she friends with Sharon Hackett?"

"I think so. Why?"

"Sharon's throwing a party tonight. House up on Skyline. Chances are that Linda will be there."

"Are you going?"

"It depends on whether I find myself in dire need of a beer and boisterous companionship."

Brian spoke without taking his eyes off the stunted dimensions of Stone's bonsai pine tree. "Consider yourself in need," he said.

Sharon Hackett's house was located on the uppermost ridge of the Berkeley hills, which commanded a stunning view of the whole Bay Area. The building was a New Age medley of glass and exposed beams surrounded by redwood decks that jutted out toward the Pacific. The road was already lined with cars and even before crossing the drawbridge-like entrance ramp Brian recognized the pounding din of a serious bash.

Their hostess greeted them at the door, pecked at their cheeks and pointed them to the bar. Through the floor-to-ceiling bay windows Brian could see the Emerald City skyline of San Francisco and the Golden Gate, its crimson spans engulfed by a frozen wave of fog.

"How does a comp lit lecturer afford a place like this?" Brian asked, accepting a vodka and mango juice cooler.

"She doesn't." Stone pointed across the room at a wan fellow with a balding pate. "He does. Some kind of computer whiz over at Lawrence Livermore. They're engaged. Beauty and the Brain."

Stone's conversion to Zen Buddhism had unleashed a streak of brutal honesty. "Truth is beauty," was his new motto. Brian considered Stone's reductionist profile of their hosts. Cruel, yes, but doubtlessly accurate. It didn't matter how rich, or talented, or happy a person was, they could still be boiled down to a few well-chosen words. How would Stone describe me, Brian wondered: Ethnic mutt. Professional late bloomer. Would rather study the mysteries of ancient cultures than deal with his own past.

"I'm going to cruise around for a bit," Stone said.

"Fine."

The kitchen was crammed with people, drawn to the light like moths. Brian was dying for a beer, but he wasn't up to fighting his way to the refrigerator. A James Brown song came on and people started to gravitate toward the living room. Brian scanned the faces in the thickening crowd for Linda, poised between hope and dread.

"Three Serpent must also be a good day for partying."

It was the woman from Sproul Plaza. Her T-shirt was emblazoned with the words: DRUG-FREE BODY.

"Hey, I was only—"

"Don't apologize," she said. "Everybody knows that St. Cloud is a tribal trickster. I didn't recognize you from class."

"He's my advisor. I'm doing field work for my Ph.D. in Mexico."

Drug Free shifted her weight forward. "I love Mexico, what's your dissertation about?"

"Aztec ritual sacrifice."

"You mean tearing out people's hearts? That kind of sacrifice?"

"Yeah, that kind."

"Groovy," she said.

Brian turned his attention back to the party. Someone had lowered the lights and a few couples were getting aerobic on the hardwood floor. He spotted a flash of long blond hair and moved closer just to make sure. Even before he got a look at her face he knew it wasn't Linda. She would never jiggle and shake like a belly dancer. Her movements tended to be fluid and sensuous, reflecting years of yoga and modern dance. Brian decided to check out the other rooms, all of which had skylights and sliding doors. Brian wandered out to the deck, where an outdoor hot tub had been built into the corner. The tub was surrounded by a ring of discarded clothes and voices emanated from the cloud of steam.

"Get your ass in here, Mendoza," Stone's voice called out. A woman giggled.

"No thanks. Maybe later."

Brian ducked back into the house and joined a group gathered around a computer terminal. A woman with a bulky glove on one hand and protruding goggles over her eyes flexed her fingers and dropped her jaw. "I just saved the world!" she yelled.

"It's a virtual reality generator," the man beside him explained. "It's a simulated battle between space stations in the stratosphere."

"I take it you designed the program."

"Philip Atwater," he said distractedly. "I expect you're a friend of Sharon's."

"Brian Mendoza. And I expect you work with computers."

"I'm sorry, what did you say you do?"

"I'm an anthropologist. Doing some field work in Mexico."

"Have you ever played Tomb?"

"Tomb?"

"It's another virtual reality program. Synthesizes the experience of excavating the tomb of an ancient Egyptian pharaoh. Lots of secret passages. Stuff like that. It was written by a former archaeologist."

"It sounds like you've played it."

"Oh, sure," Atwater said. "But I got wiped out in a cave-in after twenty minutes, so I can't tell you how it ends. Besides, it's not my area of expertise."

"What is your area of expertise?"

Atwater's face lit up. "Killer micros," he said.

"Killer what?"

"Micros," Atwater repeated. "Microprocessors. Do you know anything about computers?"

"Not much."

Atwater grunted. "Well, I'll try to make this as simple as possible. It's kind of like killer bees. One can't really hurt you. But thousands attacking at once can be deadly."

Sharon Hackett joined them and, realizing that Atwater was talking about his work again, frowned.

"Honey, are you talking about your killer computers again."

"Killer *micros*," he corrected.

Sharon gave Brian a conspiratorial look. "I don't understand it either. But the government thinks he's brilliant."

"Damn, they're getting through!" The player was frantically trying to hold off a horde of invading aliens.

"Philip and I are getting married in June," Sharon said.

"Congratulations."

"He's taking me to Canyon Ranch for our honeymoon."

"Listen," Brian said nonchalantly, "I thought Linda Hinton might be coming by tonight."

"That's right," she said, as if seeing Brian for the first time. "I forgot you two went out together."

"Do you expect her to show up?"

Sharon shook her head. "I really don't know. She's been really freaked out by the prospect of being a mother."

"She's married?"

"Engaged. To some guy from San Francisco. Didn't you know?"

There was a commotion in the room as the player was obliterated by a simulated nuclear explosion.

"Do you have a phone I could use?" Brian asked.

"Sure. In the master bedroom."

He pulled a tattered piece of paper from his wallet and dialed the number. His fingers seemed to move in slow motion. The first ring went on forever. Then an interminable silence. Then the second ring. He suddenly remembered when she had first told him she might be pregnant. They had talked about it. Late at night, alone in bed. They'd even discussed names. Thomas for a boy. Susan for a girl. A few weeks later it was official. There was never any question. It was a unanimous decision. She'd wanted the abortion, hadn't she?

"Hello?"

Hadn't she?

"Why didn't you tell me, Linda?"

"Brian?"

Her voice was little more than a whisper. Had he woken her? What time was it?

"Why didn't you tell me?" he repeated.

Brian could hear his own breathing in the receiver. When she spoke the words were clear and sharp.

"Because it's none of your business," she said and hung up.

Dial tone. He found Stone in one of the bedrooms and told him that he needed to borrow the car. Ten minutes later he was pounding on Linda's door. When the light blinked on he took a step back. The door opened a crack. He could see that the chain was still on.

"What do you want from me?"

"I want to talk."

"There's nothing to say."

"I'm sorry, but I disagree. If you don't let me in, I'll spend the night on your porch. I'm sure your neighbors wouldn't mind."

She opened the door again, this time all the way, and Brian stepped inside. It was a momentous occasion. Someone should be here to take a snapshot, he thought. But there was no one else there. Just the two of them, standing apart like strangers.

"Aren't you going to offer me coffee or something?"

"Are you out of your mind?"

She was angry. He could see that. Her hair was disheveled and her cheeks puffy. Her robe was pulled tightly around her body, a gesture probably intended to deemphasize her sex but one that had the opposite effect. Brian tried to see things from her angle. They had been lovers. He had gotten her pregnant. Their parting had been less than amicable. After more than a year of silence, just as she was about to begin a new life, he had called her up in the middle of the night and demanded to see her. Now he was inside her house and she was steaming. Under the circumstances, he figured, anger was a positive sign.

"Can we at least sit down like civilized people?" he suggested.

She held up her hands and shook her head like someone witnessing a miracle. "What do you know about civilized people?"

"Quite a bit, actually." He knew it was a tactical error to be flip, but her attitude was starting to annoy him. Just to rub it in, he took off his jacket and sat down.

"Who the hell do you think you are?" she said.

"I'm the man you used to love, remember?"

"Sure, I remember you. You're the man who knocked me up and then went camping with the boys to get his head together. You're the man who didn't even have the decency to take me to the clinic."

"That's a lie," he countered. "And you know it. It was a week before you were supposed to get the abortion. You're the one who took off to L.A. without telling me. You're the one who left me a Dear Brian note on the table, asking me to move my things out. Is that your idea of civilized behavior? You think it was a picnic for me wondering what the hell was going on?"

"I was scared," she said softly. "I felt abandoned."

Something in her seemed to bend. She slumped down in the nearest chair and he could see she was on the verge of tears. He was afraid of what the sight of her crying might do to him.

When she spoke again the anger was gone from her voice. "Brian, this is all such old news. I have my own life now. It doesn't include you. Now, will you please, please just leave?"

Her pleading almost broke his resolve, but he wasn't ready to go yet.

"I don't know what I was thinking when I came over. Maybe I was kidding myself. I guess it was the shock of hearing you were pregnant."

Linda's expression went awry. "*Pregnant?* What on earth are you talking about?"

Brian felt a slight tremor, the epicenter right under his feet.

"Sharon Hackett just told me you were freaked out about becoming a mother."

Linda's outrage melted into pity.

"Oh, Brian . . ." she sighed. "His name is Jim Levinson. He's a lawyer and he's got a two-year-old son named Ben."

"Is he a good man?" The words felt odd on Brian's tongue.

"Yes, he's a good man," she said. "And a good father."

"Sometimes, when I think about us, I really wish . . ."

"I know," she said soothingly. "So do I."

"I guess I really fucked things up."

"We both did."

Brian closed his eyes, trying not to lose control. Then he felt her next to him, her long fingers massaging his neck. "Poor Brian," she said soothingly. "Poor, confused Brian." Her touch felt so right, so knowing. He turned to face her and her robe fell open. It had always been so natural with her.

Her hand met his and gently pushed it away.

"Let's not make the same mistake twice," she said.

11

"I would ask you if you enjoyed your trip, but final farewells to loved ones are never pleasant." Zapata opened his arms in avuncular sympathy. "Please accept my condolences," he added. "I didn't learn about your grandfather until after you left."

"Thank you, Professor."

Zapata settled back into his chair. "As you know, Mexicans have a very different attitude than Americans about such things. All men fear death, naturally. And no one grieves louder than a Mexican widow. But in this country, death is not something that happens at the end of a life. Instead, it is a part of life. Death follows us everywhere, from cradle to grave, and the souls of the dead continue to live with us. For that reason, perhaps, we Mexicans are not afraid to look death in the face and laugh. The laughter is not frivolous but one of knowledge."

Brian wondered if the phrase "we Mexicans" was meant to include him. It was strange to be sitting in Zapata's office, chatting about the afterlife. This was not the businesslike museum director that Brian had met on his arrival. Zapata's demeanor had changed. He was now projecting the persona that came across so well in his books—an erudite uncle expounding on a favorite topic.

"The Mexican Day of the Dead," he continued. "It is much like the American Halloween. But the devils and goblins of Halloween are apparitions, ghosts that are banished by the light of day. Not so to us. To Mexicans, the echoes of the dead are very real and impossible to ignore."

"Especially when they are discovered under Catholic cathedrals," Brian said.

"Quite so," Zapata agreed. He gazed directly at Brian. "What did your visit to the site tell you?"

Brian now knew the real reason he had been summoned by Zapata. He swallowed and tried to make his argument as clear and concise as possible.

"There's no question that the site represents a major discovery," Brian asserted. "I understand that the cell was older than the structure that once existed above it, yet many of the objects found inside were from Period VII, just prior to the Conquest."

Zapata pushed his glasses against the bridge of his nose. "Go on."

"Well, I'm convinced that whoever used the tomb was more than just an ordinary priest in Quetzalcóatl's temple. Or, at the very least, his motives were not ordinary. I think he had a secret agenda, an agenda that took him, and possibly several others, on a journey far away from here."

"And do you know where he was going?"

"Yes," Brian said. "At least I think so. When I was at Atetelco, I found glyphs that match the ones under the cathedral. I'm waiting for verification, but I'm pretty sure that they're also from the same time period, which I guess to be no more than a few months before the fall of Tenochtitlán."

"But you don't believe that Atetelco was the priest's final destination."

"No. I believe he was actually heading south—for Yucatán."

"Do you have any ideas as to the composition of the priest's cargo?"

The query took Brian by surprise.

"What cargo?"

Zapata's fingers drummed on the desk. "It's not such a strange question, really," he said as he produced a handkerchief from his pocket and wiped his lenses. "It's traditional that religious pilgrims carry an offering. From what you've just told me, I would assume that this priest—if in fact he existed—was on a religious mission of some sort. So it logically follows that he would be carrying an offering or gift. A precious bundle. Are you familiar with the term?"

"No," Brian lied.

"Torres maintains that you cannot be trusted," Zapata said. "Is there any basis for his suspicions?"

"Well," Brian said lightly, "I'm not working for the CIA, if that's what you mean."

"Please, don't misunderstand," Zapata went on. "We are under a great deal of strain these days. There have been leaks to the press. This business about the cathedral site has become a political"—he groped for the word—"albatross."

Zapata clasped his hands together. "As you are aware, the dig has become a sensitive issue in certain circles. There are some kinds of information that, if revealed to the public prematurely, can be potentially damaging."

"Like the Xotl codex?" Brian asked.

Zapata allowed himself a brittle smile. "Like the Xotl codex," he repeated.

Brian felt the muscles in his neck tighten. He was on dangerous ground now, and the risk he was about to take made him giddy with fear.

"I've read it."

Zapata should have been shocked but he remained as serene as the Buddha. "I know," he said mildly. "The guard reported you after the first night."

Now it was Brian who was flabbergasted. "You knew but you didn't say anything?"

At last, Zapata showed surprise. "Why should I have?" he asked.

"It was important to ascertain your motives. Once I realized that you were working alone and that your interest in the codex was not larcenous, I decided that helping you along could be advantageous."

"So you granted me access to the dig." Brian felt the blood rush to his face. "You've been toying with me."

Zapata gravely shook his head. "Brian, I'm going to be perfectly frank with you," he said. "I find your ideas highly speculative, even more so than Professor St. Cloud."

"You spoke to Larry?"

"Not long after you joined us here, I thought it would be wise to know more about your background. Please don't blame him. I requested that he keep our conversation confidential, a matter of professional obligation. He spoke very highly of you, but admitted that when it came to research you sometimes relied more on inspiration than documentation."

Brian felt like the wind had been knocked out of him.

"I can see that you think you have been betrayed, but I assure you that it is all routine," Zapata said with the assurance of a man who held all the trump cards. "Besides, your position may be better than you think. As director of the museum, I am prepared to continue helping you with your work—both in terms of research and resources. All I ask in return is a certain degree of loyalty. I know that you have spent time at the country home of Alejandro Villalobos. I know that he is interested in your work. Exactly why, I don't know. It is something I would like to understand better. Have you told him anything about the codex?"

"Nothing that hasn't been in the newspapers," Brian said.

Zapata visibly cringed at the reference. "Yes, the newspapers. I'm sure I don't have to remind you that our conversation—like everything here—must remain absolutely confidential."

"No, sir. You don't."

"That's good." The words carried an implicit threat. "If you adhere to these rules, I promise that you will be given total access to all the museum's resources, including an opportunity to read the remaining installments of the Xotl codex as soon as they are translated. In addition I will personally guarantee to help you eventually publish your findings in the United States. Do we have a deal?"

Brian felt like someone about to jump off a very high diving board.

"What about Torres?"

"Don't worry about Torres," Zapata said. "He no longer has any jurisdiction over you. From this moment on you will be working directly for me."

Brian walked back to his desk in a daze. Guillermo came by to welcome him back and offer his condolences and apologize for Laura, who had been avoiding him since their trip to Atetelco.

"She's acting like a child and I told her so," Guillermo said, slapping his arms against his sides in a gesture of helplessness. "Go talk to her. She thinks you were using her friendship to get to the codex."

"That's ridiculous."

"I know, but she has to hear it from you."

"I'll try."

He found her in the depths of the library using a magnifying glass to study a copy of the Borgia Codex, the book of prophecies. Brian recognized one of the symbols he had seen on the walls of the cathedral tomb. The glyph showed an undulating serpent pierced by an arrow, with rivulets of blood spurting out in every direction.

"It means drought and famine, doesn't it?"

"You don't need me to tell you what you already know," she said and he was amazed at the sharpness in her voice. She tried to leave but he gently held her arm.

"Laura, if you don't want to be my friend, that's your choice, but just hear me out first. I know you think I used you, but that's not how it was. I knew about the Xotl codex because I'd been reading Torres's copy."

Her mouth opened into a perfect circle. "But how . . . ?"

"I did it at night when everyone was gone. It was wrong, I know. But they knew all along. They wanted me to read it."

"They?"

"Torres and Zapata."

"But why?"

"It's too complicated to explain, but you have to believe me. I was trying to find out what you thought about the codex because I was trying to understand what I was reading. There was no one else I could talk to, no one else I trusted. And it's still true. Your friendship is very important to me."

Her eyes were moist when she looked at him. "I could lose my job," she said.

"I know. I'm sorry. I promise not to ask you a single thing more about the codex, all right?"

"I knew you couldn't be a bad person," she said with some of her old sweetness.

"I'm glad to hear it," Brian said. "But I could still use your help."

"Oh, Brian . . ."

"It's just one little word, a Nahuatl word. I couldn't find it in the dictionary."

He knew he had piqued her professional curiosity when she asked, "You already looked in the dictionary?"

Brian repeated the word that the old man in the church at Amatlán had whispered to him.

"*Yaxactun*," she repeated, frowning with concentration. In her braids and flowered cotton dress, she looked like a schoolgirl puzzling over a difficult homework assignment.

"I'll have to double-check to be certain," she apologized. "I don't want to tell you the wrong thing."

"No hurry. Take your time."

Torres arrived a few minutes later and went straight to his midday meeting with Zapata. When he emerged he was like a man enclosed in a block of ice, a reaction Brian had anticipated. An uneasy hush fell over the office and Laura and Guillermo avoided the chill by burying themselves in their work. Brian hadn't mentioned his deal with Zapata and he was pretty sure Torres wouldn't either. A little later, when Torres passed Brian on the way to the water fountain, he looked right through him without a blink. As far as Torres was concerned, Brian had become a nonentity who no longer occupied space in the same dimension. Maybe he was right. In exchange for academic gain, he'd bartered away his independence and agreed to join Zapata's cult of secrecy. Maybe Laura had been right not to trust him; the very thought of being on the same side as Torres made him nauseous. One thing was certain: Marina was correct about Zapata and Villalobos being sharks of the same species. For weeks he had observed their Darwinian power plays from the sidelines with morbid fascination. Now he was in the tank with the maneaters, treading water.

It didn't help Brian's mood when he returned to his desk to find it loaded down with a fresh stack of computer pages. The printouts were accompanied by a curt memo from Torres informing him that he was still expected to help Guillermo collate the inventory files when he wasn't working on "special projects." Brian cursed under his breath. He had won the battle, but the cold war continued.

To distract himself, Brian poured himself into the work, escaping into the printed stream of pots, idols and silver pendants, which he sorted by age, size and material before entering them into a separate ledger. The work was gratifyingly mindless and the morning sped by. When he looked at his watch it was almost noon. Brian picked up the phone. He knew that *The Globe* had a 1 P.M. deadline. If Marina had a story running in the next day's edition, she would be there. The operator answered and Brian asked her to put him through.

"I'm sorry, Marina Soto has taken a leave of absence," she told him.

Brian tried her home number. The answering machine picked up and Marina's voice told him that she was out of town for a few days on an assignment. Brian didn't leave a message after the beep.

At lunchtime Brian politely declined Guillermo's invitation, needing time alone to digest the events of the morning. He knew just the place. Heading along República de Venezuela to the Mercado Rodríguez, he entered the market and took a seat at one of the taco stalls sandwiched between overflowing bins of papayas and radishes. Across the clotted aisles skinned baby goats hung from their hoofs and shouting women in flowered aprons haggled for a pound of frijoles under murals by Bracho and Gamboa. As always, the vivid smells and colors soothed his senses—it was like an instant trip to the country in the center of one of the world's largest cities.

A little girl proffering sesame candy tugged on Brian's trousers. Her hair was pinned back with combs in the shape of prancing pink tigers.

"Cuánto?" he asked.

"Dos pesos."

He took the candy and paid her double. A tentative, shy gracias, then she was gone.

Brian took a bite of his taco, irritated by his own paranoia. Anyone else would be ecstatic; the endorsement from Zapata was an anthropologist's dream come true. But several details nagged at him. Why, for instance, was the esteemed doctor so interested in Xotl's cargo? And then there was the disturbing revelation that he'd been under surveillance without his knowledge. Were Guillermo and Laura in on it too? he wondered.

Brian pushed the notion out of his mind and opened the day's edition of *The Globe*. The lead story was about Nava's order for the arrest of Raúl Tolsa, the deputy director of Pemex, the government oil monopoly. Tolsa was wanted for pocketing government money earmarked for a new refinery. There was a picture of the fugitive, and Brian recognized him as the man he had seen on his second visit to Villalobos's house in Tepoztlán. The powerful oil workers union had responded by calling a national strike that could bring the country to a standstill. Pressure was building for Nava to take a strong action in the crisis. Meanwhile, the rebel uprising was gathering strength in the eastern and southern regions. The article ended with a quote from a cabinet minister promising that El Presidente would soon take his case to the people in a state of the nation message from the National Palace.

Paying the check, Brian decided to pick up a few avocados for La Madre, hoping he could entice her to make him a batch of her velvety guacamole. He ambled among the vendors, many of them garbed in the dusty white trousers and banded sarape of the campesino, his eyes roving the stalls for the shiny green skins. From behind a bin of brown jícama root, the girl with the green tigers in her hair waved to him. Brian waved back, noticing a man, her father probably, dozing on a stool nearby. Brian touched the man's shoulder and he started, reaching for something that had slipped under his sarape. A pistol clattered to the ground and the crowd of shoppers flinched at the brittle sound. At the same instant, through his peripheral vision, Brian saw a dozen other men stiffen and reach under their clothes. In the strange hush, a parrot shrieked and muttered to itself. Slowly, and without taking his eyes from the man's sweating face, Brian backed away and walked deliberately through the crowd toward the exit, away from the eyes and guns of the peasant army.

My dreams are changing. The premonitions of disaster continue, but now the invaders' faces are brown as well as white. The image confounds and saddens me. Does this mean that our people will turn against one another? Or perhaps it is another trick being played by Smoking Mirror, a web of confusion spun by the spider of the night, a wicked ruse meant to cloud my mind and deflect me from my goal? I am doing my best to purify myself and fortify my body and spirit for the tribulations that I know lie ahead. Each morning I rise before the others and make an offering to our god and protector. The rite is always the same: I take a sharp thorn and pierce my penis, letting the blood drip onto a strip of bark paper. Then I place the paper in the fire and pray as the yellow smoke rises through the clouds to the Fourth Sky, the House of the Lord of the Dawn, the realm of Venus, where my master Quetzalcóatl sits on a throne of light and guides my every thought and action.

In the weeks since we bade farewell to our besieged city we have been blessed with much kindness. Without the help of my fellow priests, we would have never made it this far. The brotherhood of Quetzalcóatl is much stronger than I ever suspected. His memory is revered not only in Teotihuacán, but as well in the south, in the hills of Amatlán, and beyond in Cuetlaxtlan and Tochtepec. I have also learned that there are others like me who have had the same dreams. Their visions have added details to the pictures in my head and have strengthened my resolve to complete our mission.

Our group has grown to nine. Acama, who joined us at the Eye of the Window, is a tall youth with a flashing smile who has pledged to guide us as far as Mixtlán, which marks the southern extreme of the Aztec empire. After that, we will have to chart our own course in the land where monsters dwell. Citlax, or Great Bear, and Zacatuche, or Volcano Rabbit, are warriors assigned to protect our party by the high priest of Tepantitla. Both of our escorts live up to their name. Great Bear is hulking and fearsome, and Loma trembles in fear whenever he treads near her. Volcano Rabbit is slighter of form, but his strength lies in his sharp senses and fleet movements. He has already saved many days from our journey by scrambling to the top of nearby hills and choosing the best route from his vantage point. Together they constitute a formidable duo, and I sleep more peacefully thanks to their presence.

Tonatiuh is a willing and enthusiastic student but I sometimes wonder if he has the patience and discipline to live up to his calling. Seated around the fire, I notice his furtive glances at Loma, and I worry that his attentions are motivated more by the demands of the flesh than brotherly benevolence. I consider saying something to him, but I cannot find the words. And why should a boy in the flowering of his manhood listen to an elder who carries the experience of life like rocks in his sandals? Despite my sagging flesh and bending bones, I am not too old to remember the hot fevers of my youth. Back then the feckless advice of the elders had only made me feel more isolated in my torment. What did they know? To me they were corpses, their passions shriveled up and dormant from years of neglect.

I decide on a more subtle course of moral suasion. Instead of trying to close Tonatiuh's senses, I will open his soul. I clap my hands and our band of pilgrims gathers around, all except Zacatuche and Citlax, who remain on the perimeter of our camp, their ears tuned to the night music of the open country. Tonatiuh, as usual, sits directly across from me, crosslegged. Acama and Loma sit to either side of him, with the slaves taking their places behind. I see the fire's reddish glow on their rapt faces and suppress a sigh. Their unblemished innocence makes me feel ancient.

"We are travelers on a sacred journey," I begin. "And the path we have chosen has taken us through mountain passes and flowering fields, across arid plains and rolling rivers. Our goal is clear, but the route has been difficult, with many twists and turns and unexpected barriers. So it is with the path to truth and wisdom. And there can be no truth or wisdom without knowing the Life-Giver, the dual one, the one who holds the world in his hands and dwells in the Thirteenth Sky."

I pause and the silence is filled with the singing of frogs and crickets and the dry rustle of burning wood.

"Listen to the words of the Toltec poet:

> *"Where is the place of light*
> *Where he who gives life hides himself?*

Where shall I go?
Oh, where shall I go?
The path of the god of duality.

"Is your home in the place of the stars?
In the interior of the heavens?
Or only here on earth
is the abode of the dead?"

Looking at Tonatiuh, I ask, "What does this poem mean? Can you
tell me?"
Tonatiuh has his answer ready.
"The poem asks where it is that god dwells. In the netherworld, the
heavens or the world of men."
"And do you know the answer?"
"The answer is all three."
"Can you finish the poem?"
"Yes," Tonatiuh says proudly:

"You live in heaven;
You uphold the mountain,
The world is in your hands.
Awaited, you are always everywhere;
you are invoked, you are prayed to.
Your glory, your fame is sought.
You live in heaven;
The world is in your hands."

"Good," I say. "Now listen to this:

"And the Toltecs knew
that many are the heavens.
The celestial god is called the Lord of Duality.
Which means he is king, he is Lord, above the Twelve Heavens."

"Who can tell me the meaning of this poem?" I ask.
This time Acama speaks up.

"It is about the first god, the beginning of everything. It means that the Lord of Duality is above the world and the other heavens."

"And does that also mean that the Lord of Duality is also above all the gods in the universe?"

"Yes."

"And if that is so, then is the Lord of Duality also above the god Quetzalcóatl?"

Acama starts to answer, then falters. "I don't know," he mutters.

"No one is above the god Quetzalcóatl," Tonatiuh blurts out.

"But now I am confused," I say. "How can the Lord of Duality be above the god Quetzalcóatl and yet not above him?"

"He is inside," Loma says quietly.

"Inside what?" I ask.

"Inside everything."

I allow myself to smile.

"So the Lord of Duality and the god Quetzalcóatl exist together in the same being?"

"Yes."

"Very good," I say. "Now who can tell me about Ce Acatl Topiltzin-Quetzalcóatl?"

"He was the king of Tula," Tonatiuh says, eager to reclaim his place as star pupil. "He was a wise and gentle ruler who loved his people and preached sobriety and abstinence and practiced self-sacrifice in the name of spiritual purity. Then a tragedy fell upon him and he exiled himself to the paradise of the south, where he disappeared into the sea and vowed to return someday."

"And what was this tragedy that befell him?"

"He was tricked by the sorcerers of the evil god Tezcatlipoca, the Smoking Mirror."

"And how did they trick him?"

"One day, when the good king was ill, one of Tezcatlipoca's sorcerers came to him disguised as an elder and gave him some medicine to drink. But the medicine was actually pulque and he became drunk and lost control . . ."

"How did he lose control?"

"He summoned his sister to the palace and forced her to commit incest with him."

"He allowed physical desire to debase his love for his sister?"

"Yes," Tonatiuh answers quietly.

"Very good," I say. "And what lesson do we learn from this story?"

"That sexual abandon and degeneracy are contrary to the pursuit of goodness and wisdom."

"Correct. Now tell me, Tonatiuh, how do you look on Loma?"

At first, Tonatiuh is startled by the question, then I see the blood rise to his cheeks and I know the arrow has reached its target.

"As a sister," he murmurs.

"I could not hear you."

"As a sister, teacher." His eyes flicker at Loma, who is staring into the fire.

"You have learned your lesson well," I say. "Now say your prayers and sleep. We still have a long journey ahead of us. Evil will test us every step of the way, even in our dreams. But I have faith in your unwavering strength."

Tonatiuh rises and takes his leave without looking at me. Loma, too, is noticeably subdued. One by one the others stand and bid me good night. Alone again, I wonder if I have been too harsh. I have grown to love Tonatiuh like a son, but this is not the time for fatherly indulgence. He must be tempered for the tribulations that lie ahead. There is so little time to prepare him for the initiation. Smoking Mirror is at this very moment plotting our defeat, priming his minions in the facile arts of subversion. During the lesson I sensed the evil spirits hovering outside our camp, fearful of the light, circling like hungry animals. This is no place to lower my guard; I must be endlessly vigilant. The frogs and crickets sing their guttural song to the stars. I pull the blanket around me and stare at the fire until the log burns down to cold ashes . . .

The Monte de Piedad, or national pawnshop, was a stately edifice that marked the spot where Captain Hernan Cortés and his army stayed as guests of the emperor Motecuhzoma. Now it was a center for loaning money to the poor and not so poor, accepting personal property as collateral, just as Motecuhzoma had hocked his empire to the Spanish conquistadors. Thanks to the Xotl codex, Brian knew that Motecuhzoma was not a dupe of history, as commonly believed, but a savvy

212

actor in a cosmic tragedy, playing to a celestial audience from a script written in Aztec blood.

Brian made his way up Avenida Republica de Brazil to the Plaza de Santo Domingo, in the old section of Mexico City. Dodging the milling lunchtime crowd of tourists, office workers, housewives and squads of stampeding children, he came to a row of men sitting at wooden tables under an umbrella of peeling Colonial arches. Each man sat before an antique manual typewriter with a ream of blank paper stacked at his side. Guillermo had once brought Brian here to see the scribes who pecked out letters on rusty Smith-Coronas for the unfortunates who couldn't write themselves. The scribes had gathered here for as long as anyone could remember, and even in the age of the electronic fax there was still a healthy demand for their services.

Brian took his time, interviewing several until he found one who was free for immediate hire. He wore a crumpled green suit, dingy white shirt and an orange striped tie at least an inch too wide. His thinning black hair was brushed back behind his ears, framing a forehead like a dry riverbed.

"I would like you to write a letter for me," Brian informed him.

"Of course, señor." The man licked his thumb and lifted a blank page. "What kind of letter?"

"A love letter."

The man ran his tongue over his teeth.

"A love letter will cost you more."

"But I already know what I want to say."

"It doesn't matter," the man retorted. "It will still cost you extra."

"If I am telling you what to write, why should the cost be more than any other letter?"

"Do you wish to write the letter yourself, señor?"

"No, I don't."

"And why is that?"

"Because I want it to be perfect."

"You want it to be a serenade of pure poetry," the scribe intoned, "without creaking verbs or sour notes of faulty grammar."

"Something like that."

"Tell me, señor, is your love a living thing or a dead thing?"

"She's very much alive."

The man chuckled and shook his head. "Not the object of your love, I mean the love itself."

"It's still living. I think."

"Then, like a delicate rose, it must be transplanted with skill, or its meaning will wither and die before it reaches the heart of your loved one."

"I see," Brian said. "How much will this operation cost me?"

"Ten dollars."

"Isn't that a bit expensive? That guy over there said he'd do it for five."

The man spat on the ground.

"Cheap words convey cheap sentiments, señor."

"How about seven dollars."

The scribe pinched his lips together.

"Seven dollars for one page."

"It's a deal."

The scribe aligned the paper in the roller and carefully advanced it into place. Then he squared his shoulders and paused with his fingers hovering over the keys.

"And what, may I ask, is the lucky lady's name?"

"Marina."

"Ah, Marina. A beautiful name, señor."

The scribe pecked out the date and waited.

"Dear Marina," Brian began. "I was wrong—there is a rabbit in the moon . . ."

When Brian got back to the office, Laura was waiting to talk to him.

"I think I've figured it out," she announced. "But let me ask you something. Are you sure that the word you told me is Nahuatl?"

"Well, no, I'm not sure of anything. I just assumed—"

"That's what I thought," she said, her braids bobbing with excitement. "It was driving me crazy at first. Then I figured it out. *Yaxactun* isn't Nahuatl at all; it's classic Maya."

"Maya?"

"Yes. That's what confused me at first. This particular language was prevalent on the Yucatán peninsula up until the tenth century. The key is in two parts. The first part is *Yax*, which means great or

214

principal. The second part, *actun*, means cave or cavern. The article is implied."

"So it means the great cave."

"Yes," Laura said, her eyes shining. "That's it, the great cave. Does that help you?"

Brian gave her a grateful buss on the cheek, causing her to bloom with color. But he scarcely noticed; his thoughts had returned to the tiny church at Amatlán. The great cave. It made some sense—there were plenty of them in the area. But why would the old man speak to him in Maya?

Brian spent the rest of the afternoon working on the inventory sheets and collecting everything he could find on the god Xólotl, which wasn't much. His library search at Berkeley had turned up zilch, and all the other sources had merely confirmed what he already knew. He carried the pile of books and folders back to his desk and sorted through the material, painstakingly assembling a portrait of a deity that seemed to simultaneously exist in several places and nowhere at all.

Stumped, Brian copied the information in one of his notebooks and tried to concentrate on the museum printouts. He wanted to catalogue a few more columns of artifacts before quitting time. He had whittled the pile of pages down to just a couple of inches, or what he estimated to be about a day's worth of work. Brian's finger moved down the column and stopped:

OBJECT DESCRIPTION—OBSIDIAN KNIFE; HUMAN BONES; INCENSE BURNERS INSCRIBED WITH REPRE-SENTATIONS OF GOD XÓLOTL; UNIDENTIFIED TOOLS; CERAMIC FRAGMENTS; GLYPHS ON WEST AND SOUTH WALLS.

COMMENTS: REPORTED BY LOCAL TOURIST SUPER-INTENDENT, DONATO NEGRETE (23 CALLE HIDALGO, OXKUTZCAB). SECONDARY CHAMBER ATTACHED TO UNDERGROUND SHRINE UNCOVERED BY SEISMIC DIS-TURBANCE. EVIDENCE OF POSSIBLE TOLTEC OR AZTEC RITUAL SITE. CARBON DATING PENDING. NEGRETE HAS SEALED AREA UNTIL FURTHER INSTRUCTIONS FROM THIS OFFICE.

DIG LOCATION: LOLTÚN, YUCATÁN.

The flash of light came from a point on Calle San Jerónimo, directly in front of Brian's building. La Madre was perched coquettishly on the stoop, a hand cupped to one ear as Esmeralda preened on her shoulder.

"Now look into the camera," Greg Stone urged, "and pretend that you are on a tropical island, a paradise where the sun shines all the time and dinner drops from the trees into your lap."

The camera flashed again, capturing La Madre in another pinup pose.

Brian tapped on his friend's shoulder. "May I see your photo permit, señor?"

Stone spun around and broke into a boyish grin. "Ladies and gentlemen," Stone exclaimed as he pointed the camera at Brian and clicked away, "there he is: the great American anthropologist returning to his base camp after a hard day at the office!"

"Real funny," Brian said. "Now will you put that damned thing down for a second?"

Stone was wearing baggy camouflage shorts, a Hawaiian shirt depicting a nineteenth-century shipwreck and cherry red high-top sneakers. His auburn locks were awry and his handsome face was bristling with a week's worth of stubble.

"We don't look like we're in the same country," Brian noted.

"A few hours ago we weren't."

"Where's your stuff?"

"At the Camino Real."

"Very swank, señor."

"Perks of the trade," Stone said slyly.

La Madre had insinuated herself between the two men and was tugging on Brian's sleeve.

"Dile que yo quiero una fotografía."

"She wants a copy of the picture you just took," Brian translated.

"No problemo," Stone said. "I automatically make copies for all my models."

"And one too for Esmeralda," La Madre added in English.

Stone looked at La Madre's parrot, then back at Brian again.

"She's into birds," Brian explained.

"Unbelievable," Stone said, but Brian could tell that his landlady was destined for Stone's personal collection of prized portraits.

"So whatever happened to the end of the world?" Brian inquired as they mounted the stairs to his apartment.

"They postponed it."

Brian guffawed.

"No, really," Stone said. "Annihilation Annie put it off until July. The town council revoked the cult's building permit, so they're falling behind schedule on the bomb shelter. This is nice. Very, ah, collegial."

"Spare me the compliments. Anyway, I'm glad Annie decided to put the Big Bang on hold."

"She's a great gal, actually. A certified wild woman."

"You like anyone who's certifiable."

"But plain bonkers doesn't cut it," Stone corrected. "They've got to have a finely twisted imagination. Big Bang Annie's crazy like a fox. Do you know how much money she's making?"

"Nothing would shock me."

"Besides, she gave me a complimentary shelter pass." Stone pulled out a laminated plastic badge bearing the church's mushroom cloud insignia.

"Are you planning to use that thing?"

"Absolutely," Stone said. "I might do a whole photo essay. How's this for a title: Thermonuclear Afterglow in the Arms of Annie Armageddon. Kinda catchy, don't you think?"

"Just stay away from the Kool-Aid."

But Stone was out of earshot, leaning out the window with his telephoto. "It's fucking Wild Kingdom down there!" For Brian, Stone was living proof that energy equaled matter times the speed of light squared.

"Hey, I just remembered something," Stone shouted over his shoulder.

"What's that, Greg?"

"You still owe me a tequila!"

As Brian had imagined, Stone proved a quick study in the finer points of tequila y sangrita. In the middle of their second round, he surveyed the cantina they were in and raised his glass. "I like this drink," he said, "I like this city. I like this crazy enchilada of a country."

The two men kicked back their shots.

"When was the last time you were here?" Brian asked.

Stone studied his empty tumbler. "About four years ago. I was in Cabo for a story on marlin fishing."

"I was there two weeks ago."

"Business or pleasure?"

"I went for pleasure and got the business."

Stone showed his sympathy by signaling for another round. "She's a diplomat's daughter," Brian continued. "A journalist. Her name is Marina Soto. We had a disagreement about the moon."

"Sounds cosmic."

"It was—for a while anyway."

"And now it's history?"

"I don't know. I'll find out tomorrow. I've asked her to meet me."

Their drinks arrived and Stone threw down a fifty peso bill. Brian tried to pay but Stone waved his money away.

"Save your lucre, pal. I'm charging this to the company store."

"Doing what?"

"Well, AP and the newsmags for starters. This country's about to rip itself apart, in case you haven't noticed."

"I've noticed."

"I figured I'd stake things out before the entire international press corps shows up for Nava's speech." Stone raised his glass. "Anyway, here's to love and second comings."

Brian took another drink and felt the strain of the day dissolving away.

"Besides," Stone said, "there are some things I'd like to do while I'm waiting for the kettle to boil. This place is crawling with good copy. For instance, have you heard of Superbarrio?"

"The masked champion of the slum dwellers? Does he actually exist?"

Stone scowled. "Of course he *exists*. Even if he doesn't, it's still a great story: Robin of the 'Hood. I'm also thinking of doing a piece on this radiation guy."

"Chávez."

"Right. You know anything about him?"

"Just what I've read in the papers. Marina was covering it."

"Is she as pretty as she sounds?"

"And twice as smart. Maybe I can try to get you in touch with her."

"Sounds like you'd better get in touch with her yourself first. No offense intended."

"None taken," Brian said glumly. "Unfortunately it's the truth."

"It pains me, amigo, to see you in such libidinal grief," Stone said. "Which is why I'm going to insist that you accompany me to Puerto Vallarta for a week of frivolous degeneracy."

"Is there any other kind?" Brian asked.

Stone pondered this. "I would, if pressed, argue that there is such a thing as serious degeneracy. It's a matter of how much one is willing to risk to fulfill one's desires."

"Point taken," Brian said, but he already had a different kind of excursion in mind. "Listen, I've got a better idea. How about a trip to the Yucatán instead?"

Stone dumped the salt container on the bar and, using his finger, traced the outline of Mexico in the white powder. He pointed to the hooked knob of the Yucatán. "Is that where you're talking about?"

Brian nodded. "Give or take a few grains."

"Isn't it full of jungles and jaguars . . ."

"And ruins and rebels and some of the world's most beautiful beaches."

Stone squinted as if trying to imagine such a place. "Did you say rebels?"

"They attacked a busload of tourists a couple of weeks ago. The Maya have a long history of rebellion. It's called the Cult of the Talking Cross. The ministry of tourism is understandably nervous."

"And why," Stone asked, "are you so interested in this particular part of Mexico?"

"I have my reasons."

"Try me."

"I'm looking for somebody."

"Anybody I know?"

"Doubt it. He's been dead for more than four hundred years."

"So it's unlikely I went to high school with him," Stone speculated.

"He was an Aztec priest named Xotl. He might have been carrying something intended as a sacred tribute to the god Quetzalcóatl."

Stone was grinning again. "You're talking about buried treasure, aren't you?"

Brian squared his shoulders. "Maybe. I can't say for sure. All I know is that this bundle was very valuable to him, so valuable that he took a hike from Mexico City to the Yucatán just to deliver it."

"And I suppose you know where in the Yucatán he was headed."

Brian looked his friend in the eye. "I found something today, a dig report. It gave me a pretty strong clue."

"Who else knows about this?" Stone was suddenly serious, a journalist protecting his lead on an exclusive story.

"Nobody," Brian said. "The site was just reported to the museum a few days ago. We'd be the first to check it out. Could be a very big story. There might even be an article in it."

"In which case you'd need some good photos. Hey, I know an editor at *National Geographic* . . ."

Brian raised his hand. "No editors. Not yet, anyway. This stays between the two of us. Consider it a spec assignment. Besides, there's a chance that we won't find a damn thing."

"I can deal with that risk," Stone said. "What does your boss at the museum think about all this?"

"He doesn't know. And I'm not sure I'm going to tell him."

Stone was drawing a bull's-eye in the salt map, the rings radiating outward from the peninsula's center.

"Are you suggesting some freelance excavation?"

"All I'm suggesting," Brian said, "is that we take a little sightseeing trip to the Yucatán."

"Right," Stone said, playing along. "Two college buddies on a road trip. And if we just happen to stumble on a priceless treasure or two, I'll just happen to have my camera loaded."

"You've got it."

Stone became serious again. "You know, I knew you were ambitious, but I never thought you were the type to break the rules."

Brian held his friend's stare. "The rules are different down here. I'm different down here."

"Oh yeah?" Stone asked. "How so?"

Brian groped for words to express the strange tension that he felt inside, like something struggling to shed its skin. "It's hard to explain," he said. "Nothing looks or feels the same to me anymore. Something's changed. It's right in front of me. But I can't put my finger on it."

"Maybe you don't need to," Stone said as he used his hand to wipe away the spiraling vortex of salt.

12

The pyramid at Pino Suárez was located in the middle of one of Mexico City's busiest subway stations. Like so much of Mexico's pre-Columbian past, the small stack of concentric white ovals had been discovered by pure chance when federal workers blundered onto it while digging a Metro train tunnel. In deference to Ehécatl, the god of the wind to whom the temple was dedicated, the monument had been enclosed in a glass-walled pit so that commuters could glimpse a piece of their Aztec heritage while rushing to the office.

Brian scanned the street-level plaza that had been built above the pyramid. Off to the south, the sky was bruised by gathering rain clouds. The jaundiced light spilled across the endless streams of people and automobiles and suffused the air in shades of marmalade. She was still half a block away when he picked her out of the crowd, her assertive stride cutting a straight path through the chaos of vendors and bargain shoppers. She was in the same navy suit she had worn when they met and Brian felt bewitched all over again. When she noticed him watching, her pace slackened, becoming tentative as she closed the distance between them.

"Thanks for coming," Brian said.

Her eyes stabbed him for a second. Then a cloud passed overhead, softening the harsh shadows around her mouth.

"I don't have much time," she snapped. "I'm in the middle of a story."

Brian nodded and handed her the perforated strip of paper ballots.

"What are these?"

"Lottery tickets."

"I know that." She ran the accordion strip of colored paper through her fingers. "Why?"

"I figured those were about the same odds that you'd show up."

Her smile was grudging. "Well, it looks like you won your bet."

"No," Brian said. "At least not until I know we're friends again."

"Is that all I was to you," she asked scoldingly, "a friend?"

"Marina." He reached for her hand but she pulled it away.

"Friendship is nothing without trust," she said.

"I know that. I'm sorry. I was wrong. I've been wrong about a lot of things lately."

"Like the man in the moon?"

The teasing lilt of her voice gave him hope.

"I guess you got my letter."

"It only took me about two seconds to figure out you didn't write it—flowery metaphors just aren't your style."

The memory of Cabo weighed on the conversation like an anchor.

"I guess something got lost in the translation."

"Not everything."

He tried to gauge her expression, but she had turned to look at the temple.

"How are things at the paper?" he asked. "They said you were on assignment."

"I tried to quit," she said to the temple. "I was so angry at them."

Brian took the opportunity to move a few inches closer.

"But they didn't let you."

"No." A slight breeze lifted her hair from her face. "I couldn't do it. There's too much going on. It scares me sometimes. Being a journalist is the only way I know how to help, to be useful."

She pulled a cigarette from her purse and Brian hurried to light it. He cupped his hands around the match and her fingers reached up and brushed his. As she inhaled, her eyes rested on him and a kind of truce was declared. They agreed not to fight, not to hurt each other. The rest was subject to negotiation and the healing intervention of time. Still, her body language warned him to tread lightly.

"Are you covering Tolsa's arrest?" Brian asked.

She looked at him with surprise. "Didn't you hear?"

"Hear what?"

"Tolsa got away. There was a shootout at his house in Chihuahua and he escaped. The federales are searching the whole country for him."

"What about the strike?"

"It's already begun, but they say there's enough gasoline reserves for another month. Of course, that hasn't stopped the prices from going up already."

The din of the city was joined by the rumble of distant thunder.

"Can Nava hold on much longer?" Brian asked.

"Only if he does something very dramatic, something that will show the people he is serious."

"Like what?"

"Like dissolve the government and call a referendum for a parliamentary democracy."

"You think he would actually do that?"

"According to my sources he will announce the measures in his address to the nation."

"When?"

"Soon."

"Jesus," Brian said. "Will the people go for it?"

"The people are ready for change—with or without their leaders," she said, and Brian felt the zeal behind her words. "The system isn't working and everybody, even Nava, knows it. It's time for the Revolutionary Party to live up to its name."

"If it's not already too late."

"It's never too late," she said. "At least I pray to God that it isn't."

"Me too," Brian said, shuddering at the specter of political upheaval. If the chaos and the killing came, all he had to do was get on a jet and three hours later he would be safe in the U.S. Mexico would become a mirage, a colorful experience, a dramatic anecdote that he could use to entertain his friends. But for Marina, and for millions of Mexicans, there would be no easy escape. If and when the storm came, they would have to find their own shelter.

"And you," Marina asked. "How is life at Templo Mayor?"

"Tolerable. I'm planning a trip to the Yucatán next week. A hunting expedition of sorts. If I bag what I'm looking for it could be big news."

"Don't do me any favors, Brian," she said sarcastically. "Professor Zapata might not like it."

Her comment stung him, and for a moment she became a stranger again. Maybe he was just kidding himself by thinking that their relationship was salvageable. After all, they had grown up on opposite banks of the Rio Grande, and their view of each other would always be muddied by that fact. It might be easier if they just chalked the whole thing up as a cross-cultural fling that had run its course. Then he saw that her lips were trembling and his resentment changed into something much more nebulous. She didn't hate him; she was only trying to protect herself by pushing him away.

"I didn't mean to get you into trouble," he said. "I thought—"

"You didn't get me into anything," she said petulantly. "Can't you see? It was my own decision and nobody else's. You play the sensitive man, but you're even more dangerous than the machos who mistreat their women. At least they're honest. You say you care but you still interpret everything through your own self-importance. When will you understand: you don't control my career and you don't control me."

He grabbed her wrist and she tried to twist free.

"Let me go!"

"Not until you listen."

She stopped struggling and he relaxed his grip. "I'm not the enemy, Marina. We may be from different countries, but we want the same thing."

"And what is that?" she asked suspiciously.

"The truth."

"The truth," she scoffed. "Now you sound like the fool who wrote that letter."

"I am the fool who wrote that letter," Brian said. "I told him what to write. Maybe he overstated my case. Maybe not. You're terrified that I'll tell you that I love you and not mean it, and I'm terrified to say it because it might be true."

She started to walk away, stopped, and raised her hand to her eyes. She was still vacillating between flight and tears when he put his arms around her. "You don't have to say anything," he whispered, "you don't have to decide anything. Just promise me that I can see you again."

Her tears anointed his neck. There was no redemption in Marina's embrace, but Brian was grateful anyway. Just being able to hold her was enough. They stayed that way until the first drops began to fall on the plaza. Brian didn't mind getting wet because he had just cleared up a major misunderstanding about his own nature. All this time he had been convinced he was one of those men who out of fear, or habit, or just plain selfishness, were incapable of commitment. But in fact it was just the opposite. He wasn't afraid to hold on; he was afraid to let go.

"We're going to drown," Marina said as she gently pulled free.

"It wouldn't be the first time I got in over my head."

"Maybe we both did."

He reached for her hand again and she moved away. "I've really got to get back to work," she said.

"Not until you promise that I'll see you again." Her expression became wary and he quickly added, "as a friend, if necessary."

"I can't tonight," she said, tying a rose pattern scarf over her hair. "Call me tomorrow."

He stood there until she had sprinted across the street and around the corner, until the vendors and pedestrians had scurried for cover and the downpour had soaked him to the skin. Then he took a parting glance at the pyramid and started back toward his apartment. He walked without hurry, like a man out for an afternoon stroll, his hands clasped behind his back, his face turned up to greet the falling rain.

Even without Diego to guide him, Brian had no trouble finding his way back to Tepoztlán. The highway from Mexico City was well marked and he directed Stone to the turnoff without mishap. When Los Borrachos came into view, the sight of the brawny peaks gave him a visceral charge, as if the knowledge he brought with him had made him privy to some of their power.

"That's where we're going," Brian said, pointing, and he could see that Stone was intrigued. Brian was enjoying the chance to play the role of guide for a change. It was Stone who usually instigated their adventures, but Mexico had become Brian's turf, and revealing it to his friend instilled him with proprietary pride.

They were close to the outskirts of town when Stone pulled over onto the dirt shoulder and killed the engine.

"What's wrong?"

"Don't you see it?" Stone asked as he loaded his Nikon.

"All I see is a cemetery."

"Exactly. I'm going in there. Wanna come along?"

"No thanks. I'll wait."

"Suit yourself," Stone said. "I won't be long."

Brian sat in the car and watched as Stone pushed open the rusty metal gate and went in. The cemetery was deserted and the air vibrated with insects and the dry rattle of wind through the weeds. Stone moved among the candy-colored tombstones like a zoologist hunting for rare specimens, vigilant for that fleeting moment of inspiration. When the camera was "hot," Stone didn't just look through the lens, he *became* the lens, oblivious to everything except the images he was coaxing onto film. For Stone, capturing a good picture provoked a Kodachrome catharsis that he liked to describe as sex in two dimensions. Stone reached into his bag for another roll and waved. Then he was off again, ducking and weaving like a commando through the graves, until Brian lost track of him altogether.

Parked in the blistering sun, the car quickly became a toaster oven and Brian climbed out, preferring to wait in the shade of a lone oak about thirty feet away. He was almost under the tree when he noticed the boy leaning against the trunk.

"Buenos días," Brian said.

The boy nodded and shifted his weight. He was wearing a Bart Simpson tank top, huarache sandals and a Mets baseball cap.

"Americans?" the boy asked in accented English.

Brian nodded and motioned to Stone, who had just emerged from the cemetery gate.

Brian asked, "You live in Tepoztlán?"

Instead of answering the boy pointed off toward the mountains. He said his name was Bill. When Brian called him Guillermo, the boy corrected him.

"Not Guillermo, señor. *Bill*."

Bill liked Americans because he wanted to go to the United States and get a job. He had friends who had gone to Texas and earned a month's pay in two days. "They said all I have to do is cross the river and I can stay with them," Bill said in Spanish. "In a few weeks I'll be able to buy a car."

"But what if you get caught crossing the border without papers?" Brian asked.

Bill tugged sullenly on his cap until it nearly covered his eyes. "If I get caught, I'll go back again. Even if it takes a hundred times or a thousand times. California and Texas belonged to Mexico. The Border Patrol can shoot us and beat us and put us in jail, but they can't stop us from going home again."

"Do you know about the birthplace . . . ?" Brian wrestled with the Spanish, ". . . el lugar de nacimiento del dios."

The boy cocked his head. "La cueva del nacimiento de Quetzal-cóatl?"

"Right. Have you been there?"

The boy rose to his feet and used the cap to dust off his pants. A hank of reddish brown hair hung down over one eye, giving his stance a rakish tilt.

"Yes. Many times."

Bill was born in the hills outside Amatlán. He and his father lived on a small ranch near the base of La Ventana, where they eked out a living selling cactus and whatever else they could grow on their small patch of land. He had climbed La Ventana ever since he was a boy and, yes, he had seen the sun pierce the needle on the sacred days.

In the old days, when his father was a boy, the cave contained artifacts and the remains of a small altar. But anything of value had been long since stolen or sold to the museums.

"Have you ever noticed any drawings on the walls?" Brian asked.

Bill nodded vigorously, describing pictures of wise men and slaves carrying bundles on a journey. Brian described the symbol of the descending god.

"Yes, I have seen it," Bill said.

"Anything else?"

"A girl. A naughty girl."

"Why was she naughty?"

Bill giggled and looked down at his feet. "Because she was like this," he said, holding his arms out around his belly.

The bamboo gates of Villalobos's villa were open so they drove right in and parked near the main house, next to two cars that Brian didn't recognize. Out on the patio, the table was set for dinner but no one came out to greet them. Even the mountains, their flanks obscured by a smoky haze, seemed to be keeping their distance.

Stone already had his camera out and was scanning the property with a light meter. "So this is how the poor Mexicans live," he quipped as they crossed the lawn. "*HG* would love it."

"Hello?" Brian called out.

When there was no response, they circled around toward the pool but the water was placid, the tennis courts abandoned.

"The master appears to be out," Stone intoned. They were heading back toward the front of the house when the men turned the corner. Brian counted four, a quartet of endomorphs straining the seams of their business suits. He had seen their ilk around the house before, and he even thought he recognized one of them from his previous visit. So Brian wasn't alarmed until they grabbed Stone's camera and started taking it apart.

"Hey, you can't do that," Stone protested, but the film was already dangling in the sunlight like a spent party favor. The men surrounded them, two behind and two in front. Brian looked over at his friend. Stone looked pale, his face twisted between amazement and anger.

"Who sent you?" one of the men demanded in Spanish.

"Nobody," Brian said. "My name is Brian Mendoza. I'm a friend of Don Alejandro."

The inquisitor hesitated, then ordered one of the other men to the house. A moment later, Diego appeared with the messenger following a few steps behind.

"Release them," Diego barked, and the men obliged. For one startling instant Diego the genial chauffeur had become a decisive lieutenant in Villalobos's private army. The men retreated to the house and Diego became his old affable self again. "Are you all right, Mr. Mendoza?" he asked deferentially.

"I guess so. Why did—"

"I'm terribly sorry, señor. A terrible mistake. As you know, these are tense times in Mexico. A man of Don Alejandro's stature cannot be too careful."

"Well, he just was," Stone said.

"Is this yours?" Diego asked, holding the film up in his hand.

"They took it from my friend's camera," Brian explained. "We were coming to see Alejandro."

"I understand," Diego said. "I'm very sorry but Don Alejandro had to go into Mexico City on business. He's very busy, but I'm sure he would like to see you as soon as he is available. Would you like me to have him call you?"

"Yes, Diego. Thank you."

"Once again, please accept my apologies. But I suggest that you call first before your next visit."

"Thanks for the tip," Stone said. Then, as they crossed the lawn to the car, he added under his breath, "I really like your new friends."

"I can't believe what just happened," Brian said.

Stone eased the car onto the pitted dirt road that led back to Mexico City. "*You* can't believe it. You're not the one who almost got his camera busted. Who was that guy?"

"Diego. He's Alejandro's chauffeur."

"He sure didn't seem like a chauffeur."

"He's never been like that before. He was almost a different person. At the end, when he apologized, that's how he normally acts."

"Look, I don't know what your pal Villalobos is up to, but I can tell you he's no businessman. Those Doberman thugs were for real, they were packing heat and they meant business. Did you see the way they went for my camera?"

"Yeah. I did," Brian said, tired of Stone's haranguing. "Now will you just shut up about it?"

After a few minutes of driving in silence, Stone turned to Brian and said, "How did you get mixed up with someone like Villalobos?"

"I met him at a party," Brian said. "He's a kind of an entrepreneur. Wealthy. Eccentric. Politically connected."

"So is he afraid of getting busted by Nava or something?"

"I don't know. I don't think so. He's too smart for that."

"What's your connection with him?"

"He's an anthropology buff. He's interested in my work on ritual sacrifice."

"It seems like a lot of people are interested in your work these days," Stone said.

But Brian was thinking about what had just happened. Diego had told them that Villalobos was in the city, and the absence of the Mercedes bore him out. But as they were getting into their car, Brian had glanced back at the house. It could have been his imagination or a trick of the light, but he was sure he'd seen someone watching them from the window of Villalobos's study.

The garbage heaps of Nezahualcóyotl smoldered like funeral pyres, their noxious miasma wafting over the outskirts of Mexico City. Brian held a handkerchief to his nose and turned away from the burning refuse, wishing that he'd never allowed himself to be talked into coming along. Stone planned to do a series titled "Villages of the Damned" for *Life*. The point of the piece, Stone explained, was not to exploit the pain and misfortune of helpless people, as Brian had accused him of doing, but to call attention to the peripheral dangers of radiation use in medical science. "It doesn't matter if you're talking about chemical spills in India, hurricanes in South Carolina or atomic disasters in Mexico," Stone had said. "The poor always suffer the most. Don't take my word for it, come and see for yourself. Besides, my Spanish stinks and I need an interpreter."

They had been wandering in the world's largest slum for a good half hour without seeing a single radiation victim. The directions that the hospital gave them had stopped making sense as soon as they left the main highway and entered the puzzle of rutted dirt lanes and makeshift dwellings. When the street they were on became too narrow, they had parked the car and paid one of the local urchins to guard it. Inquiries for Pancho Chávez had been answered with mute stares and Brian had begun to simply ask "radiation?" in the hopes that someone would get the idea. "I hope they don't think we're offering them cesium," Stone remarked. When Brian pointedly invited him to find a better way, Stone kept busy by taking ghetto stock shots.

Brian was ready to give up the whole enterprise when his radiation query was answered by a vigorous nodding of a young man's head. A few minutes later, they were inside one of the tin shacks looking at a woman with bandages covering both of her hands and arms. Since she seemed to assume that they were from the hospital, she readily removed the dressings to show them her wounds. Brian was sickened by what he saw—purple welts and patches of discolored flesh that had begun to peel off like cheap wallpaper. After that, Brian stayed outside while Stone took pictures.

Waiting for his friend, Brian got a firsthand look at a world he had only glimpsed in documentaries and news magazines. Yet what impressed him the most was not the wretchedness of the lives around him but the degree of human dignity that managed to exist in spite of it. Once he got used to the aromas of burning rubber and open sewage, Brian realized that Nezahualcóyotl was not a uniform sinkhole of poverty but a complex community defined by infinite shades of disadvantage. While some of the dwellings were little more than cardboard boxes with a door cut into one side, others had stucco walls, foundations and even electricity, the voltage pirated from the main power lines with wires that had been stitched together from scraps and odd pieces. Several of the shacks had working televisions and rudimentary plumbing. Instead of the ennui and indolence that he had imagined, there were ample signs of industrious ingenuity. Even the poorest hovel evinced a humble pride of ownership. Brian saw ceilings plastered with flattened soda cans and walls papered with bread wrappers. Many of the houses had a yard or garden planted with beans or maize or herbs that went into the dishes he could smell simmering over open fires. And everywhere he looked the oppressive weight of want was lifted with the gay pigments of a Mexican fiesta—pink, aqua, lime and yellow—and, occasionally, a solitary white cross.

One house in particular caught Brian's attention. The structure was a lopsided collage of metal sheets, wood planks, plastic bottles and broken shards of tinted glass. Each side was dominated by a different primary tint, giving the place the whimsical appearance of a child's drawing. A plastic pink shower curtain served as the front door and the windows were screened by the radiating spokes of discarded bicycle wheels.

"How did you know?" Stone asked.

"Know what?"

"That Chávez lived here. This is his place."

Before Brian could react, Stone had pushed aside the shower curtain and stepped inside. Brian followed, not at all sure that journalistic license gave them the right to barge into strangers' homes, but unable to control his own curiosity. The first thing he noticed was the lingering reek of disinfectant. Then, as his eyes adjusted to the interior light, he found himself standing in a living room with a flat plywood roof and a dirt floor. The cramped dimensions and the round windows gave the place a vaguely nautical atmosphere, as if the house had run aground on the shoals of greater Mexico City. Except for the shower curtain and a couple of gaping light sockets, the rooms were devoid of furniture, clothing or any other sign of human habitation. While Stone fired away with his Nikon, Brian peeked into the two windowless cubicles that had apparently served as nurseries and inspected the cramped alcove of the kitchen. He opened the single cupboard mounted over the wood-burning stove. No pots, utensils or plates. Not a scrap of food. Just a few startled cockroaches running for cover.

A small crowd had gathered outside. The murmuring gang of neighbors peeked in through the spoked windows, but no one crossed the threshold.

It dawned on Brian that they were trespassing in somebody's home without the owner's permission. "I don't like the look of this," he said. "Let's get out of here before those people lynch us."

"Maybe they can tell us what happened."

They stepped outside and were enclosed by a circle of wary faces. Brian introduced himself and waited for an interrogation, but no one questioned their right to be there. It obviously wasn't the first time strangers had invaded the Chávezes' house. When he began to ask questions, the neighbors just stared blankly. Then a woman in a blue smock spoke up. She lived two houses away and had known the family ever since they had arrived from the countryside two years before. She had seen the magic rock but Chávez wouldn't let her touch it. "Gracias a dios," she said, sinking to her knees and crossing herself. The ice broken, others freely offered their opinions.

"What did they say?" Stone wanted to know.

"They think the cesium was a piece of heaven that fell to earth. They think it was a message from God."

"What kind of message?"

"The arrival of Judgment Day, the end of the world. They believe Chávez was chosen by God to spread the word."

"That explains this," Stone said, pointing to a corner of the living room. A framed picture of Chávez and his family lay against the wall. A battery of candles and religious charms surrounded the photo. Chávez was smiling, and a girl of about four years old sat on his lap with a headless doll in her hands. Brian stooped down and picked up a small plaster object that had been nestled in the strands of a beaded rosary.

"Look familiar?" Stone asked.

Like a man reading Braille, Brian traced his finger over the figure, which held in its hands two circular objects. "It's Tezcatlipoca, Smoking Mirror, the god of death and destruction."

Brian pulled up to the wrought iron gate and waited for the security guard to come around to the car window.

"I'm here to see Don Villalobos," Brian told him in Spanish.

"Name?"

"Brian Mendoza."

The guard scrutinized the clipboard in his hand, nodded, and swung the gate open. Brian followed the hedge-lined drive through a manicured paradise of trees, flowering shrubs and rose gardens. The grounds of the mansion were surrounded by a high cement wall topped off by shards of broken glass. A peacock preened on the lush lawn, its emerald head tilted suspiciously in Brian's direction. He had heard of the opulent estates of the Chapultepec Hills district, but it was still hard for Brian to believe that he was less than thirty minutes from the slums of Nezahualcóyotl.

Villalobos was waiting on the veranda in his customary slacks and open-necked shirt. He seemed much more at ease than the last time they had met. After greeting Brian with a warm abrazo, he led the way into an airy saloon of whitewashed walls and red tile floors. The furniture was upholstered in pale kid leather and the coffee table was a sculpture of glass supported by a tortured chunk of bronze. Framed paintings hung from the walls. Brian didn't need to ask to know that they were originals.

"With a house like this, I don't know why you would ever need to go to the country," Brian observed.

Villalobos made a knowing murmur. "It used to be the residence of the Spanish ambassador," he said. He noticed Brian admiring a series of small renderings of vivid sunsets. "Do you like them?"

"Very much. It looks like the work of one of the Impressionists."

"I quite agree," Villalobos said. "But we are both wrong. They are Riveras."

"Diego Rivera, the muralist?"

Pleased, Villalobos said, "They are the exquisite afterthoughts of a great genius. He painted them at the end of the day, using whatever oils were left on his palette."

"I would have never guessed."

"You are hardly alone," Villalobos said. "Rivera was indeed a great muralist, but his artistic expression had many other forms that are unfortunately less well known. You see, before he developed his own style, Rivera passed through many different phases, but the world sees only the most obvious one. That, my friend, is the story of Mexico! We are trapped in the prism of frozen perceptions. Rivera too. As you can see on that wall over there, his career included a Cubist period. And this one behind me—"

"El Greco."

"Yes," Villalobos confirmed. "The Greek, as the Spaniards called him. Born Doménikos Theotokópoulos on Crete. The island of paradise."

"A paradise like Tepoztlán?"

Villalobos's smile evaporated.

"Diego told me about what happened yesterday. I'm terribly sorry. Those men are like animals, and sometimes they slip off the leash. Believe me, I don't like them any more than you do, but they are necessary for security reasons. You see, in America, success is celebrated and the wealthy are admired. To Mexicans, success should never be flaunted, and those who have it must enjoy the fruits of their labor behind guarded walls. It's a difference in national psychology. An American sees his neighbor driving a Cadillac and he says, 'How can I get one too?' Whereas a Mexican would say, 'Does he really deserve it?' "

A servant appeared with a bottle of scarlet wine and two glasses. Villalobos turned to Brian. "I took the liberty of ordering some Beaujolais."

When they were alone again, Brian asked, "Do you think Nava can really reform the system?"

Villalobos tasted the wine and nodded before answering. "No one person can reform the system. There must be a consensus. Any constitutional change must have the support of both the elite and the people."

"Do you support him?"

Villalobos sat back with his hands on his knees.

"I support whatever is best for my country," he said opaquely.

"And how do you decide what is best?"

"It is not for me to decide. I leave that to the forces of history."

"But don't you—"

"Please, Brian, please." Villalobos held his hands up beseechingly. "I am so tired of politics. It's all anyone talks about anymore. I am much more interested in hearing about your work at the museum. Have you made any progress?"

"Well, yes, actually," Brian said. "I think I know where Xotl was headed, and I'm beginning to understand why."

Villalobos leaned forward in his chair.

"That's very exciting, Brian. Does Zapata know this?"

"No."

"Be careful of him, Brian. All he cares about is his reputation and that damned museum of his. He'll ruin you if you get in his way."

"Thanks for the warning. But I think I've figured out how to protect myself."

"And the precious bundle," Villalobos asked. "Have you ascertained its nature?"

"Not yet. It could be gold, or bones, or something else."

"Bones?"

"The key is the Xólotl myth," Brian explained. "I think our traveling priest identified with the god, particularly his role in the creation of mankind."

"The bones of the Sixth Sun," Villalobos mused, "the future race of men."

"Maybe. I think that Xotl was trying to revive Quetzalcóatl so that he could fight Cortés, the impostor. I'm also pretty sure that Xotl was planning to reenact the creation myth. But I won't know for sure until I reach Xotl's final destination."

"Fascinating," Villalobos said. "When do you leave?"

"This weekend."

"Good," Villalobos said. "The sooner the better. And are things going with La Malinche?"

"You mean Marina."

"Yes, of course. I apologize. Have the wounds of misunderstanding healed?"

"I think so. We're having dinner in Garibaldi Plaza tomorrow night."

"Ah, Garibaldi," Villalobos said. "What a wonderful place. The mariachis are the sound of Mexico's soul—so alive and full of passion."

"I've never been," Brian said, putting down his glass, "but I'm looking forward to it."

The peacock's shrill screech intruded through the window. "An ungainly sound for such a beautiful creature, don't you think?" Villalobos observed. "Those birds are living proof that mother nature has a cruel sense of humor."

"Something strange happened today," Brian said. "I was at

Nezahualcóyotl, the house of the man involved in that radioactive accident—"

"Accident?" Villalobos asked doubtfully. He rotated the wine glass in his fingers. "Are you familiar with the Aztec rite known as the New Fire Ceremony?"

"Yes," Brian said. "Every fifty-two years, at the end of the Aztec century, a man was sacrificed to the sun god and eviscerated. A fire was lit inside his corpse and people with torches waited in line to take part of the fire back to their homes. The flame signified the rebirth of Huitzilopochtli . . ."

". . . and the certainty that the sun would burn for another fifty-two years," Villalobos added, his eyes lit by some interior source. "A coincidence? You're the anthropologist, Brian. You tell me."

Brian felt a twinge of foreboding, a creeping fear that he could no longer trust logic to explain what was happening. "I'm not sure anymore," he said.

The splinter of a smile crept across Villalobos's lips. "Ambiguity paves the way for the deepest understanding," he said. "Did you ever notice how one can see a faint star better by not looking directly at it? Our peripheral vision is actually more sensitive to light than the part that lets us see clearly."

Brian felt a wave of vertigo, like a high-wire acrobat afraid to look down and lose his balance. "There's something else I don't understand," he said.

"Ask me anything," Villalobos said, spreading his arms in a gesture of accommodation.

"If you were here yesterday, then who did I see watching us from your study window in Tepoztlán?"

Villalobos's arms dropped. "I'm sorry," he said, "but I can't tell you that."

"I thought there were no secrets between friends."

Villalobos rose and laid a fatherly hand on Brian's shoulder. "You mustn't be offended. It's for your own good, really. It's vexing, I know, but even in the pursuit of ultimate truth, some questions are better left unanswered."

• • •

The Camino Real was Mexico City's most famous hotel, a favorite of movie stars, moguls and visiting heads of state. But Stone told Brian that his only reason for staying there was the fountain that thrashed outside the glass-enclosed lobby like a miniature tsunami. "It's like those wave machines they have in Arizona," Stone had said. "Before I leave I'm going to take a surfboard in there and hang ten."

Brian stared at the hypnotic whirlpool of green water and conjured the absurd image of Stone doing radical maneuvers on the mechanical waves. He shook his head and continued through the split-level reception area and past the Rufino Tamayo mural to the elevators. Stone opened the door in a towel, his health club physique still dripping from the shower.

"Hi," he said. "I'll be ready in a minute. The key to the mini-bar is on the dresser."

Brian helped himself to a beer and sat on the bed munching cocktail peanuts and watching Spanish MTV. A teen idol type, his hair in a fifties pompadour, crooned into a microphone while a synthesizer band pumped out a generic rock background. Brian pressed the remote control and settled on a dubbed version of *48 Hours*. Stone came out of the bathroom and glanced at the screen. "I never knew this movie was set in Spanish Harlem," he said as he pulled on his trousers. "Come to think of it, Eddie Murphy does look sort of Puerto Rican."

"I'll tell him you think so. Hurry up, Marina's meeting us at the restaurant."

"Keep your shirt on." Stone ran a comb through his hair and reached for his jacket. "So I guess the letter worked, eh?"

"I guess. But I think she wants it to stay platonic."

"Give her time," Stone said, closing the door behind them. "The girl just stopped hating your guts, right? By the way, what did you tell your boss?"

"I told him I was going to see the ruins at Uxmal."

"And he bought it?"

"Hook, line and temple."

They hailed a mini-taxi outside the hotel and Brian told the driver to take them to Garibaldi Plaza. When Brian had asked Marina what kind of place it was, she'd said only, "It's something everyone who comes to Mexico City should see at least once."

As the car halted for a red light on Reforma, a boy darted out in front of the traffic and started juggling a trio of striped balls. His face was painted white with a clown's sad eyes and oversized red lips.

"Damn," Stone exclaimed when he saw the juggler. "I knew I should have brought my camera."

"You'll have plenty of chances to burn film tomorrow," Brian said. "Tonight is for fun, not art."

"I resent your implication that art is not fun," Stone said archly.

When the light turned green, the juggler ran among the cars collecting coins from the drivers. Brian passed a dollar bill through the window and the boy's face broke into a rubbery smile.

The cab let them off at the edge of a large plaza ringed by restaurants and bars. Music suffused the air. Mariachis of every size and shape, their tight pants and short jackets embossed with gold thread and studded with silver buttons, loitered under the trees and around the fountain smoking cigarettes and tuning their guitars. Several of the troubadours had lashed their instruments with rope to the smaller branches, as if the tools of their trade might sprout legs and wander away unless properly tethered.

In the center of the plaza, a small crowd had gathered around a trio playing a woeful ranchera. The onlookers joined in on the chorus, a soaring crescendo of unrequited love that brought tears to the eyes of the burliest men.

Brian followed Marina's directions to a spacious saloon on the far corner of the plaza. The doorman took one quick look at Brian and Stone and lifted the velvet rope stretched across the entrance. She was already seated in one of the booths that ran parallel to the bar. True to the spirit of the surroundings, she wore a flared skirt and white blouse with a delicate lace trim. It was a far cry from the uptown attire she usually wore, and it reminded Brian of the night that they became lovers.

"You look beautiful," Brian said, and he kept his eyes on her long enough to show that he meant it. "Marina Soto, I'd like you to meet my former roommate and present friend, Mr. Greg Stone, the best photojournalist north of the Rio Grande."

"So you are not the best south of the Rio Grande?" Marina asked teasingly.

"I am when I'm in Mexico."

Brian started to order a beer but his two companions wouldn't hear of it, insisting they all start with a shot of tequila. When Brian reminded Marina that he and Stone had a plane to catch, she brushed aside his concern. "As my father likes to say, today is today and tomorrow is tomorrow."

"The mañana syndrome," Brian said dryly. "But what about the things you neglected to do the day before?"

Marina shrugged. "It's too late to change the past."

"I hope that's not true," Brian said.

Their drinks arrived and Stone raised his glass toward Marina. "To the woman who stole my best friend's heart."

"Oh really," she said, "I didn't know it was missing."

Brian tipped his glass against theirs and drank, determined to change the subject. Stone and Marina were like antipodal magnets, inherently alike yet prone to resist each other.

A mariachi band had begun to serenade the next table, and the sweet violins and tangy horns were like an elixir. No sooner had the first band finished when another began. Brian recognized the sound instantly; a sweet filigree of notes stretched over lusty guitars.

"They're from Veracruz," he said, and Marina squeezed his hand in affirmation. "But why haven't they come to our table?"

"You have to pay them," Marina explained. "The musicians are for hire."

"Then we should make sure they have plenty of work." Brian excused himself and went over to negotiate with the band leader. When he returned a minute later, Stone and Marina were in the midst of an animated discussion.

". . . but I like to shoot with Kodachrome film and my memory only turns out Polaroids," Stone was saying. Then to Brian, "I told her that I missed my camera and she said it is better to be a participant than an observer—kind of a strange view coming from a journalist."

"Why do you say that?" Marina asked.

"Because journalists are by nature objective, unless you happen to be one of those reporters with an axe to grind."

"You mean with a point of view."

Stone leaned forward across the table. "The camera doesn't lie, but journalists often do."

"You're wrong," Marina said, bristling with indignation. "The camera lies by what it leaves out. Lenses distort reality. Filters alter the light. The shutter freezes motion."

"And I suppose you think reporters capture reality without a personal bias," Stone snickered.

"Excuse me," Marina aimed her finger at him. "I never said that. But you've raised a valid point."

"Oh, thank you, señorita," Stone said sarcastically.

"You're welcome," she shot back without missing a beat. "The fact that a journalist's name is attached to every story is a reminder that the events being described have been filtered through a human mind. What makes pictures so dangerous is that they carry this false mystique of objectivity—since a picture is taken by a machine, people assume it is true. They are more likely to see it as a factual document."

Stone turned to Brian. "Do I look like a machine?"

"No," Brian said through gritted teeth. "You look like someone who has forgotten his manners."

"Ouch," Stone said calmly. "You see," he said, turning back to Marina. "I can't be a machine. Brian just kicked me under the table and it hurt like hell. Machines cannot feel pain."

Marina looked at Brian. "Did you really kick him?"

"I didn't bring him here to trade inanities with my date."

"That's insulting," Marina said.

"I didn't kick him that hard."

"I mean to me. You act as though I can't fend for myself in a simple conversation."

"Yeah," Stone chimed in, "we were exchanging ideas, not bodily fluids. Is that all right with you?"

"I don't believe this," Brian moaned, covering his eyes with his hand.

"I think he's angry with us," Stone said.

"Maybe we were too intellectual for him."

Laughter. At his expense. Stone excused himself to buy another round, and Brian felt Marina's slender fingers on his. She was looking at him with concern, but her eyes were crinkled with humor.

"I'm sorry if we got you angry," she said, "we were just having fun."

"You two have the strangest notion of fun," Brian said, but he was already responding to her touch.

"What can I do to make it better?" she asked soothingly.

"Kiss me," he said. And she did. From somewhere nearby, the harpist led the band into the first notes of "La Guacamaya."

"You remembered," she said.

Brian nodded as Stone returned with a tray of fresh tequilas. "Well, so much for trying to foster a cerebral atmosphere around here."

Stone peered at Brian like a doctor checking the condition of his patient.

"I feel much better now," Brian told him. "And I apologize for losing my temper."

"No apology necessary," Stone said. "But for being such a dope, I condemn you to two shots of fermented maguey juice."

"Not maguey," Marina corrected, "agave. Pulque is made from maguey."

"She's right," the harpist agreed.

"A toast," Stone said. "To friendship and agave and love."

As they clinked their glasses together an old man with a Polaroid camera came to their table, hawking snapshots at four U.S. dollars each. Stone bought the whole roll, taking pictures of the band, the bartender and even several of the patrons. They stayed for several more songs, until everything was spinning in a pinwheel of light and laughter. Stone was the first one to come to his senses, paying the check and leading the way to the door. They crossed the plaza to the street, where he managed to pour himself into a cab. His last words were, "I love to fly hung over."

Alone, Brian and Marina strolled in the shadows as a single mariachi strummed a romantic ballad. "I want you," he said, squeezing her tight.

"I want you too," she replied. "But not like this."

"I'm not drunk."

"Yes you are. Besides, being a gentleman, you have no choice but to respect my wishes."

"You're right," he said, deflated. "I guess this is good-bye."

Marina kissed him again. "Until tomorrow anyway."

"What did you say?"

"I've decided to come with you," she said. "I've already bought my ticket."

"You're joking," he said, suddenly sober.

"You need me," she explained. "I know this country; I can help. Yucatán is very dangerous right now. I don't want to have to write your obituary."

13

Zacatuche is healing. The wounds were not deep and soon he will be able to walk again. The Zoquean bandits also killed one slave and escaped with some water and half of our food. Many other things were lost in the struggle, but I count ourselves lucky. Tonatiuh fought well; he has the heart of a warrior. He saved Zacatuche's life by jumping on the attacker from a boulder and killing him with his own spear. As I feared, the Place of Thorns is rife with unknown perils. The plants are becoming strange to us and we refuse to eat them for fear of being poisoned. When we come across a friendly village we are sometimes able to barter for our dinner. But I have traded most of our beads and other valuables and worry that without help we will soon starve.

Acama left us at the southern border of the One World, shortly after the news came that the invaders had been driven out of Tenochtitlán. He *begged us to return with him, saying that the danger is now past. But I know this is not so. I will not be fooled, for Quetzalcóatl has spoken to me about the end of the Fifth Sun, a terrible time when brother will turn against brother and vultures will feast upon the flesh of the dead.*

Despite my words, I could see hesitation in the faces of the others. It was the first serious test of our faith, and Tonatiuh did not disappoint me. I told him of my vision, described the cunning trickery of the white strangers, who will return again in greater and ever more ruthless numbers. "I will follow Xotl and honor the wishes of our lord Quetzalcóatl," he said, and I saw the others bend to his will as they would to their leader. I know now that he was sent to me by Quetzalcóatl and that he will not fail me at the crucial moment.

Our Lord has said that his cousin Tláloc will give us sanctuary, but we are entering the land of the Mysterious Ones, who do not know our gods. At night I dream of an awesome city built in the jungle. There are stone serpents crawling down the stairs and pictures of young warriors adorning the surrounding temples. The biggest temple is a four-sided pyramid topped by a square that tears a hole in the heavens. The hole becomes dark and solid like a tunnel or a cave. I am inside a cavern in which a ceremony for Tláloc was taking place. I know this because I am the priest. I am holding a dagger in my hand. Then all is awash in red and I am awake staring at the morning star. The dream leaves me troubled. Quetzalcóatl has promised to show me the door to the Thirteenth Sky. But how will I recognize it. Could it be the temple in my dream?

We continue south beyond the Land of Life. Already we have seen signs that we are entering an enchanted world unlike any other. After many weeks of unrelenting savannah and chaparral, the land has suddenly turned green and the air is moist and heavy with heat. In some places the trees have become so numerous that they blot out the sun. The plants, which are richly abundant, seem to have been touched by a magician's wand. There are flowers the size of a man's hand and trees that appear to be upside down, their roots growing from the branches down into the earth. The animals who live here are also strange. Monkeys, which I had previously only seen tethered in the imperial zoo of the emperor, are plentiful. They dangle from the trees and chatter like angry merchants as we pass. They seem to tickle something in Loma, who laughs girlishly when they appear. There are other creatures too, impossible an-

imals that seem to have been formed by the nightmares of a madman. One has the head of a weasel and a long neck that ends in the body of a fox, except that the paws are like a man's fingers, black and fleshy and tipped with claws. Another is like a pig whose snout has been stretched like dough, making a hairy trunk that it uses to root for plants and small insects. There are snakes of many sizes and colors, birds of dazzling plumage, and insects and butterflies of every shape and hue. Not all the denizens of this emerald paradise are so benign. On several nights, when the fire is low, we have heard the jungle tremble at the growl of the jaguar, a sound so terrifying that even the fearless Citlax becomes watchful and uneasy.

Just as the land has become fertile and blossomed, so has Loma ripened like some soft-skinned fruit. Despite the hardship of our travels, she does not complain or question our purpose. She seems to understand that her role is to nurture the blessed magic inside her. As if in response to Loma's transformation, Tonatiuh has himself sprouted into manhood. He has become taller and broader and his features have sharpened handsomely so that it is now Loma who watches him with furtive longing. His gait, once gangling and awkward, has become steady and assertive. His easy, carefree laugh has been replaced by the brooding silence of a young adult. I have done my best to accelerate his education in the ways of Quetzalcóatl and he has listened and learned well. I know that a time will soon come when I have no more to teach him. His knowledge is maturing, and its fruit will soon be ready to nourish the gods. Already they are opening his mind to their secrets. One day we happen upon a field covered with millions of blue moths, and when they take wing together it is as if a cape of shimmering feathers has risen to meet the sky. Seeing this, Tonatiuh turns to me and says, "I understand now; we are entering your dream."

Thirty thousand feet above the Land of the Mysterious Ones, Brian stuffed the photocopy of the codex back inside his bag and picked at an airline breakfast of soggy bacon and eggs. Could Xotl be the father of Loma's child? The concept was troubling, not the least because it blatantly violated the ethics of the Quetzalcóatl cult. But if Xotl and Tonatiuh weren't responsible for Loma's pregnancy, then who was?

Marina stirred beside him, her head resting lightly on his shoulder as she slept. Across the aisle, Stone was immersed in an airline flight magazine, a pair of complimentary headphones dangling from his ears. He had gallantly offered to trade seats with Marina so that they could sit together, but it was obvious that he resented the unexpected addition to their party. Travel had a way of magnifying even the smallest tensions, and Brian knew it was up to him to smooth out the rough spots and keep the peace.

Ideally, they would have made the trip by land, stopping at Palenque and other places that Xotl and his companions might have lingered for food and water. But there was neither time nor money for such an elaborate expedition. Besides, Brian wanted to be able to explore his theory without the help or hindrance of Zapata and Villalobos, who seemed to orbit around his life like two celestial bodies in cosmic opposition. His connection to each of them was clouded by conflicting facts and the gnawing apprehension that he was being manipulated for some purpose he still couldn't fathom.

There was another reason too: in some numinous way his own quest had become a mirror image of the priest's pilgrimage. Like Xotl, Brian was risking everything on the gamble that he was right. He knew what it was like to listen to one's heart and plow ahead against the odds, to make the inner leap of faith over a chasm of doubt. If Brian failed now, he would never again have the courage to follow through on his convictions. Like Xotl, he had reached a place where his fears and dreams intersected and pointed in a single direction. There could be no turning back; the road led only forward. And so what had initially begun for Brian as an academic exercise, a means of professional validation, had taken on a personal urgency that went deeper than any manmade excavation.

Over the past few weeks Xotl had become increasingly real to Brian, until he could almost visualize the stooped figure of the renegade wise man, wrapped in his soiled white robes, both isolated and empowered by his vision, pushing on against fatigue and worry to achieve his sacred mission. At times it seemed as if Xotl had intended his tangled string of clues to be discovered by Brian and no one else, as if his voice alone could have reached Brian over the din of intervening centuries and compelled him to listen. It was impossible, Brian knew, yet he found himself heeding the call of the dead magus like a man possessed, or a boy stumbling in the dark as he tried to follow in his father's faded footsteps.

Brian reached into his flight bag and unfolded his map of the Yucatán. Curving out from the horn of Mexico like a scorpion's stinger, the peninsula was divided into the state of Campeche in the west, Quintana Roo in the east and Yucatán in the north. Campeche and Quintana Roo were colored green, indicating tropical and semitropical forest, with blotches of blue for mangrove swamp. A wide band of orange for dry scrub forest took up most of the state of Yucatán, from the Colonial city of Mérida to the border town of X-cán some two hundred miles northeast. This surprised Brian, who had always imagined the Yucatán as an unbroken expanse of rainforest crawling with iguanas, coral snakes and crocodiles. Obviously, Brian had a lot to learn about the Land of the Mysterious Ones.

Their plan was to land in Cancún, rent a car and drive south down the Caribbean coast of Quintana Roo as far as the Maya fortress of Tulum. From there they would backtrack to Playa del Carmen and turn inland on the road to Mérida, stopping along the way at Chichén Itzá. From Mérida it was less than an hour's drive to Loltún. Brian was well aware of the odds against them. Hundreds, perhaps thousands of cavities and underground springs riddled the limestone under the riverless plateau like the pores of a giant sponge. Only a handful had been explored and even fewer were open to the public. Loltún was a relatively obscure cave located in the heart of the Maya Puuc region, near the town of Oxkutzcab. The closest city of any size was Mérida, a good fifty miles away by winding roads that were well off the principal tourist track. His strategy was to find Negrete first and then get him to lead the way to Xotl's subterranean shrine.

The stewardess removed his tray and the fasten seatbelt sign blinked on. Brian put the map away and nudged Marina awake. "I will never drink tequila again," she murmured. Stone, who had also dozed, was trying, in vain, to sweet-talk the stewardess into bringing back his breakfast.

"Boy," Stone said as he yawned and rubbed his eyes. "I just had this terrible dream that I was hung over and trapped in a flying bus."

The plane dropped through the clouds and Brian looked down at the main coastal highway, a linear strip that bisected the thick carpet of green. Then the jet banked over the Caribbean and the window filled with a dozen shades of blue, the colors progressing from pure sapphire to aquamarine. Brian had read somewhere that the site for Cancún had been selected during the 1960s by a currency-hungry computer, and the assembly line of high-rise hotels that hugged the shore seemed to confirm that rumor. As they leveled out for their approach, Brian glimpsed a lone telephone pole and several decapitated palms, their tops blown off by the remorseless breath of a Stage Five hurricane.

Stepping out onto the tarmac, Brian was embraced by a blast of humid air. "Qué rico," Marina said, basking in the tropical warmth. They hurried through the terminal and rented a jeep from the Mexican branch of Avis.

By luck or farsighted design, the coastal road from Cancún to Tulum was built several miles back from the sea, providing a much-needed buffer between the shore and the speeding traffic on highway 307. To reach the beach, Brian took a ninety degree left turn onto one of the myriad unpaved roads and followed it to a hidden cove with a small sandy beach and a restaurant overlooking a pristine lagoon. Below them, a handful of people were snorkeling in the transparent water amid flickering schools of angelfish and blue chromis.

Brian ordered a beer and watched the swimmers frolic in the chain of translucent pools. "Look at that," Stone said, pointing to a wedge of gravel that poked into the ocean. "That's a breakwater for a marina. Plans for a Carlos and Charlie's can't be far behind."

"From what I've heard it wasn't always like this," Brian said. "As recently as the fifties the Yucatán was the kind of place where tourists were kidnapped and roasted on spits for dinner."

"You're kidding."

"No, it's true," Marina broke in. "Yucatán was the last part of Mexico to be conquered by the Spaniards. There were many violent battles. Until very recently, the Maya were quite inhospitable to outsiders. From what I know about the Cult of the Talking Cross, they still are."

"What about the Cruzob leader?" Stone asked her. "The guy they call El Grito."

"It means the Shout," Marina explained. "His real name is Eduardo Garza. They say he is a Maya descendant who was trained in the arts of destruction by the Shining Path guerrillas in Peru. He is thought to be responsible for the latest revival of the Cult of the Talking Cross, an armed insurrection that almost drove the Mexican army out of the Yucatán in the 1850s. According to the legend, a white cross appeared in a vision to the Chan Santa Cruz Indians and told them to attack the foreign invaders who were trying to take their land. It almost worked. At one point they had the garrison at Mérida surrounded and cut off. They would have wiped it out if it hadn't been for the flying ants."

"The flying ants?"

"Just before the final assault on Mérida," she continued, "a cloud of flying ants filled the air. For the Indians, the ants were a signal from the gods that it was time to harvest their crops. Since they would rather die than offend the deities, they dropped their weapons and headed to their farms. It gave the Mexicans a chance to regroup and counterattack, and within a few years the rebels were forced to surrender."

"Interesting," Stone mused. "But something tells me the Cruzob won't make the same mistake twice."

"Not likely," she agreed. "Garza has given the Cruzob teeth as well as a tongue by marrying the fierce nationalism of the Maya ancestors to the tactics of modern-day guerrilla warfare. He is also a master of media manipulation. So far he's only killed a handful of tourists, but the bad publicity is costing Mexico millions and giving quite a headache to the minister of tourism."

"You sound as if you admire him," Stone observed.

"He's a murderer and a megalomaniac," she said tartly, "but his link to the common people is very strong. The Indians love him. He understands their dreams and they repay him by risking their lives. That kind of passion can change the world. Yes, I respect him for that."

"Do you think I could get Garza to pose for me?"

Marina gaped at him like he was deranged. "Sure," she said, "but it would probably be the last picture you ever took. No one outside the Cruzob has ever seen his face. He moves among the villages like a shadow. There are those who think that he doesn't really exist."

"What do you think?"

Marina shrugged. "It doesn't matter what I believe. The movement is real. The rifles and bombs are real. The rebellion is real."

"What about the Cruzob?" Stone persisted. "If there are so many of them, how hard could it be to find a few to interview?"

"Haven't you been listening?" Marina asked, her voice rising. "These people are not a tourist attraction—they're revolutionaries. And they'll kill you if they think it will help their cause." She looked at Brian. "Is that why you two came down here, to risk your lives for a few snapshots?"

"Not exactly."

"Then why?" When Brian didn't answer, Marina leaned back in her chair and crossed her arms. "Well?"

Brian hesitated. Keeping her in the dark could be dangerous, but telling her too much might be just as bad. "It's research for my dissertation," he said finally. "We're going to see a man about some artifacts. It's museum business."

"I understand that," she said. "But you could at least have the decency to tell me where we're going."

"Just trust me. I promise I'll tell you all about it when we get closer."

"Well, I'm sure you lovebirds will work it out," Stone said. "Meanwhile, maybe Marina and I can do a piece on the Cruzob together. I'll take the pictures, you write the words."

Marina's eyes shifted to Stone. "You think you can use me to get to the Cruzob and then you fly off and sell your pictures to magazines around the world. No thanks. Besides, I'm already on assignment for *The Globe*. Of course, if you want to take some pictures on spec and submit them, I can't stop you."

Stone whistled in admiration. "You drive a hard bargain, señorita," he said with a phony Texan drawl. "Let's see who gets the story first and then we'll negotiate the terms."

"No problem, hombre," Marina said, taking up the gauntlet.

"That's just great," Brian said grimly. "This trip is going to be hard enough with you two playing dueling deadlines."

"Don't worry," Marina said. "We're professionals, remember?"

Brian threw down some money on the table and stood to leave. "That's what worries me."

Back on the road, Brian coaxed the jeep past a herd of hollow-haunched cows and onto the main highway. He drove fast enough to overtake several tourist buses beginning their day trips from Cancún. Stone fiddled with his lenses and struggled to enunciate the signs posted along their route.

"X-Caret . . . Akumal . . . X-Cacel . . . Tan-cah . . . Strange language," he murmured.

"Only when you say it in English," Marina retorted.

They were about twenty kilometers from Tulum when they hit the first roadblock. Two men in olive green fatigues were waving the traffic down while a third questioned the drivers. The green trucks flanking the road were not empty; Brian estimated there were about a dozen well-armed men in each.

"I went through this once in Acapulco," Stone said. "Just give them twenty bucks and they'll leave you alone."

"I don't think that's such a good idea," Marina said. "These aren't federales; they're Mexican Army regulars. Let me do the talking and keep your camera out of sight."

The officer in charge approached the jeep, his eyes hidden behind aviator sunglasses. He was about their own age, Brian guessed, but he already had the pelvic strut of a man who was used to wielding power. The patch over his left breast pocket bore the stenciled letters COL. TREVIÑO. He asked for their passports and they handed them over.

"Turistas?" he asked, his glasses trained on Brian and Stone.

"Periodistas," Marina corrected, explaining in Spanish that they were there to do a story on tourism in the Yucatán. She handed him her press pass, which the soldier scrutinized for a good thirty seconds.

"Your destination?" he asked in fractured English.

"Oxkutzcab," Brian said.

Treviño frowned as he flipped through their passports. He stopped on the pages with their pictures and ran his thumb over the official seals as if expecting them to rub off. "Only terrorists go there," he said, letting the implication hang in the humid air.

"*The Globe* is hardly a terrorist newspaper, señor," Marina said. "In fact, several government ministers sit on its board of directors."

"I know about your newspaper," Treviño answered brusquely.

"Then you also know that my reasons for going there have nothing to do with terrorism," Marina said. "If you wish to contact my editor and explain to him why the media is being barred from Oxkutzcab, I'm sure it would make a very good story for tomorrow's edition."

The officer turned and looked at the parked army trucks, and for a moment Brian thought their bluff had been called. "That area is dangerous," Treviño warned, handing back their passports. "The roads to Chichén Itzá, Mérida and Uxmal are protected. But the small towns are crawling with Cruzob. The terrorists will shoot anybody they don't recognize. If you go there, we are not responsible for your safety."

After they had driven a while, Stone said, "Would you have really called your editor?"

"Sure," she said. "But if they had decided to stop us there would have been nothing he could do."

He whistled and put his feet up on the dash. "So much for the power of the press."

Brian pressed on the accelerator, grateful that, for the moment at least, the noise of the wind had drowned out their voices.

At the turnoff for Tulum, Brian parked next to a souvenir shop hawking rows of Iguana T-shirts and baseball caps with PYRAMID POWER stitched across the bill in neon letters.

"You don't actually expect to find anything here, do you?" Stone asked.

"No, but there's something I'd like to take a quick look at."

Immediately upon passing through the stone arch that marked the entrance to the seaside ruins they were approached by a throng of men in white shirts offering to be their guides. Brian rebuffed them politely and led his companions across the sloping lawn to a building that their guidebook identified as the Temple of the Diving God.

Stone pointed to the small relief carving on the north facade. "Isn't that the same god you were looking for in Tepoztlán?"

"Maybe," Brian said. "See those things coming out from the sides?"

"Yeah."

"Some of my colleagues have interpreted those as wings. They think this might be the manifestation of a bird or honeybee god."

"But you don't," Marina said.

"No, I don't. And if we're on the right track, I think I'll be able to prove it."

"What's that big one over there?" Stone pointed to a square structure ahead of them.

"That's the Castillo," Brian told him. "It's the biggest building on the site."

"I'm going to check it out." He rummaged in his bag for a telephoto lens. "I'm pretty sure I can sell this as stock to the travel mags."

"Help yourself," Marina said, but Stone was already bounding across the grass. They watched Stone work the site like a Nikon-bearing commando, stopping, kneeling, firing off a few shots, then trotting off again in pursuit of a better angle.

"He looks at the whole world through the lens of his camera," Marina observed. "It's funny, at first I couldn't understand how you could be friends with someone like that."

"But now you do?"

"I'm beginning to," she said. "I think he's your alibi."

"Alibi for what?"

"He helps you hide from who you really are. He brings out your objective, voyeuristic side. He's the gringo in you."

Before he could argue she grabbed his hand. "Come here, I want to show you something." She led him to the other end of the site, to an outcropping of rock that overlooked a postcard perfect beach embraced by vertical bluffs. "It's so beautiful," Marina sighed. "It's just the way I remember it."

"You've been here before?"

"Once. When I was a little girl. Before the tourist buses started coming."

Perched above the placid blue sea, the temples of Tulum sparkled like gems on a setting of silver stone. Had Xotl been here too? It was certainly possible. The Maya city of Tulum had collapsed by A.D. 1000 but there was little doubt that the site had remained a religious mecca well into the sixteenth century. He looked out over the expanse of flat blue water and tried to imagine the Spanish explorer Juan de Grijalva sailing past Tulum for the first time. It was Grijalva's description of

Tulum's majestic walls and towers that had drawn Cortés to the uncharted shores of the New World.

Spotting them from the base of the Castillo, Stone waved and disappeared behind an ancient wall.

"Why wouldn't you tell me we were going to Oxkutzcab?" Marina asked.

"Why didn't you tell me you were on assignment for *The Globe*?"

"I said it just to shut him up," she said. "He thinks the Cruzob are ready to pose for *People* magazine. It'll be a miracle if he doesn't get us all killed. Now answer my question."

Brian looked out over the wrinkled blue skin of water. "Can't you see I'm just trying to protect you?"

"Really? It looks to me like you're trying to protect yourself." Stone shouted and waved to them from one of the nearby temples. "Or maybe him."

"He has nothing to do with it."

"Then why is he here?"

"Because he's my friend."

"And what am I?"

"Marina, don't talk like that."

"Then give me a reason not to."

He answered her by taking her in his arms. As he kissed her, Brian sensed they were not alone and opened his eyes. Beyond the beach and jagged cliffs, Stone was standing on the flat summit of the Castillo, his telephoto pointed in their direction.

The road to Chichén Itzá was a narrow gash of blacktop bordered by unbroken walls of dense jungle brush. The unrelenting curtain of green, hemmed in by the cloudless sky, made Brian claustrophobic, and he found himself longing for the next town or intersection—anything to break the numbing monotony.

Marina, her hair trapped in a white visor, was engrossed in her notebook, while Stone kept busy by cleaning his cameras and humming old Beatles songs. Now and again they passed a smoke-spewing tourist bus headed for Chichén Itzá, but the traffic was lighter and the roads were so haphazardly marked that Brian worried he would miss the turnoff. He gripped the steering wheel tight when he saw an army convoy moving up in the rearview mirror, but the soldiers showed no interest in them as the pea green trucks barreled past.

"I guess they've met their bribe quotient for the day," Stone muttered as he aimed a can of compressed air into the core of his telephoto.

"Let's hope so," Brian said.

They were a few miles from Chichén Itzá when Brian pulled over at a roadside stand for cold drinks. A gang of jabbering children quickly surrounded the jeep and he had to wade through a thicket of small arms and hands to give Stone and Marina their Cokes.

"Hurry up, the vender wants the bottles back."

"What are those kids saying?" Stone asked.

"They say there's a cenote over behind those trees," Marina told him. "A big one."

"What's a cenote?"

"It's a kind of spring or natural well."

"So? I thought it rained here all the time," Stone said, draining his soda.

"Actually, Yucatán is a huge piece of limestone," Marina told him. "There are no rivers and the land can't absorb the rain so it gets very dry. The water in cenotes comes from underground streams. It's exceptionally clean. The Maya believed that cenotes were sacred."

"The kids say they'll take us there for a dollar each," Brian said, starting to get behind the wheel.

"What are you doing?" Stone asked him.

"I'm getting in the car."

"Don't you want to see the cenote?"

"I thought you were tired of tourist traps."

Stone shook his head in dismay.

"Do you see any tourists around here? C'mon, Bri," he teased. "Where's your sense of adventure? Marina just said cenotes are sacred. You can't get a better recommendation than that."

Brian regarded Stone warily.

"He's right," Marina agreed. "You should see it."

Brian said, "Then let's all go."

"No, thank you," she said. "I've seen cenotes before. I'll stay here and watch the jeep." She wiggled her fingers over her shoulder. "Don't fall in."

By now the clique of young tour guides had grown to at least a dozen. Small hands latched on to their fingers, belt loops and pant legs, pulling them along while the older kids led the way with ceremonial authority. Stone was enjoying himself immensely. "Lighten up, Livingston," he called as he turned and snapped Brian's picture. Then he was gone behind a clump of cactus. When Brian rounded the corner Stone and the boys were already squatting by the rim, staring into the gaping abyss.

Reflexively, Brian lurched back from the precipice. Stone whistled a falling note. "It's not the Grand Canyon, but I'm impressed," he said.

The cenote was at least a hundred feet in diameter with crumbling walls that plunged straight down into its murky depths. Gnarled tree roots jutted out from the exposed earth and small birds swarmed in the shadows like bees in a jar. As Brian and Stone stared, one of the boys tossed a rock into the shady maw. There was a long silence, then the hollow plunk of water. Another boy appeared with a length of rope tied to a metal pail. He let it down until it was invisible, then reversed his movements and hauled it back to the surface.

"Tomen. Se puede tomar."

"They want us to drink it," Brian said.

Without hesitating, Stone dipped in his hand and brought it to his mouth.

He swallowed and smacked his lips. "Delicious," he said. "Go ahead. Live dangerously."

Brian took a sip. The water was cool and clean, with a filtered sweetness that sang on his tongue.

"It tastes good," he admitted.

Stone paid the two ringleaders, and asked Brian to make sure they understood that the money was to be shared equally among them. The boys did a dance of affirmation and dashed off, a dusty stampede of chattering children in their wake.

"She doesn't like me much, does she?" Stone said as they walked back to the car.

"I wouldn't say that," Brian replied, grateful that he didn't have to look him in the eye. "She just has a different way of seeing things."

"Communists usually do."

Brian stopped and looked at his friend. "You've got to be kidding."

"I wish I were," Stone said. "Did you hear the way she was talking about Garza, like he was Robin Hood or something? She might not be a card-carrying commie, but I know a true believer when I see one. Personally, I don't give a shit. It's what I see her doing to you that gets to me."

"What is she doing, Greg?"

"I don't know, it's like she's recruiting you or something. The little comments, the sexy come-ons, the whole PC package—it's like a game to her, like she's trying to trick you into being somebody you're not."

"Oh, I get it," Brian said, mocking him. "She's a conniving Cruzob seductress and I should thank you for being here to save me from her evil spell because you know who I *really* am."

"That's right," Stone said. "Hey, don't get me wrong, amigo, I don't blame you. I mean she's a nice piece of ass. Just don't—"

Brian punched Stone in the chest before he could finish the sentence. The blow was mainly ceremonial—just hard enough to shut him up. Stone touched the spot where Brian had hit him, his eyes glittering with disbelief.

"Greg, I'm sorry," Brian said.

But Stone just brushed past him. "Fuck you, Brian," he said as he stalked down the trail. "Fuck you both."

Behind the wheel again, Brian drove in silence while Stone sulked in the back seat. If Marina noticed the strained atmosphere in the car, she didn't show it. Brian felt rotten about what had happened at the cenote, but he was still too irritated by his friend's insensitivity to apologize. Stone had found a vulnerable spot and zeroed in, ignoring the warning signs, until Brian had lashed out in an act of emotional self-defense.

Brian avoided Stone's eyes as they carried their bags through the arched lobby of the Mayaland Hotel. They checked in and took two adjacent rooms—one for Marina, one for the boys—in the modern wing of the building, with its unobstructed view of Chichén Itzá's domed observatory, and agreed to rise early the next morning to beat the tourist swarms.

On their way to the dining room they were approached by a

stocky dark man with a quarter-moon smile and thick raven hair. He had the typical oval face and squat physique of the Maya, and wore a white shirt, blue slacks and sandals.

"Excuse me, Señor Mendoza?"

"Yes."

The man acknowledged Brian with a deferential bow. "Pleased to meet you, señor," he said in a high-pitched, slightly nasal English. "My name is Jorge Cartas. I would be honored to have the pleasure of being your guide to Chichén Itzá."

"Thanks, but we don't need a guide," Brian said, but Cartas persisted, following them down the hall and into the hotel lobby. "I have been trained especially to provide information that could make your visit more enjoyable," he said. "There is much of interest that I can show you."

"I'm sure you can," Brian said diplomatically, "but we are planning to visit the ruins very early . . ."

"That is not a problem," Jorge said. "I can meet you here in the lobby at five A.M. or even four A.M., whenever you wish. I have friends at the gate who will let us in before the grounds open to the public. Otherwise you will have to wait until nine o'clock like everyone else."

Cartas tilted his head, waiting for a verdict. Brian looked at Stone and Marina, who both shrugged as if to say, Why not? Despite his reservations, Brian said, "Okay. Six o'clock. Right here in the lobby."

Jorge shook hands with all three of them. "Thank you for your confidence, señor," he said, his smile more incandescent than ever. "I know that you will not regret it."

"Tenacious fellow," Stone observed when he was gone. "I just hope he doesn't bore us to death."

"How bad can it be?" Marina asked. "Besides, you might even learn something."

After a subdued dinner of Yucatán chicken and rice, Brian walked Marina back to her room. She kissed him good night, but didn't invite him in. In the boys' room, Stone was already in one of the two single beds with the lights out. Brian undressed in the dark and slipped into the sheets, wondering if his roommate was still awake.

"You know, physical violence is a good way to end a friendship," Stone said from across the room.

"Yeah, I know," Brian said. "I didn't want to do that. It's just the way you were talking about her . . ."

"I admit I was wrong, in style if not substance," Stone said. "The way I see it we're all stuck with one another, at least for now, so we might as well try to get along. Just don't expect me to roll over and play dead the next time somebody picks a fight."

"I won't. It's just that I have to see this thing through, wherever it leads me. I need a little more slack."

"You can hang yourself with it if it makes you feel better," Stone said dryly. "Now shut up and go to sleep before I change my mind."

The next morning Jorge was waiting for them in the restaurant under a huge mural of a stalk of corn giving birth to mankind. While they had coffee and pan dulce, Jorge sipped black tea and told them about the two years he had spent living with relatives in Austin, Texas, studying English at night, and earning his tuition by going into the desert to collect mesquite, which he then sold to suburban Texans who burned it in their barbecues. "That's when I learned that money makes people insane," Jorge said, shaking his head. "They were rich enough to own a stove, but instead they paid for the privilege of cooking over a smoky fire."

"Sounds like you really miss the U.S.," Stone said facetiously.

"Only the Cowboys," Jorge said, not getting the joke. "I love American football."

The sun was strong, but not yet oppressive, and pockets of cool air lingered in the shade. As they walked toward the ruins, Brian was aware of the lingering scent of night-blooming flowers and the soft crunch of the earth under their boots. Picking up the thread of their conversation, he asked, "So, Jorge, you don't live around here?"

"No, I live with my family outside Mérida."

"It must be nice to live in such a beautiful part of the world."

"It was more beautiful before the Spaniards and the Mexicans came," he answered.

"Have you seen any rebels," Marina interjected. "The Cruzob?"

"Yes, I have seen them."

"We saw some army trucks on the highway. Do the rebels have a chance?"

"The rebels will win," Jorge said adamantly. Then, like a passing squall, his gentle disposition returned. "But what do I know? I am not a political man, I am a tour guide and now it is time to earn my pay." He stopped and dramatically raised his voice. "Before you, señores and señora, is the tallest structure in Chichén Itzá. The Maya called it Kukulkán."

The pillbox summit of a four-sided pyramid rose like a mirage above the tree tops. Its jagged symmetry was both massive and exquisitely precise, timeless and indelible. Vertical stairwells flanked with carved panels marched up each side; a cosmic ladder to the gods. At the base, a pair of serpent's heads, their stone fangs bared, seemed ready to strike. Though he had seen it in photographs a hundred times, Brian was still impressed.

"The Spaniards first arrived in Chichén Itzá in 1533," Jorge began, "and even put a cannon on the top of Kukulkán to defend it. But they were unable to conquer the indigenous Maya and a year later they were forced to abandon the site. Chichén Itzá's Classic phase lasted from the fifth century A.D. to about 1100, when the Toltecs arrived from the north. The Toltecs ruled Chichén Itzá for the next two hundred years. It was during this time that the temple was built in dedication to the priest-king Kukulkán, who is also known to the Aztecs as Quetzalcóatl."

They had entered a large grassy plaza the size of a football field. Though he had never been there before, Brian felt a shock of recognition as Jorge took them around the compound of meticulously restored buildings. The ball court, with its elegant Temple of the Bearded Man, reminded him of his game with Villalobos. But it was Kukulkán, with its crystal-cut beauty, that struck the deepest chord.

Though lesser in scale than Teotihuacán, there was something sublime in the shapes of the buildings around them, an otherworldly genius that superseded ordinary notions of time and space. By 1521, Chichén Itzá would have been a ruin, overrun with wild vegetation and abandoned by its people. But there was no question in Brian's mind: Xotl would have come, even if nothing but rabbits and monkeys were there to greet him, if only for the chance to see it with his own aging eyes.

At the base of the pyramid, Jorge picked up a stick and began to draw on a patch of dirt. "The Maya were very advanced astronomers and architects," Jorge told them. "And Kukulkán reflects the Maya mastery of both." Using his dirt blackboard to illustrate the axial alignment of Kukulkán with the equinox and solstice, Jorge explained how the pyramid was a physical representation of the cosmos. Each side of the temple had ninety-one steps, which, if added to the top platform, equaled 365, or the number of days in the solar year. He also described how during the equinox the serrated shadow created by the temple's steps became a serpent's body slithering down toward the ground.

"Where is the serpent going?" Marina asked.

Jorge beamed at her. "No one has ever asked me that before. Follow me and I will show you." The makeshift pointer still in his hand, Jorge led them north from the temple to a wide stone-paved path. He informed them that they were walking on one of the sacbe, or white roads, that were built by the Maya to connect their cities. After going about two hundred feet, Jorge stopped at the rim of a cenote, smaller but not unlike the one that Brian and Stone had drunk from the day before.

"The Maya believed that this was the dwelling place of Chac, the god of rain, whom the Aztecs called Tláloc," Jorge declared. "As you might guess, he was an extremely important deity. During the drought, children and young adults were sacrificed to Chac to make him happy and bring the rains. After a purification rite, the victims jumped—or, who knows, maybe they were thrown—into the cenote and fell to their deaths."

"Want another drink, Stone?" Brian teased.

"In 1885," Jorge went on, "the U.S. consul to Mérida was a man named Edward Thompson. Thompson purchased Chichén Itzá and the land around it for seventy-five dollars. He had heard the stories about the ancient sacrifices of virgins covered with gold and jewels. Between 1903 and 1907, with the help of Harvard's Peabody Museum, he conducted the first excavation into the bottom of the cenote. Mr. Thompson was a smart man. He discovered about fifty skeletons along with many objects of jade, and precious metals. Most of the skeletons were of young boys and girls, so perhaps he was partly right about the virgins."

"What happened to the treasure?" Stone asked.

"That is something *everybody* asks me," Jorge said with a decorous smile. "Thompson smuggled the objects to Harvard in a diplomatic pouch. When this was discovered, the Mexican government expelled him and started a lawsuit to get the treasure back. Many years later, the Peabody returned most of the objects. Most, but not all."

Brian was staring down into the cenote as he heard Stone's shutter click a few feet behind him.

"What about caves?" Brian asked. "Did the Maya ever use them for sacrifice?"

"There is some evidence of that," Jorge answered. "If you came from the east coast you passed the Cuevas de Balancanchen. A shrine to Tláloc, the Toltec rain god, was found there along with some ritual objects, mostly pottery, I believe."

"And what about Loltún?"

"In the Puuc region?"

"Yes."

"A shrine was discovered there, yes. But the caves there are very deep, so who knows? I have only been there once."

"So it's possible that there might be other shrines there that haven't been discovered yet."

"Oh, yes," Jorge confirmed. "It's possible."

"Sounds like we're on the right track," Stone said. Brian shot him a look that said shut up, but Jorge caught it. His black eyes narrowed as he stared at the two strangers.

"Señores, it is a very bad time to be sightseeing in the Underworld," he said.

14

Brian twisted the knob on the jeep's AM radio, but the speakers only hissed and spat like angry beasts. He clicked the set off; it was too noisy anyway to hear anything over the steady whine of the engine. Marina was dozing, her hair doing a hula in the wind. In the back seat, Stone was slumped down with his hands behind his head, his eyes hidden behind his polarized dark glasses. Brian's friend had kept his word, but his self-conscious civility only seemed to have widened the rift between them. The change in their relationship was barometric, a subtle shift in the wind that signaled bad weather ahead.

"Where are we?" Marina asked, rubbing the sleep from her eyes.

"Mérida," Brian said as they entered the colonial capital of Yucatán. "Do you have a place for us to stay?"

"Not here," Marina answered. "The fax lines were down so I couldn't make a reservation."

"I guess we're on our own. Greg, why don't you look in the guide-book."

Stone flipped through the pages until he found the right chapter. "Mérida is known as 'the White City,'" Stone intoned, "because—and I quote—of the residents' fondness for lime whitewash and for wearing traditional white huipils, guayaberas and panama hats. Sounds like a great place to shoot a Clorox ad. Here's a hotel: Casa del Balam. It means House of the Jaguar. Four stars. Restaurant. Pool. Parking."

"Just as long as it has a phone," Marina said.

"And hot water," Brian added. He was hoping to connect with a local anthropologist that Guillermo had said might be able to give them some logistical tips before they headed on to Loltún. He still hadn't shaken off the mood of foreboding that had gripped him at Chichén Itzá. Jorge's warning about the Underworld had been spoken in utter seriousness. Was he a rebel sympathizer, or just an ordinary Maya with a mystical bent? More to the point, was there any difference between the two?

Brian navigated the tidy streets past houses with red and blue tin doors and noticed that the city's sobriquet was still accurate. The buildings, many of which were actually white, were clean and well maintained. The inhabitants, in their bright clothing and bustling gait, displayed a modern, almost cosmopolitan flair that he hadn't seen anywhere else in the Yucatán. Bougainvillea and roses dangled from window boxes and couples strolled in the main square past outdoor cafés with tiled fountains. Despite its age, the place had a youthful energy, and Brian remembered reading somewhere that Mérida was also a college town.

Yet, for all its genteel charm, the city seemed oddly anxious, a white flower blooming in the shadows. Even now, more than a hundred years after the Caste Wars, Mérida had the compressed, introverted stance of a besieged city. The town was like an island surrounded by a foreign army, except that it was the city itself that was foreign and unnatural here. It was almost as if the rebel-infested jungle were a ravenous animal, biding its time, sending its rotting, sickly-sweet breath on the midnight breeze, patiently waiting for the right moment to storm the gates and drag Mérida, kicking and screaming, back into the sixteenth century.

Contrary to its savage moniker, Casa del Balam turned out to be delightfully civilized, with a Colonial decor that rang true to the city's history as a bastion of European influence. Their room overlooked an almond-shaped swimming pool and a patio decorated with cement replicas of Olmec idols. Once they were settled in, Brian got on the phone and started calling the numbers that Guillermo had given him. There was no answer on the first two. The third call was answered by a Mexican woman in Spanish.

"Está Señor Bill Sonnichsen en casa?" Brian asked, assuming he was speaking to the maid.

"This is Mrs. Sonnichsen," the woman replied in English, informing him that her husband was expected home in half an hour.

Brian stopped by the adjacent room, where Marina was making a call through to Mexico City. The television was tuned to a Mexican news station and Brian watched it while Marina was on the phone. Despite increasing signs of civil unrest, the U.S. was backing President Nava, at least until his address to the nation, which was scheduled in a few days. There were rumors that the Mexican leader was planning to announce sweeping democratic reforms and terms for a truce with the opposition. The report added that Raúl Tolsa had evaded a nationwide manhunt and was still at large. The broadcast ended with a picture of the fugitive.

When Marina hung up, Brian was staring at the screen with disbelief.

"Is something wrong?" she asked.

"No. I don't know. I'm not sure anymore," he said. "Tolsa is with the opposition, isn't he?"

"Not necessarily," she told him. "He has many friends and many enemies both within and without the government. We won't know whose side he's on until he is caught." She stood behind him, her fingers massaging his shoulders. "We may never know," she said distractedly.

"What's wrong, Marina?"

"Your political instincts are very impressive," she told him. "We just got a tip that a renegade faction of the PRU is going to try to block Nava's announcement."

"I thought Nava was the leader of the PRU."

"He is, and that's what makes him so dangerous to the reactionaries. He's the only one in the country who has the power to make real change. I need to be back in the capital day after tomorrow. The opposition is holding a meeting with Nava at the end of the week."

"What happens if they can't reach an agreement?"

"Then there'll be a civil war."

"I'll have what I came here to get by tomorrow night," he said. "In any case, I'll make sure that you get to the airport in time to make your plane."

"Thank you."

There was a knock on the door. It was Stone, saying that Sonnichsen was on the line. Getting on the phone, Brian told him the reason for his call. The anthropologist cordially explained that he had plans for later in the evening but would be happy to meet them for a drink at the hotel. A half hour later, Sonnichsen was already waiting for them in the bar when they came down. A tall, solidly built man in his forties with thinning blond hair and a dun-colored beard, his blue eyes were pale almost to the point of being colorless, but his long face was kind and intelligent. Like many northern Europeans, he spoke flawless English and smoked hand-rolled cigarettes.

He had come to Mexico fifteen years before for a two-week vacation and wound up staying six months. "When I went home for Christmas that year I felt like a man who was suffocating," he said. "Everything seemed the same—the people, the language, the cars. Denmark is a small country, homogeneous, set in its ways. I felt like a foreigner there. I decided to come back and try to live here. My parents and my friends said I was crazy. That's when I knew I was making the right decision. Then I met Consuelo and fell in love. We were married and had two children—Jens and Christina. Now this is my home."

Sonnichsen described himself as a "photographic anthropologist." His book on Mexican graveyards had been published in Denmark, England and Germany. "But I can't get a publisher in Mexico," he added with a strangled laugh. "The government pretends to care about the Indians, but they only have money for the dead cultures. When you talk about the living Maya there is suddenly no interest."

He held up his large hands in frustration. "You're surprised? Just look at the Mexican television shows. You only see white faces, Spaniards and Europeans. Mexico can't stand to look at its own face."

"Maybe that's because its face is always changing," Marina said. "Mexico is still a very young country."

"And what about the rebels?" Stone asked.

"The rebels are not the problem," Sonnichsen said sternly. "The system is the problem. The people are simply tired of being ignored. The government builds statues of Indians in Mexico City. But here nobody cares about them. In terms of uncovering the past, the Cruzob have been more effective than all the anthropologists. They are bringing the past into the present, you see."

Sonnichsen had spent the previous two years taking pictures for a book about the agrarian life of a small village north of Mérida. The book would follow the annual cycle of a milpa, or small corn field, from planting to harvest. "The Maya saw the world as a flat layered square," he explained. "At the corners, four bearded gods called Be-cabs held up the sky. In the center of the earth stands La Ceiba, the Tree of Life. The roots of La Ceiba stretch down into the Under-world, and the branches touch the heavens. For the Maya, corn is not just good to eat, it is the source of life itself. For them, farming is a re-ligious act."

"I bet you've seen some pretty interesting fertility rites," Stone speculated.

"I'm going to one tonight. The village is holding a ceremony for Chac, the rain god. The outcome will predict the weather for the growing season. I've never known them to be wrong. You're welcome to come if you like. Very few non-Mayans ever get a chance to wit-ness it."

"Can I bring my cameras?" Stone asked.

"Yes, but you'll have to ask permission before you take any pic-tures."

"Count me in," Stone said.

"I'd like to get on the road pretty early tomorrow," Brian said. "When will this thing be over?"

Sonnichsen looked at his watch. "It starts about now and goes all night, but I'm only staying a few hours. I'll have you back long before dawn. We can all leave right now in my van."

Marina yawned. "It sounds wonderful, but I'll never make it. Maybe next time."

"Greg, why don't you go?" Brian suggested. "I want to hit the hay early so I'll be fresh in the morning. You can sleep while I drive."

"Are you sure?"

"Yeah, I'm sure."

"Well, I guess that settles it." Stone rose from the table. "Give me five minutes to pack my cameras. I'll be right back."

While they waited for Stone to get his equipment, Brian asked Sonnichsen about the road to Loltún.

"That's rebel territory," Sonnichsen said cheerfully. "But I would be more afraid of the army if I were you. They can be unpredictable when you get out of the cities."

"What about Loltún?" Brian asked. "Is it safe to be there?"

A hand-rolled Prince dangled from Sonnichsen's lip while he pondered the question. "It depends on why you are going."

Just then Stone rejoined the table, and Sonnichsen rose to say good-bye. After they'd left, Marina became much more relaxed and animated. Brian had planned to eat at the hotel, but she insisted that they have dinner at one of the outdoor restaurants near the church of Santa Lucía. The menu was a mix of local Yucatán and Lebanese specialties and Marina talked Brian into trying the pepper steak and labne, a thick yogurt sauce served with fried Arab bread.

"Delicious," Brian said after taking a bite. "I have to admit I'd never thought I'd be having good Middle Eastern food in Mérida."

"Actually there's a very large Lebanese population in Mérida," Marina said.

"I'm lucky to be with such a knowledgeable woman," Brian said, lifting his wine glass in a toast.

"The luck is all mine," she said sincerely, and Brian's doubts dissolved in the balmy tropical night. Witty, smart and sensuous, this was the Marina that had bewitched him.

"I love you," he said impulsively.

She drew back and laughed softly. "How can you love a woman that you don't even trust?"

"I do trust you. It's just that there's so much at stake. I figured the less you knew the better off you'd be. I'm bending the rules, Marina, and if something goes wrong, I don't want you to be involved."

She laid her hand on his arm. "Can't you see that I'm already involved?"

The touch of her fingers was making his skin tingle. "There's a good chance that I've found the key to the new codex," he said. "I found it buried in a routine excavation report. Not even Zapata knows why I'm here, or that I'm traveling with a journalist. If he did he'd have my head on a platter. And yours too, probably."

"So why did you invite me here?"

"Well, actually, I didn't."

"That's true," she admitted. "But I know this country much better than you do. Anyway, it's Villalobos you should be careful of."

"Why do you say that?"

"There are rumors that he's involved with a group of reactionary terrorists."

Brian came to a decision. "There's something else you should know," he said. "I saw Raúl Tolsa, just before the warrant for his arrest was issued."

"Where?"

"In Tepoztlán. He was visiting Villalobos."

"So it's true," she gasped.

"What is?"

"That he's plotting against the government."

"I don't believe that," Brian said, clinging to the clarity of Amatlán, the bond of wordless understanding. "He's my friend."

"Are you sure? What will it take to convince you?"

"Some proof would be nice."

"Proof." Marina said it like an expletive. "I've never been bitten by a shark, but I know they have teeth."

Brian laughed in spite of himself. "Oh yeah? How sharp are they?"

She played along, baring her own perfect set. "Very sharp."

"And very beautiful," he said.

She peered at him through hooded eyelids. "I suppose you think you can change the subject by flattering me."

"Can't I?"

"You are hopeless, Mendoza. God, why do I even try? I know you

271

won't listen to reason, but please at least think about what I've said."

"It's a deal," Brian agreed. He took a drink of wine before adding, "It must be terrible to live in a world where there are monsters lurking behind every door."

"Sometimes the monsters are real," she said.

By mutual agreement they managed to avoid politics and anthropology for the rest of the meal and afterward they strolled around the zócalo, hand in hand, content to savor their privacy. Somewhere, out beyond the city limits, the rebels were lurking, plotting their tryst with history. But for the moment at least the threat of insurrection seemed distant and unreal, like a foreign plague or a nightmare from another century.

Brian walked Marina to her door and this time she pulled him inside, her arms coiling around his body like perfumed vines, dragging him away from civilization into the humid swamp of sensation, until he lost his bearings and the jungle devoured him completely.

Stone was supine on the bed and fully clothed when Brian returned to their room to shower and pack. He sat up and yawned, lifting a hand to fend off the morning light. "When the cat's away . . ." he said with a groggy leer.

"Not that it's any of the cat's business," Brian retorted. "How was your Chac ceremony?"

"Well, I doubt my experience in the bush was quite as rewarding as yours," Stone said drolly, "but I think I got some good shots. I also got a serious case of brewer's flu from the local white lightning. I'll say this much about the Maya, those people really know how to throw a party."

"Now that you mention it," Brian said, "you're looking a little rough. Are you sure you're up for the drive?"

"You bet," Stone assured him. "A shower and a cup of coffee and I'll be raring to go."

They had just passed the town of Muna, about fifty kilometers south of Mérida, when the second roadblock came into view. Brian brought the jeep to a halt and waited as two officers approached the driver's side and asked for identification. Just as before, soldiers huddled in trucks parked along the shoulder. But unlike the troops outside Tulum, these men looked alert and battle ready. There was nothing lackadaisical about the way they gripped their guns as they scrutinized the jeep. This was no routine patrol of a well-traveled tourist route; these were fighters who had crossed out of the safety zone and into enemy territory.

Marina greeted the men in Spanish, and after a terse exchange the jeep was waved through.

"They didn't look happy to see us," Brian said.

"They weren't. There's been some guerrilla activity near Uxmal and they're not letting any more people in until the area is secure. There's a curfew in effect from Mérida down to the Campeche border."

"So why did they let us through?"

"I told them Colonel Treviño had given us his personal authorization."

"The honcho with the sunglasses?" Stone said.

"Yes."

Stone crossed his arms and leaned back in his seat as Brian accelerated. "I always wanted to do an insider's photo essay on Mexican jails," he said.

The monotonous flatness of the lowlands gave way to undulating hills as they passed the turnoff to the road to Uxmal. The ruins of the ancient Puuc city were known to be almost as impressive as Chichén Itzá, but Brian decided to skip it. He wanted as much time as possible to track down Negrete and inspect the cave before the curfew forced them to return to Mérida for the night. Every few miles, Brian would slow down and consult the map, just to make sure they didn't take a wrong turn.

Brian half expected to round the next bend and see another army truck blocking their way, but no soldiers appeared to delay their progress. The whole morning, in fact, they only saw two other cars besides their own, both heading in the opposite direction. The jeep seemed loud and conspicuous as they sped through vast oceans of shrubs and tall grass, a perfect cover for guerrilla snipers. Brian didn't allow himself to relax until they saw a sign that told them they'd reached their destination. A few kilometers more brought them to the grimy storefronts and shuttered thatched shacks of downtown Oxkutzcab.

Brian consulted the scrap of paper onto which he'd copied Donato Negrete's address.

"We're looking for 23 Calle Hidalgo."

"That's simple enough," Stone said, surveying the rutted dirt streets. "All we need are some street signs."

Marina laughed. "This isn't San Francisco," she said. "We'll have to stop." Brian parked the jeep in front of a small store and went inside to get directions. For a minute he thought the shop was closed, then he spotted the eyes of a little girl spying at him from behind a potato chip display.

"Buenos días," Brian said, but before he could get out another word, the girl scurried behind a curtain at the back of the shop, leaving Brian alone with the dusty stacks of canned peaches, bulging bags of rice and crosshatch-stacked bars of creamy dulce de leche. The curtain moved again and a small, dark woman emerged. She was dressed in a white huipil and translucent plastic slippers. Her eyes drank him in like dark pools of oil.

"Could you tell me where Calle Hidalgo is?"

The woman merely glared before retreating behind the curtain.

"What did they say?" Marina asked when Brian got back to the jeep.

"The proprietress wasn't very cooperative."

"No lo creo," Marina exclaimed. "You are helpless without me. Start driving and we'll ask someone else."

Brian turned the jeep around and started slowly down the main thoroughfare. "Look," Stone said, pointing down a side street. "How about that kid on the bike."

Brian cut a hard right and sped up until he was abreast of the boy, who looked about ten. Still pedaling, the boy tried to veer away but Brian stuck with him.

"La casa de Donato Negrete?" Marina shouted. In what seemed to be a single motion, the boy pointed toward the end of the block and peeled away from the road into a grove of banana trees. Brian drove about a hundred feet down the street and parked. "It's got to be around here," she said.

"Which one do we try?" Stone asked.

"All of them," Brian said.

They began at the middle of the block and worked their way toward the edge of town. The first house appeared to be abandoned, its walls out of line with the foundation, as if a giant had shoved against it. The second, though equally humble, showed signs of occupation—brilliant flowers grew along the stone path and a bicycle with flat tires leaned against the side. Brian could hear voices inside and as they approached the door. He knocked and waited, knocked again, but no one answered. The third house was a blue stucco building with a wrought iron door embellished by yellow curtains. The stucco was cracked and in need of paint but the yard was tidy and free of weeds. From inside, Brian could smell the inviting aroma of breakfast. He was about to knock when the curtains were pulled aside by a fleshy man with a mouth that seemed too small for his face.

"I'm looking for Donato Negrete," Brian told him. "We're here from Templo Mayor."

The mouth stretched into a genial grin. "Come in please," the man said in carefully pronounced English. "I've been expecting you."

Our camp is on the banks of a gadding stream. Loma and our two remaining slaves are off gathering firewood while Citlax hunts for game. Tonatiuh and Zacatuche have remained with me to plot the next step in our journey. It has been many weeks since Quetzalcóatl came to me in my dreams; we have nothing but our instincts and the stars to guide us. I am about to suggest that, for lack of a better plan, we continue south and follow the river downstream, when I hear human cries for help. We follow the sound to a small clearing where the Mysterious Ones are holding Loma and the two slaves. The war party is made up of six men, the tallest of which would only reach as high as Tonatiuh's shoulder. But they are nimble and strong in a way that tells me they would make formidable fighters. Even if Citlax were with us, there would be nothing for us to gain by a battle. We are exhausted, outnumbered and lost in a land that is

alien to us. I am relieved to see more curiosity than hostility in their faces. The eyes are large and almond-shaped and their foreheads slope downward with the same angle as their flat noses. They carry spears and lances; and leather bands are fastened to the muscles of their arms and legs. Their leader wears a splendid cape of quetzal feathers and a necklace of polished green stones.

Zacatuche, whose uncle married a Maya woman, speaks a few words of the language and willingly acts as translator. The leader calls himself Pacal, after his ancestor who once ruled the place they call the City of the Clouds.

"Ask him to let the woman and the slaves go," I instruct Zacatuche. "They are no threat to him."

At this, Pacal steps forward and replies, "And you, stranger, are you a threat to us?"

"No," I say. "We come in peace. We are pilgrims on a mission from our god."

"And of which god do you speak?"

"The Lord Quetzalcóatl."

"We know of no such god."

"Then why do you wear his plumage? Your cape is made from the feathers of the sacred quetzal, and your necklace of green rocks found in the earth. Quetzalcóatl is the Plumed Serpent, the god of wisdom and creation, he who dove into the Underworld to retrieve the bones of mankind to form the Fifth Sun, who walked the earth like a man before diving into the sea and reappearing in the heavens as the morning star."

Pacal is nodding and his body becomes more relaxed. "Yes, I know of this god," he says, "but his name is Kukulkán. He does not dwell in the City of the Clouds. You must follow the sacbe to Chichén Itzá and there you will find his temple."

"What is the sacbe?" I ask.

"The white road," Pacal says, raising his arm to the east. "It is many days in that direction, across the river to where the mountains meet the flatland. There you will find the white road. It will take you to Chichén Itzá and beyond."

Pacal has begun to turn away when I speak in desperation. "We are tired and hungry and lost, my liege. And you are wealthy and wise. Pray, can we stay with your people a short while before we set out on this arduous journey?"

Pacal looks at me with a mixture of annoyance and resignation. Clearly he would be glad to avoid the trouble of feeding and housing seven strangers, but to deny aid to a band of pilgrims would be to invite punishment from the gods. And there was also the risk—however unfounded—that, if turned away, hunger and desperation might drive us to rob or attack his people. Finally, I have made a deliberate point of appealing to his pride. No man, particularly a chief, wants to admit to strangers that he is poor or lacking in social amenities.

"Is this the full number of your party?" Pacal asks warily.

"All but for one."

"And where is he?"

Before I can call out, Citlax steps out from behind a tree and carefully lays down his spear.

"Truly this one is more fairly counted as two," Pacal observes.

The Maya are pointing and laughing at Citlax. At first Citlax is unsure how to respond, then he too begins to laugh. Compared to them he is a giant. They come closer for a better look at the behemoth before them, touching his arms and wide shoulders. They regard him with respect, but there is neither fear nor awe in their eyes.

We arrive at Pacal's village near dusk. The buildings are made of wood with small cloth-covered doorways and thatched roofs. A few of the larger, more important buildings have been covered in an outer layer of stucco. Loma is assigned to share a hut with several young village women. The men in our party are housed in one of the stucco houses adjacent to Pacal's palace. I notice that several Maya warriors are posted outside our house. Pacal, it seems, is as prudent as he is hospitable.

After we have washed and been fed, I am summoned to a meeting of the village elders. I ask that I be allowed to bring along Tonatiuh, who is my religious acolyte, and Zacatuche, who acts as my translator. After much nervous murmuring, the guards relent. I am pleased to see that the Maya have a respect for holy men that is akin to that of my own people. As honored guests, we are invited to sit at Pacal's side. There is more food and two Maya priests play ceremonial music on drums and wooden flutes. Light and silky, like a flag fluttering in the breeze, the music is rich with nuance, yet I notice that Pacal's sandals are worn thin, and his cape is frayed along the edges. The Mysterious Ones, despite their unbending pride, seem to suffer from a glory that has gone before them. It is there in Pacal's eyes, a subtle pall of solitude, like *someone doomed to reside in the vacant house of memory.*

Over special libations and fine tobaccos, he asks me the purpose of our journey and I repeat that we are on a pilgrimage to pay tribute to our Lord Quetzalcóatl, known to him as Kukulkán. I do not mention the precious bundle, but I describe to him the splendors of Tenochtitlán, with its wondrous mountains and lakes and floating gardens. In turn I learn from Pacal that he is the descendant of a line of kings that reaches back to the time of the Fourth Sun. "My fathers once ruled a great city that rivaled the heavens in its majesty," he tells me. "Tomorrow I will show you where it stood."

"And what was the name of this place?"

"Palenque."

"And what happened to this city, my lord?"

"At first the gods smiled on my fathers and Palenque flourished. But then the gods became displeased and abandoned them; they feared that Palenque would become more beautiful than heaven. They no longer smiled upon the city and the people languished. There was drought, then storms of fire, then pestilence. The crops would not grow, and the cattle would not give birth. The earth became barren. Then the others came."

"What others, sire?"

"The ruthless hordes from the south. They took our women and placed the heads of our dead warriors on sticks. The people left the city and returned to the jungle. Now this village is all that remains. The greatness that was our nation is remembered by the spirits who reside in the City of the Clouds."

Pacal inhaled from the pipe and released a ring of smoke from his mouth. "Tell me, traveler, has Kukulkán abandoned your people?"

"No, he has brought us here and will watch over us until our mission is completed."

"And what mission is that?"

"To create a new race of men, to give birth to the seed of the Sixth Sun." Pacal is impressed, yet despite my confident words, I feel strands of doubt tightening around my heart.

The next day Pacal keeps his promise. The trip is not far and soon we are stepping over the white bones of a dead city. The ruins are of different shapes and sizes—some are tall and gracefully slender, others are low and box-shaped—all with shrubs and trees growing through the crum-

bling roofs and cracked plazas. Even in its egregious state, Palenque is a wondrous sight. There is an observatory, a ballcourt, and a majestic palace with a tower that rises through the creeping mist. I strain to imagine this place as it must have once been, a thriving polity that rivaled in sophistication and beauty any city in the One World. Who were these people, I wonder, and why did the gods desert them? As I survey the desiccated remains of this fabulous place, I am filled with a sense of dread. I know now that if I fail the same fate awaits my own home. In my mind's eye I glimpse the twin towers of Tláloc and Huitzilopochtli defaced with the dirt of centuries, their exquisite carvings and murals obliterated by a funereal layer of dust. Will some stranger someday stand on the wasted shell of Tenochtitlán and have the same thoughts, feel the same fears for his own people?

At dawn we rise and gather our belongings. It is time to begin our search for the white road. Before we take our leave, Pacal fills our bags with food and presents me with a large chest ornament made of brilliant feathers.

"To protect you on your journey," he explains.

I bow before him in gratitude. "Thank you, my liege. We will tell Quetzalcóatl of your infinite kindness."

"Only the tears of mankind are infinite," he answers. Then Pacal lifts his hand and the Maya retreat into the jungle.

As we make our way north the path traverses a series of waterfalls and traces the edge of a steep cliff draped with flowering vines. From our vantage point we see that the forest flattens out ahead into a carpet of green extending as far as the eye can see. The trail dips again and we find ourselves descending into a lush river valley. The sun is blinded by a cataract of fog, making it difficult to gauge our direction. I raise my staff to take another step and then we hear it. The throaty ululation rumbles through the valley like a peal of thunder and a breathless hush descends over the valley. I see Citlax slowly turn his head until his ears are trained toward the river.

That night, as we huddle around the fire, no one dares speak of the jaguar. We nibble at the food that Pacal gave us—tortillas, mashed corn and pumpkin, tomatoes and pineapple—and engage in subdued conversation, pretending not to listen to the chorus of screeching bats and nattering insects. Tonatiuh is withdrawn and pensive; I sense he is steeling *himself for the coming rites. He will make a good priest and his personal power will be sharpened by acute knowledge. Loma's belly has swollen to the size of a watermelon. In a few more weeks she will be unable to travel. But by then, the gods willing, we will have reached our destination.*

There is no moon when I awake. The sound comes again, a snarl that seems to emanate from the bowels of the earth, only this time the source is barely a stone's throw away. The slaves are whimpering, quivering mounds under their blankets. Beneath the dense canopy of trees the darkness is almost tangible. "Don't move," Citlax whispers. Against the backdrop of the smoldering coals, I see his silhouette crouching low, holding a spear at the ready. I grope in the darkness for something I can use as a weapon and my fingers close on the feathered breastplate. In the roaring stillness I can hear the rushing river and then, much closer, a tree branch snapping. If only I could see! Something impels me to toss the breastplate onto the coals and within seconds the glossy plumes burst into flame. Only a few feet away, exposed by the fire of feathers, the jaguar prepares to pounce. In the same instant, Citlax's spear slices through the air next to my head. The cat screams in pain and I can smell its breath, hot and fetid, the exhaust of a mighty killing machine. As the animal writhes and claws at the air I see my form reflected in his jaundiced jaguar eyes. They are the beckoning portholes of an injured demon, twin mirrors of shining yellow and black, the eyes of a god named Smoking Mirror.

Two days later, at the mouth of the valley, where the mountains pan out to a vast wooded mesa, we cross a cactus-filled arroyo and take our first steps on the white road. The sight of the stone-paved avenue, straight as an arrow and as wide as six men, cheers even Citlax, who has been grousing ever since the jaguar got away with his best spear still impaled in its ribs. Again I marvel at the ingenuity of the Maya. Hundreds of years after the fall of their empire, the road they built still admirably serves its purpose. The speed of our progress more than doubles; it takes only a few more days to reach the ruins of Chichén Itzá.

For the first time since leaving Tenochtitlán, we find ourselves in the company of fellow travelers. Most are farmers, laden with fruits and vegetables they will sell in the marketplaces of the small towns and villages that dot the land. On several occasions, however, we encounter other pilgrims who are on their way to Chichén Itzá or the holy ruins of Tulum, a fortress shrine said to be located on a cliff overlooking the sea. With Za-

catuche's help, I am able to converse with them over a shared meal of beans and toasted tortillas and maybe a cup of pulque. From these fragmented interviews I have gleaned that the great temple of Kukulkán is indeed located at Chichén Itzá. It is there that a bearded man who called himself the Plumed Serpent built a new kingdom on the ashes of the Maya civilization. I have also heard stories of a sacred cave near Uxmal where many sacrifices were made in the name of Kukulkán. I am sure now that the Kukulkán the Maya worship is none other than Quetzalcóatl, the Plumed Serpent.

As we approach the outskirts of the fabled city my heart beats faster. Suddenly, looming above the trees is the box-shaped tower of the temple of Kukulkán, just as it appeared in my dream. We enter the spacious courtyard and Tonatiuh asks, "Is it the one we seek, teacher? Is this the doorway to the Thirteenth Sky?" But I am too moved to speak or even stand. I drop to my knees in the shadow of the splendid house of my Lord and pray thanks to him who dwelt there. The dream was real. Quetzalcóatl has not forsaken me. I lift myself up and Tonatiuh is looking at me, his eyes urgent with excitement as he repeats his question.

The time has come to give him the answer.

15

B rian lifted the spoon of menudo and tasted his childhood in the piquant red soup. The tripe and white hominy kernels stirred memories of his father, hunched over a bowl on a Sunday morning, swearing that there was nothing better in the universe to cure a nasty hangover. Brian had always hated the stuff, but now it went down easily, as if his weeks in Mexico had altered his taste buds along with his other senses.

Negrete refilled Brian's cup with hot café con leche and ordered his wife to bring them more tortillas. They were all wedged around the table between the wash basin and the charcoal stove in Negrete's cramped kitchen. In the next room, a woman in a black shawl sat motionless in a wooden rocker, a tattered Bible clutched in her fingers.

Breakfast in Oxkutzcab had not been on the itinerary, but as soon as Negrete learned that they hadn't eaten he insisted that they join him. It was simple peasant fare, and the tortillas were fresh and steaming hot from the grill. Generous in spirit as well as body, Negrete seemed delighted to have visitors from the big city "that can talk about something besides donkeys and corn." Besides, the last thing Brian wanted to do was offend their host. For their purposes, it was important to have him relaxed and fully cooperative.

Negrete slurped his coffee and beamed at his guests. "Good?" he inquired.

"Delicioso," Marina answered.

Stone, his mouth full, nodded and made a thumbs-up sign.

"You can't get food like this in the capital," Negrete blared, taking a pinch of oregano and sprinkling it into Stone's bowl. "Now you will get the full flavor!"

"Thanks," Stone said. "What's this white stuff anyway?"

"Where did you learn to speak such good English?" Brian asked Negrete.

"In Arizona," he replied, his voice becoming thick with nostalgia. "When I was younger, I lived in Tucson with my uncle and sold used cars. Chevys. Buicks. You name it."

"Did you go to school there too?"

Negrete shook his round head. "The University of Mexico. Archaeology and American literature."

"And you've been the superintendent of Loltún cave for how long?"

"Four years," Negrete said, his chest swelling with pride. "No one knows the caves better than I. Not even the bats."

"So why did you wait so long to report the find?" Brian asked.

"The other men asked me the same question," he said with a trace of irritation. "And I will give you the same answer: because the tomb never existed before. About five weeks ago, there was a seismic disturbance of some kind—my mother-in-law says it was a sign from God, but what does she know?—it broke a hole in the wall and there was the tomb. I investigated it the very same morning and reported it immediately."

"What other men?" Brian asked.

"Why, your colleagues from the museum, of course. They came

to collect the artifacts and said you'd be along shortly to examine the glyphs. That's how I knew you'd be coming." Negrete's cheeks puffed out in alarm. "Is something wrong?" he asked. "I followed proper procedure, didn't I?"

"Yes, of course you did," Brian said, regaining his composure. "It's just that we didn't expect them to arrive so soon. We were hoping to photograph the artifacts while they were still in situ. I'm sure you can understand."

"Oh, yes, well, these things happen," Negrete said, his features relaxing. "Luisa," he demanded, "come here and serve our guests more coffee."

As casually as possible, Brian pumped Negrete for details about his other visitors. Two men identifying themselves as Muñoz and Rosas had arrived at Negrete's house the night before and told him they were there to retrieve the artifacts. Rosas was a short man with Maya features; Muñoz, who did most of the talking, was taller and wore a mustache. They had taken several small green stone idols and pendants, some broken pots, and an obsidian knife with a jade handle. To Negrete's knowledge, there had been no sign of gold or other treasure. The men packed the objects in boxes and drove away in an unmarked van.

"Forgive me for saying so," Negrete told Brian, "but it seems strange to me that they did not advise you that they were coming. You do all work together, do you not?"

"We certainly do," Stone said sanguinely. "It's just that the museum is so large, with so many departments. You know what a nightmare the bureaucracy can be. The papers are probably sitting on our desk as we speak."

"You don't have to explain that to me," Negrete said, rolling his eyes. "I understand all too well. It took me three weeks just to get the new report forms from—"

"You mentioned some glyphs?"

"Yes. The markings are quite extensive. They almost cover the entire east wall. I was surprised that Mr. Muñoz and his companion were not more interested in them, but they only had eyes for the book."

"The book?"

"The codex. I had never seen it before. Muñoz found it in a cavity inside the stone altar. It had Indian drawings and inscriptions in Nahuatl."

"Are you sure it was Nahuatl?"

"I only got a very short look at it, sir. Muñoz and his friend left right after they found it. They seemed to be in a hurry."

"I'll bet they were," Stone said.

Brian's stomach turned. He could almost hear Torres's mocking laughter. Someone had tipped him off. But who? On the slender chance that they'd left behind some clue, Brian turned to Negrete and asked, "Will you take us to see the glyphs?"

The fat man wiped his chin and extricated his bulk from the unfortunate chair. "Nothing would give me more pleasure!" he boomed. "It's not a very long walk—no more than three or four kilometers. It's very good for the digestion. Unless, of course, you have a car, in which case it would be much better to drive."

With Stone and Marina in back and Negrete squeezed into the passenger's seat, they set out toward Loltún. At one point they passed a farmer who raised his hand in greeting, but Negrete pretended not to know him. As Brian drove, they traversed a stretch of denuded land. "It used to be green like the rest," Negrete explained, "before the peasants cleared the forest so they could grow corn. But without fertilizer and room to rotate their crops, the topsoil is exhausted after a few seasons and the land becomes useless. Now not even the insects want it."

Brian stared at the naked land, so barren and hopeless under the grinding sun, and struggled to stave off the fear that their journey would prove equally fruitless.

"Turn here," Negrete said, directing Brian down an unmarked dirt road to a small parking lot.

"You are fortunate," Negrete explained, "the army has closed the roads, so you won't be forced to share the cave with tourists."

"Lucky us," Stone said, reaching for his camera bag.

As they neared the entrance to the cave, Negrete shook his head and cursed. "Cabrones," he muttered, using the sole of his shoe to rub off a white cross that had been painted on a large boulder. "It's the second time this month."

"Cruzob rebels?" Stone asked.

"These are not rebels," Negrete growled. "They are just common vandals. They are children who need to be taught some respect."

"What about the cave?" Brian asked as Negrete led them through a thicket of trees toward a shrub-covered escarpment. "Could they have taken anything?"

"They didn't touch it," Negrete replied.

"How do you know?"

"Because it's sacred ground." Negrete let out a bitter laugh. "They think they are muy macho, but they are actually superstitious old women. They fear the ghosts of their ancestors more than the army."

The opening to the cave was smaller than Brian expected and if not for the metal gate that marked the entrance he would have walked right past it. Negrete scrambled into the bushes and returned a moment later with two flashlights. "The electrical power in this part of the country is not very reliable," he apologized. "Don't worry. These will give us plenty of light. Industrial strength Eveready. My uncle sent them to me from Arizona."

He handed one of the flashlights to Brian and led them into a depression that widened as it corkscrewed into the earth. Brian was instantly enveloped in dense, stagnant air. He had always thought of caves as places that provided a cool refuge from the heat of the day. But this one was stiflingly warm. Rivulets of water trickled down the tunnel's walls like sweat.

"It's the humidity," Negrete said as they descended into the murk. His voice took on a pedantic authority as he described how the limestone caves had been formed over eons by hundreds of underground springs and rivers. They walked for at least a mile, through apertures and vaulting chambers adorned with rippling curtains and dripping stalactites, across natural bridges and gurgling rivers that splashed into bottomless gorges, until Brian could almost believe that the surface world of men was merely one level in an endless filigree of corresponding layers. After a while, as Negrete had predicted, Brian's eyes grew accustomed to the dark and the battery-powered beam became less a means of vision than a way of focusing his attention on a particular place or object. As they continued deeper into the cave, their speech became sparse and then ceased altogether, until the only sounds they heard were the steady slap of their shoes on damp rock and the thrilling rush of unseen water.

The cavern floor pitched upward until it slanted at a forty-five-degree angle. Here and there a few crude steps had been chipped out of the rock, but most of their climb was up a ramp of slick stone. Negrete urged them to hold on to the guy rope that had been bolted to the limestone wall to keep from slipping.

"We're very close to the tomb of Tláloc," he said, "but I want you to see something else first," he said.

The passage took on a trapezoidal shape, with the walls slanting away obliquely. Then the ceiling opened up and what they saw brought them to a halt.

"Unbelievable," Stone said as he fumbled in his camera bag. "The folks back home will never believe this."

They were standing near the bottom of a subterranean dome a hundred yards in diameter and almost as high. In the center of the space an immense tree stretched from the floor of the cave up to the roof, where sunlight poured in through a gaping hole. A vortex of tiny, chattering birds spiraled among the branches.

"La Ceiba," Negrete announced. "The Tree of Life. You can understand why the Maya believed that its roots reached into the Underworld and its branches touched the heavens."

As the birds whirled around the tree's vertical axis, Brian had a sense of a faceless clock being wound, the spinning funnel of birds coiling time in its motion. A burst of incandescent light reflected off the rock around him as Stone fired off a shot, but the synthetic glare seemed wan and feckless.

Negrete turned to his guests. "Now I will take you to Tláloc's tomb," he said.

The vibrating din of the birds followed them for a while as they retraced their steps for about forty yards and turned left into an arched threshold. The walls became smoother and more cylindrical, as if a huge snake had bored through the rock. Brian held out his arms and his fingers brushed against the sides until the tunnel flared into a room about twenty feet in diameter. Stepping inside the shrine, Brian recognized the hollow plunk of dripping water. Along the walls, he could see the display cases, boxy and out of place in this world of sinuous curves. In the center of the room, on a stone pedestal, stood the statue of Tláloc.

"The god of rain and abundance, the Lord of the Southern Paradise," Negrete said.

"How old is he?" Marina asked as Stone fiddled with his tripod.

"The statue, we think, dates back to the ninth or tenth century, but, of course, the god himself is much older." There was something in Negrete's tone that made Brian want to see his face, but their guide had turned away. "What you came to see is over here, against this wall," he announced, shining his light to a spot between two display cases that had been cordoned off with a piece of rope. A crude sign warned visitors to keep away from the excavation-in-progress.

"Are you doing any digging?" Brian asked.

"Of course not," Negrete said, "but the turistas don't know that."

Brian pulled the rope aside and aimed his light at the spot where the floor and the wall intersected. The hole was just large enough for a man to crawl through. The displaced limestone bricks lay scattered outside the chamber, as if some force had pushed them out from the inside. By examining the crumbling opening Brian could tell that the blocks had been laboriously fitted together to within a fraction of an inch. The tremor had been a lucky fluke; without it, the chamber might have remained hidden for countless centuries more.

Stone joined them, his equipment unpacked and hanging from his shoulders. "Well, I assume we didn't come this far just to stare," he said.

Brian turned to their guide. "Would you like to lead the way?"

"No, gracias," Negrete averred, gesturing to his stomach. "Understand, it's difficult for a man of my dimensions."

"I'll wait with him," Marina said. "I'm slightly claustrophobic. Brian, you and Greg go ahead."

Crouching on all fours, Brian crawled through the threshold. Then he was inside, alone. Without stopping to think, he scrambled to his feet and winced as his head smacked the ceiling. The room spun for a moment as Brian regained his balance. He cursed and gingerly touched the rising lump on his cranium.

"You all right?" Stone called from somewhere near Brian's feet.

"I think so. Just be careful when you stand up. It's pretty low clearance in here."

A moment later, Stone was half standing next to him. The chamber was about eight feet square, with a narrower annex at one end. The air was acrid with dust and the faintest whiff of copal incense.

"I guess I got spooked," Brian said, trying to ignore the dull pounding in his head.

"Gee, I can't imagine why," Stone retorted. "By the way, what are we looking for?"

"Anything we can find."

Starting at the nearest corner, Brian used his flashlight to scan the walls of the narrow tomb. At first the light only reflected on stone and blotches of something that looked like dried molasses or resin. Then the first glyph appeared, followed by another and another.

"Jesus Christ," Stone whispered. "It's Aztec porno."

Brian's understanding of pictograms was still rudimentary, but what he was able to glean made his mouth go dry. The faded pictograms told a story, the story of a priest of the cult of Quetzalcóatl-Xólotl, the Descending God.

Brian tried to hold the light steady as he moved the beam across the inscriptions. First came the crossed insignia of Tenochtitlán, Xotl's home. Then the image of the priest himself, performing a bloodletting and burning sacred paper bearing the emblem of the Feathered Serpent . . . Curling speech scrolls indicating the vision serpent speaking to Xotl, and on the next line, a woman and the Feathered Serpent in coition . . . The girl alone in her bath with a snail, the symbol of maternity . . . Something he couldn't decode, followed by a temple pierced by an arrow, meaning war or some disaster . . . Footsteps: a journey . . . The symbol of the Southern paradise . . . A second priest . . . The girl, adorned with a diving serpent . . . A cave, probably Loltún . . . A knife . . . Blood trickling down in a sign of sacrifice . . . Then, in quick succession, the symbols for birth, death and the Thirteenth Sky . . . The last few glyphs were faded beyond recognition.

"Looks like someone must've had a hell of a party in here," Stone muttered as he began to set up his camera.

Negrete's round head poked through the breech. "Fantastic, isn't it?" he said, his voice compressed by the rock walls. "The altar is over there, about ten feet to your left."

Stone fired his flash—a blinding bleached light. When Brian opened his eyes again the glyphs were still there, branded into his aching brain. He shut his eyes again and the after-images of the glyphs danced like ghosts behind his eyelids. Bright green, then blue, then yellow, then red. The figures floated through his mind like a neon circus, the gods and mortals swimming in inky space as they performed their lurid passion play.

Brian braced himself against the wall. The dizziness passed, but his head was still throbbing as he swept his beam toward the end of the room. A long gouge in the floor marked where the stone slab had been dragged from the wall and upended. The codex had been hidden in a slotlike depression engraved with small figures. Brian took a step forward and felt a sharp object under his shoe. He bent down and used his fingers to dig it out of the dirt. Too light for stone, he thought it might be a piece of wood or ceramic and held it under the light. It was a fragment of bone, possibly human. Most likely a finger or part of a vertebra. The realization that it might belong to Xotl made him gag. Suddenly starved for air, Brian tried to take a breath, but the darkness closed in around him, pinning him under its weight as he broke into a cold sweat.

The neon figures reappeared, dancing away toward a pinpoint of blazing light. Brian tried to follow them, but something interceded, a swirling presence that blotted out everything else. It surrounded Brian, entering his lungs, filling his brain with myriad shades of indigo and licorice, ash and sooty coal. It was a color defined by the absence of color: the airless void of deepest space. Black like the Master of the Night, the King of Chaos, the Obsidian Knife, the Smoking Mirror.

Brian struggled in vain against icy fingers gripping his heart, squeezing his ribs, sucking out his breath. Then the darkness receded and Xotl was before him, his eyes turned to the heavens, his mouth open to speak. Straining to hear him, Brian could almost touch the priest's robes and feathered headdress. Xotl raised his hand and moved his lips. The words were strange, like the ones in Brian's dream, but the tone and cadence were familiar, soothing and strong, and he knew he was no longer in danger. As Xotl turned and flew into the

290

light, Brian recognized the voice of his dead father.

At the four corners of the world the Becabs began to cry, their tears coursing through a million underground arteries, feeding subterranean springs and rivers, rising against gravity to the roots of trees and underground caves. Gradually, like a leaf floating to the surface, Brian became conscious of the sound of dripping water. Marina and Stone were kneeling beside him, their anxious faces illuminated by the flashlight. Behind them, the statue of Tláloc peered down from his frog throne.

"Gracias a dios," Marina said.

"You okay, buddy?"

"I'm fine," Brian said, propping himself up on an elbow. "I'm not sure what happened."

"You got a nasty bump on your head, that's all," Negrete said. "We must get you outside right away."

Negrete and Marina helped Brian to his feet while Stone packed up his equipment. With every step he felt a little better, and by the time the bright circle of the cave entrance came into view, his headache was nearly gone.

"We should get you to a doctor," Marina said, trying to lead him to the jeep.

"No, really, I'm okay," he said. "Just let me sit down for a minute."

They rested near the visitors center, under a tree flecked with bright yellow blossoms. Two barefoot children, a girl of about eight and her younger brother, approached them with bottles of ice-cold orange soda. As the girl negotiated a price with Negrete, Stone raised his camera and snapped the boy's picture. The boy giggled with delight as Stone reached out to ruffle his raven hair and hand him a dollar.

Marina came over to where Brian was sitting. "I'm sorry, mi amor," she said, giving him a consoling hug. "But maybe it's better this way."

"Oh yeah, how's that?"

"If somebody wants this codex so badly, maybe it's best that you give it up before something really bad happens."

Brian was incredulous. "Are you serious? What could be worse than this?"

"Don't be angry at me, Brian. I know how much this means to you."

"Do you? Zapata duped me, used me, lied to me. I can't just let that go. I can't let him get away with it."

"How do you know it was Zapata?"

"The information came from a museum report. No one else even knew I was coming to the Yucatán, except Villalobos."

"That's still not proof."

"Whose side are you on, Marina?"

"I can't talk to you when you're like this."

"Then don't talk to me."

Brian stood up and walked over to join Negrete, who had plopped down to enjoy his drink in the cleavage of a nearby boulder.

"Thank you," Brian told him.

"Don't mention it," Negrete said, taking a thirsty gulp. "A cold Fanta is one of the few civilized pleasures of this place."

"For the tour, I meant, and for helping to get me out of there. I'd like to reimburse you for your trouble."

"No, no," Negrete insisted. "I don't take money from colleagues. All I ask is that you speak well of me to your superiors in La Capital. In any case, you shouldn't thank me. If you must thank someone, thank the Aztecs who built the tomb, and, more importantly, thank Tláloc and Quetzalcóatl for giving it power."

"I just want you to know that we appreciated it."

Negrete nodded, looking oddly regal perched on his throne of rock.

"The gods speak to those who listen," he said. Then, almost as an afterthought, added, "You heard them, didn't you?"

Negrete was staring at Brian with a strange smile, a knowing, fearless grimace, the same mirthless grin he had seen on the stone face of Tláloc.

Loltún was twenty minutes behind them when Stone turned to Brian and said, "So it looks like you were right after all."

"About what?" Brian asked, his eyes on the road.

"About the cave, about there being something valuable inside. Kinda funny how those guys showed up just before we did, don't you think?"

"Yup," Brian said tersely.

The knowledge that someone had beat them to the cave by mere hours was still like a knife in his ribs. At least he now knew for certain that Loltún had been Xotl's final destination. Someone had been sacrificed there, who and why remained unknown. The answers were no doubt in the Loltún codex, which Brian was now certain he would never get to see. Zapata and Torres had played him perfectly, giving him just enough rope to lead the way to his precious bundle. Had they followed him, or had they known where he was headed all along? The very thought of it made him want to yank the steering wheel out of its socket.

"You know," Stone mused, "I can't help thinking about Negrete's description of the two guys from the museum."

"What about it?"

"Well, it could just be a coincidence, but when I was out with Sonnichsen, he mentioned a couple of anthropologists from Mexico City had been around asking questions about Loltún too."

"Why didn't you say something sooner?"

Stone shrugged. "It didn't seem very significant at the time. But it does now."

"It sure does," Brian said.

As they drove to Mérida the road became a squiggle of looping curves. Now that they were on their way home, the prospect of a rebel attack had all but disappeared from Brian's mind. So he was more annoyed than alarmed when he was forced to slam on the brakes to avoid crashing into another army roadblock.

Two soldiers, their rifles cradled in their arms, barred their way. "No pase," one of them shouted, pointing back the way they had come.

"They're crazy if they think we're going back," Brian said under his breath. In Spanish, Marina asked to see their superior, but the soldiers ignored her.

"They don't seem to speak your language," Stone observed.

"Maybe they'll understand this," Brian said as he honked the horn. The soldiers started at the strident beep, their eyes narrowing with anger.

"Brian," Marina warned. "Please don't do anything stupid."

"Quiero hablar con el comandante," Brian repeated. He honked the horn again, and this time there was a shout of warning from one of the trucks.

"Quiero hablar con el comandante!"

Torn between hostility and duty, the soldiers rocked on their heels. Then the one who had spoken mumbled something to his comrade and the shorter of the two trotted off behind one of the trucks. A minute later the man returned a few steps behind his cursing superior. It was Treviño.

"Oh, great," Stone said. "It's the jefe máximo."

When he recognized them, Treviño's mouth broke into a wide, malicious grin.

"So, I see you refused to take my advice," he said to Marina in Spanish.

She responded in an even, professional tone. "We had government work in Oxkutzcab. Our business is done and we're heading back to Mérida for the night. We have no argument with you. Please tell your men to let us through and we'll be out of Yucatán tomorrow."

Treviño came around to the driver's side of the jeep. He leaned forward until he was close enough for Brian to see himself in the mirrored lenses.

"I don't give a fuck where you were or what you're doing," he said in Spanish, "but I can tell you that nobody is crossing this barricade. There has been rebel activity in the area. Uxmal has been evacuated. So has Tecoh on highway 18. You have two choices: you can go back in the same direction you came, or stay here under my protection until the road reopens."

"When will that be?" Marina asked.

Treviño crossed his arms. "It could be in a few hours, or a few days or a few weeks," he said. "The rebels don't tell us their plans. And if you honk that horn one more time I will personally order your vehicle to be confiscated." Treviño showed his teeth again and marched off behind the trucks.

"What did he say?" Stone asked. When Brian gave him the gist, Stone looked at his watch. "It's three thirty," he said. "If we take the back roads and don't make too many wrong turns, I figure we could be back in Mérida in three to four hours."

"Should we chance it?"

"If we stay here I'll miss my plane," Marina said.

Brian made a U-turn and began retracing their route to Oxkutz-cab. Their plan was to swing back past Loltún and make an arc through the villages of Maní, Teabo and Mayapán. According to their map, the road ended at Mayapán, but Negrete had assured them that an un-paved section extended another thirty kilometers to Sotuta, where they could catch a main road and circle back to Mérida from the east.

Defying an officer of the Mexican Army momentarily boosted Brian's spirits, but he couldn't completely shake the feeling that all the roadblocks and wrong turns were merely symptoms of his own lack of direction.

They smelled Maní before they actually saw it—a faint perfume of charcoal and cinnamon and burning rubber. The shacks along the side of the road became more numerous, then a neighborhood store appeared. Brian slowed the jeep to avoid a pack of mutts fighting over a shapeless lump. The center of town consisted of a few mud-stained white buildings decorated with murals hawking Pepsi and José Cuervo tequila. A group of young men wearing straw hats, jeans and huaraches leaned against a wall with a large white cross painted on it. As Brian drove past, Stone lifted his camera and clicked off a few shots. The men didn't move, but as Brian drove by he could feel them scrutinizing every detail of the jeep and its three passengers.

Stone leaned forward and spoke to Marina. "Those guys were Cruzob, weren't they?"

"How would I know?"

"You know," Stone said. "I saw the way you looked at them."

"You're crazy," she said, reaching for her cigarettes.

The road became steeper and they climbed a small hill with a view of a massive stone cathedral. The church, with its massive bell towers and flying buttresses, seemed incongruous and out of scale with the town that surrounded it. Then the cathedral was behind them and the road dipped into a thicket of mango trees before fork-ing off into two directions. Brian slowed down, looking around for somebody who could give them directions. But the sole witness to their dilemma was a mangy burro who watched askance from his stall beside a banana tree.

"Buenos días, amigo," Stone said, and the donkey stamped his hoof on cue.

"He says it's that way."

"What does the map say?" Marina asked.

Stone spread the guide across his knees.

"It says this road doesn't exist."

"I agree with the burro," Brian said.

"If you're wrong, we're screwed," Stone said. "Let's go back to town and get directions."

Unwilling to suffer another pointless delay, Brian tossed a coin into the air. "Heads is left, tails is right."

"Heads," Stone said.

Brian showed the coin. "I guess it's unanimous." He put the jeep into gear and took the road to the right, following it until the pavement turned to dirt and they were traversing a large cornfield. The plants were still young, no more than a foot or two high, and the stubble of tender green stalks stretched out toward a wooded rise in the distance. Stone was craning his head, as if admiring the scenery, scanning the horizon for someone who could help them. But they were going further into the corn, toward the arid brown hills, away from everything.

"I think we should go back," Stone said.

"I agree," said Marina.

"It just isn't my day," Brian said as he wheeled the jeep around. They were halfway back to the highway when he saw a truck coming toward them. It was an old Chevrolet pickup with heavy-duty tires and a busted headlight. A dozen or so farmers with machetes in their hands were stuffed into the cab and perched on the flatbed. The truck was about twenty yards away when it halted in the middle of the road, blocking their way.

"Christ," Brian groused as the campesinos clambered off. "They could have at least left me some room to pass."

As the campesinos came closer, Marina dug her fingers into Brian's arm. "Brian, don't stop," she said. "They're Cruzob."

But it was too late; the jeep was already surrounded with men holding long steel blades. One of the rebels ordered them to get out. "Andale," he said coldly.

"You want money?" Brian asked him. "Quieres dinero?"

"Fuck you," the man said. "Let's go."

"To where? Adónde?"

He pointed to the shallow irrigation ditch that divided the road from the corn fields. The soaked soil gripped Brian's shoes as he stumbled over a chain of muddy puddles. Meanwhile, another man had found Stone's camera bag and began methodically ripping open the rolls of exposed film.

"Hey, what the fuck are you doing?!" Stone shouted. As he reached forward, one of the bandits stopped him with a neat chop across his forearm. Stone dropped to one knee holding his good arm up to fend off another blow, but Marina had distracted his attacker with her demands to speak directly to his superior. Obviously unaccustomed to such a verbal onslaught from a woman, the man shrank back and called to one of his companions while Brian went to help Stone, who was still squatting in the dirt, gripping the gash in his arm and repeating the word "shit" like a mantra.

"How bad?" Brian asked.

"I can't tell," Stone said through gritted teeth. "It doesn't hurt yet."

Brian pulled Stone's hand away to get a look at the wound, which was on his forearm just above the wrist. Almost to the bone, it was oozing blood at a dangerously steady rate. Brian quickly ripped the tail of his shirt into three strips, wrapping a makeshift dressing around Stone's arm and knotting it tight. "That should hold it for a while," he said to Stone, who was pale and alarmingly quiet.

"How is he?" Marina asked.

"Okay, I guess. But we need to get him to a hospital."

"I'm going with these men to see if I can work out a deal with their leader, a man named Loya," she said.

"You're not going anywhere with those guys."

"Brian, there's no time to argue. They think we're government agents. Our only chance is if I can make a deal with them. I can do that better without you. Besides, Greg needs you here. I'll be back as soon as I can."

"Marina, no," Brian shouted, but she was already in the jeep with one of the guards, driving away in a cloud of yellow dust.

The rebels bound their wrists with sisal twine and blindfolded them. Brian and Stone were forced to kneel in the mud under the blaring sun. So this is how it ends, Brian thought, on a dirt road in the middle of nowhere.

"This man has got to get to a hospital!" Brian shouted. When he felt Stone slump against his side, his anger ignited.

"Listen to me, you Maya motherfuckers! I said this man needs medical attention!" Brian searched his memory for the Spanish word for mercy. Was it misericordia? Yes, that was it. "Misericordia, por favor! Let us go and we won't report you to the federales!"

He was rewarded for his linguistic efforts with a well-aimed kick to the kidneys. Brian doubled over in pain, the rich aroma of damp earth filling his nostrils. Some time passed. Two hushed voices, the discreet murmur of the Mexican peasant, confided out of earshot. Then there was only the whisper of the wind sifting through the corn. Brian was thirsty, but knew there was no point in asking for water. In his mind's eye the field around them became an undulating pool of green, cool and refreshing, the gentle current of leaves carrying him toward the shore and Marina's waiting arms.

The old-crone squawk of a vulture jolted Brian back into reality. He could almost feel the negative touch of its shadow rippling over the corn. His thirst was replaced by fear. A naked animal loathing that started in his gut. Was the buzzard descending now, its greedy talons extended in anticipation? How could something so ugly be blessed with flight? It was almost as if the buzzard denied its true nature until it had swooped to the ground, folded its feathers and hobbled with its tottering clown walk toward a rotting meal, warmed to tender perfection by the naked sun.

Empowered by his fear, Brian decided he had nothing to lose by getting up. But as he started to stand a hand shoved him back down against the dirt. So their guards were still there. But while Brian was glad to be alive, there was something about it that was very wrong. By now they should have killed them or let them go. And what had happened to Marina? Was she dead—or worse? Hours passed—or were they minutes?—as time seemed to melt in the afternoon heat.

Brian had imagined the sound so many times that when the low drumming of the engine finally reached his ears, he dismissed it as another cruel hallucination. Even when the jeep came to a halt a few feet away, he still wasn't convinced that the straining squeal of the brakes or the hot breath of the engine were real. But there was no other way to explain the crunch of boots on the dirt, or the careful hands that cut their bonds and freed his eyes, or the sight of Marina's face floating over an emerald sea of corn.

16

"What the hell took you so long?" Stone was lying in a hospital emergency room in Mérida with twelve stitches in his arm when he looked at Marina and asked the question.

"I already told Brian," she said, taking a drag from her second cigarette. "Loya, the Cruzob comandante, they couldn't find him at first, or maybe they were just trying to confuse me. Anyway, when the men saw you taking pictures, they thought we were government spies."

"So you told him we were press, and that killing us would be bad public relations, and he decided to let us go, no problemo." Stone's voice was dreamy from the painkiller but his eyes were sharp. "But first, I'm sure, he gave you a personal description of the utopia that he's going to build right after he kills anyone who disagrees with him."

"Something like that."

"So you made a deal: my camera and film in exchange for our freedom. Not a bad bargain. Or did they just owe you a favor for being such a good friend of the revolution?"

"How can you talk like that," Marina demanded, "after I saved your life?"

"But that's just it," Stone said. "You *did* save our lives. One minute we were dead meat, and the next minute we were free. Amazing. Almost as amazing as the way someone got to the cave just before us. Funny how they knew exactly where to go? Any ideas, Marina?"

She wheeled on Brian. "Is that what you think?"

He had convinced himself that it was gone, but the faint impression of doubt was still there, like a stubborn stain that wouldn't wash out. "No," he said unconvincingly. "I don't know what to think."

Marina stubbed out the cigarette and stalked over to the office to speak to the receptionist. When she came back Brian tried to touch her but she shrank away and reached for her bags.

"What are you doing?"

"Just get out of my way please."

"Not until you tell me where you're going."

"I'm going outside to wait for my cab. If I hurry I can still make the last plane to Mexico City. Now let me pass."

Brian followed her out to the curb, trying in vain to grab the bags away from her. "Marina, please, don't be stupid."

"I've already been stupid," she snapped, "stupid to think that we could ever be together."

"Marina, don't do this. Greg doesn't mean what he's saying. It's the drugs they gave him. He's just confused, that's all."

The taxi pulled up and she climbed in. "No, Brian, you're the one who's confused. I know now that I can't be with a man who doesn't know what he thinks or even who he is. You have to decide. Until you do, there's no chance for us."

Just before closing the door, Marina hesitated.

"Brian?"

"Yes?" He was tired of arguing, tired of trying to decide.

"If you still care anything for me, just do me one last favor."

"What's that?"

"Leave Mexico. As soon as you can. Go back to your beloved California."

"You know I can't do that."

"You must," she said with real concern. "Something is about to happen. Something dangerous. It won't be a good time to be in Mexico."

"What's going to happen?"

"Please just do as I ask. It's better if you and your friend go. For once, believe that I'm telling you the truth." Then she turned and spoke to the driver and the cab was gone.

Brian stood alone on the curb for a minute, trying to get his emotional bearings. The idea that he'd never see her again didn't make sense, so he pushed the possibility out of his mind, concentrating instead on the imperatives of the present. He let his feet wander in the warm tropical night until he knew what he was going to do. Then he went back to the hospital to get Stone.

After Brian had helped him to the jeep, Stone slumped down in the passenger seat, his arm in a sling. "I guess I really fucked things up for you, didn't I?" he said.

"No." Brian turned the key in the ignition. "I fucked them up for myself."

After a night of fractured dreams, Brian checked out of Casa del Balam and drove Stone to the Mérida airport. Along the way they traded banalities, as if nothing out of the ordinary had happened. But when they pulled up to the terminal, Stone swiveled in his seat and asked, "So what really happened to you in that cave yesterday?"

"I'm not sure," Brian said, shuddering at the memory of the cold black void.

"You know," Stone said as he hoisted his bag out of the back with his good arm, "I'd figured you were acting funny because of your love thing with Marina. But now I'm beginning to think all this Aztec hocus-pocus has really gotten to you."

"I don't expect you to understand, Greg."

Stone lifted his arm in surrender. "Hey, don't blow a fuse, all right? You sure I can't talk you into coming back with me?"

Brian shook his head and tapped his thumb on the steering wheel.

"Thanks anyway. I need some time to sort a few things out."

"Suit yourself, amigo," Stone said. "Look, I know you've had enough of people telling you what to do, but just promise me that you won't go back to Loltún. It's not worth it."

"Don't worry. I'm headed in the opposite direction. Besides, somebody's got to take the jeep back to Cancún." When Stone shot him a dubious look, Brian added, "You're just jealous because you can't come along. You'd better get going before you miss your flight."

The friends shook hands. "You'll always have an address in the real world," Stone said.

"I appreciate it." Brian looked at Stone's bandaged arm. "Sorry about that."

"Me too. Good thing I bought traveler's insurance."

Stone took a few steps toward the terminal and stopped. "Did Marina sell us out?" he asked over his shoulder.

"I don't think so."

"Whatever you say, compadre," Stone said. Then he waved with the back of his hand and ducked through the glass doors.

Brian watched Stone's plane quiver through the rising heat waves and put the jeep into gear, accelerating until Mérida was behind him and his windshield was splattered with dead bugs. Sonnichsen had been quite cooperative when Brian had called him the night before to ask about the two anthropologists who'd mentioned Loltún. Muñoz was a mestizo from Mexico City whom Sonnichsen had never seen before, but Rosas was a local, a Maya who worked as a part-time guide at a luxury campground called Bali Hi, on the Quintana Roo coast near Playa del Carmen. Brian's plan was to find a hotel in Playa and then pay a visit to Señor Rosas.

Brian drove east with the urgency of a man who had nothing left to lose, his thoughts scattering in the hot wind. He broke his stride only once, for gas and a fast lunch, pressing on until he could feel the temperature dip in anticipation of the sea. A swath of azure ocean came into view and Brian found the Playa del Carmen turnoff. The town had originally made its mark as the main landing point for the ferry to the island of Cozumel, but as the strip of beachside restaurants and hotels had grown so had its reputation as a raffish, low-key resort. Brian parked the car and walked out to the dock, where herds of tourists were clambering aboard an air-conditioned water shuttle equipped with airline seats and video screens showing Road Runner cartoons in Spanish.

At the end of the dock stood a man with an iguana lounging on the brim of his sombrero. The iguana was wearing a tiny T-shirt emblazoned with the words BLUE TURTLE HOTEL.

"Dónde?" Brian asked the iguana man.

"Aquí." He pointed north along the strip of white sand. Deciding he would come back for the jeep later, Brian pulled off his shirt and shoes and started walking along the shore. The sand sifted through his toes as he dodged naked blond toddlers frolicking in the wash and dusky college boys in Ray-Ban sunglasses showing off for lissome women stretched out on towels that screamed CALIENTE!

The Blue Turtle was just what Brian wanted: relaxed and quiet and within easy walking distance of the cheap restaurants and bars on Quinta Avenida. Brian rented the upper floor of a duplex cottage with a palapa roof, tile floors, and a small terrace facing the sea. After retrieving the jeep, he changed into trunks and strode out into the surf, letting the waves slap against his legs and chest. He dove in and surfaced in time to see the shadow of a large fish swimming through the blue mass of a breaking wave.

Back on the beach, he stretched out on his towel, watching the unfocused glint of seawater roll down the hairs on his forearm. He thought about Marina and Stone and gravity, the inexorable, downward tug of matter. He could feel it pushing down on him, grinding his chest into the sand. One moment so subtle one was hardly aware of it, the next so strong it was almost unbearable.

"Would you like to play?"

Brian raised his head off the towel.

"Excuse me?"

"I said, would you like to play a game of backgammon?"

He had noticed her before: a lithe brunette in her early thirties, black Lycra suit perfectly molded to her taut body. A few feet away, her male companion was settled into a lounge chair, engrossed in a paperback novel, his eyes shaded by the bill of a Valvolene cap.

The woman treated Brian to a fetching smile. "You play, don't you?" she asked with a slight Southern lilt. "I promise to go easy on you." Before he could object, she brought her towel over and sat cross-legged in front of him.

"Brown or white?"

"Excuse me?"

"Which color of stone do you like?"

"Whatever."

"Then we'll roll to see who goes first."

Her boyfriend peered at them from under his cap. "Maybe he doesn't want to play, Christine." Then to Brian: "Don't let her strong-arm you into anything."

"Was I talking to you?" she asked peevishly. "Just go back to your book, Matt."

Christine explained the rules to him as they rolled the dice. "I go first. Is it all right if I'm brown?"

"That's fine."

"You might feel better if you talked about it, you know."

"About what?"

"About whatever it is that's bothering you. That's the value of making friends with strangers. Besides, we're not the judgmental type." Christine rolled the dice and moved two stones toward her side.

Brian watched as the pieces marched across the board to the cadence of chance. "It was something I wanted very much, I thought I had it, and now it's gone."

"So maybe you were never meant to have it."

"Maybe."

"Does it matter that much?"

He scooped up some sand and let it sift through his fingers. "That's what I'm trying to figure out."

"I'm sorry," she said.

"Why?"

"Because it's none of my business really. I mean, a lot of people come here to forget their troubles."

"I'm not sure I want to forget."

"Then maybe," she said as she bumped one of his pieces, "you should be trying to remember."

Matt and Christine Connor lived in a brownstone in New York City, where Matt worked as a sporting goods salesman. They were both originally from Richmond, Virginia, but didn't meet until the night Christine ran into Matt at an art gallery opening in SoHo. Within minutes they had discovered a mutual appreciation of Diebenkorn's Ocean Park series. They had honeymooned at the Blue Turtle, arriving two days after the hotel had been washed away by a hurricane.

"You know, Albert," Christine said.

"It was Gilbert," Matt corrected her.

"Well, it was a male hurricane, that's for sure. The point is that there was nowhere to stay. There was nothing here but tree stumps and dead fish! Hard to believe, isn't it?"

"Sure is," Brian said.

"It was *beyond* imagination," Christine recalled, picking up the tale. "A few minutes after we arrived, Simon showed up. Our knight in Coppertone armor. He owns the Blue Turtle and another place up the beach called Bali Hi. Anyway, he sat us down and told us not to worry, he'd have our honeymoon suite ready in a couple of hours. And that's exactly what happened. The Maya came out of the jungle and out of nothing, nothing except the jungle itself, they built us a palapa with fallen fronds right on this spot. There was a hammock in the front facing the water. The Indians brought us food, and after dark we went back to their village and sang and drank and danced under the stars. They were wonderful to us."

"It was like some kind of time warp," Matt remarked.

Christine nodded. "We were like Adam and Eve. We ran around naked most of the time. I mean, it didn't matter because we had the whole beach to ourselves. We come back here every year just to remember, just to give something back."

"You say this guy Simon owns Bali Hi?"

"Oh yeah. It's a great place. The floors in the dining room and the bar are just sand and at night the Maya light torches along the paths."

"I'm looking for a man named Rosas. I think he works for Simon as a guide."

"Oh, you mean George," Christine said.

"No, this guy is a Maya."

"George is a Maya," Matt told him. "He leads tours to Tulum and Chichén Itzá. Are you a friend of his?"

"Sort of. I really need to talk to him. Do you know where he hangs out?"

"At Bali Hi, he's got a little office there." Christine looked at Matt for confirmation. "We always see him having dinner."

"Yeah, the best place to catch him is usually at the bar or in the restaurant after he brings the groups back."

"And when is that?"

"Oh, you know, dinnertime. Drinks start at about seven thirty. Everybody sits down at about eight. You should go anyway, the food's really good."

"I think I will."

"Great," Christine chimed in. "We're going too. We'll introduce you to Simon and you can sit at our table. If anyone can tell you where George is, it's going to be Simon."

Later that evening, before heading over to Bali Hi, Brian tried to call Mexico City. Playa del Carmen's long-distance phone office was located in a cement and glass building crowded with sunburned college kids calling their parents for more money. After waiting his turn, Brian gave the number to a harried young Mexican girl who punched the numbers into a switchboard and waved him to one of the semi-private booths along the wall. When the *Globe* operator answered Brian asked to speak to Marina Soto. Miss Soto is out of the office on assignment, he was told, would he like to leave a message? No gracias, Brian said and hung up.

Bali Hi was just as Christine and Matt had described it—an upscale tent camp clustered around several palapa-covered buildings on a wide private beach. As Brian passed through the bamboo entrance, Maya with blazing torches moved in the twilight lighting oil lamps along the landscaped paths. The dinner crowd, mostly professionals with a sprinkling of celebrities and yahoos in Hawaiian shirts, was already gathered around the self-service bar, trading stories about pyramids and coral reefs. Off in the corner, a guitar and bongo duo was doing a credible rendition of calypso. Christine was standing near the bar, waving for Brian to come over.

"Hi, I'm glad you made it. That's Simon Lowell over there." She indicated a barrel-chested man of commanding girth and a cropped white beard chatting with a small group. When he delivered the punchline of the anecdote, his listeners erupted into gales of laughter.

"C'mon," Christine said, tugging on his arm, "let's have a drink and then I'll introduce you. Matt's right over there."

"You haven't seen George by any chance, have you?"

"Not yet, but I promise I'll tell you the second that I do."

Matt was in the midst of making a pair of Planter's Punches. "Hey, there he is," he said when he saw Brian. "Can I fix you one of these?"

"Sure, why not."

"That's the spirit," Christine said, moving her hips to the bongo rhythm.

While they drank Matt gave Brian a quick rundown on Simon Lowell: he was a retired Colorado surgeon who had first come to the Yucatán twenty years ago on his own honeymoon. His wife, a Mexican heiress who preferred Gucci to guacamole, had long since divorced him and gone back to Denver, but Lowell's love of Mexico—and his legal claim to some prime beach front property—had endured. His first guest house was built for friends who were coming to visit. They had such a good time they offered to help him with expenses. He refused, but said they could pay him a small rental fee whenever they came back. Since then, Lowell's guest plan had grown to more than a hundred tents and cottages, not including the twenty rooms at the Blue Turtle.

Lowell was working the crowd like a politician, shaking hands and waving as he moved in their direction. Spotting Christine, his arms flew open. "There she is, my sweet Virginia belle!" he roared, sweeping her up in a fatherly embrace. "Hiya, Matty. I hope you don't mind if I steal your beautiful wife!"

"Just don't spoil her too much. Simon, this is Brian Mendoza. He's staying at the Blue Turtle too."

Lowell gave Brian's hand a crushing grip. "Nice to meet you, Brian. Welcome to Bali Hi. I hope you'll stay with us for dinner tonight." Lowell gestured to a large round table in the center of the candle-lit dining room. "There's always an interesting meeting of the minds."

"Thank you, I just might. By the way, I'm looking for a man named George Rosas. I understand he might be here tonight."

Brian could sense Lowell's guard go up. "Do you mind me asking why?"

"I'm an anthropologist, working on my Ph.D. thesis at Templo Mayor. I heard that Rosas was at Loltún cave a few days ago. I'd like to hear more about it."

"That's reasonable enough," Lowell said. "And if you're who you say you are then you'd know the name of the director at Templo Mayor."

"Are you talking about Xavier Zapata?"

"I certainly am," Lowell said, slapping Brian on the back. "I'm sorry about giving you the third degree just now, but we get all types in here and I just wanted to make sure you were legit. I hope I didn't offend you."

"Not at all."

"Good. Georgie is due back anytime now with a group that went to Cozumel. Stay for dinner and when he comes in I'll introduce you."

"Thanks."

"Don't mention it. Always happy to further the cause of science."

The band finished their set and there was a round of musical chairs as everyone found their seats. Brian took his place between Christine, who sat next to their host, and Judy Hampton, a British travel writer from London. The far side of the table was taken by Matt, then Monica Ramp, a blond actress from New York, and her manager-boyfriend, Scott Durkin, a men's clothing manufacturer who kept craning his head toward the other tables.

Hampton spoke first, her question directed at Durkin. "Having any luck?" she asked, her pencil poised over her notebook. Durkin and his star were supposedly scouting for locations for an adventure film.

"Well, sure," he said lackadaisically. "I mean this whole country is one big movie set. Mexico is perfect for us—it's dirt cheap and it's pretty and none of the extras use coke."

Lowell frowned.

"It was a joke," Durkin said.

"Of course." Hampton stopped writing and put her notebook away. There was an awkward lull while the soup course was served.

Brian directed his attention to Lowell. "Have you ever had a movie filmed here before?"

"No, never. Unless you count the TV news crews that came down after Gilbert."

"It must have been awful," Monica said sympathetically.

"It was a scene right out of hell," he said gravely. "Christine and Matt were here. They'll tell you I'm not exaggerating. Practically all the trees were down. The roads were jammed with debris. It took us two hours just to get through from the main highway. It usually takes ten minutes, so you can imagine what that was like. When we finally got through, the buildings, the tents, everything was gone, blown away."

"What did you do?" Hampton asked.

"I'll tell you, madam," Lowell said, casting his spell over their corner of the dining room. Even Durkin looked enthralled. "My whole life, twenty years of hard work, everything I'd ever cared about, was in ruins, destroyed. All that was left was a palm tree stump, right about where this dining room is now. I'm not ashamed to say it. I sat down on that stump and bawled like a baby. I thought it was over. And then I saw feet."

"Feet?" Durkin guffawed.

"A circle of brown feet standing around me in the sand." Lowell went on. "It was the Maya, the people of this land. Don't ask me how, but they had survived, and they had come to offer their help. I was speechless, overwhelmed. Then the one we call Joe, he still works for us, looked at me and said, 'When do we start?' And I said, 'Tomorrow.' And the next day we started to rebuild. It began with one tent, down on the beach where the turtles lay their eggs, which went to these two beautiful people right here." Lowell beamed at Matt and Christine. "Now we've got ninety-five units in three locations with no vacancies," he said proudly, "and we owe it all to our friends who come back year after year, and the spirit of this blessed land and the hardworking Maya people."

It was a bravura performance. Across the table, Durkin was scowling skeptically.

"That's a wonderful story, Mr. Lowell," Hampton said. "But I hope you never have to endure another hurricane."

"I'll be long gone by the next hurricane."

"You mean you'll leave Bali Hi?" Brian asked.

"In five years, maybe six, I'll be out, forced to sell."

"But, Simon, I thought you owned this land," Christine said. "How can they make you leave?"

"The politics of profit," Brian said.

Lowell nodded grimly. "You've all seen the atrocities they're building up at Cancún. High-rise cattle runs with a beach that could be anywhere in the Caribbean. Of course, it hardly matters since most of those folks never even leave the pool. They might as well be in Miami. No contact with the people. No sense of the culture. They don't even need to change their money. Visa and American Express spoken here. I've resisted that all of my life. But there comes a point when you just have to cut your losses and run. Last year the Mexican government declared the whole coast of Quintana Roo a tourist development zone. It's only a matter of time before this place is under twenty stories of cement with a neon sign flashing 'Bienvenidos.' "

The others laughed but Brian kept his eyes on Lowell. "So where will you go from here? South?"

"Your friend is a smart man, Chrissie. That's right, Mr. Mendoza. Belize. The last untrammeled Eden." Lowell's chest inflated. "I've got the land picked out already. A piece of paradise on fifty acres."

"Oh, but Simon," Christine lamented. "You can't leave Mexico. It just wouldn't be the same without you."

Lowell rubbed his thumb and index finger together. "They need the dolares," he answered. "Money makes the world go round and the Mexicans are no different. It's their country, after all."

"But isn't that the problem, really?" Heads swiveled at Durkin, who looked surprised to hear himself talking. "I mean, just like when Bali Hi was blown down and the Maya were all standing around waiting for you to tell them what to do."

Lowell squinted and rubbed his beard. "I'm not sure I follow you, friend."

"I mean, they might be hard workers and all but it takes a civilized man like yourself to motivate these people, to give them direction. Just like America was a bunch of savages and buffalo until the settlers came along. Well, in a way, it's the same with Bali Hi. It was your idea, you saw what was possible, and now they want to take it away and claim it for themselves."

Lowell looked uncomfortable. "I appreciate what you're saying," he said diplomatically, "but you've got to remember that I didn't make this beach; it was already here. All I've tried to do is keep it from getting spoiled." Lowell looked up and smiled. "Hey, Georgie, come over here. I want you to meet somebody."

A Maya in a Bali Hi T-shirt was walking over to join them. When Lowell stood up to greet him Brian did too.

"George Rosas, this is . . . I'm sorry, Brian, I don't remember your last name."

"Mendoza," Rosas said, smiling nervously, "nice to see you again." It was only then that Brian recognized him as Jorge Cartas, the guide who'd given them the tour of Chichén Itzá.

Consternated, Lowell said, "I didn't realize you two already knew each other."

"Neither did I," Brian said. Lowell shrugged and sat down again, leaving them standing alone.

Rosas giggled uncomfortably. "It's a funny coincidence, no?"

"No," Brian said, trying to control his anger. "Where is the codex you took from Loltún?"

"What codex, señor?"

"The one you took from the cave, you little son of a bitch. Sonnichsen told me that you went there two days ago with a man from Mexico City. A man with a mustache named Muñoz—or was it Torres?"

"I'm sorry," Rosas said, backing away, "I don't know anything, señor." He tried to make a run for it but Brian lunged in time to grab his shirt and yank him off his feet, sending the both of them lurching into the next table, triggering an avalanche of glasses, plates and cutlery.

Pinned to the floor in a prone position by his attacker, Rosas was still struggling to flee, his arms making futile swimming motions through a pool of sopa de tortilla and mole amarillo. Before the other diners could react, Brian reached for a dinner knife on the floor and pressed it against Rosas's neck.

"Tell me where the codex is or I'll cut your lying throat!"

"I don't know!" Cartas screamed as he squirmed in the puddle of spilled soup. "He said his name was Muñoz and that he worked for the Museum of Anthropology. He hired me to give you a tour of Chichén Itzá and then to take him to Loltún. He flew back to Mexico City with the artifacts today. He paid me in cash. That's all I know. I swear on my mother's grave!"

Brian felt hands grabbing his arms, pulling him up off of Rosas.

"Está loco," Rosas yelled as he struggled to his feet. "Crazy fucker!"

"That was incredible," Christine marveled. "You totally blew my mind, Brian."

Lowell surveyed the wreckage and looked at Brian with something akin to disappointment. "I'm sorry, Mr. Mendoza, but I'm going to have to ask you to leave."

"I apologize for ruining your dinner party," Brian said as two men led him to the door and pushed him out.

The beach was desolate and vague in the moonless night, and for the first few minutes he walked blindly, still hyperventilating from anger and adrenaline. Then his pulse slowed and the shame and pointlessness of what he'd done began to sink in. As much as he didn't want to believe it, Rosas seemed to be telling the truth. The Loltún codex was already in Mexico City or beyond, being read by its new owner. Playa del Carmen had turned out to be a dead end, and Brian had run out of ideas.

Bolts of lightning scrawled across the clouds and crabs scuttled underfoot as he trudged toward the lights of the Blue Turtle. With every step, the darkness around him seemed to enter into his pores, until it was no longer an exterior condition, but something inside, a black hole, a bottomless pool of negative space that threatened to engulf his soul and everything around it.

When he reached the Blue Turtle, Brian bought a fifth of tequila at the bar and took it up to his room. The balcony had a good view of the water and he sat there and sipped from the bottle, watching the ocean liners from Cozumel trace the invisible horizon like floating chandeliers. After a while, his brooding was interrupted by a persistent knocking. He ignored the noise and after a few minutes it stopped. Then he was alone again, with nothing to distract him from his vigil. In the beginning, the change was imperceptible: the deepest black becoming something lighter, evolving by immeasurable increments into gray. Then the gradual inclusion of color—an inky purple, followed by navy and royal blue. Now the ghostly strip of sand and the horizon itself, a thin line etched with God's ruler, neither bent nor straight, yet always true.

Brian screwed the cap back on the bottle and slipped on his trunks, his mood reflected by the predawn gloom. Small waves lapped gently at his legs as he waded into the water. He swam directly out to sea, with steady even strokes, conserving his energy for maximum distance.

A month before the accident, Miguel had taken Brian on a week-long camping trip in the mountains. It didn't matter that Brian's father had never before shown any particular interest in the outdoors, or that his mother didn't complain a bit about being left behind. All he could think about was that he and his dad would be sleeping in a tent under the stars, two friends on a great adventure. It was the happiest week of Brian's young life. They fished for rainbow trout, explored caves and redwood forests and studied the soft dirt along the wilderness trails for bear tracks. One morning they found one, a deep impression with a ring of paw marks, and Miguel helped Brian make a cast with plaster of paris so he could take it to school for his science class.

On the last night of their trip, Miguel lit a fire under an umbrella of stars and fixed two cups of hot chocolate.

"Do you know why we took this trip?" Miguel asked, suddenly more serious than Brian had ever heard him.

"No."

"Because you're no longer a boy. You're a man. Do you know what that means?"

"Sort of."

"A man is someone who can be counted on. A man is someone who keeps his word. Understand?"

"I think so."

"A man doesn't say I think so. A man says yes or no."

"Yes."

"Promise that if something ever happens to me I can count on you to take care of your mother."

"Nothing's going to happen to you, Dad."

"I know, but promise me anyway."

"I promise."

Father and son shook hands, like real men, and then Miguel took Brian in his arms and hugged him hard. Brian hugged him back, confused and a little scared. He had told his father that he understood, but he didn't really. There was too much happening all at once, too many things that had never happened before this week. He had never been camping with his father. He had never been a man. And he had never seen his father cry.

The sky was getting lighter. Up ahead, a strand of pearly clouds absorbed a spectrum of pinks and ripening yellows. Brian kept swimming. From a mile away, the shore that had seemed so solid just a few minutes before looked thin and insubstantial, a watercolor landscape of green and white squeezed by widening borders of water and sky. His arms felt like lead but he kept moving. He swam against the tide, alert to the unfurling fins of fish, the ecstatic growth of the reefs, and the cold, greedy grip of the ocean floor. A pelican, its large wings flapping in slow motion, wheeled above him and dove, bobbing to the surface a few seconds later with breakfast in its beak. The sun grasped the clouds above him, hauling itself above the horizon, and the sea shimmered and caught fire. With a shudder of wings and water, the pelican whipped the air and rose into the blaze of a new day.

And then, in a way that defied logic or words, Brian understood what his father had been trying to tell him. He had known it talking to Walter at his grandfather's funeral. He had known it in the black depths of the cave at Loltún. In some buried part of him, he had known all along.

Brian's hair was still wet as he stood in the long-distance telephone office and waited for the operator to dial the number.

"Hello?"

"Mother, I want to know what really happened to Dad."

"Is that you, Brian? What in heaven's name . . . Have you been drinking?"

"You know who it is, Mother, and you know I'm not drunk. No more playing dumb, Ma. It won't work anymore. Answer the question. Why didn't you ever tell me that my father killed himself?"

The scratchy silence of surprise.

"Who told you that?" Her voice sounded brittle, like a twig about to snap.

"Nobody. I figured it out for myself."

A wave of interference drowned out her next words. Brian plugged his other ear with his finger.

"I can't hear you, Mom. You've got to speak up."

"He wanted to protect you," she repeated.

"Protect me? Protect me from what?"

"I can't talk about this on the phone, not like this. When you come home I'll try to explain."

"What makes you so sure I'll come home? You'd better explain it to me right now."

Another hiss of satellite static.

"He was afraid you'd be ashamed of him."

"What do you mean ashamed?"

"Your dad was sick, Brian. He wanted us to be provided for after he was gone. That's why it had to look like an accident. He wanted us to be financially secure."

Brian gripped the receiver like a lifeline.

"What do you mean he was sick?"

"Your father had cancer, Brian. He didn't have that long to live. He said he didn't want to give the insurance money to doctors and hospitals. He said he wanted his son to have it."

The room around Brian became blurred and distorted, as if immersed in water.

"You mean you knew he was going to commit suicide? Why didn't you stop him?"

He strained to hear her reply. "I didn't really believe he would do it," she said. "I thought it was just talk. Believe me, I tried to argue with him, I told him it was a sin in the eyes of God, but he wouldn't listen. In his mind he was already dead."

Las Cruces, like most of the bars in Playa del Carmen, passed through several incarnations in the course of a single day. Mornings were for tourists seeking a cheap breakfast on the open-air patio while they waited for the ferry to Cozumel. By midafternoon, when the sun became hot enough to melt the plastic forks that came with the huevos rancheros, the gringos would retreat to their air-conditioned rooms, leaving the place to a hardier clientele. For the next few hours Las Cruces would become the domain of the Mexican locals, who preferred to sit in the dark interior sipping beers and watching boxing and news on the satellite TV while the bartender swatted flies and stocked the cooler with cases of Corona and Dos Equis.

The breakfast shift had just tapered off when Brian walked in and took a secluded seat at the bar. He'd barely taken his first sip of tequila when a vaguely familiar face appeared on the oversized TV. It was Francisco Nava, his boyish features partially obscured by a battery of microphones as he stood on the balcony of the National Palace in Mexico City. The only other patron, an old man nursing a tequila con limón, watched as Nava delivered his long-awaited address to the nation. The bartender turned up the sound and the president's voice, impassioned and urgent, intruded into the room as a few other regulars wandered in.

". . . I will not lie to you, my people," Nava was saying. "Our proud nation is facing one of the worst crises in its long and proud history. Mexico is besieged by debt and poverty, by armed insurrection and the threat of foreign intervention. We are under attack by enemies from without and from within as self-proclaimed patriots foment chaos in the name of democracy."

The camera zoomed back to take in the tide of humanity spilling across the zócalo. It began as a low rumble, a chant repeated over and over, gathering force until it poured out through the speaker.

". . . DEMOCRACIA! . . . DEMOCRACIA! . . . DEMOCRACIA! . . ."

Nava held his hands up, waiting for quiet.

"I swear to you here and now that these reactionary forces will fail. Why? Because they are wrong. When they say Mexico is finished, they are wrong. When they say history is on their side, they are wrong. When they say the will of the people is with them, they are wrong. When they say that Nava is against change, they are wrong . . ."

There was a smattering of perfunctory applause as the camera cut to the waving flags of the ruling party.

"It's the same old bullshit," the old man muttered at the screen.

"Those who chant the slogans of hate, who seek to inflame the divisions within our nation must not be allowed to win," Nava insisted. "The poor, the young, the rich and the old must dream together. Then and only then can the reality of our once and future glory come to pass . . ."

There was a round of halfhearted cheers from the government faithful in the audience.

"My fellow Mexicans, I know that you are tired of hearing talk, the talk of politicians who offer words in place of action . . ."

More cheers, this time louder.

"For that reason, I see it as my duty to take the first step on the path to greatness. I hereby announce free, multi-party, democratic elections to be held one year from today. Furthermore, I vow that the government will ensure that the elections are fair and represent the true will of the people."

There was a moment of confusion as the significance of Nava's pledge sank in.

"Madre de dios," someone in the bar said. "The son of a bitch actually did it."

"Now, since there is nothing left to divide us, I ask you to join hands with me, my people, and let us walk together into the future."

Nava raised his hands up in a victory salute.

"Viva México!"

The response was thunderous.

"VIVA!"

The cheering grew louder, a tidal wave of sound that drowned out everything else.

"VIVA MÉXICO! VIVA NAVA!"

Even the drunks of Las Cruces burst into applause, and Brian realized that this was history in the making.

"VIVA MÉXICO! VIVA NAVA! VIVA MÉXICO!"

There was triumph in the president's eyes as he turned to leave the dais. He took a step and seemed to stumble, losing his balance. Hands rushed to help him. Then a final glimpse of Nava looking suddenly tired, a blot of red on his white shirt.

For a few seconds, the camera drifted aimlessly. Then the announcer's voice returned, rattled and high-pitched. "What? Are you sure? My God! The president has been shot. I repeat: President Nava has been shot!"

The old man, his eyes still on the screen, shook his head sadly. "God have mercy on the president," he said. "God have mercy on us all."

17

Black smoke smudged the sky over Mexico City as Brian's cab inched toward the center of town. After Nava was shot Brian had gone straight to the long-distance phone office, but the line of callers was already halfway down the block. Realizing that he'd never be able to reach Marina on the phone, Brian went back to the Blue Turtle, checked out, and drove as fast as he could to Cancún. Getting a flight into the capital had been surprisingly easy; most people were trying to avoid it. Still, the waves of panicky tourists clamoring for a direct flight to the U.S. had contributed to the atmosphere of impending doom.

"Andale, idiotas!" the driver exclaimed, cursing the stalled traffic that had trapped them on Reforma. It was the same all over the city, he told Brian. The chilangos, terrified by the prospect of chaos in the streets, were leaving for the countryside. Meanwhile, rural residents fleeing from the rebels were flooding in. Everyone else was making last-minute forays to pick up relatives or stock up on food before locking themselves in their houses. The latest word was that the president was alive but gravely wounded. The opposition denied responsibility for the assassination attempt, but no one believed them. The provisional president, Alfonso Aranda, a party veteran who opposed free elections, had declared martial law and ordered the army to move against the rebels, who had responded by launching all-out offensives in Guanajuato, Mérida, and San Cristóbal de las Casas. In the north, U.S. troops were massing along the border, ostensibly to hold back the flood of refugees, but most Mexicans were already bracing themselves for an American invasion.

"If Nava dies," his driver told him, "the yanquis will come into Mexico just like before, and no one will be able to stop them. Mexico will become another state, just like California."

The taxi was moving again. Brian looked out his window at a city seized by a political paroxysm. Graffiti, not just white rebel crosses but also the insignias of the opposition and the ruling party, were emblazoned on walls and buildings. Garbage littered the streets and small fires smoldered in the gutters. Yet the sidewalks were crowded with people, most of them running, or moving at a pace accelerated by fear. The scattered pop of gunfire echoed in the distance, causing people to twitch, an involuntary spasm of anxiety, as they hurried to a safe place. And amid the hubbub of civilian panic, strangely quiet men sat alone or gathered on the street corners, watching with reptilian patience, intent on their ruthless vocation. When the fighting broke out and the rule of law unhinged, they would slither through open doors and windows, taking whatever they could. More than the army, more than the rebels or the Americans, this is what the people feared: the roving bands of bandidos that preyed upon the defenseless masses whenever social order broke down. Their crimes were beyond politics and outside the law, except maybe the law of survival; they did what they did because it was their predatory nature.

The taxi turned down Avenida Juárez and stopped in front of the Latin American Tower. Inside the steel and glass lobby Brian was immediately stopped by a trio of security guards. Brian would be allowed up only if he consented to a search and left his bag downstairs. He had expected to find a buzzing hive of journalistic activity, but the newsroom was eerily empty. There were only a few reporters in their cubicles, typing frantically on computer keyboards.

"I'm here to see Marina Soto," Brian told the receptionist.

"She's out covering the crisis, like almost everyone else."

"Listen, I just got into town and I really need to reach her," Brian said. "If you told me what her assignment was, maybe I could track her down myself."

"That's really not our procedure, sir. But you can leave a message if you like."

"No I can't. You see I'm a source for her story, and I think she'll be very disappointed if we don't connect today."

The receptionist mulled over Brian's lie. "She's supposed to be at the National Palace for a press conference at four o'clock. I can't guarantee—"

But Brian was already out the door, dashing for the elevator.

Outside, Avenida Pino Suárez was lined with a band of military green. The soldiers were standing at ease, their rifles slung over their shoulders, but Brian knew their posture could change at any moment. When he stopped to drop his things off at the apartment, La Madre had told him the opposition was planning an illegal rally the next day in Alameda Park. If the demonstrators marched on the zócalo, the army was expected to open fire.

The rumor rang true when he reached the National Palace, which was transformed into a fortress. Tanks, their turrets aimed low, guarded the main entrance and machine gun barrels bristled from sandbag emplacements on the roof. The troops stared ahead with unseeing eyes, like a battalion of apparitions.

The palace had several entrances, but Brian had no way of knowing which one was being used by the press. "Periodistas?" he asked and one of the guards motioned around the corner to the north side of the building, where it shared a side street with Templo Mayor. Brian used his museum pass to get inside the museum compound, which had been closed to the public, and by remaining behind the wrought iron fence, he was able to get to within shouting distance of the entrance. After a few minutes, a man in shirtsleeves carrying a camera exited through the doorway. Then a larger group started filing out. She was the tenth person through the door. Her head was down, looking at the notebook in her hand, and Brian had to wait until she was almost at the corner before he could be sure.

"Marina!"

She turned around, but the momentum of the group was pulling her in the opposite direction.

There was something inherently unnerving about the empty museum. Deprived of the sound of squeaking shoes on polished floors and hushed human voices, the spot-lit displays took on a slightly ominous energy. The masks and pointed daggers ceased to be mere artifacts; they were reclaimed by their dead owners, spirits that otherwise crouched in the corners of the hermetic glass cases. It was the lingering presence of death that gave the objects their power to fascinate and instruct. But without the counterweight of living beings, the sterile aura of decay was overwhelming.

The elevator was out, so Brian mounted the steps to the third-floor reception area and let himself in. The office was abandoned, the floor unswept and littered with unfiled papers. Brian crossed through the library stacks to Torres's office. The door was open and everything of value, including the plaster Chacmool, had been removed. Noticing a piece of blue paper crumpled in the waste basket, Brian picked it up and pressed it flat. It was a memo from Torres to Zapata, mentioning a few last-minute bits of business before the Templo Mayor offices were moved to temporary quarters at the Museum of Anthropology in Chapultepec Park. Brian was about to toss it away when he noticed the final item:

> Re: Brian Mendoza. Pursuant to our earlier discussion, I have confirmed that phone calls made from Mendoza's line were to the editorial offices of "The Globe" and that he and a "Globe" reporter were on the same flight to Cancún last Tuesday. Suggest disciplinary action when/if he returns.

"I thought you were too smart to come back, but now you've proven your own stupidity."

Brian slipped the memo into his pocket and turned to face Torres. "Thanks for the vote of confidence. It looks like there've been a few changes since I left."

"A few, yes," Torres said. "We've moved the offices to Chapultepec."

"What better time for a trip to the Yucatán?"

"You would know better than me," Torres said smugly. "Anyway, the army has made working here temporarily impossible."

"You're the last person I ever expected to have a problem with authority," Brian taunted. "Don't tell me you're turning into a democrat, Arturo?"

Torres flinched at Brian's impertinence, but kept his frozen smile. "Joke while you can, Mendoza. You won't laugh when you learn the consequences of breaking an executive order."

Brian pulled the memo out of his pocket. "You mean this?"

When Torres declined to answer, Brian shook his head in disdain. "Arturo, you disappoint me. You hate someone for weeks, plot tirelessly to bring about his downfall, and this is the best you can do? Do you really think Zapata gives a damn about any of this bureaucratic bullshit?"

Brian tossed the memo into the wastebasket.

Torres's smile slackened, but the loathing in his eyes was undimmed.

"Rules, as any true scientist knows, are made to be broken," Brian continued. "New information supersedes old assumptions; natural laws are rewritten. I'm afraid you've let your emotions cloud your judgment. All Zapata cares about is getting certain information from me. I think you're the one who should be worried, amigo."

Brian rang the buzzer of Marina's apartment for several minutes before she answered, and even then she opened the door only a few inches, like someone trying to remain incognito.

"Who told you I was here?"

"Nobody. After I saw you at the National Palace, I checked back at the paper. They said you hadn't come back, so I figured you might be home."

"So it was you who called my name."

"Yes, it was me. Now will you please let me in?"

The door didn't budge. "Brian, there's nothing more for us to say."

"I disagree. Now open the goddamned door."

She reluctantly did as he asked, locking the door behind him. "I asked you to leave Mexico," she said irritably. "You should have listened."

"I did listen. That's why I'm here." The television was on and a newscaster was pointing to a map of the city that showed the positions of the government troops and the opposition's planned route. The two lines intersected at the National Palace.

Brian nodded at the TV. "You knew Nava was going to be shot, didn't you?"

"No." Marina shook her head adamantly. "I knew *something* was going to happen, but I didn't know what. I knew that Villalobos and his kind couldn't afford to let Nava succeed."

"Villalobos again!" Brian shouted with exasperation. "What the hell do you know about Villalobos?"

"Much more than you realize."

"What?"

"You mean he didn't tell you?" she asked snidely. "Yes, your dear friend Villalobos. He called me just before we left for Yucatán and offered me an interview in exchange for information."

She had spoken out of anger, and Brian could see that she already regretted telling him. Was this what she'd been trying to protect him from?

"What kind of information?" Brian asked.

"About you. About your work. About your trip. He also told me that the Fifth Sun would be ending very soon and that a new era for Mexico was about to begin. When the president was shot, I knew what he meant."

"But you refused his offer."

"Even if I didn't love you," she said chidingly, "I would never do anything to compromise my integrity as a journalist. Besides, you should know by now that I would never betray you."

"So why didn't you tell me sooner?"

Marina stared at him accusingly. "I wanted to, but when you couldn't even trust me enough to tell me where you were going, I decided you didn't deserve to know." She balled her fists and shook them at him. "You make me so angry sometimes! Afterward, I don't know . . . I decided that if you left Mexico, then there was no point. It didn't seem to matter anymore."

"So your sudden decision to come to the Yucatán was prompted by the man you claim to loathe so much," Brian said, almost enjoying the irony.

"I'll admit I became curious," she said, leaning over to light a cigarette. "The journalist in me wanted to know what everyone was so interested in."

Brian slumped in a chair, overwhelmed. He looked at Marina, alluring as ever in black jeans and a contoured knit top, and found it impossible to be angry.

"And what do you think now?"

"Frankly," she said, exhaling smoke, "I still don't get it. There aren't any answers to be found in the past. The only answers are here, right now, in the present."

"What about the future? Don't you think we still have one?"

She extinguished her cigarette. "I'm sorry, Brian. I can't think about that right now. Besides, you've got more immediate worries."

"What's that supposed to mean?"

Her stare was incredulous. "You haven't heard?"

"Heard what?"

"Tolsa. He was found dead in his apartment last night. He had been stabbed in the heart with an obsidian knife."

Brian sighed. "And you think Villalobos is behind it."

"Who else?"

"But why would Villalobos take the risk? He's already rich. There's nothing more he can have."

"You don't understand," Marina said. "For some people the status quo is their life, it is the source of their power. Nava tried to change that and it almost got him killed. This attack came from within the power structure. He wasn't shot by the rebels, he was shot by the enemies he made inside the government. They needed a scapegoat. Tolsa was already a fugitive and he had a perfect motive."

"So you think his own people killed him to take the heat off themselves."

"He was sacrificed to the power elite," Marina said. "They have the perfect alibi by making it look like the rebels did it."

"It's still hard for me to believe," Brian said. "Alejandro's ambitious. But a cold-blooded killer?"

"Understand me, Brian. I know he can be charming. Men like that always are. Snakes like that have many skins. Hypnotized by the serpent's charm, the victim hardly feels the venom."

"Oh, come on, Marina," Brian said. "You make him sound like some kind of monster."

"If he did what I think he did, then he is a monster. Tell me, does Villalobos know that you saw Tolsa at his house?"

"Unless he was blind, I would think so. We practically walked into each other. Why?"

"Because you might be the only one who can link Villalobos with Tolsa. Think about it. Whoever killed Tolsa could be looking for you too."

Brian had to laugh. "Now you're telling me that I'm on somebody's hit list?"

"It's not funny, Brian. You could be very dangerous to these people. If they're willing to try to kill the president, why would they even hesitate about you?"

Brian held up his hand. "Wait a minute. Assuming that you're right about this, what am I supposed to do? Hire a bodyguard and carry a gun? Or is this just a way to get me to leave the country?"

"Don't be ridiculous," Marina said, pacing now, an unlit cigarette waving in her hand. "If they wanted you dead you'd never make it to the plane. But there is a way to protect you."

"And what's that?"

"Go public with your story."

It took a few seconds for him to understand.

"You mean the press?"

"Give me an exclusive interview," Marina said. "I'll protect your identity. No one will ever know. The minute this story hits the papers, you'll be safe. You won't matter to them anymore."

Brian wanted to tell her she was crazy, that she was imagining things. But then he thought back to the ominous atmosphere at Tepoztlán, the Aztec dagger he had held in his own hands, and Villalobos's parting advice not to ask too many questions, and he felt himself waver.

"When would you do this?"

"Tonight," she said bluntly. "We can still make the morning edition. There isn't a moment to waste. Just repeat what you told me about Tolsa and Villalobos and I'll do the rest."

Marina went to her desk and returned with a portable tape recorder. She checked the batteries and placed it on the floor between them. Even dressed like a teenager with her hair awry, she assumed a professional pose as she readied a pen and notebook.

"Wait," he said as she reached for the record button. "What will happen to Villalobos?"

"That depends entirely on what he has done. In the end, it may turn out to be no more than a temporary embarrassment, or he might be sent to jail for conspiring to kill the president."

"But what if he's innocent?"

She looked at him directly, and for a second her voice took on the caring tone of a lover. "I'm afraid that if you don't do this you might not live long enough to find out."

Brian closed his eyes for a moment, trying to quiet the conflicting voices in his head.

"Okay," he said. "Turn it on."

La Madre's birds were her life, and she would rather die than see a single one suffer. That was how she explained her decision to open her cages and let them go. Brian tried to talk her out of it, but the old woman was adamant, insisting instead that he help her banish her winged family from the only home they had ever known.

There was a great commotion of startled squawks and flapping wings as Brian carried the cages up the stairs to the roof. The cages weren't heavy, but their bulky size and the outraged sounds coming from inside made for nerve-racking work. At last, La Madre's aviary was assembled on the tar launching pad. Brian stood back, marveling at the old woman's feathered menagerie. There were over a hundred birds in all, some fifteen or twenty species in a kaleidoscope of colors. It was clear that La Madre was no ordinary ornithophile; she was a breed unto herself, a wingless human who spoke the bird language and dreamed bird dreams.

La Madre's children seemed to know what was coming. They twittered and chirped in their castles of wood and wire, as if alarmed by the notion of being released into the smoldering city.

"Hush, my babies," La Madre cooed. "Don't worry. Soon you will be free to fly away to safety."

"Madrecita," Brian pleaded. "Think about what you're doing. These birds aren't wild, they can't fend for themselves. They'll be cat food before they know what hit them."

He saw her thin shoulders shudder at the thought, then she turned and wagged a bony finger at him.

"Don't talk about my babies that way," she scolded. "I told them what to do if they see a cat—they must flap their wings with the speed of the wind—and rest only in tall trees. But they mustn't fly so high that the hawks will see them. That would be just as dangerous. In the morning they must fly south, where their cousins are waiting for them in the land of warm nights and sweet fruits. They're good listeners; they know what they must do."

Brian made a final attempt to deter the old woman with logic. "And what about you," he asked her. "You live for these birds. What will you do with yourself when they've gone?"

"Esmeralda has agreed to stay and keep me company," La Madre said, puckering her lips at the green parakeet on her shoulder. "I will miss my babies, of course. It makes me very sad to make them go. But with the trouble coming, I am happier to know that they are safe in the forest, far away from the guns and the fighting. They don't like loud noises. The fireworks make them very nervous every year on Cinco de Mayo. So imagine with bullets!"

La Madre pursed her lips at the thought.

"No, it would make them crazy," she concluded. "It would be too much. But the worst would be if a bomb fell on the house. Or what if there was a fire and I couldn't get them out? No, sir, that would really kill me. More certainly than a heart attack in my bath or standing in front of the firing squad, that would be my finish."

Perhaps sensing that Brian had run out of arguments, she went over and patted him on the back. "Someday you'll have your own children," she said consolingly, "and maybe you'll understand." Then, with a quick look at the morning sky and a long sigh of resignation, she ordered him to help her free her babies.

There was a great rustling of wings and craning of feathered necks as La Madre and Brian approached the cages. The cockatoos were particularly upset, screeching like prisoners on death row. But then La Madre leaned over and whispered something that made their sulphur crests rise up like yellow fans, and the other birds, watching intently, grew quiet.

La Madre had determined that the largest birds should go first, since it was their responsibility to look out for their smaller relatives. From her position near the cockatoos, she gave Brian the signal to release the parrots. Brian opened the cage door and stood back respectfully, aware that a parrot's beak could sever a man's finger. The birds, two females and a male, preened for a moment, showing their pointed tongues before beginning a rocking, sideways dance toward the exit. The male reached the opening first. His left eye, a beady bull's-eye in a circle of red and green, regarded Brian warily. Then, with one foot comically extended, it seemed to teeter on the edge until the powerful push of its wings took it airborne. There was another flailing of green wings as the females followed and Brian watched them circle overhead in huge, graceful corkscrews.

"Wait, my darlings, wait for your cousins!"

Next came the cockatoos, showing off their egg-yolk plumage. Then the toucans and the ravens, who flew off with a final scream of "Hello," followed by the blue jays, cardinals, finches and smaller parrots. Sparrows were next, then the parakeets and canaries and several species Brian had never seen before. The last to go were the hummingbirds, their gossamer wings whirring as they hovered over La Madre's head and floated up to join the swirling airborne pageant. Twice more the birds circled, squawking and tweeting with a wistful exaltation, then veering off in a great fluttering swarm to the promised land of the south.

"Fly away, my darlings," La Madre cried. "Yes, fly, fly, good-bye!" And there were tears in her eyes as she held her arms up to catch the rain of falling feathers.

The winged messenger comes flying from the north, lifted by the breath of Ehécatl, the jewel of the wind. It circles overhead in great spirals, crying out my name as the earth shudders and the trees bow down before its power. Great gusts blow through the branches, cracking limbs and scattering leaves, and I know that this is not the benign wind from the south or the life-giving wind that presages Tláloc but the dreaded breeze of devastation, the last furious gasp of my beloved Tenochtitlán.

The vulture dips lower, its shadow racing around me, until I can feel the dry heave of its wings, taste the viscera in its broken beak. Closer and closer, around and around, until our shadows merge and the fear is left behind with my human shape. Oh, yes, Great Lord, I should have known. There is nowhere to run, no escape, not from you, not from knowledge, no matter how terrible or strange.

Rising above the trees, I flex my talons and with a powerful beat of my wings head north, riding the waves of hot air to gather speed, hurrying toward my homeland. Below me, the land shows its true face; its forests like thick hair, its rippling hills like muscles, its rivers like pulsing veins, all bound together by a brown skin stretched taut between the oceans. How beautiful you are, my world, my earth, how generous to let me see you this way, with the sharp focus of a bird of prey rushing toward its awful appointment. From my place in the sky even Teotihuacán, the fabled door to the Underworld, looks puny and insignificant. I scarcely give it a glance, my attention already riveted on the shroud of smoke hanging between the volcanoes ahead. I fly faster until the outskirts of the city are below me, the farms and houses etched flat like Tonatiuh's drawings. But this is no painted illusion; people are running and screaming as they pour like ants from the causeways that lead from the city. Skimming across the surface of Lake Xochimilco I am sickened by what I see: a waterlogged graveyard of floating bodies, broken carriages and capsized boats. The lake's fair waters are stained with blood, the shore littered with bloated corpses. My nostrils detect the reek of decaying flesh and I fly on, resisting the urge to stop and fill my belly.

Gliding over Tenochtitlán, I see the black hand of Tezcatlipoca at work, crushing the city in his fatal grip, his army of white demons overcoming all resistance. Lightning sticks flash around the temple of Huitzilopochtli, where a battalion of Eagle Warriors is making a desperate last stand on sacred ground. They fight with valor, but our spears are no match for the glittering weapons of the bearded strangers, who slash and stab from the backs of their huge four-legged beasts. And following close behind, like a plague of rats, are rampaging hordes of Tlaxcalan warriors, gleefully pursuing their mission of murder and arson. Aztec men, children and older women are mercilessly slaughtered, their blood filling the gutters of the narrow streets. Only the comeliest women are spared, herded like chattel for the pleasure of the Tlaxcalan captains. A single scream, a wail of pure terror, rises above the din and I wheel to see a young maiden trying to escape a bearded devil on the temple of Quetzalcóatl. Realizing she is trapped, the girl turns to face her attacker, who pins her arms with one hand and begins to loosen her garments with the other. The unfolding atrocity is beyond belief. What manner of monster would defile a woman on a site of saintly devotion? Inflamed by the demon's sacrilege, I swoop down, hovering just long enough for the intruder's mouth to open in wonder, before sinking my talons deep into his eyes.

Blinded, the invader staggers back, roaring like a wounded bear as blood streams down his face. Inspired by what they have witnessed, my countrymen let out a great shout of defiance and fight on with renewed fury, taking the lives of several startled demons who were closing in for the kill. But the reversal is fleeting; before long the Aztecs are overwhelmed by sheer numbers and enemy archers aim in my direction. I know that the battle of Tenochtitlán has been lost. Engulfed by fire, bathed in blood, the Fifth Sun has ended and the future has begun.

Dipping low between the smoldering rubble, I hear Tlaxcalan arrows rip the air around me. With a final cry of anguish I flee the dying city, escaping high into the unscathed southern sky, my wings singed and battered, my heart burnt and broken.

18

The silver Mercedes pulled away from the curb and glided through the milling crowd on Calle San Jerónimo. Hurrying to catch the Metro, Brian didn't notice as the car drew up alongside and slowed to match his gait.

Diego poked his smiling head out through the driver's window. "Buenos días, Señor Mendoza," he said amiably.

Brian halted in his tracks, too surprised to speak. Diego stopped the car, climbed out and opened the rear passenger door. From the back seat Alejandro Villalobos waved. "Brian," he called. "What a co-incidence! Get in and I'll give you a lift."

Brian looked around, fighting the instinct to bolt.

"If you insist, I'll get out and walk with you, but it is much more pleasant to ride, don't you agree?"

Warily, Brian approached the car. "I'm surprised to see you out in public," he said.

Villalobos pursed his lips. "It's true that, for the moment at least, La Malinche has put me in an awkward position," he said. "The accusations have been damaging, of course, but I forgive you since I can see how certain events may have led you to the wrong conclusion. Besides, you have helped me in other ways that you don't even know yet."

Brian still hesitated.

"Please," Villalobos said with a touch of exasperation. "You have nothing to fear. Get in. I have something I want to talk to you about."

Brian climbed into the plush interior, amazed at the power Villalobos still had over him. He tensed as Diego sealed the door with an airtight thud.

"Ah, much better," Villalobos said, settling back into his seat. "I knew you were a reasonable man. Now, where are we going?"

"The Museum of Anthropology."

"In Chapultepec? Diego, you heard the señor."

As the car moved forward, Brian felt unease laced with anticipation. "I'm sorry that our relationship has become so strained," Villalobos said with honest regret. "I'm a man who prides himself on keeping his friends."

"Is that what you told Raúl Tolsa?"

Villalobos grimaced. "Tolsa," he said, as if even pronouncing the name was a bother. "He was not a friend; he was a curse. The damage that little man has caused. Qué lástima! A real tragedy. But we all make mistakes, don't we?"

"It seems to me that your mistake was thinking you could change history," Brian said.

Villalobos seemed to find great irony in Brian's words. "Did you hear that, Diego? From the mouths of niños."

Diego's eyes flickered in the rear-view mirror. They were gentle and smiling, and Brian felt himself being won over. The charm of the serpent, Marina had said. He was indeed a most amiable devil.

"You are still young, but someday you will learn," Villalobos said, a mist of nostalgia in his eyes. "None of us can change history, Brian. That is particularly true in Mexico, where the gods still rule our human intrigues. Democracy will come because the time for it has arrived, not because of Nava or Tolsa or anyone else. If civil war comes with it . . ." His voice trailed off. "It wouldn't be the first time the world has ended."

"And when it's over, you and your kind will be there, waiting to pick up the pieces."

"We are necessary, but we are not important," Villalobos said matter-of-factly. "Mexican blood is heavy, it holds us down, ties us to the earth. All of us, rich or poor, we bleed the same."

"But some bleed more than others."

A shadow passed over Villalobos, and for an instant his profile became cold and lifeless, a statue made of ashes.

"What will you do now?" Brian asked.

The light shifted, and Villalobos became his animated self again. "I am planning a trip to Europe," he said airily. "Not because of the news reports—that is a trifle, a temporary nuisance. I am leaving because the situation here has become too unstable. When things calm down, I'll return. Nava was right about one thing: Mexico is bound for greatness. The prophecies are clear: after the heavens turn black, the seed of the future will take root. From the Obsidian Sky, a new sun is born. Meanwhile, I have people here who will look after my interests."

"I'm sure you do."

"I realize what you must think," Villalobos said, "but you should believe me when I tell you that you are wrong. I confess that in my life I have done many questionable things, but trying to kill the president is not one of them. It's true that Tolsa was organizing a conspiracy. Since I am a man who is known to have some influence in this country, he came to me to ask for my help. I said no, or to be exact, I did not say yes. He left Tepoztlán not knowing my final position, which is exactly what I wanted. I contacted some mutual friends, and we all agreed that Tolsa had to be stopped. But by then it was too late. It wasn't too late, however, to make Tolsa pay for his crime. The dagger was a signal to certain men very close to the president and elsewhere. It was a message that the old ways are dead and a new age has dawned in Mexico."

Villalobos peered at Brian, trying to gauge his reaction. "I see that you remain unconvinced," he said. "That saddens me. I can only hope that future events might change your mind. I understand your confusion, but don't let it blind you."

Brian looked at Villalobos, dashing in his blue blazer and red Hermès tie, and wondered how many more personas were hidden behind that unflappable, well-groomed exterior. Brian had already met Villalobos the country gentleman, Villalobos the mystic, Villalobos the savvy political power broker. And now he was being introduced to Villalobos the avenging angel, the unfairly maligned, behind-the-scenes dispenser of cruel justice.

"So now I'm supposed to believe you're actually one of the good guys, is that it?" Brian said harshly. "A fugitive who spends the night at your house pops up later with a knife in his chest, but it's not your fault. You've been linked to a plot to assassinate the president, but you expect me to believe it's all just a terrible misunderstanding . . ."

Exasperated, Villalobos said, "I don't expect you to believe anything, Brian."

"So then why did you pick me up?"

"I wanted to warn you."

The Mercedes lurched to a halt and a woman with a child in her arms pressed up against Brian's window, her face framed by a gaily patterned rebozo. There was something shocking about her proximity, the pleading intimacy of her expression. Brian had an impulse to get out and help her, to give her money, to know her name. Then the car moved on, and she was lost again, a colorful detail in the huge canvas of the city.

"Warn me about what?"

"Have you spoken with Zapata since you got back from Yucatán?"

"No."

"Good," Villalobos said. "There's something you should know before you see him. He never intended to let you see the codex at Loltún. He was just using you to find it."

"That much I've figured out myself," Brian said bitterly.

"By now you must have realized it wasn't he who took the artifacts from Loltún."

"But then who . . . ?" Brian began, but Villalobos's smile had already answered his question.

"Don't worry; they are in a safe place," Villalobos reassured him.

"And I promise you that the codex will eventually be returned to its rightful owners, the Mexican people."

"I still don't understand."

Villalobos flexed his manicured fingers. "It's quite simple, really. You see, Zapata had possession of the first part of the codex. Like me, he suspected that it could ultimately point the way to another discovery. When he realized that you were making progress in the search, he decided to encourage you, hoping that you would ultimately lead him to Xotl's precious bundle."

"But you got there first."

Villalobos tipped his head in tribute. "Thanks to you, Brian. Your connection between the Xotl drawings and the Loltún artifacts was a stroke of inspiration. A first-rate piece of anthropological deduction. I salute you."

"Jorge Cartas, or should I say George Rosas, he was one of your spies, wasn't he?"

"He was hired by Muñoz, who was working for me."

"And was Marina working for you too?"

Villalobos raised an eyebrow. "She told you about our conversation?"

"Yes. She also said you tried to bribe her to spy on me."

"It's true," Villalobos nodded, looking quite pleased with himself. "When I realized that you were in love with her, I had to make sure she could be trusted. If anyone could corrupt her it was me. But Marina stayed true to her captain. Did you know that the real Malinche bore Cortés a son, yet they never married. Instead, she was betrothed to one of Cortés's trusted lieutenants. A sad ending to one of history's great love stories."

Brian's chest swelled with feckless rage. He had been like an insect caught in an invisible web, pinned and helpless as unseen powers plucked at the strands. "But what about the treasure?" he asked. "The precious bundle. Isn't that what you really want?"

Villalobos shifted his weight and gave his cuffs a slight tug. "What you fail to understand, Brian, is that the key to the treasure can only lie in the book of knowledge, the Loltún codex, which I now possess. It will be a few more weeks before we can decode it. Then perhaps we will learn the fate of the Spaniards' lost ransom—if it really does exist."

"But why bother? How much richer can you get?"

"Don't insult me," Villalobos said. "Do you really think I care about the money? The gold itself is of no value to me." He faced Brian, his eyes ablaze. "Think about it! A window through the centuries. A time machine on painted parchment showing the way to the lost treasure of Motecuhzoma. One of the greatest mysteries of all time, solved by the Book of Xotl and the Book of Tonatiuh."

"The Book of Tonatiuh," Brian whispered. It made sense that Xotl's disciple would carry on the scriptures. There was no question now that Villalobos actually had the codex.

"Zapata possessed the first half of the riddle, but not the second," Villalobos continued. "It would have sealed his glory to be able to present the nation with the complete codex as well as jewels of Motecuhzoma!"

"But now there will be two codices," Brian said. "The Zapata Codex and the Villalobos Codex."

"The second of which will soon be made public," Villalobos said, his eyes gleaming. "A gift from myself to the people of Mexico."

Incredible as it seemed, Brian knew now that Villalobos was serious. But another mystery still hung in the air.

"Why are you telling me all this?"

Villalobos clasped his hands and stared into the tangled foliage of Chapultepec Park. "Zapata and I are alike in many ways," he explained. "We want many of the same things. Yet we are doomed to struggle against each other, to make sure that the other does not get too powerful—or too weak."

"The Flowery War," Brian said. "Eternal combat between opposing forces."

Villalobos gripped Brian's shoulder with affection. "You've learned your lessons well. Now you must find the wisdom to use that knowledge properly."

But Brian's ego was too bruised to respond. "So this is all just part of some vendetta between you and Zapata," he said. "You both used me in your battle of wills."

Villalobos retracted his hand. "You joined the battle too, Brian. You've been fighting since the first day you came to Mexico. Besides, none of this would have been possible without you. I thought you deserved to know that you hadn't failed, that your theory had borne fruit." He smiled at Brian fondly. "Someday I will find a way to prove that your friendship was not misplaced."

The Mercedes arrived at the main entrance of the National Museum of Anthropology.

"So what will Zapata do when he finds out I don't have the codex?"

As Diego leaped out to open Brian's door, Villalobos extended his arm. "That," he said as they shook hands for the final time, "is what I presume you are about to find out."

Insulated from the seething city by ten-foot fences and glass walls, the National Museum of Anthropology was an air-conditioned island of calm. The only sign of the turmoil gripping the capital was a doubling of the number of security guards, who stared nervously at the growing number of campesinos gathered on the lawn around the building. Dressed in worn blankets and sandals, the people watched and waited, as if expecting the ancient gods to break out of their glass cases and speak to them. For the mestizo masses, the icons of their ancestors were the only true rivals to the political leaders of the republic.

Brian entered the lobby and paused to admire the rectangular patio with its umbrella-shaped fountain before asking the jittery guards for directions to Zapata's temporary office. Frisking him, they pointed to a warren of tan cubicles, where Brian found the right door and knocked.

"It's open," Zapata called out. He was wrestling with the ribbon cartridge of an IBM Selectric, his fingers smeared with carbon.

"These damned machines are the curse of the literate class," he groused. "I would shake your hand, but mine's covered with ink." He waved Brian to a chair. "Ah, well, more proof of Murphy's Law, eh? Anything that can go wrong sooner or later will." Zapata wiped his fingers on a paper towel. "I must confess, I really didn't know when to expect you back. Not that you've missed anything. Our records, our staff, our country—everything is in chaos!"

"Shades of Tezcatlipoca," Brian said.

Zapata chuckled. "Yes indeed," he said, "or maybe just Xotl's ghost coming back to haunt us."

"The thought has crossed my mind."

"So," Zapata exclaimed, "tell me about your trip! Have we made anthropological history?"

"I was hoping you could tell *me*."

Zapata's smile curdled. "We both know you went to Yucatán to find Xotl's grave. We had an agreement. In exchange for my support we would share the artifacts or information that came into your possession. I have provided you with total access to the museum archives, including the final installments of the Xotl codex. Now it's time for you to deliver your part of the bargain."

"I'm sorry," Brian said. "But I can't do that."

Zapata's face darkened a shade.

"And would you please tell me why not?"

"I think you should ask Torres."

"Arturo? What does he know about this?"

"I think it's only fair that we give him a chance to answer that question himself."

Zapata touched a button on the intercom and asked his deputy to join them.

Brian could feel the wheels of fate turning in his direction, gathering momentum like a runaway roller-coaster. Zapata pushed his glasses back on his nose and cleared his throat. "I should warn you that the Mexican government takes a very dim view of foreigners who attempt to smuggle artifacts out of the country," he said gravely.

"Are you threatening me, Professor?"

"I am simply saying that if you are withholding anything from me I will be forced to turn the matter over to the police. To make your position worse, we have a record of your phone calls to *The Globe* that are in flagrant violation of my directive."

"I think the police have enough to worry about these days," Brian said. "Besides, I already told you, I didn't find anything."

There was a discreet knock and Zapata told Torres to come in. Brian's presence seemed to throw him off balance for a second, but his superior sneer quickly reasserted itself.

"Arturo," Zapata said evenly, "it seems that Mr. Mendoza thinks you have something to confess to me."

Torres glared at his antagonist. "And you believe him?"

Zapata's eyes traveled back to Brian.

"Don't take my word for it," Brian said. "Call Donato Negrete at Loltún."

Nonplussed, Zapata asked, "And what would that accomplish?"

"He can confirm that by the time I reached Loltún two men identifying themselves as museum employees had already been there to collect a number of artifacts from a hidden chamber dedicated to Quetzalcóatl. It seems there was also a codex, a sequel to the one found under the cathedral."

Zapata's voice was tight with anger. "And what makes you think Arturo was there?"

"Negrete described one of the men as tall and slim with dark hair and a mustache."

"That's ridiculous," Torres blurted. "Even if it's true, that description fits half the men in Mexico."

"True, but how many of those men preside over an office that registered and catalogued Negrete's discovery? I found out about it by looking through the printouts that Torres gave me himself."

"It's a lie!"

"Let's find out," Zapata said. It took a few minutes for the operator to make the connection to Oxkutzcab and a few more for Negrete to be called to the phone. When Zapata introduced himself, Brian smiled, imagining the caretaker's reaction to a personal call from the director of Templo Mayor. As Negrete confirmed Brian's story, Torres's smirk disappeared. Zapata slammed down the phone, his face pale with rage.

"There must be a mistake," Torres stammered, shrinking before Brian's very eyes. "It's a trick of some sort . . ."

"Or maybe it's just another case of Murphy's Law," Brian speculated. "Well, Professor, I guess you can go ahead and call the police now, but it's not me who'll be going to jail."

Torres looked stricken. "I swear I had nothing to do with it," he said, seeking Zapata's averted eyes. "It couldn't have been me. I can prove I was in Mexico City the whole time. I have witnesses—"

"Shut up, Arturo," Zapata snapped, his anger aimed far beyond the walls of the museum, as if staring into the face of an unseen enemy.

• • •

Sirens screamed in the distance as Brian hurried across Chapultepec Park toward Reforma. Under the flowering trees, clusters of families seeking refuge huddled in makeshift shelters fashioned from blankets and coarse twine. They were the ragged harbingers of a new tent city; the founders would soon be joined by others seeking refuge from the furious streets.

Getting a cab was hopeless, so Brian tried the Metro, which, miraculously, was still running. For now, at least, life went on underground. Brian joined the crush of bodies on a train to Alameda Park and was aware of an almost palpable sense of dread among his fellow passengers. A child was bawling, and though she was nearby, Brian couldn't see her. The disembodied sobs, so dejected and frail, seemed to speak for all the people pressed together as the train hurtled down the tracks. And Brian had a sudden rush of empathy for the ordinary Mexicans, the anonymous citizens who stubbornly clung to habit while the skies descended and the gods of the Underworld rattled their bones.

Brian ascended a flight of stairs to the surface, where the crowd of demonstrators had expanded to several thousand. There was an ugly buzz in the air, and Brian noticed machetes dangling from the arms of many men. Someone else carried a box of stones and another passed out sticks with nails driven through one end. Brian backed away slowly toward the Latin American Tower wondering if a thousand Davids would have a chance against Goliath.

In the *Globe* offices, Marina waved to him as she cradled a telephone under her chin and scanned a news service printout. Unlike before, the newsroom was a swarming hive of activity. The impending crisis was like a clarion call to the reporters, who had gravitated to their offices as if responding to some biological signal.

While he waited for Marina to get off the phone, Brian went to the window and looked out over Mexico City. The cloud of smoke was thicker now, hanging over the valley like a shroud.

. . . And the sky will divide and the Lord of the Night will enter the world . . .

Off toward the horizon, he could see the plumes of individual fires and he hoped that La Madre had locked herself in as she had promised. Looking down, he noticed the demonstrators massing in the park, assembling around their leaders, rending the air with their banners and fists.

"Democracia!" they shouted in a wrathful chorus. "PRU afuera! Democracia!"

From the opposite bank of windows Brian looked out over the Palace of Iturbide, named for the first post-Conquest emperor of Mexico, up Avenida Madero to the zócalo and the National Palace. The army was dug in behind the ornate Colonial walls, braced for battle. Still, there had been reports of a possible revolt among the soldiers, many of whom supported Nava and the cause of democracy. The troops had been ordered to shoot to kill, but nobody could say for certain if they would obey their commanders and fire on the people, or join the masses in rebellion.

Marina joined him at the window and he clasped her hand.

"There's still time for us to get out," he said.

"It's already too late," she replied. "The demonstrators will begin their march at noon. I have to be there."

Brian looked at his watch. Noon was less than an hour away.

"Some of us are going to the Hotel Majestic to report from the balcony," Marina said.

"I thought the zócalo was sealed off by the army."

"It is. But my photographer has an uncle who knows of a way in through the basement. That was the manager of the hotel on the phone. He's sending someone downstairs to open the door and lead us up. I'll meet you at your apartment when it's over."

She started to move away but he held on to her hand. "I won't get separated from you again," he said. "If you have to go, then I'm coming with you."

"But it's too dangerous," she started to say. Then she saw the determination in his face and relented. "Maybe you can help Pablo with his camera equipment."

They set out for the zócalo twenty minutes later with Pablo and another reporter named Jesús. Avoiding the main intersections, Pablo took a circuitous route around Plaza de Las Tres Culturas, the site of the final battle of the Conquest, and dropped Jesús off to cover the opposition as it marched on the zócalo. Parking in an alley near Calle Palma, they entered a covered arcade that led to a large cantina with ceiling fans and plastic stools at the bar. Jesús embraced the bartender and a moment later they were all walking single file past the kitchen and down some dark stairs to a vaulted cellar.

"This used to be part of the old sewer system," Pablo explained. "But now it's used as an alley by the businesses between Palma and the zócalo. My uncle knows about it from when he was a busboy at the hotel. He says they used to come back here to smoke marijuana." The bartender mumbled something to Pablo. "He says that's the entrance to the cellar of the Majestic."

They were standing before a rusted steel door that rolled on metal wheels. The bartender banged on the door and waited. When nothing happened, Pablo cursed and banged again.

"Are you sure this is the right door?" Marina asked. "The manager told me he'd be waiting for us."

Brian picked up a brick near his feet and hammered on the door with all his might. Silence. A distant scraping sound was followed by metallic clicks, then a thunderous creak as the door rolled aside.

The hotel manager was there, looking over the shoulders of two busboys. "First the door was blocked by a refrigerator," the man explained breathlessly. "Then we couldn't get the key to work."

Bypassing the lobby, they rode the elevator directly to the rooftop cocktail lounge. A few intrepid travelers were sitting at the bar, drinking and trading travel stories about dysentery and black market money changers. They hardly noticed as the reporters trooped through the room. "Hey, we're stranded tourists," one of them called as Marina led the way to the terrace, "want to interview us?"

From their vantage point on the Majestic's balcony, Brian could see the army hunkered down in a V formation that stretched across the zócalo from the palace to the cathedral. The wrought iron fence where women in shawls usually proffered rosaries and religious postcards had been fortified with sandbags and metal sheets. Almost directly below them in the western corner of the square, a contingent of municipal riot police stood by with truncheons and shields. A bullhorn blared the warning that the zócalo had been declared a security zone, and that anyone found in it would be subject to arrest and detention.

"What about the people in the hotel?" Brian asked.

Pablo said dryly, "I don't think the army wants to arrest a bunch of drunk Americans—they have enough problems."

Brian glanced at Marina, who was crouched on a lounge chair scribbling away. "What are you writing about? Nothing's happened yet."

"Those police down below are not in a defensive formation," she said. "Look at them. They are waiting to attack from behind after the demonstrators enter the square. Pablo, make sure you get a picture of that."

"You mean it's a trap," Brian said.

"It will be important afterward, when the government claims it did everything it could to prevent bloodshed."

"Too bad Mexico doesn't have the Pulitzer Prize," he said admiringly.

"There are more important rewards," she said quietly.

Brian was about to say something when Pablo pointed up Avenida Madero. "Atención," he said. "They're coming."

Brian heard them before he saw them; a dull ominous roar, like football fans after a bad call. And beneath that, like a throbbing heart, the sound of drums.

Boom . . . "Democracia!" . . . Boom . . . "Democracia!"

The first banners came into view, crimson and green letters on a field of white: JUSTICIA. LIBERTAD. PRU AFUERA. ARANDA AFUERA. Some carried just the naked poles, others placards and small signs. The mob was mostly men, mostly young, but there were also women, some of them carrying infants in their arms. The demonstrators were closer now, and Brian saw on their faces the same joyous rapture as that of the religious processioners he had seen in Tepoztlán. The chanting flood of humanity poured down Madero, swirling and sweeping along everything in its path like a river overflowing its banks.

The mob reached the edge of the square and hesitated as the two armies faced each other across the zócalo. Then it began to push forward like a living organism, sending out tentacles that probed the open plaza while the main bulk of the group flowed behind them. The crowd was eerily quiet as it tested the army's resolve. No more than forty yards away, the soldiers held their ground, gripping their ri-

344

fles to their chests. From below the terrace came the squeak of plastic shields being raised into position.

"My God," Marina whispered. "It's happening."

Then, just when it seemed that the shooting would start, the crowd stopped advancing. It was as if the two groups were separated by some invisible buffer. Suddenly, what had threatened to be a riot took on the orderly shape of a mass protest.

"What's happening?" Brian asked.

Marina leaned forward for a better view.

"I don't know."

A platform, raised on the shoulders of a dozen men, appeared between the demonstrators and the palace guard. Lifted by a ladder of hands, a man, dressed in white with a red sash across his waist, stood on the platform and addressed the crowd with a bullhorn.

"My people, the time for fighting and killing is over. These guns that point at our hearts must remain quiet. It is time for the voices of the people to be heard. It is time for democracy!"

The crowd let out a throaty cheer.

"Who's that?" Brian asked.

"That's Gaspar Zamorra, the opposition leader," Pablo told him. "I've got to get closer. I'm going down."

"Be careful," Marina warned.

A minute later Pablo appeared on the square below, several cameras dangling from his shoulders. He turned and waved before heading off toward the edge of the crowd gathered around Zamorra.

"I can't believe they're letting him talk," Brian said.

Marina nodded and scanned the plaza. "The authorities are confused," she said. "They were expecting an all-out offensive. But the opposition has surprised them by mounting a peaceful demonstration right under their noses. If the soldiers attack now it would be an unmistakable instance of cold-blooded murder."

Across the zócalo, a CNN TV crew was filming Zamorra's speech, broadcasting it live to the whole world.

"The crimes of the government must be forgiven—but never forgotten," Zamorra was saying. "For democracy to function, the leaders of the nation must be accountable to the people. The people must be heard, the people *will* be heard!" He turned to face the palace, shaking his fist as he issued the challenge. "Listen!" he cried. "Listen to the voice of the people!"

The deafening roar rose like a wave against the palace. The onslaught of sound grew in volume until the windows of the hotel began to rattle and a flock of startled pigeons took off over the cathedral like a winged blessing. Still, the noise increased, until the buildings and all of Mexico seemed to vibrate in sympathy. First one soldier's arm flew up, then another as they put their weapons down and stepped forward. Brian could feel the rising surge of elation, like the rumbling of a dormant volcano. The cameras wheeled to catch the image as the soldiers voted with their feet for change.

Brian heard a tinny pop, like the report of a toy pistol. In front of the cathedral, a young soldier crumpled to the ground, shot by one of his own officers. As the crowd roiled in confusion, the deserting soldiers froze, unsure of which way to turn, some running back behind the sandbags, others diving into the crowd. More shots rang out. In the center of the throng, Zamorra's bodyguards formed a circle around their leader, their guns at the ready, as they rushed him out of danger.

"Oh my God!" Marina shouted. "Did you see? They shot him in the back!"

The crowd was roaring again. Only this time it was the growl of a wounded animal, a scream of rage that demanded vengeance. A barrage of rocks peppered the palace, breaking a dozen windows and causing the soldiers to duck behind their sandbags. At the same time a sudden rush of protesters broke through the army line and spilled into the undefended ruins of Templo Mayor. The mob paused, intoxicated by its success, then spilled over the ruins toward the museum itself. There was a shattering of glass as they poured inside, only to reemerge moments later dressed in the beaked helmets and feathered breastplates of the Eagle Warriors.

"Look over there!" Brian shouted, unable to believe his eyes.

Swinging a stone-handled machete, a man wearing a clay skull mask charged the police and was cut down with a bullet. Another group, their limbs wrapped in the leopard skins of the Jaguar Knights, stormed the barricades around the cathedral, impaling terrified gunners with their gold-tipped lances. Bat-faced fighters made feral, inhuman screams, galvanizing the mob, which redoubled their assault on the startled security forces. A few of the young troops, convinced that they were being attacked by demons, began to fall back, pursued by howling packs of coyotes, vultures and grinning skeletons. Even the opposition leaders were momentarily struck dumb by the surreal spectacle of Aztec warriors venting their wrath on the disoriented Mexican Army.

"It's the end of the Fifth Sun," Brian said numbly. "It's happening again."

Caught by surprise, the soldiers retreated in disarray. Then, regrouping at the gates of the National Palace, the government forces began a lethal counterattack, aiming their guns above the crowd, then lower. In the center of the zócalo tear gas bombs mushroomed on the pavement and the demonstrators began to scatter, their hands covering their eyes and mouths. The phalanx of riot police, medieval in their black suits and helmets, began their rear assault on the crowd, clubbing people from behind and dragging them away to waiting vans.

"Look, there's Pablo," Marina said. Emerging from a plume of smoke, the photographer was staggering blindly toward the hotel as the line of police blocked it off.

"He'll never make it," Brian said, springing for the stairs. Before anyone could stop him, he unbolted the front doors and ran out into the plaza. The rally had disintegrated into a vicious free-for-all, as both sides ran amok in a scrimmage of bullets and knives. The soldiers were advancing from their positions around the palace, using bayonets and live rounds to beat back the crowd as they began a sweep of the plaza. A riot cop was lifting his truncheon over Pablo's prostrate form as Brian tackled him from the side. Pinned flat under the heavier man, Brian felt the baton crushing his larynx as he clawed helplessly at the plexiglass visor. Then the policeman's grip suddenly went slack and his pupils rolled into his head. Brian pushed his limp body off and struggled to his feet in time to catch a glimpse of his savior, a youth in a duality mask who let out a victory cry before melting into the madness.

Pablo was on his knees, clutching his left arm.

"Are you all right?" Brian asked as he helped him to his feet.

"I think it's broken. But I can walk."

A cataract of tear gas wafted across their path as Brian and Pablo hobbled back to the hotel. Brian felt an acrid stinging in his eyes and nose, as if he had just inhaled horseradish. His vision blurred, then went dark as his eyes swelled shut. He pushed ahead blindly until he felt a familiar hand on his arm.

"Here, put this over your eyes," Marina told him as she handed him a wet bandana. "Your heroics are going to get us all killed!"

Before Brian could respond, a fusillade of machine gun fire tore into the hotel, sending glass and plaster raining down across the entrance. From the plaza, a commander's voice ordered his men to search the buildings for snipers.

"The hotel is no good," Marina said. "We'll have to find another way out."

Still blinded by the tear gas, Brian was engulfed in an inferno of sulfurous fumes and anguished screams, howling sirens and explosions. The boy in the mask hovered in his mind's eye, his triumphal shriek adding to the cacophony of chaos. As he stumbled ahead, Brian flinched at every volley of gunfire, bracing for the bullet that never came. Then the sound of fighting gradually receded and there was only the urgent slap of running feet as Marina held his hand and guided him to safety.

It was nearly dusk when they staggered into the Latin American Tower. In the hard fluorescent light, surrounded by the swank furniture and high-tech accoutrements of a modern news organization, what they had just been through seemed all the more unreal.

Brian slumped against a stack of newsprint in Marina's cubicle while she went to fetch a blanket and some coffee. The violence of the zócalo had left his nerves vibrating like a tuning fork and he had to steady his cup with both hands to drink. "It's not safe to go out after the curfew," Marina said. "We'll spend the night here. Zamorra is in hiding and the opposition is in disarray. The soldiers are cracking down all over the city. It will be over by morning."

"Over?"

"The shooting, I mean. The rest of it is just beginning."

"What about outside the city?"

"In Yucatán and Chiapas, the Cruzob are retreating. I don't know about the other provinces. It's hard to get information."

"By the way," Brian said, "there's something you should know." She listened intently as he told her about his last conversation with Villalobos. "I promised him our talk would remain confidential."

Marina nodded. "Don't worry," she said. "I won't use it in my story. Nobody would believe it anyway."

"Thanks."

"And Zapata?" Marina asked.

"I almost had him convinced that Torres took the codex."

For the first time all day, Marina smiled. "I wish I could have seen their faces," she said.

"It was priceless. The bad news is that I've worn out my welcome at Templo Mayor—or what's left of it."

Marina became somber again. "Will you miss Mexico?" she asked.

"No," he answered, "because you're coming with me. I've made my choice. I want to marry you."

She sat back in her chair and crossed her arms. "I'm very happy for you, Brian, but what about me? Don't I get to decide?"

It was not the reaction he'd expected. "I thought you would be glad—"

"Glad to move to California and get a green card? You think you can lure me to Los Angeles with the prospect of U.S. citizenship? Or do you expect me to get a job cleaning houses for your neighbors?"

"Marina, that's not fair," Brian managed to say. "In Mérida, you said—"

"I know what I said," she replied, her voice softening, "but too much has happened. Mérida seems like such a long time ago."

Brian took a sip of coffee, but it had become cold and tasteless. "Marina," he pleaded, "don't do this to us. I want to be with you, even if it means staying in Mexico."

"You know Zapata would never let you stay here."

"Look, I don't give a shit about Zapata. I'll get out of anthropology if I have to. It wouldn't be the first time I changed careers."

"You don't mean that. And even if you did, I wouldn't let you do it. Anyway, that's not the reason I won't marry you."

"Then why? I thought you loved me."

"I do love you. But it's not so hard to understand, really. You don't belong here and I can't leave. My work, my life is here. My country needs me."

"I need you too, Marina."

"No," she said. "You don't need me, you *want* me—there's a difference. You think that by having me you can regain a part of yourself. But it's already there. It always has been. Besides, you have plenty of time to find the right woman."

"You're the right woman," he said hoarsely.

"No, I'm not. I never was," she said, stubbing out the embers of his hope. "And if you're really honest with yourself, you'll see that I'm right, that this is the only way it could ever end."

Brian leaned against the pile of papers in dejected silence. "Sometimes I think you really are La Malinche," he said bitterly.

"Maybe I am. I'm sorry, mi amor. Try to understand."

"I'm trying," he said without conviction.

"Now get some rest. I want to start writing while everything is still fresh in my mind."

Brian looked at the blank computer screen. "What are you going to say?"

"I'm going to say that I just witnessed an end and a beginning—the end of the old Mexico and the beginning of a vibrant new nation."

"That's funny," he said, "you're starting to sound just like Villalobos."

She kissed him gently and returned to the desk, the light dancing in her hair as she flipped through her notes. Brian pulled the blanket around his shoulders and watched her work. He fought to stay awake but quickly drifted off, lulled by the staccato music of the keys as Marina typed her story.

19

Sailboats skidded across San Francisco Bay, their wakes like chalk on the slate blue water. Summer had finally surrendered to the cool exhilaration of October, and the sharp autumn air was like a tonic. The fog had receded behind the Golden Gate and the velvety hills of Marin County stood magnified and brushed clean by the Pacific breeze.

Berkeley was charged with anticipation of the coming term; students hurried across the campus in a collective rush. Brian searched the passing faces for some sign of shared experience, a mutual recognition that they too had passed through a threshold that had no name. But he saw only the waning lassitude of beach houses and transatlantic jaunts; carefree memories fading faster than a summer tan.

Brian traversed the winding wooded pathway toward the Bear's

Lair. St. Cloud was at the same table, hunched over a plate of fries and a thick stack of class registration cards. When St. Cloud glanced up and nodded, Brian took a seat and waited.

"Native-American philosophy," St. Cloud announced. "I've got twice as many undergrads as the room can handle—the price of being in vogue. Didn't you know? It's become chic to have a Navajo rug in your den, or an Anasazi pot on the mantel, or a sweat lodge in your backyard—solar-heated, of course."

"Can't you get a bigger room?" Brian asked.

"Sure, they'll give me one of those stadium-sized auditoriums. I can use a mike and work the stage like Mick Jagger. Wear leopard leotards and turn my teaching into a spectacle of primitive libido."

Brian grinned, but his teacher's expression remained sour. St. Cloud shuffled the cards and pushed the stack across the table.

"Cut," he said.

Brian divided the stack into two parts. St. Cloud took the smaller pile and put a rubber band around it. Then he picked up the rest and dumped them in his pocket.

"I guess what they don't know won't hurt them," Brian suggested.

"By that measure, most of these kids are invincible," St. Cloud quipped. He took a golden fry and daubed it in the red pool of catsup. "I read the outline for your dissertation," he said casually, "showed it to the dean too." St. Cloud chewed slowly, milking the moment. He fixed Brian with his laughing blue eyes. "Until Mexico signs an extradition treaty with the University of California, it looks like we might have to offer you a degree."

"Thanks, Larry." Brian surveyed the suddenly quaint contours of his alma mater. "I owe a lot to this place."

"Well, you have a funny way of showing your gratitude. You'll hate UCLA, unless you happen to like swimming pools and perfect weather."

"I'll survive somehow," Brian said. "It's something I have to do."

"Do you have a place to live?"

"I'll be living at home for a while. My mom and I have sort of patched things up. I think it'll be good to spend some time with her."

"You sure this is what you want?"

"I think so." Brian shrugged. "But who knows? Maybe I'll come crawling back on my knees in a few weeks begging you to hire me."

St. Cloud chewed thoughtfully before responding. "I'd like to think so, but I won't hold my breath," he said. "In any event, you know you're welcome here when you finally come to your senses."

Brian's teacher wiped his fingers on his napkin and gazed over the distant peaks of some internal landscape. "I'm sorry things didn't turn out better for you down south."

The words lingered in the air like skywriting. St. Cloud rose to leave. "I never say good-bye to my friends," he said, gripping Brian's hand. Then he was off, his proud head cutting through the sea of students like a prow.

Brian sat alone for a few moments before rising to join the pedestrian flow on Telegraph Avenue. He had the house to himself since Stone was in Wyoming, shooting a story about climbing the Grand Teton range. He had already sent Brian a postcard of the massive peaks at sunset. "One wrong step and it's buenas noches," Stone had written on the back. "But just imagine the view on the way down!"

As he fished in his pocket for the key to the front door, the landlady, who lived next door, waved from her porch. "Oh, Brian," she called. "A man was by to deliver something for you. He wouldn't leave it outside, so I put it in your room. I hope you don't mind."

Brian thanked her, closing the door behind him.

The package, about the size of a telephone book and wrapped in plain brown paper, was waiting on the coffee table. He picked it up and shook it. Nothing moved. Whatever it was had been carefully packed. He ripped away the paper to find a wooden box with an envelope taped to the cover. Brian unfolded the letter and moved his eyes over the meticulous, angular scrawl:

Dear Brian—
I hope these color Xeroxes of the Villalobos Codex and Laura's translation will help you with your work. It seems that our friend Xotl was successful after all. I look forward to your analysis, which I'm sure will merit publication in several languages.
—Tu amigo para siempre, A. Villalobos

Brian put the note aside and prayed that this wasn't some cruel hoax. The box, with its dull reddish patina and gold hinges, was real enough. The top and sides were embossed with an exquisite pattern that looked vaguely Moorish. He nudged the latch free with his thumb. Then he gingerly held the lid from both corners and lifted it open.

Grandma Sara's garden was blooming. The flowerbeds were vibrant with fuchsia, red bottlebrush and purple hyacinth. But nothing compared to her roses. The buds were already unfolding in shades of yellow, red and the palest peach. Even the thorns looked beautiful, the triangular blades reaching out from the stem, patiently waiting for anything that came too close.

Brian knocked on the screen door. He heard the syrupy strains of a soap opera theme, then footsteps retarded by old age.

"Grandma, it's Brian."

Tentative fingers fumbled with the lock and even through the wire mesh he couldn't help noticing the thick bluish veins on her hand. She opened the door and took him into her arms, enveloping him in the scent of rouge and hair spray.

"Mijito! Come in, come in."

"I can't stay long. I just came to take you to the cemetery."

"Yes, thank you, m'hijo." In her black dress and lace shawl, she bore an uncanny resemblance to the old women he'd seen kneeling at the pews of the Metropolitan Cathedral. "Please, m'hijo, come here. I want to show you something."

She took his hand and led him into the bedroom. The curtains were drawn and the room was suffused in a kind of perpetual twilight. He vaguely recognized the faded floral wallpaper, the heavy varnished furniture. A clock ticked loudly, its face discolored by the years.

"Here," she said, pointing to a box on the top shelf of her closet. "It's too tall for me, m'hijo."

Brian reached up and pulled the box free, nearly gagging on the dust that came down with it. He took the box out into the living room and set it on the couch. Even before she opened it he knew it was full of photographs, memories that had been sealed away for decades, a hiding place for ghosts. Sara's hands shook as she rummaged through the contents. Then, one at a time, she began to show him the pictures.

They were old snapshots, mostly black-and-whites with a few blurry squares of color. Some were still mounted on brittle cardboard with dates and names scribbled in the margins: Don Daniel as a young man, looking rakish in a forties-style suit. Himself as a baby. His parents' wedding portrait.

Then Brian was holding a picture of his mother that he'd never seen before. She was young, in her early twenties, prim in a white cotton dress. Her whole life lay ahead of her, yet her eyes were gentle and understanding, as if looking through the years to this very moment.

"It's yours," Sara said, pushing the photograph into his hands.

"Thank you, Grandma."

"You're welcome," she said, closing the box. "Now let's go before your grandpa gets tired of waiting."

As they walked to the car she clutched his arm tightly and he could feel her drawing strength from him. Brian wondered if Don Daniel had ever beat her. If he had, Sara had kept it to herself, suffering with the dignity that came so naturally to Mexican women. The very thought made Brian's blood simmer. The syndrome was deeply ingrained in Latin culture: the macho who uses brute force to mask his weakness; the woman who uses silence to hide her strength. At least Marina would never be a passive victim. She belonged to the new breed of Mexican women—educated, outspoken, cosmopolitan. The old ways were dying. But the transition was gradual; the pattern would have to be broken one life at a time.

The cemetery stood on the crest of a hill that overlooked a looping section of the Long Beach Freeway. Off in the distance, Brian could see the downtown skyline jutting up behind scraggly palm trees. Brian parked and helped her out of the car.

"Mira qué hombre guapo. What a strong, handsome man my mijito has become. You always protected me. Siempre. Remember what you did to those boys?"

"What boys, Grandma?"

"The boys who stole my Christmas lights."

"I don't remember."

"Yes you do. You were just a boy. Like this." Her hand hovered near her waist. "Some bad boys from down the street were stealing the Christmas lights from my tree in the front yard. Your mother brought you to stay with your grandpa and me for the holidays and when I told you, you said, 'Grandma, I'm going to watch out for those boys, and if I see them stealing your lights I'm going to give them a whipping.' And you took a big stick from the garage and hid in the bushes out front to wait for them. And sure enough, when they came into the yard you jumped out with your baseball bat and scared them away. You were very brave, mijito."

She let out a wheezing chuckle and Brian held her tighter. He wondered if the story was true. He tried to picture himself as a pint-sized avenger chasing off thieving intruders, but the image was faded and out of focus.

As they climbed the hill toward Don Daniel's grave, Sara grew pensive. "Your grandpa is waiting for me, mijito," she said, and Brian cringed at the words.

"Don't talk like that," he chided. "You're going to live a long time, Grandma."

"It's okay, mijito," she said gently. "I don't mind. I will live in your memory." She took his hand and held it against her bosom. "Will you remember me, mijito?"

"Yes," Brian said, and he felt something well up inside of him. "I'll remember you."

"Good," she said cheerfully. "Then I'll never die."

When they reached his grandfather's plot, Sara knelt down to pray. She spoke to her husband, saying how much she missed him, but all Brian could think about was the story Sara had just told him. It bothered him that he couldn't remember. What else had he forgotten? He tried in vain to picture his grandfather's face and it occurred to him that he had no right to be there. So Brian turned and walked away, hoping his grandmother wouldn't notice. He was halfway back to the car when he noticed a simple tombstone. The inscription leaped out at him: MIGUEL MENDOZA, BELOVED HUSBAND AND FATHER, 1926–1964.

He wanted to run away but his legs wouldn't move. He stood there on the soft grass, watching the wind bend the green blades, feeling the ineluctable weight of the whole planet under his shoes. A hand touched his arm. Sara was looking at him, her face wrinkled in concern. "Qué tienes, mi chulo? My beautiful boy. What's the matter?"

At first, Brian didn't know how to answer, then the words found their way to his lips.

"Help me remember, Grandma. Tell me about my dad."

20

The sun is falling behind the trees as we arrive at the mouth of the sacred cave. In the last few hours of light we clear away the vegetation and set up our camp at the rim of a nearby cenote. The next morning, as Venus rises in the east, Xotl tells me that he has dreamed his death; he has seen his own corpse in the tomb of Tláloc, not far from the Tree of Life. I fear that the master has gone insane, or worse, that he has not, and that we will soon be descending into hell. But Xotl makes me understand. He reveals the true intent of our mission and I see the courage in his eyes. I know now that I will die too if he asks it of me. But his final request, as I will soon learn, is much worse.

   Xotl has become more attentive to Loma, and I understand that she is part of his vision, that he has chosen her and brought us all to this place according to the will of Our Lord. The Plumed Serpent marked her with the proper sign and placed her among the virgins who had been charged to serve the deceiver called Cortés. She has seen the carnal face of the Smoking Mirror, Tezcatlipoca. Thus the Evil One, Xotl tells me, has sown the seeds of his own undoing. Loma's child, half human, half god, will have powers beyond any common man, and the birth cries of the precious bundle will echo throughout the universe.

For the next few days we spend most of our time in the cave searching for the tomb in Xotl's dream. Inside the tunnel, our way lit by torches, we see vast chambers with tall spikes growing from the floor like jaguar teeth and meandering streams of singing water and wide lakes as smooth as mirrors. Each day we emerge with the bats at sunset and trudge back to camp exhausted and shaken by what we have seen. Meanwhile, Xotl's prayers to Our Lord become more ardent and my teacher's manner pensive and withdrawn. Still, there are moments of joy that remind me of the mentor I once knew. Our discovery of the Tree of Life is cause for great exaltation. Stunned by the blessed sight, we give thanks to Our Lord for guiding us safely through the bowels of the Underworld. And though it is a place we have never been before, Xotl turns and moves with assurance into another passage that opens into a room with a gurgling pool and an altar built by our Toltec ancestors. Upon entering the sacred chamber, we fall to our knees and begin to pray. For the world of dreams and the world of men had become one, and there is no longer any doubt that our master is endowed with the power of prophecy.

After more prayers and an offering of copal, Xotl points to an indentation in the wall. "Here," he commands. "This is where we dig."

The work is arduous and takes many days. Each pot of dirt is carried out by the workers, while the rest of us search for the stone that will serve as an altar. We find it on the edge of a nearby field and it is several more days before it has been hewn to Xotl's design and carried to the site of his inner vision. At last all is ready, and a mood of uneasy expectation descends over our camp. That evening Citlax returns from his hunt with a worried expression. He was chasing boar when a pair of white and red birds flew across his path. When the birds lighted on a branch, the limb broke. He did not see the birds fly away, but when he went to where the branch had fallen there was nothing there. Xotl listens gravely, but without being disconcerted.

He looks at me and asks, "What say you, Tonatiuh? What do you divine in Citlax's vision?"

At first I do not speak; I am unaccustomed to hearing our leader address me as an equal. Then I remember the lesson of the Divine Couple. They had been picking flowers when they broke a tree branch and left it to bleed. As punishment they were transformed into birds who often carried daggers in their beaks. They were messengers of Quetzalcóatl and their appearance foretold disaster.

"Our Lord and Lady Butterfly, a bad omen," I say, and Xotl nods in agreement. I have proven myself worthy, yet I do not feel glad. Instead I feel the lonely burden of the holy man, he who must remember the writings and locate the significance of every occurrence. Now I too feel the keen ache of knowing what others do not know, seeing what others cannot see.

Xotl looks at me with eyes that pierce my soul. "The sky over Tenochtitlán is blinded with smoke and the temples lay in ruins," he tells me. "Our fair home is no longer. The Fifth Sun is finished."

It will be many weeks before news of the fall of the Aztec capital reaches our camp, but I realize at that moment that the world as we knew it has ended. The others begin to weep, but my sadness stays buried inside me. Tonatiuh the child-man is dead, and I mourn him with the fleeting remnants of my youth.

A strong wind from the east is blowing, sending leaves fluttering around us. I shiver, though I am not cold. "It is time," Xotl announces. "We must make the final preparations." And just then, as if his words have penetrated Loma's womb, she cries out and clutches her belly. This time the midwife nods to us as she applies a damp cloth to her mistress's forehead. The quickening has begun. Loma is placed upon a litter and while Xotl shouts instructions to the carriers, I run off to dress and gather my things. Besides my bedroll and extra food and water, I select several objects: a bag of incense and torches, some fine brushes and paint and a soft blanket. Lastly, I remove from its deerskin sheath the knife that Xotl gave me on the day I became a tlamacazqui. Even under the brooding sky, the blade gleams like a jet of black water. Then, as if looking at it too long might cut my eyes, I quickly replace it in the bag and hurry to join the others.

The bone-rattle of thunder shakes the trees as Xotl and I lead the procession into the cave. Again, I am swallowed by the maw of Mictlan, the downward sloping passage with walls that tremble and make unnerving shapes in the torchlight. We move in silence, but my ears are ringing with the wet slap of our sandals on the stone floor. In the flickering light, Xotl's eyes are hollow black sockets and his mouth is a cracked line of resolution. As we walk together in the humid darkness, through the string of pearl-shaped chambers leading to the Tree of Life, I remember the first day we met in his chambers, and I see again the sanctity in his eyes that told me he would not betray us. Rightly, I trusted him, that thin, bent apparition in his immaculate robes, the man who would become my teacher and spiritual father and enlist me in his faithful mission. How I love him, this wizened holy man with the heart of a lion, so imposing and regal in his formal vestment of gold and white. If anyone can save our people, it is Xotl, high priest of the Plumed Serpent and confidant of Quetzalcóatl, the Descending God, who will harvest the seed of the Sixth Sun and lead us back to our rightful home at the crossroads of the One World.

The floor slopes down again and I know we are approaching the shrine of Tláloc. The group waits in the outer chamber and the air is harsh from the smoke of our torches. I move inside to light the incense burners as Loma is carried into the altar room. She is no longer moaning but a sheen of water, like the finest silk, covers her face and arms. Xotl and I lift the hems of our robes and follow into the dim compartment, where Loma is stretched out on the slab of carved stone, her body rigid with pain. I want to comfort her, but I know I must prepare the paint that I will use to record this moment.

The art of writing is another gift that Xotl has given me, and the measure of its power is clear. I try not to waver as I apply the pigments to the damp walls and inscribe the record of our journey. Xotl is praying and preparing the ritual sacraments. He hands me a small bag of herbs and holy plants, which I swallow. Loma is no longer quiet. Her body quakes with the toil of childbirth and her screams fill the underground chamber until my ears ache. At the same time I recognize the transforming effects of the potion. The room becomes larger and every detail jumps out at my eyes. A flood of well-being enters my body and my mind becomes lucid and wakeful. Xotl's pupils reflect my state and confirm it; nothing is different, yet everything has changed. The gods are coming closer. I can feel them roaming the passages of the cave, swimming in the underground rivers, gathering outside the walls of the altar room, waiting to enter.

Xotl bids me to come forward. Along one side of the altar, forming a semicircle around Loma's writhing body, he lays out a collection of charms and tiny figures, each one representing a stage of the ceremony and its accompanying prayer. I recognize the inverted figure of the Descending God, the star that fell on its head and entered the Underworld, and several other objects associated with Quetzalcóatl: a white conch; a pair of twisted shell ear caps, representing the womb; a serpent pierced by an arrow and bones, indicating self-sacrifice; maguey cactus spines for bloodletting; a serpent pierced by its own tail, the sign of the beginning and the end in perfect conjunction.

I have seen them all before, have been lectured on their powers, yet placed together in a chain of relation, I look upon them with new understanding, for they are nothing less than a depiction of Xotl's entire purpose. Their meaning is suddenly as clear to me as the tears that sting my face.

"Teacher," I call above Loma's cries of agony, "I am ready to serve Our Lord."

"Good," Xotl says. "I knew that you would not fail me. Now do what must be done." Then he lies down next to Loma, who is convulsing in the final throes of labor, and undoes his robes. Our eyes meet again and I feel his strength flowing into me, flooding my senses like an underground river as I grip the sacrificial blade. Xotl puts the conch to his lips and the sound is like a curtain parting in the clouds.

The roof of the chamber opens above us, and we drift up with the wisps of smoke until I see the treetops and the flat jungle spreading toward the horizon. As we ascend into the blue depths of the First Sky, Xotl is beside me, pulling me higher, until the clouds are drifting under our feet and the land and the seas are stretched thin across the sphere of the world. We rise further still, until the light is no longer coming from above but emanating from the earth itself, and in the darkening twilight I see the blinking firmament of the Second Sky. There, etched in chains of diamond-bright stars, are the outlines of the skirt of Ometéotl, the god of duality, the tiger Tezcatlipoca, the great bear Citlaxonecuilli and a million more. Then the sun itself, dweller of the house of the Third Sky, bows its furious head as we rise further, past the Fourth Sky, the realm of Venus and Our Lord Quetzalcóatl, on to the Fifth Sky, a bowl of darkness alight with darting comets, and higher still, past the skies of Smoking Mirror, Little Hummingbird, and the regions of White, Yellow and Red, until we hover on the edge of the final barrier. I am willing to go on, but my guide hesitates, as *if waiting to be loosed from the last tether that ties him to the world of men.*

In the underground chamber that holds our mortal bodies, I hear Loma's urgent wails and the nurse's shouts of alarm. As if watching from a profound distance, I sense the fetus straining in Loma's tortured womb, dragging her life out with it, until, with a final feckless exertion, she lies limp on the blood-soaked slab, her eyes inchoate with the knowledge of her own death. Then Xotl's voice, much closer to my ear, urges me to close the circle of creation as the wriggling bundle emerges from Loma's lifeless body.

"Now," the voice commands. And as I plunge the knife into Xotl's naked chest I feel his spirit ascend beyond the Twelfth Sky, to where the gods are born and reborn and the deities nourish their ability to be eternal and transformed.

Fighting to stay conscious, I lift the infant from the corpse of its dead mother and cut it free. Then I wrap the child in the blanket and carry it out of the cave and into the moonless night after which he would soon be named.

In one fateful day I have lost a father and gained a son, and I know that I will devote the remainder of my life to the task of raising my trembling charge to manhood and tutoring him in the ways of the Plumed Serpent and the glorious history of his people. As I write this, I know that Loma's offspring will be named Obsidian Sky and that he will become a teacher who will preserve the memories of his ancestors. Because the wisdom of Xotl must never be forgotten. It must be repeated and copied down in every language, so that the gift of his sacrifice will live on in the heart of Obsidian Sky and his children, and the children of their children, for as long as the blood of the gods flows in our veins and the morning star rises in the newborn dawn.

About the Author

Guy Garcia is the author of the novel *Skin Deep* and a contributor to the anthologies *Iguana Dreams: New Latino Fiction* and *Pieces of the Heart: New Chicano Fiction*. A native of Los Angeles, he is a graduate of the University of California at Berkeley and Columbia University. His journalism has appeared in *Time, The New York Times, Rolling Stone, Interview, Premiere, Harper's Bazaar,* and other publications. He lives in New York City with his wife and son.